<u>The Diary of a Canadian Nobody</u>

A responsible account for respectable people,

by
Arthur Lakelady

Copyright © Statement

DEDICATIONS

For my family, without whom this book would never have happened. The inspiration they provide and the time they allow me for imagining and typing makes everything possible.

Also, for AC whose thoughts and suggestions make Arthur's life outside the family so stressful and interesting. I hope life has treated her more kindly than her dream for her future prophesied and she has not died of a non-disfiguring illness while lying in a sumptuous bed surrounded by grieving lovers.

Author's Note:

This story takes place in a time that was real and the news items mentioned on the days throughout are also real BUT the characters in the story are NOT. They do borrow from my family, people I know or knew, and me but they are still fictional characters -- no one behaved as they do in the story. To summarize, this book, dear Reader, is FICTION.

Foreword:

Over the past years there's been many successful books based on diaries and it seems to me that there should be room for one more. Peter Mayle may have his year in Provence, Bridget Jones her year in London, the Edwardian Lady her year in the countryside, and so on, but a Canadian edition has been missing.

I'm convinced Canadians can be just as cutely quirky as the residents of Provence, as sexually slippery as Londoners, or elegantly intellectual as Edwardians; even those of us out here pioneering in a harsh land and climate, at Whitebay, on the outermost eastern fringes of Metropolitan Toronto. We too have a story to tell and posterity requires, no, history demands, it to be told.

Why, you may ask? Well, Peter Mayle makes sport of the Provencal contractors who don't turn up for work. My experience of Ontario contractors is they are equally as difficult to start, and, when it's happening to someone else, it's equally funny. All our friends thought so anyhow.

Bridget Jones, when she's not trying to stuff goodies into every orifice of her body, makes fun of gyms. We Ontarians know gyms and they're serious stuff; as my own experience, recorded here in this diary, will demonstrate.

The Edwardian Lady may find that first fragile violet blooming in spring and record it with pride but it's nothing to the feeling you get on watching your daffodils wilt in a tropical Ontario sun, the day after they first bloomed -- when the snow melted.

Other, cheaper diaries begin on January the first. This one does not, which makes it different right from the start and proves we Canadians are just as uniquely quirky as everyone else is. This one starts on September 1st because that's the day I thought about writing a diary and did indeed start writing it. I've had to use two diaries to record my year, but what the hell anything goes in modern art. It will also allow my publisher to claim, quite honestly, that the buyer is getting TWO for the price of ONE. (My Public Speaking course says 'start with a joke' to break the ice and that was *the joke*.

From now on, everything you read here will be a serious account of life in the early 21st Century -- history demands it.)

This diary introduces a new family to the realm of literature -- the Lakeladys, Alys, Lance, Gwen, and me, Arthur. I should give you some background before we get into the diary proper. My father used to be obsessed with his family name, and its allusion to the stories of the Knights of the Round Table, so he named his children after the characters in the stories. I was fortunate, as the eldest boy, I got Arthur; my brothers Galahad and Gawain, were not so lucky. Growing up, I swore I'd never impose such ridiculous names on my own children and stuck firmly to that until I met Alys, who was also besotted by the Middle Ages. I did my best, but Alys is a very determined woman at times and anyway Lancelot and Guinevere can sound quite modern when shortened to Lance and Gwen.

Alys's love of the Middle Ages comes from reading too many romances as a child; parents be warned, not all reading is good for you. She fell for the noble ideals, the demure feminine gentleness of the heroines and the lusty valour of the heroes. Alys feels the world would be a better place if we all followed that ancient code of chivalry; those good old days, when men were monsters and women were worse. I agree with her because I daren't do otherwise. Alys appears to have chosen Empress Matilda or Kate from Taming of the Shrew as her models, which seems to point to a weakness in her idyllic vision but it may just be my inability to comprehend. In fact, I know it's my inability to comprehend because Alys says so -- often.

Before today, the Lakeladys were just your typical unrecorded Ontario family, unsung heroes of the modern world. When this bursts upon the astonished public, they will undoubtedly become as famous as the Pooter's or the Mayles, or the Jones' are. This will no doubt mean Mrs. Lakelady getting mobbed in the local supermarket, the children being beaten senseless at school, and Silky, the cat, being catnapped for cash but I'm prepared to risk it for my fifteen minutes in the Sun (preferably snuggling with the Sunshine Girl).

Arthur Lakelady,
3 Merlin Crescent
Whitebay, Ontario.

p.s. No cash will be passed over for Silky so don't waste your time.
p.p.s. Or the kids either. You have been warned.

p.p.p.s. Finally, I know you'll say you don't believe our address. Well, you're wrong. It's real and when we saw the 'For Sale' listing we just had to buy the house. (Sadly, it's not actually named after the magician, Merlin; it's in a subdivision named for birds of prey. I've circulated a number of petitions to have the rest of the subdivision streets renamed to a Round Table theme but they have all been mysteriously lost.)

September 2001:
A New Diary

Saturday 1:
Raining hard. Finished re-reading Diary of a Nobody and reason, quite correctly, that the world needs a Canadian voice in Diarists and never so much as at this time. There have been Canadian diarists or, at least, diarists who wrote in Canada but they were all in the past. Posterity requires this era in Canada's history also be captured by a simple, homespun ordinary man-in-the-street who, in his simple, homespun ordinary way, will shine a light on the darkness that is all about us at the dawning of this new Millennium.

I sat down to write but Alys immediately insisted I stop wasting my time and take part in choosing tiles for our kitchen and bathroom and, although it cost me some precious diary time, it's as well she did because heaven knows what would have been on the floor if I hadn't. Perhaps promising twelve-year-old Lance the 'final say' wasn't one of our better ideas but he's always been so conventional in the past. You would have put money on him choosing a regular blue or brown. I don't know what's got into him lately. Perhaps it's puberty.

I called my father back home in England. He has conjunctivitis in one eye and feels very unwell. He can't get out because he can't see through the gummy mess sticking his eyelids together. Gawain, my youngest brother, lives with him but doesn't like to leave the house (being called Gawain has a lot to do with that) and watches videos when he's not at work. I think they may starve now that Dad's health is failing.

Here in Ontario, the inquiry into the Walkerton disaster last May wrapped up. For those of you not familiar with this particular man-made disaster, flooding in farm fields carried manure into the town's water supply, which, despite Ontario and Canada being a developed country in the 21st Century, failed to deal with it. Nine people died. The enquiry has exposed the amazing way small Ontario towns run their affairs as much as anything; nepotism reigns in the hinterland

and lack of qualifications isn't a bar to people doing technical work. I've no doubt it was considered a triumph over 'qualification discrimination', at the time.

Sunday 2:
Choosing tiles is the most difficult part of the process or, at least, I hope it is. After yesterday's trawl around two tile shops with a sulking Lance, Alys and I trawled around another three on our own today. We didn't choose any tiles, there are so many to pick from, but I was able to settle down to my diary when we got home because Alys and I were no longer on speaking terms.

I intend for the diary to become like Pepys' Diary, a record of our time that will be used by historians in centuries to come. Thus, it will include comments not only on the family, the nation, international events (where they impinge on the Lakeladys) and the climate, this last part being vitally important to future generations in proving Global Warming -- or not. I hope my various readers will skip the parts they don't like and concentrate on the parts relevant to them. (You can skip the whole thing if you like, provided you buy it and not wait for the library to provide you with a free copy.)

It's time I told you something about the Lakelady family. Alys, Mrs. Lakelady, is tall for her weight, blonde when the occasion demands it and is a strong, read fierce, supporter of me doing well at work. Gwen, our daughter, takes after her Mother physically but I like to think has my most endearing characteristics. Lance, our son, does take after me and I look exactly like Pierce Brosnan or Sean Connery (either of those Celtic movie stars) would look if they were shorter, stockier (but thinner on top), and bespectacled. Silky, our cat, is a long-haired slut who spends most of her life on her back with her legs in the air, seducing passers-by into tickling her tummy, or arching her back lewdly at anything vaguely male. Fortunately, she has been fixed or we'd be the proud possessors of a strange collection of hybrids.

Monday 3:
The Head, President and CEO of the company I work for, an American, Mr. Al Genuflecten-Grovel, announced last Friday that he is reorganising the company again because, apparently, none of the previous four re-organisations cured our problems. For a wild moment, I imagined Mrs. Genuflecten-Grovel timidly asking her

husband to decorate the living-room, all the while hoping and praying he doesn't begin by levelling the house like he did last time she suggested a change of wallpaper might brighten up the place. Perhaps he has more sense at home, where the damage he does hits his own wallet, unlike work where the damage he does hit ours but gets him more stock options and a bigger bonus. Mr. Genuflecten-Grovel is a firm believer in the notion that activity equals achievement, despite all the evidence to the contrary

I tried hard not to think the company's problems were created by the constant mania for re-organisation, because I'm 'management' and must put on a brave face for the definitely sullen employees. I wasn't successful in convincing me; I only hope it works on the employees. Not only are we downsizing this time, but we're also spinning off divisions too and the announcements sound like an advert for 'Crazy Zee's Carpet Emporium' -- 'Everything must go!' 'No reasonable offer refused!'

Today, senior management told us about the Restructuring Team they've already formed of, you guessed, senior managers who will award themselves plum posts in the new organisation, as they always have in the past. I am full of foreboding. After the last re-organisation, I spent a year in a windowless broom closet before I was given an office with a window and staff again. Gerry, a colleague at work who is a bit of a comic, says my change in fortune was 'when they realised I couldn't take a hint.' Whatever the reason, it was 'a close run thing' as the Duke of Wellington said about Waterloo. (My Public Speaking course says apt quotes from famous people are good too.) The only concrete fact we got from today's announcement is that the re-organisation will be complete by the end of the year so we can start the New Year in a new leaner shape. Some hope!

Went to the gym, as usual. Did usual routine, 20 minutes running and walking on the treadmill, followed by abs and arms machines. It is still no easier despite it being almost a year now since I started; perhaps the sinking feeling in my stomach from the fire sale announcements made me weak.

In the afternoon, a strange thing happened. A woman I've never seen before came into my office and said, 'Are you Arthur Lakelady?' I replied I was. She handed me a small, heavy package and left before I could say anything more. I felt a little like my namesake must have felt when the Lady of the Lake handed him

Excalibur; i.e. I wasn't sure this was a blessing or a curse. When I felt a steady pulsing beat coming from the package, I left my office quickly and called Security. Since the downtown Anthrax scares of last year, we've had lots of memos on what to do with strange packages and I'm proud to say I followed the procedures perfectly, clearing the floor, isolating the area, and everything.

My performance was commended right up to the moment news of it reached the thirty-fifth floor when the CEO's Admin Assistant realised my fifteen-year service clock was in danger of being detonated by a Police SWAT team. I still feel that, had there been some ceremony attached to the handover, I wouldn't have jumped to the, as it turned out, wrong conclusion. I didn't press my case, however, to the Senior Executive-Vice-President of Human Resources; instead, I listened politely to his not-so-polite speech absolving his office of all blame. It wasn't a good day at work.

Tuesday 4:
Didn't get to the gym because of an important meeting. Can't now remember what it was about. Work was very uneventful because everyone stood around the water cooler and coffee stations discussing the re-organisation. I kept away. I don't want people to get the impression I have so little to do I can stand around chatting all day and I wish the others in our department felt the same way. Who knows who is watching? I could be swept away with the others if the department I'm in is considered redundant. I should warn Mr. Ogilvie, the Department Director, of the danger the rest of his staff are placing us in.

In the evening, I intended to write a speech for my next Public Speaking course assignment but Alys insisted we start tearing up the linoleum on the kitchen floor. She is still annoyed about my not liking the pink tiles on Sunday. She says she knows I'll never lay tiles as long as there's a covering on the floor so she wants the covering removed.

Linoleum is tougher than it looks and we'd cleared only a small portion before bedtime. Unfortunately, we found another layer of the stuff immediately below the one Alys no longer likes. Sadly, she doesn't like the lower layer either.

Gwen started working at the local leisure centre last night as a swimming instructor and lifeguard, which is well paid and a good start to her Running-Away-To-University fund. I mention this because it is having an unfortunate side effect on Silky, our cat, and me. Silky likes to lie on my legs when I settle down for the last few minutes before bedtime. Normally, she sleeps there till we turn off the late night news about 10:45, at which point she jumps off and hides under the coffee table till we've gone to bed. (We don't know why she hides under the coffee table; presumably, it's some kind of race memory of cats being thrown out of the house down the ages.) With Gwen working late, any phone calls for her are also late. These calls terrify the sleeping Silky and she leaps off my knee in fright. Tonight is only the second night and already my thighs are torn to shreds by her claws. If this continues, I will have bled to death by Friday.

Wednesday 5:
Got to gym, usual routine -- still no easier. Work was again at a standstill while people discussed the lack of new announcements from the restructuring team and what it all meant for them. I think our bosses may be right. There must be too many people in the company because nobody's working and yet nothing has stopped working. It's as I've long suspected; I'm the one keeping the whole place going. I'm more than ever determined not to join the chattering groups in the halls.

The price of tiles is frightening. I worked it out in the morning and reviewed our household accounts in the afternoon. I wonder if Alys is fully aware of the cost of her whim?

Alys, it seems, is aware of cost and means to continue. We do better removing linoleum this evening and lift it almost all the way to the patio door. Lance helps until I suggest he be a little more careful with the utility knife. He returns to his Mephisto III game on the computer, sulking. It must be puberty.

Silky had another go at my thighs when Gwen called for a lift home. Should I get tetanus shots?

Thursday 6:
Didn't get to the gym because I had an important meeting where I'm told I am to be 'Acting Director' while Mr. Ogilvie, the real Director, is on a training course next week. I tell Alys by phone and she asks, "Will you get more money?" I check with Mr. Ogilvie, who says, scornfully I thought, "Yes, 2% more." Alys says it's not enough and I should demand more. Persuade her not to come to the

office to 'have it out' with Mr. Ogilvie by telling her I will discuss it with him personally. Become very busy and don't have time to see Mr. Ogilvie.

Didn't join the 'chattering classes' in the corridors and watering holes but worked on my Public Speaking speech for next Tuesday night instead. My topic is Globalisation and the Individual. I think I'm well placed to talk on that considering what I've gone through at work this past ten years -- unlike our politicians who promote the globalisation concept. They don't see any global competition in their industry; instead, they see growth in their business because of it. Is this the real cause of globalisation?

When we lifted linoleum all the way to the patio doors, we found the underlying linoleum very discoloured. Lance, who was helping again, stomped heavily on the patch then, when nothing exciting came of that, unwisely began jumping up and down on the spot. I was just thinking fondly about the way that pubescent kids flip between angry adults and cheerful children when he went right through the floor. Not right through so he landed in the basement; only one foot reached the basement, breaking the false ceiling down there and leaving the rest of him howling on the kitchen floor. His leg was very badly scratched, almost as bad as mine after a week of Silky's claws, but his pride was what really got hurt when I called him an idiot. After Alys had treated his wounds, he went off to sulk at the computer. Alys says it's cute that Lance has called his Mephisto III 'villains', Arthur and Alys. Personally, I don't like the way 'Arthur' and 'Alys' are tortured, mutilated and then killed, night after night. Is this healthy?

Friday 7:
Got to gym, usual routine and still no easier. Later, on our local commuter train, the GO train, I commented on this to Gerry and am told, "Going 2 or 3 times a week is just maintenance. You need to do much more to get any improvement." I sarcastically asked him how he would know seeing as he's never done any exercise since leaving High School.

Gerry was indignant at my assumption that he does no exercise and ranted on, for most of the journey home, about the Extreme Frisbee game he plays at an isolated farm up north every other weekend. The game, so far as I could tell, is played with Olympic weight discuses, a large pack of junkyard dogs, and a lot of flammable liquids. It sounded unlikely but no more so than the Fear Factor game show on TV.

Gerry, apparently, subscribes to Extreme Runner magazine, which recommends two periods of running every day. Each run should last 5 hours with a brief cool-down period between for taking in a high protein and carbohydrate meal (previously known as 'lunch' and later as 'power lunch'). Said meal to consist of 'Extreme'-ly rare T-bone steak (2 lbs. post-cooked, bone removed weight) in a 4 lbs. bowl of 'Extreme'-ly a la dente pasta drizzled with 'Extreme'-ly extra virgin olive oil and cilantro. If you don't follow this regime there's no benefit; no sexily toned torso on the runner and hence, no sexily toned model on the runner's sexily toned arm.

I made extremely satirical snorting noises but secretly wonder if he isn't right, certainly one year of what I'm doing has done nothing for me. I go into shock at seven minutes, a cold, clammy sweat breaks out everywhere as the sane part of my mind realises that, despite telling the rest of me there isn't a sabre-toothed tiger anywhere in sight, the irrational rest of me isn't going to stop. At 9 minutes my breath goes, hot sweat pours out at 11 minutes, and I'm walking by 13 minutes. By 17 minutes, I'm crawling on all fours (actually, at the beginning – now only metaphorically).

Regarding the olive oil mentioned above, I don't know much about the sex life of olives (I dropped biology early at school but I have heard some olives do get stuffed though until now I believed it was cookery term). [Note: check to see if that last part is really a joke or not] {Note to self: remove last note before publication, particularly if first note is confirmed as a joke]. But it seems to me 'Extreme and extra' are redundant phrases in describing virgins. One is either not a virgin or one is; no matter how many sweaty fingers have tested the fruit.

After work, I put a piece of wood over the hole in the kitchen floor and continued lifting linoleum.

Saturday 8:

This morning, as I waited to turn left out of Merlin Crescent onto the main road, I was looking to the right for a gap in the traffic when on my left side there was a thump that shook the car. Then a young woman in spandex shorts and a loose T-shirt skittered across the hood in front of me before falling off the other side. I jumped out, very concerned, but fortunately she was uninjured. She was shaking with fright and I couldn't help noticing her breasts had come out from her bra and they were jiggling about like anything. I had a strong urge to calm her with a big hug but felt it safest not to.

After she'd gone, and I'd settled down, it came to me I must work harder at my Public Speaking course, and perhaps add Assertiveness Training as well. I need more 'visibility' because this isn't the first time this has happened. Once, when I was younger, I was knocked from my motorbike and trampled by a pedestrian who failed to see me while crossing the road to catch a bus. Today's incident is particularly puzzling. A Ford Taurus station wagon isn't a small car and pale blue isn't a camouflage colour so I can only put this and the earlier mishap down, in some way, to my lack of 'presence.' Fortunately, no one at work seems to have noticed my invisibility. I expect that's the effect of the Public Speaking.

Continued to Home Terminal, our only remaining local (because it's global) home renovation store, and bought new chipboard and sub-floor, all the while wondering if I shouldn't have done more to calm that beautiful young cyclist; her breasts spoke of considerable agitation. I was also worried the accident was my fault because maybe I was so preoccupied with things and did something wrong. What if her Dad is a lawyer?

At lunchtime, I called my dad, who was not a lawyer. He was a nurse and retirement has left him too much time to diagnose himself. His conjunctivitis has spread to both eyes and he has new medication. It's so bad he can't see to watch TV. I decide not to mention how shaken I am by the cyclist incident or weakened by my Silky-lacerated thighs.

We have finally chosen some tiles. A nearby store, the Olde Worlde Tile Shoppe, had tiles we could agree on so we bought them and a neat border that sets them off brilliantly. We were so pleased with our success that Alys and I celebrated with a coffee and doughnut at Timmy's Coffee Emporium.

Sunday 9:
The reason Lance went through the floor is because water has seeped in under the patio doors and rotted the chipboard. I spent the day clearing out the remaining loose chips and preparing to lift the broken panel. That means lifting the lower layer of linoleum, which turns out to be glued to the floor. I let Alys and Lance work on the linoleum while I tried to raise the broken wood. They started

squabbling and I refereed for a time till I got sick of it and grounded Lance for a week. I wanted to ground Alys because she was the one causing the problem but didn't dare. Lance took this very badly and stormed off to his room, no doubt to mutilate 'Arthur' and 'Alys' again. We hadn't finished raising the linoleum by evening so we gave up for the day. Actually, Alys had worked herself up into such a state we fell out, despite my best efforts to placate her, and she stormed off to shower. I took this as a sign my shift was over too.

Later, when Alys was safely out of earshot, Gwen told me, very forcefully, that I had to stand up to Alys more and not always take her side. Gwen says it's bad for Alys to always get her own way. I agree, weakly, so she'll go away and stop scolding me but the thought of my life if I took Gwen's advice returned as nightmares and kept me awake most of the night. I'm writing this at 4 am! (Note to self: remove this part before publication.) It will be good for Gwen to go away to University and for me too if she's going to start pushing me into fights with Alys.

Thought from the early hours: In the olden days, when kids reached adulthood they were given the key to the door. Nowadays, sensible parents change the locks.

Monday 10:
This is the week I'm 'Acting' Director. I would have been more pleased if Mr. Ogilvie hadn't ordered me to seek Gerry's advice if anything came up, and if he hadn't also made every one of his direct reports 'Acting Director' before me -- when I'm the oldest. Actually, I think I'm the oldest Section Manager in the whole corporation but I daren't confide that to Alys. She may make a fuss. As well, now that I think about it, all the other section managers got to be 'Acting Director' for longer periods of time -- like Mr. Ogilvie's vacations. I wonder if I should make a fuss?

My section's work on administrative procedures is progressing nicely. We have ten procedures out for First Internal Review, seven out for Second Internal Review, four out for Third Internal Review and two out for First External Review. Not bad, considering we've only been going four years and there's considerable resistance to the whole concept of administrative, or any other kind of, procedures. We're fighting every inch of the way against appalling apathy.

Didn't go to the gym, awaiting important Directorial calls. There were none.

In the evening, continued lifting linoleum with Lance and Alys, who has graciously forgiven me for her bad temper last night. I estimate we will still be lifting linoleum at Christmas because the glue is in fine shape after all its years of service. I wish I knew whose glue it was, I'd write and commend them on their product. However, I expect they are out of business now because nobody would need to buy the stuff twice.

Back to normal on the Silky scratched thighs front, and I mean front. Perhaps I should lie face down on the couch on alternate days to spread the damage. Perhaps Gwen could stop work? I don't want to stop Silky sleeping on my lap because if she does this much damage when we're friends I can't imagine what she'd do if we weren't.

Lance had an accident cycling to school today; he was very badly shaken and scratched so he lay on the couch all evening (until I kicked him off so Silky could have her evening sleep). Alys fussed around him, foolishly encouraging him in the worst way. I don't think there'll be any real men left in the world soon, the way we coddle boys nowadays.

Tuesday 11:

On the morning GO train, Gerry and I joked about it being the International Day of Peace; it said so in our free commuter newspaper. The idea of peace in this world seemed unlikely at 7 am and it seemed ludicrous by lunchtime. My first inkling that this wasn't just any old 'international day of peace' came about 10 am when Renee, my Admin Assistant, said a plane had crashed into the World Trade Center in New York. I murmured suitably sad phrases; other people's aerial misfortunes make me uncomfortable because I'm not a good flyer, and I continued with my essential work. The news that a second plane had hit the building and one had hit the Pentagon as well sent my stomach into free-fall.

"Everybody's watching it on the Emergency Centre TVs," Renee told me, so we elevated ourselves to the 25th floor to join the rest of the company's staff crushed in the Centre or peering through the door.

Our Emergency Centre is well equipped with TVs and seeing myriad planes crash into myriad buildings was grotesque. As the buildings collapsed, the crowd began to edge out of the room. Perhaps the knowledge they were on an upper floor of a tall building in Toronto and not so very far from the airport was beginning to make itself felt.

"Shouldn't we evacuate?" one of my staff asked me and I was tempted to say flippantly that I already had when I realised they were genuinely frightened and needed a serious managerial answer.

After reassuring my staff, I returned to my desk where the phone was ringing. It was Alys, who reminded me we knew someone in the World Trade Center. She's doing an MBA correspondence course and the University's MBA office was on the first floor of the WTC. She'd been talking to them only the week before about her last and next assignments. The pile of rubble I'd just seen on TV probably included her assignments and the pleasant woman who'd received them. It's hard to believe that this touched our lives even though we are so far away.

Didn't go to the gym, too sickened by events.

When I got home, Alys told me my night class is cancelled. No one wants to do anything today and we didn't do linoleum lifting either. Carrying on with normal life seemed wrong somehow. At least, in the coming days, I'll have more time to prepare my speech; the presentation is now next Tuesday.

Wednesday 12:

It turns out the Olde Worlde Tile Shoppe can't get our tiles and we must choose some new ones. They are closed by the time I get home so Alys says we'll go tomorrow and I'm to get home early, which will be easy to do now that I'm Director. 'Say you're going golfing,' was her sarcastic suggestion, when I argued I should set a good example and stay later, not leave early. But maybe I will leave early; Alys would be happy and no at work one will ever know. I haven't had one Director-type call or meeting since the week began.

I booked my car into the usual place for its usual service. Really, the fact I've mentioned that tells you how dull a day it's been. No work was done at work; everyone was poring over newspapers and listening to the radio for the latest on terrorists. I'm worried we'll lose momentum on the new 'Expense Report' procedure. Luckily the 'Application for Unpaid Leave' procedure is at the external review stage or it too would be at risk.

Went to the gym because I can't go tomorrow if I'm leaving early. Also, tonight is the night!

The evening wasn't any more exciting than the day. Lance refused to help his mom lift linoleum so I had to leave the hole in floor and scrape linoleum instead. Alys brought in the garden spade from the garage and we used that, but it's still backbreaking work. The spade occasionally digs into the wooden sub-floor and gouges it. At first, that upset me because all those gouges will have to be filled if we're going to lay level tiles but by 10 pm I no longer cared and now the floor is a mess. Alys refused to speak to me after I muttered this was a dumb idea more times than she cared for.

After collecting Gwen from work and before going to bed, I reviewed my naked body in the closet door mirror. Today is the first anniversary of my starting the gym and I'm taking stock. I look like one of those 'before' and 'after' photos, only it's the 'before' photo when it should be the 'after' one.

Height -- 5ft 9 and three-quarters ins., down from 5 ft 10. What's going on?

Weight -- up 5 lbs. Action: I will record my progress every Monday and Friday from now on to increase focus on this challenge (that's modern management speak for sort out my problem).

Body Mass Index (BMI) – 27.5, up from 27 a year ago.

Waist -- 36 inches, exactly as it was a year ago. My waist is the whole reason I went to the gym. I've been a 34 in waist man since I was twenty and the sudden jump up in pant size shocked me into action.

Muscle tone -- same. No sign of rippling 'washboard' abs yet.

Folds of flab on stomach -- no discernible change. There's still, at least, two inches worth when grabbed by an unfriendly hand. In this case Alys's unfriendly hand, her sharpened nails tell me she hasn't forgiven me for the 'dumb idea' comments.

"I like a man with love-handles," my beloved beanpole quips cattily.

We won't be spoon-hugging in bed tonight.

Thursday 13:
On the train, I recounted the floor saga to Gerry and he says I'm doing it all wrong. Extreme Renovator, another magazine he reads, recommends leaving the linoleum in place. A suggestion so sensible that I have trouble believing he read it properly. However, my faith in human nature is restored when he continues, 'But they don't recommend tiles.' What I should have done is called in a redi-mix truck and poured an inch of concrete on the floor, topping it off with

solid marble slabs shipped specially from Sicily. That's the only floor covering being laid this year by extreme renovators.

Is it possible Director's do nothing? I ponder this question all day because I have even less work this week than I normally have when I'm responding to Mr. Ogilvie's insatiable demands for updates, reports, graphs, feedback, strategic plans, etc. If Mr. Ogilvie's sole purpose is to make work for me and the other section managers, and my sole purpose is to carry out the work he invents for me, what am I to make of my career, the company's future prospects, and the capitalist system in general? I'm glad when four o' clock arrives and I can go home. I don't share my doubts about the future of capitalism with Gerry or Alys. They would point out the flaw in my reasoning and I'd feel stupid. I'm certain to spot the flaw soon enough without their assistance and I'll laugh at my fears privately.

Leave early (so no gym) and, with Alys, wander around the Olde Worlde Tile Shoppe looking at alternate tiles and borders. Unfortunately, we are back at the stage where we can't agree and we leave, barely speaking, without choosing anything.

I began work on the hole in the floor, which took my mind off the flaw.

Friday 14:
Today, my last day as Acting Director, was quiet and I was able to concentrate my mind on the flaw (not the floor) in my reasoning about the capitalist system and, I'm ashamed to admit, was unable to spot it.

And nothing vaguely Directorial was required of me. I considered calling a meeting of all my, well, Mr. Ogilvie's, direct reports but didn't -- because I knew they wouldn't come. Few of them have been in much this week at all. No doubt they too have been under-utilised without Mr. Ogilvie's constant demand for updates. I spent the afternoon writing a 'handover' memo from me to Mr. Ogilvie so he would know what happened while I was in charge. By four o' clock I hadn't filled one side of a sheet of paper so I decided to give him a 'verbal update' on Monday morning.

On the train, Gerry asked me how I liked being Director and I replied vaguely by laying heavy stress on the extra work and responsibility. He nodded and said that's what he'd found the three times he'd been acting Director. I changed the subject.

Removing the broken chipboard panel from the floor wasn't

simple and my temper was not improved by listening to Alys, Lance, and Gwen laughing at a 'Simpsons' episode about home renovation on the family room TV. Eventually, I stopped work -- right after hitting my kneecap with the mallet as I tried to bash off a recalcitrant piece of board. Alys was so disgusted with my language she refused to spoon-hug in bed again. I think we may be growing apart.

Weight: minus 1 lb. Good.

Saturday 15:

I call dad. His conjunctivitis is better but he has a blocked tear duct and needs an operation. Gawain is prostrate after injuring his back reaching for a fallen videocassette. My bruised knee doesn't seem so bad today and I don't mention it.

The floor panel is finally out. Unfortunately, a piece of it is under the sliding patio door frame and can't be removed without removing the door, which means I have nothing on which to support the new panel all along that edge. After studying the problem, I bought a 2x6 plank, cut it into pieces, sealed it with wood preserver, and nailed the pieces to the beam under the door. Of course the new panel still didn't fit because it couldn't get under the doorframe and I had to cut an inch off the full length of the panel. I covered the new panel with water sealant and nailed it down with pounds of nails. Alys, Gwen and Lance went out for the day so as 'not to be in the way.' They had a good time, except Lance bashed his knee on the car door and he's now hobbling around in a comical fashion. Of course his mother is paying him all the attention he wants. Maybe I should make more fuss about my aches and pains, particularly my bruised knee.

Sunday 16:

After sealing the new chipboard panel for a second time I sealed the new sub-floor and nailed it on top of the chipboard. I amused myself during all this satisfactory trades' work (why didn't I become a carpenter?) by imagining how Extreme Renovator would do it. My family kept out of the way again -- and had a good time again, despite Lance's bruised knee, which, I'm told, is much worse than mine.

Monday 17:

Spent all day trying to see Mr. Ogilvie and update him on what happened. I couldn't see him because he was in meetings all day.

Question: Does this help me in finding the flaw in my reasoning? Answer: No.

Didn't go to the gym, awaiting Mr. Ogilvie's call.

In the evening, I filled the gouges and other holes in the floor with wood filler and began finding beams. Every floor in this house creaks and groans when you walk on it and I'm determined this floor won't when I've finished because every loose board will be nailed and screwed to a beam. By bedtime, the floor was neatly crisscrossed with lines showing where the beams were. Tomorrow, I'll nail the boards to the beams, followed by screwing on the weekend. (I can just about remember when 'screwing on the weekend' meant something more exciting.) Some days my genius just shines.

Weight: plus 2 lbs. Not so good.

Tuesday 18:

After realising I was getting nowhere on the phone, I went along to Mr. Ogilvie's office where his secretary, a motherly lady called Eunice, told me he was busy. However, I saw him through his window hunching over something, and then swaying sideways before walking the length of his office to bend down and pick something up. I'm sure he was practising his putting. I wish I played golf but Alys won't hear of it. She says we can't afford it and anyway she isn't being left alone all weekend with the kids. Sometimes I don't think Alys is a very natural mother.

Didn't go to the gym, awaiting Mr. Ogilvie's call.

Reserved automatic screw gun for Saturday and Sunday from our local Rent-All store and calculated the number of screws I'd need if I put one screw every four inches along the beams. Then I re-calculated using every six inches to see if it was worth saving some money.

I gave my speech on globalisation this evening to the Public Speaking class and it was well received by my class leader and fellow pupils. They too are apprehensive about the future. My next speech is in one month's time and I'm mildly concerned I haven't got a topic yet.

When I got home, I told Alys about my successful first speech and she said, "That's nice, dear." With all the encouragement I give her on her MBA, only last week I took Lance and Gwen to the movies so she could revise, you'd think she could be a bit more positive for my night class.

Wednesday 19:
Eunice says, "Mr. Ogilvie is out of the office today at a meeting." Gerry says golfing. I fear that's the Directorial secret I've been missing.

The statement above led me to think of the subtle flexibility of the English language. When top honchos tell us to 'treat the company's money as if it were your own' we mere minions hear 'be careful and sparing in your use of the company's money because it's not yours' but senior managers hear 'it's your money, have fun.' I suspect that's true in every corporation in the world, except those where the owner still controls, which is why owner controlled companies grow the fastest. I haven't taken economics but I bet you could easily show that countries grow fastest when their economic engines are run by owners and stand still when the engines are being 'managed' by highly paid honchos. I think that's the real reason Japan hasn't grown for the last few years, all the original Mr. Hondas, Matsushitas, et al died around 1990.

Went to the gym because I've had a brilliant idea. My strategy till now has been to remove 2 inches from my waist and it hasn't worked. Yesterday, in another momentary flash of genius, I realised that, if I put 2 inches on my chest, the result would be the body shape I'm aiming for. I've added new arm, shoulder and chest machines to my usual routine. What's even better about this strategy is I could actually eat more to 'bulk up' as they say, which is pretty well what I'm doing anyhow.

Gwen's soccer team is still playing outdoors because Canada goose droppings made their home field unusable in the spring and early summer. Tonight's game was a tie as both teams wanted only to keep warm and stopping the game to pick the ball out of the net would have prevented that. The parents kept warm by watching from their cars. Lance's team finished outdoors two weeks ago and tonight Alys won the toss to stay home and help him with his homework.

Thursday 20:
I didn't ask to see Mr. Ogilvie today because he sent an e-mail demanding an interim progress report for his meeting with the vice-presidents (all stratum, ranks and grades) tomorrow and I spent the

day putting the report together. I wish I knew what the VPs are going to be talking about. I suspect it's to do with the re-organisation and I'd like to slant my report in a way that would help me (and my section) live through it.

My arms, shoulders and chest ache from yesterday and my new gym strategy. Still, as they say, no pain, no gain. Didn't go to gym today, doing Mr. Ogilvie's report.

President Bush has demanded the Taliban government of Afghanistan hand over Osama Bin Laden, the man the Americans blame for masterminding the WTC bombing. The Taliban say they won't hand him over without proof he was involved, a measured and restrained response you wouldn't normally expect from fanatics. As the Americans have made similar negative responses in the past to countries requesting extradition from American soil, you can be sure they will be furious at being hoist by their own petard.

When I got home, Lance greeted me at the door holding up his hand for me to see his horribly swollen pinkie finger jutting out at 45 degrees from the rest. It was a gruesome sight, pasty white between the knuckles with black circles running around the joints. It was clearly broken, something the school hadn't noticed all day as he'd injured himself playing basketball in gym class at ten o' clock in the morning. We went to the doctor's surgery where we waited 45 minutes before getting examined.

"Broken," said the doctor after about a minute's inspection. "You'd best go to the hospital. They can x-ray it and they have a Fracture Clinic where it can be properly treated because fingers are tricky. They like to get them right first time otherwise they have to be broken again and reset."

Went to Emergency and the receptionist sent us to see a nurse. "Broken," said the nurse after a minute's inspection. "Go back to reception and they'll fill in your details." Reception filled in a form and entered us into the computer. We were sent to a waiting room full of horribly sick people and we waited. An hour later, we were sent to a tiny corner in a corridor that was doubling as another waiting room, to wait again with two other teenage boys with swollen hands and fingers.

Another hour passed before a doctor came and examined the boys. "Probably broken," he said to Lance, and sent us to the x-ray department, where we waited another hour in the company of the other two who were also 'probably broken'.

After the x-raying, which lasted 5 minutes, we were sent back to the corner to wait for another hour. At which time, the doctor returned with the x-rays and dispensed his diagnoses, one was just swollen and he needed to put ice on it. The next was Lance. His finger is broken and the doctor strapped the broken finger to its neighbour with sticky tape and we were sent home just after ten o' clock at night. I don't think any comment from me could improve on this episode.

Friday 21:

After checking with Eunice, and being assured Mr. Ogilvie wouldn't want to see me today because of the important meeting he has to attend, I went to the gym to continue my brilliant new strategy.

While I was out, Mr. Ogilvie finally called me to his office. The voice message was waiting when I got back. Does he watch me go out? I rushed to his office because he didn't sound pleased but before I could explain my absence or tell him about last week he demanded to know why I'd let Gerry do everything while he was away? I didn't know what to say, then I remembered Mr. Ogilvie telling me to get Gerry's advice before doing anything and so, to make it sound like I was involved in whatever Gerry did, I reminded him of his words.

"Advice is one thing but you have to take the lead when you're Director, Lakelady," he stormed, leaving me to harbour dark thoughts about my colleague. What Directorial things did Gerry do and I didn't? I couldn't ask Mr. Ogilvie or he'd know I didn't know and I didn't want him to know I didn't know. Nor could I ask Gerry because then he'd know I knew he'd stabbed me in the back and he'd become my mortal enemy -- because nobody trusts someone they've previously cheated.

Lance's soccer team had its first indoor practice tonight. I don't stay to watch practises anymore because nowadays, the quiz comes only at the end of games. At thirteen, kids know what they do in practice isn't worth questioning but still hold the after game quiz 'did you see me do...?' Gwen, from her advanced age, no longer even does that. I rather miss it.

Weight: minus 1 lb. Good.

Saturday 22:

Dad has his eye operation booked for next week. "Being a pensioner gets you special treatment," he snaps, when I ask how come he got in so soon; he's always complaining that the British National Health Service makes everyone wait for years to have surgery because that's what he reads in his newspaper. I foolishly changed the subject by asking if his conjunctivitis is better and he says it is -- but now he's having problems with his stomach and he's going for tests on Monday. Gawain has returned to work after his back problem. He's walking with a stick, which may be permanent because something unpronounceable has gone wrong with his discs. As I am in good health, if you ignore the cuts and bruises from Silky and the floor, and aches and pains from the gym, I commiserate with my usual lack of genuine sympathy.

I told Dad about our experience in the Emergency Room and he says we'd have waited twice as long for half the attention over there. Modern day Britons believe everything is worse in Britain; it's a form of inverted superiority. If they can't be the best at everything like they used to be then they're damned well going to be the worst at everything.

Picked up screw gun and 5 lbs. of screws from the Rent-All store. Screwing all day, ha-ha. (Note to reader: That's so weak it doesn't count as a joke.) By lunchtime, I have at least a hundred screws half way into the floor. Their heads (and the drill bit) are burned beyond use, and I've had to buy another drill bit. The Rent-All man was very suspicious about what I'm doing with his tool, claiming no one has ever worn out even one end of the double-ended bit before. By mid-afternoon, I'm getting better at it and I still have one end of the new drill bit left. I stopped to break off the stuck screws and let the family test the floor for creaks. They claim not to hear any improvement. I think the Rent-All man is paying them.

By suppertime, the family gives a grudging admission of improvement. I asked Gwen, who this morning claimed she had never heard the floor squeak in the past, to walk on the floor and circle any squeaks she finds with a felt marker. This turns out not to be a good idea. Gwen now claims it all squeaks and draws overlapping circles everywhere. By bedtime, I have used the whole box of screws and Gwen says the floor still squeaks. My arms, chest, and back all ache from using the screw gun -- still, no pain, no gain.

Sunday 23:

Alys's Birthday

I gave Alys her presents quickly then zipped down to the Rent-All store for another 5 lbs. of screws and another drill bit. Fortunately, it's a different Assistant and he hands them over without comment. Screwing all day again and that's no joke, my back is killing me by the time I'm finished. However, the floor is squeak-free. Alys isn't pleased that I made so little of her birthday so we won't spoon-hug in bed -- again.

Gwen and Lance took Alys out for lunch and the day, partly as a birthday treat and partly to keep out of the way while I screwed up the automatic screwdriver -- and occasionally the boards on the floor. Lance tried to lift his sister during some horseplay while they were out and hurt his back (he's forgotten about his finger). Alys, of course, fusses over him telling him to take it easy and not strain himself. Like he would do that! If she keeps mollycoddling him this way, he'll soon be a confirmed invalid.

President Bush says he wants Bin Laden 'dead or alive.' Coming from Texas makes the President seem a little odd sometimes. Don't they have rules about 'reasonable force' and 'innocent until proven guilty' down there?

Monday 24:

Work again and Mr. Ogilvie didn't update us on his Friday meeting with the VPs so I'm even more convinced it was about our department in the re-organisation. Everyone else obviously agrees because the conversation at the water coolers is now half on terrorism and half on downsizing. It's a wonder our company keeps going with so little production from everybody. The cut and thrust of capitalism must be happening somewhere else.

George Bush told us the other day that if we're not for him, we must be against him, which suggests the President doesn't know the world very well. I'm sure half a billion people are with him, another half-billion are against, and the other six billion or more of the world's population couldn't care less. Unilaterally lumping 6 billion neutrals into the 'against' column is a bad idea. Today Mr. Bush announced that Afghanistan would be better off without the Taliban, something most reasonable observers pointed out when the US began arming these nutcases a few years back.

In the evening, after supper, Alys and I cleaned up the floor so the tile layers can start anytime. Gwen and Lance had homework so were unable to help. Lance's homework involved a lot of automobile noises, which I think had more to do with 'Stolen in Sixty Seconds' than science. I suppose computer games could be considered 'science'. And if he fails science, at least he's now trained as a car thief, a serial killer, an assassin, or a Universal Soldier. There are so many different careers opened up to teenage boys today compared to when I was a lad.

Weight: plus 2 lbs. No comment.

Tuesday 25:
Lance's birthday. He's now officially a teenager.

I know adolescents have to revolt against their parent's rules and values in order to get up enough momentum to leave the nest but today's adolescents have to pierce and tattoo every part of their bodies to get the same level of horror we excited with our long hair or short skirts. Body piercing and tattooing may not be life threatening, but they're dangerous enough. And the future can only get worse. The result of our present lax standards is teenagers have an unenviable choice, being scarred for life or, worse, not leaving home at all.

This rant has been brought to you by courtesy of Lance getting his ears pierced to celebrate his accession to teenage-hood. This puberty thing is going too far.

Wednesday 26:
Lance's sudden shift to being fashion conscious makes me feel I need to update posterity on what we men are wearing, as well as how we live. So, because nothing of any significance happened today, I'm taking this opportunity to illustrate. I wish to state clearly that Arthur Lakelady is not wearing anything reported below, or ever will. Gerry, however, likes to keep up with fashion. Now that Western men have stopped trying to achieve something, they've become quite giddy with all the possibilities opening up for them. Highlights include earrings in one or both ears depending on your 'orientation' (I'm told), jewellery or bling is very popular, the gold-ier and gaudier the better, and hair is either blonde spikes or shaved bald.

Gwen's outdoor soccer team finished their season with a loss. Next week, she'll have indoor practice at this time so the driving stays much the same, except I miss out on the traffic jams across the top of the city, at midnight, after away games.

Thursday 27:
Alys called me at work to tell me my payroll deposit was wrong; they only paid me for two days. I tried to calm her, assuring her it was just a glitch in the system and would be corrected next week but she insisted I go straight to Payroll and sort it out. I demurred until she said she'd be in on the next train. I hurried to Payroll and found that when they removed my 'step up' pay for being the Acting Director, they inadvertently terminated me. It's quite worrying, particularly at a time like this when the tiles aren't paid for and the Restructuring Team is still off-site, at a golf and country club resort, working on its lists of employees and jobs.

The other day President Bush forgot to thank Canada in a speech listing all those who had helped after the WTC tragedy. The newspapers are full of patriotic complaint. Bush says he thinks of Canada as a 'brother' and family; therefore, thanks aren't necessary. What a funny family he must live in. I suspect, like many Americans, he wasn't aware Canada was a separate country.

Grey Cup day: Canada's equivalent of the Superbowl or the F.A. Cup is today. When Earl Grey, the then Governor-General (not the bergamot-scented tea), gave this trophy to the local Rugby league, he can't have imagined the game would have degenerated into a battle of shrimps, which is what North American football players remind me of with their huge helmet and shoulder padding. And like shrimps, when you remove the hard outer shell what's left is hardly worth having. Most homes in Canada on this day are given over to TV, beer and vast quantities of junk snacks. The Lakeladys maintain a dignified observance of the ritual by missing out the unessential elements, like TV, beer, and junk snacks.

We bought a cat rug for Silky to use when she lies on my lap; that way her claws won't dig into my flesh when she leaps off. Tonight was the first opportunity to use it and Silky refused to even consider sleeping on it so, when Gwen called for a ride home, I got scratched again. Alys says I should be firmer with Silky -- she's only a cat. Which is like saying I should be firmer with Alys, she's only a woman.

Lance has volunteered to train Silky to use her rug and, reluctantly, we've agreed. It will end in tears.

Friday 28:

Alys, sensing that I'm not happy with the uncertainty at work, insisted I go and talk to Mr. Ogilvie and get some straight answers. I've decided I must put on a braver face at home; the additional stress of Alys's encouragement may be too much for my constitution. What Alys doesn't seem to realise is we remember the great heroes of old because they did what no other man was willing or likely to do; that's why we call them heroes. Most of us value a quiet, uneventful life. And those that don't value a quiet life should be identified in babyhood and given cranial electric shock treatment till they do.

Lance told us, at the supper table, he isn't happy with the uncertainty at school. He's concerned the Principal doesn't like him and will fail him without cause. Alys says she'll be at the school Monday to straighten things out with that Principal. I fear Lance has a lot to learn when it comes to school, mothers, and female psychology in general.

The 'Mars and Venus' author was right about men and women inhabiting different spaces -- but they're both on this planet. Given the choice, men would be hunting, fishing and killing each other in the Temperate Zone, while women would be murdering each other for chocolate in the Tropics. Arthur Lakelady would be quietly reading a book in Iceland.

Yesterday, the US provided its evidence that Bin Laden was to blame for the WTC atrocity. As this evidence, wholly circumstantial, comes from two agencies, the FBI and CIA, who blamed the Oklahoma bombing a few years back on Bin Laden right up to the day Timothy McVeigh's brother turned him in, I can't see many people being impressed.

Obviously, the Taliban were impressed (they can't be familiar with the FBI and CIA's recent record) because they have asked Bin Laden to leave Afghanistan.

Took Lance to soccer practice, leaving Alys to help Gwen with her homework. They weren't speaking to each other when Lance and I got home. Alys says next time, she's going to take Lance to soccer practice -- and I can do the hard work for a change! I'm rightly incensed at this remark for it was Alys who sent me off with Lance because 'she didn't want to sit around in a cold gym for hours doing nothing'. There'll be no spoon-hugging in bed tonight.

Weight: down 1 lb. Good.

Saturday 29:

Dad had his operation and is recovering. His stomach problem disappeared just before the tests and the tests showed nothing. I congratulated him on his good health -- unwisely, as it turned out. His stomach is giving him problems again and so is his back. Gawain is 'as well as can be expected' for a man of 33 who has watched TV from a horizontal position every free minute of his life. When Gawain goes, he should donate his brain to science or the television museum.

I'm very embarrassed at our North American media; they are all talking and behaving in what they consider to be brave, fierce voices, only they sound really frightened. I know the WTC event was horrific but we are allowing a bunch of Muslim madmen to help our own governments repress us back to the Dark Ages. The proper answer to intolerance is more tolerance, to fear is fearlessness, and to threats of oppression is more freedom. We're building fortresses, 500 years after castles became death-traps to those inside. I thought I'd write to an editor and make my feelings known, however, when this is published, as I'm sure it will be someday, my protest will be heard.

Last week, Renee bought airline tickets for my upcoming training course in the USA, where we all go now to learn how to be good subjects of the American Empire. I feel a bit sick at the thought of getting into a plane but intend to set a good example by not being sick, or drunk, during the flight. Still, I can't help wishing my own nerve wasn't being tested so soon after the WTC event. Over the supper table, I shared my concern, in a 'modern man' kind of way with my family, hoping (foolishly) for some cheering words that showed they cared about my safety. Lance pointed out that, statistically, he was far more at risk than I will be because every day he will be going to school and, therefore, crossing the main road at the end of Merlin Crescent. Alys agreed with him and said she'll walk him to the corner from now on. Lance, realising his mistake, tried to wriggle out of it but Alys was adamant (it's practically her middle name) and it serves the little so-and-so right! Gwen wanted to know if my life insurance money would be enough to buy her a car?

Message on our answering machine says the Tile Shoppe can't get enough border tiles to do the kitchen. Can we come in and pick some different ones, please? So we do. It's funny how easy it is to pick tiles now. We've rejected the border tiles we chose today a dozen times, every time the saleslady pressed them on us in fact. This time, and considering the different tiles we're trying to match to now, they look fine. Do tile people know their job so well they just stop their customers choosing badly?

Sunday 30:
Alys asked me to drop off our dry-cleaning at the store, which I did only to get a long lecture from the woman behind the counter that went something like this:
The shop assistant, disdainfully picking up a pair of my Silky-furred trousers, "Is this animal fur?"
Me, embarrassed because of the other six customers who were contemptuously looking at my furry pants, "Y-yes. We have a cat."
The shop assistant, "Well, in future, brush it off before you come here. I don't have time for this on a Sunday. It's our busy day."
I mumbled a brief apology and fled, vowing never to go there again. I don't often go into stores, Alys is much better at these things than I am, but this is the first time anything like this has happened.
On my return, I told the family of this peculiar incident, in a 'modern man' kind of way, and Lance said it was nothing to the way his Math teacher talks to him. Apparently, the woman is a cross between Cruella DeVille and Margaret Thatcher. Alys is going to speak to her tomorrow, right after her meeting with the Principal. I hope Alys hasn't bitten off more than she can chew, two monsters of depravity in one day is a tall order even for a gentle lady from the Middle Ages like Alys. Gwen says I'm too soft; I should have given the dry cleaning lady a stern lecture on customer relations. I wonder if Gwen could take the laundry next time?
Later, I took my car to the service place I had it booked it into, intending to leave it overnight, as I always do so they can work on it first thing in the morning. Only this time the building was empty. I wandered round the outside peering in the windows and saw no sign of life. Unwilling to leave my trusty old wagon in an abandoned lot, I brought it home and called the garage. It's too late for anyone to be there on a Sunday, of course, but the answering machine is still in service and sounds positively welcoming. I wasn't convinced and kept my car at home.
Lance decided today was the day for Silky to learn to use her rug, which he tried to do using force when she wouldn't accept bribes.

After he had got badly scratched, he decided Silky should be put down and took some convincing otherwise. Silky felt Lance should be put down and it took me most of the evening to convince her otherwise too.

October 2001:
War, Halloween and
other offences against mankind.

Monday 1:

On the morning GO train, I told Gerry my theory that tile shop assistants know their job so well they don't let customers buy poor choices. He snorted and said, "Extreme Renovator doesn't recommend tiles because there's actually only one pattern of tile and border in the whole world. All the ones you see in the stores are just samples to bring in gullible fools." He stopped short of saying 'like you' but I could tell that's what he was thinking. Fortunately, I know his snide remark can't be true because I've seen houses with different tiles. Then, I thought, maybe they just make one tile and border per year and that's why it looks like there's more than one variety. Arrive at work very depressed.

Another announcement at work today; this one says the reorganisation won't be done till 'early in the first quarter of 2002.' I'm relieved, not because this extra time for 'input to the restructuring team' will help me (my section has no friends, so more input means less chance for us at the end) but because I will, at least, be employed until Christmas. I expect Public Relations advised that laying people off before the holidays is bad PR. Called Alys and told her the good news. Even the people gossiping in the hallways sounded more cheerful.

The garage I've been using for years is no more; it seems I was their only customer. I booked the car into a different one. What did everyone know about the old garage that I didn't?

Alys had a successful day at school facing down the twin dragons. They weren't aware their behaviour had led Lance to suicidal manic depression and are extremely sorry if anything they've said (such as 'where is your homework?' or 'shouldn't you be in class?') has upset Lance. They will do better in future. Lance didn't seem as pleased with this news as you might have expected. Gwen said

Lance should just get to class on time and do his homework on time, like she does, and he wouldn't feel so persecuted. This led to a brief altercation and Lance storming out of the dining room. No doubt Mephisto III has a new villain called Gwen to be maimed and killed.

Weight: + 2lbs? And I starved myself all weekend so this wouldn't happen!

Tuesday 2:

I've finally decided on a topic for my next speech, Stress in the Workplace. Gerry says Extreme Orator recommends an 'in-your-face' approach to public speaking -- timidity and responsibility are out. They advise violently emoting passion, storming, ranting, raging, and sweating to win over your audience. Hitler and Mussolini should be your role models. Now I know where our new crop of VPs learned their oratorical skills because I've watched them all have a two-year-old's temper tantrum on stage in the past few weeks. One was so unaware of the impression he created it made us all laugh -- after we were out of his sight. He was taking questions from the floor when a seemingly harmless question, like one a party stalwart asks his own Prime Minister to fill up time and stop the Opposition asking difficult questions, made him erupt like a blocked toilet. He paced back and forth, ranting, red in the face, and thumping the table with his fist before eventually calming down. Then he said, "I get very passionate about that. Now, are there any more questions?" Unsurprisingly, there weren't.

Gwen and Lance are friends again. They had to be because Lance wanted help with his math homework and Gwen's the only person in the house who can do this new math. Alys and I got left behind in grade six. Lance is also friends with Silky again but I notice Silky hides under the coffee table when Lance comes into the room. She doesn't have Lance's forgiving nature.

Wednesday 3:

At work, normality is returning as people with nothing new to talk about go back to their desks from the water coolers and smoking rooms. We're busier too, my phone rang today, I received nine e-mails, and one of my staff, who hasn't done a stroke of work in months, asked for some clerical assistance.

Our doctor called to say she'd received the hospital's x-ray results of Lance's broken finger and could we come to see her tomorrow?

Gwen's soccer team had its first indoor practice tonight and I drove her there because she's still in the 'can't drive alone after dark' stage of her driving licence. Tonight, for some reason, I realised I shall miss driving her to games and practice when she moves on, even though it cuts into my diary time. It's what used to be called 'quality time' way back in the Eighties, when we started losing the right to have a life outside of work. (Now that the government has discovered we don't mind being economic serfs, they are taking away our right to a pensionable life after work too.)

Alys helped Lance with his homework so naturally they weren't speaking when I got home. And later, the Alys character in Mephisto had a bad night too.

Thursday 4:

Yesterday Canada agreed the US evidence for Bin Laden's guilt was conclusive. Obviously, they have short memories in Ottawa as well. The Taliban have offered talks with the US government to arrange handing over Bin Laden. America's President Bush is outraged, naturally. His daddy had a successful war (against America's old ally Saddam Hussein) and he wants one too.

Gerry wasn't on the train tonight so I had time to look about me and listen in on my neighbours' conversations. I shared the GO train's four-seat passenger arrangement with two elderly men and a sharp young salesman type, still wearing his sunglasses. They got into conversation and, from Toronto till the stop before mine, the two old codgers answered the young man's questions, telling him about their respective farms, their orchards, their fishing boat, and their day out in the big city without their wives. The young salesman, in return, patronisingly boasted of his fast life in the city moving goods and winning extra commissions. The old men nodded and wished him luck in the future as he got off. Then they settled back to discuss their CPUs, their modems, their gigabytes and their RAMs, ROMs, pixels and caches, servers, LANs, and a host of other bewildering electronic wizardry that I, who use these things every day, couldn't follow. When I got off the train I, still couldn't tell which was the 'story' and which the truth. And what did the 'fishing boat' look like?

Took Lance to the doctor who pronounced his ring finger broken. Lance and I said, "No, it's the pinkie." The doctor showed us the letter from the hospital confirming it was the ring finger and we showed her his finger confirming it was the pinkie. In the end, she compromised by sending us to have it x-rayed at the local strip plaza and replacing the sticky tape with a hi-tech metal splint because taping it like the hospital did would have it set wrong. With tremendous self-control, I forbore mentioning it was she who sent us to the hospital in the first place because, she said, they would be the best people to set it properly.

Alys and Gwen stayed home while I was on this mission of mercy, Gwen to study and Alys to tinker with the kitchen decorating while the kitchen is out of commission. When I returned, I found Alys wants to move the breakfast bar because it's in the way. As this would require also moving the cupboards underneath and reworking the countertop around the sinks, I said no quite forcefully. Alys left to stick pins in an Arthur doll I'm convinced she has hidden and Gwen said she was proud of me. She won't feel that way when her husband, sometime down the road, says no to one of her schemes.

Friday 5:
Britain has laid out its evidence concerning Bin Laden but it amounts to little more than Bin Laden has said in the past that he hates the USA. Pakistan has done a much better deal. In return for having its debts written off, huge amounts of aid shipped in, and the lifting of international sanctions against the country, they have agreed the US evidence is strong enough to indict Bin Laden for multiple acts of terrorism. So it is -- but probably not strong enough to convict him. Any competent US lawyer could, and would, win this case. As the British know, prosecuting terrorists successfully is difficult. Particularly when the terrorists, such as the Irish Republican Army, have the backing of people in a large power like the USA.

I dropped my car at my 'new' regular garage, asking them to call and let me know what a 150,000 km service, four new tires, and replacing a piece of plastic trim that was hanging from the body, would cost. By lunchtime, they hadn't called so I called them. The woman who answered sounded very flustered and said she'd phone me right back after she'd spoken to the technician. An hour later, I called again and got a different woman, who transferred me to a man in Service, who gave me a price that took my breath away. They did at least promise to call when the car was ready.

Before leaving the office, when they hadn't called, I called the garage again to confirm my car will be ready. Like last time, I was once again put through to Service but this time, it just rang and rang. After a time, a woman picked up the phone and asked who I was waiting for. I said Service, without adding any sarcastic remarks. She said, "Oh," and put me back on hold. Another eon passed before another woman picked up the phone and asked who I was waiting for. I replied Service and she put me on hold again. Then, as my train was undoubtedly rolling out of the station without me, a man picked up the phone and asked who I was waiting for. I said, thinking I had reached the Holy Grail, I was Arthur Lakelady and I was calling to see if my car was ready. He said there was no Arthur Lakelady there and he was just leaving to make a delivery. I had to call back and ask for Darla. I didn't try to explain about the Arthur Lakelady business, I just called back and asked for Darla, after that I was put on hold. There are only two kinds of people at garages, those who are not Darla and those who are -- but are too fricking busy to answer phones. Eventually, as my back up train left the station without me, a woman answered the phone and asked who I was waiting for. I said, Darla. She said, "Oh," and put me back on hold. I was just deciding to hang up and catch the next train when another woman answered and we went through the usual routine. This time, she didn't put me on hold, even though she wasn't Darla (who is?) she asked what I wanted. I told her and she said, "Yes, it's ready and don't forget we close at six on Fridays. If you don't get it tonight, you'll have to wait until Monday." A fact I had forgotten amid the pleasure of whiling away my time listening to their customer service music.

Why are late trains slow trains? Don't people who work late want to get home quickly? I pondered these questions on the journey home, amid weary account executives, corporate lawyers, and other middle-class parasites. On balance, viewing their dark-ringed eyes, swelling paunches and sagging jowls, I feel they would be better off working in a coalmine rather than in the billion cubicles of downtown Toronto.

I made it to the garage with a minute to spare and I could tell the Cashier didn't want to serve me but I remained firm and got the car back. I think Gwen may have a point concerning dealing with some people and maybe there's more of Gwen in me than I have previously imagined.

Alys, Gwen, and Lance weren't so easy to deal with when I got home, however. I'd forgotten we were going out to dinner and they were hungrily waiting at home for their chauffeur. Considering I hadn't eaten either, I thought their comments most inappropriate but I didn't say so -- because I couldn't get a word in edgeways.

Weight: minus 2 lbs. Better.

Saturday 6:

Called dad. The tests on his stomach were fine and his conjunctivitis is completely cured. This is good news, finally. Except his varicose veins are playing up and he can hardly walk. Gawain is also still unable to get about because of his discs. My two sickly relatives have been assigned a public health nurse and a cleaning lady on the National Health Service. As I'm disgustingly healthy at present, I listen in guilty silence. I know that the least a really loving son and brother could do is to fly over and make them a nice cup of tea. I wonder why Galahad is never mentioned? Decided to call and ask him.

Told dad our recent experiences with the Ontario health system and he assured me Lance is getting superlative treatment. In Britain, they'd have amputated his leg by now.

With Gwen at work all day, Alys had to go shopping on her own. I suggested she call friends but she said 'if you can't be bothered to accompany your own wife, I can't hope for more charity from others.' I remained unmoved by this plea because I had to catch up on this diary.

Sunday 7:

I asked Gwen to go for the dry-cleaning but Alys ordered me stop being a wuss and go for it myself. This time I'm to remind the old biddy at the store that the customer is the boss and I'm the customer. Alys says I'm a man and I'm not to be afraid of elderly shop girls. She laid heavy emphasis on 'girls', which was supposed to make me feel braver but didn't because I was never good with girls. I returned to the store, carrying this week's heavy load of cleaning on my heart (metaphorically), with the following results:

Shop assistant, grimly scenting blood, "Have those shirts button-down collars?"

Me, in a small voice, "Yes."

She (-Wolf), "You'll have to undo them yourself. I don't have time for that on a Sunday. It's our busy day -- as I think I already told

THE DIARY OF A CANADIAN NOBODY

you."

I don't care what Alys says. I'm not going back to that store again even for the 'half-price Sunday' discount. She wouldn't talk to Alys that way.

I called Galahad and asked him about dad. He says he's tired of listening to the old bugger's complaints and I should stop encouraging Dad and Gawain to feel sorry for themselves. He'll call me if there's ever anything seriously wrong with either of them. I rang off. I'm tempted to do as he says.

Monday 8:
War

British and American submarines fired Tomahawk missiles into Afghanistan overnight so the attack on the Taliban and Al-Qaeda has begun. In response, Bin Laden has released a videotape praising God for the WTC attack. Good old God, always there when you need him. I've noticed that, down the centuries, whenever someone has wanted to do something truly moronic or just plain evil they always claim God as their inspiration. I think it's time He spoke out in his own defence and stopped using humans as interpreters. Or hasn't He, She, or It noticed that humans always interpret the Word to suit themselves?

Needless to say, normality is out of the window again as everyone returns to the water coolers to discuss recent events. Another member of my staff has asked for clerical assistance, claiming the only way he can catch up the time lost by the past weeks' alarms and excursions is for me to get him an assistant.

Lance's doctor called. They have the x-rays. Lance's finger is still broken and he is on no account to play sports for another week. We made a follow-up appointment for next Wednesday.

Gwen has a boyfriend, someone from work. I don't see how she has time for school, work, and a boyfriend; however, I didn't say so because she would shout at me. Love is supposed to make girls go all gooey-eyed and mushy. If that's true, I can safely affirm Gwen is not in love. I think the stress of juggling such a schedule is making her cranky; well, that and Lance singing 'first comes love, then comes marriage, then comes sitting in the baby carriage' all evening.

Weight: plus 2 lbs. Worse... and better because this weekend I didn't starve myself, and the gain is no larger than last weekend when I did.

41

Tuesday 9:

We have a new system at work, brought by the Americans when they took over, for tracking problems and getting them fixed. That sounds so sensible it has to be a good idea -- and it is. But it's how you implement things that make the difference. Our system works something like this:

Someone who doesn't know anything presses a wrong button, or finds a switch in what they think is the wrong position, or watches someone do something they don't understand and they report their lack of knowledge and understanding on an Adverse Condition Report or ACR. Their boss, who hasn't seen the problem, assigns this ACR to a subject aware person, or SAP. The SAP investigates and writes a proposed action plan or PAP. The PAP is presented by the SAP to the management and executive review directorate, or MERD, who, not knowing the problem or being subject aware themselves, and like the Rotweillers they're all trained to be, rip the PAP apart and demand more investigation and more corrective actions. The SAP dutifully rewrites the PAP, removing all his or her suggested improvements and incorporating all the MERD's special extras, and re-presents the PAP to the MERD. Provided the composition of the MERD hasn't significantly altered (but it usually has) the PAP is approved and becomes a correcting requirements action plan or CRAP. The actions go into the ACR system and are assigned by the deficiency oversight and leadership team, or DOLT. Thus, any person, initiator and MERD, who is willing to publicly proclaim their own ignorance, can actively use our management system to hijack workers of other people's departments into working on their wish list.

I've taken a long time to explain this because today, to my despair, I've been nominated as an SAP. I have to investigate why someone at one of our plants blew up a piece of very expensive machinery while following a procedure we issued a week ago. Actually, it's the only new procedure we've been able to get issued since our formation at the last re-organisation, four years ago. I've arranged to meet the initiator of the ACR next week after he comes back from sick leave. Before then I've got to be trained on Root Cause Analysis (RCA).

Lance's soccer team had an extra indoor practice tonight and I had the pleasure of taking him there, leaving Alys with Gwen. I don't know what they did but it didn't go well.

Wednesday 10:

Canada joined in the war yesterday. We're sending our forces to Afghanistan just as soon as the Americans can ship them there and as soon we know what they can do to help the Americans. The papers are a bit patriotically offended at this, suggesting our boys should go on their own and do their own thing. The PM replied, diplomatically, that there are few countries that can act unilaterally, the USA (of course), the UK (to a lesser extent), and France (to a still lesser extent) and Canada isn't one of them. No one asked why Canada isn't (because the answer is we would have to spend a lot more money on defence)? They would have asked if they'd been on the RCA training course with me.

Started RCA training and learned to dig deep for failures. This is a wonderful tool that was obviously dreamed up by a rabid trade unionist. No matter what happens, the fault always lies with management. The final answer is always that the worker didn't get properly trained, or have a proper safety culture, or supervision, or have the right tools, procedures, briefings, etc. This system assumes that fully trained and experienced workers are simply robots whose every action comes from a superior being called 'the boss'. It's much the same assumption that's made about women under the law, only then the superior being is called 'a man'. Workers apparently do nothing but blindly follow orders and women are either being directed by a man, duped by a man or are reacting against the wickedness of a man; somehow, despite being human, these two groups are never actually personally wrong.

Occasionally, the result comes out that management didn't have proper training, or the right culture, etc. but even then it's their fault for not knowing what was the right training or culture and correcting it. What I don't understand is, and maybe it comes out on Day 2, if everything is management's fault and they follow their boss's orders, why isn't everything the CEO's fault and why don't we just fire him or her whenever there's a mistake? They do in Parliament when some assistant to a junior clerk leaves a top-secret folder on a bus and the appropriate Cabinet Minister resigns. RCA says we should do the same -- even though it's clearly stupid.

This deep analysis of problems fits in well with the modern world because it says someone else is always to blame, particularly if they're rich. Our modern world doesn't so much tell people not to do bad things as tell them why they have the right to continue doing bad things. We give people a licence to be mischievous or even downright evil.

Took Gwen to soccer practice and, during the drive, she told me Lance is playing road hockey after school and if I want his finger to heal I should be firm and stop him. Gwen always seems to be pushing me into fights with people; I'll be glad when she gets the next stage of her licence and can drive herself. It isn't that I disagree with her, it's just she's a little intimidating. After all, this is a girl who, at the age of ten, while refereeing a children's soccer game, stared down a soccer hooligan dad that was being obnoxious from the sidelines.

Later, I spoke to Lance and urged him to be more careful. I think that will do the trick. Talking to him as one mature, reasonable adult to another is much the best policy, whatever Gwen thinks.

Thursday 11:
Canada's Federal government has announced we will have ID cards for immigrants from now on. I can't see that standing up in a court once the present hysteria has died away.

RCA training today consisted of role-playing. We investigated a real accident that happened at work a year or so ago and presented the fruits of our thinking to the trainer, or would have done if we could have agreed on any one of the dozen root causes we found between us. I noticed the management part of the group thought the injured worker was an idiot who deserved what he got and the workers thought he was the victim of poor management. I kept out of this because I could tell from the course materials that management was to blame and I didn't want to be on the losing side. The trainer also decided not to become involved and said we'd all done well and the diversity of opinions showed how much we'd learned and how difficult it was sometimes to get to the root of problems arising from systemic failures of processes. He handed out the actual root cause found by the actual real-life team and we found that we'd been too conservative. They'd found lots more root causes than we did.

I'm not sure I learned anything on this course but the experience will help when I meet the injured worker I'm root causing with next week. One thing I've learned from dealing with Gwen and Lance's school, and from training I've been on, is that education is different today. When I went to school you learned this was this, that was that, and you were expected to remember them both for the exams. Now any answer is a good answer. Telling a pupil today they are wrong will only end in tears, and the teacher will get six-of-the-best to make sure they don't do it again.

Lance played volleyball in gym class today and had a great time till he hit the ball with his finger. The splint is bent too. I reminded him of the doctor's advice and he said volleyball isn't a sport and anyway it was only practice, not a game, so it doesn't count. I think I've sown the seeds, however, and he'll be more sensible now -- and all without fighting. Gwen has a lot to learn about managing people.

Friday 12:
Now that I'm fully trained on RCA, I looked at the information I'd been given on my ACR with a new perspective and... it looked exactly the same. I'll wait till I meet the machine operator before I do anymore. It occurs to me that if I'm to do this PAP as well as my regular work I need an assistant. Mr. Ogilvie won't like it but I think it's vital I, we, have some help.

Lance's indoor soccer team had practice, not a game so it doesn't count, and Lance had a great time till he fell on his finger. Gwen glared at me when we came home with Lance holding his swollen finger and whimpering about parents who force their kids to practice when they're injured. She took Lance away so they could plot terrible revenge on their tyrannical, ruthless dad. The coach is on my side; he says kids need to learn to play through pain. It's funny how people in the Western world insist on laws preventing workplace injuries for themselves but expect to see their favourite sports stars playing through the pain and maiming themselves for life.

Went to gym. Weight: minus 1 lb. Good.

Saturday 13:
Packages containing Anthrax spores have been circulated in the US mail system and a postal worker has died. There's talk about it being Bin Laden but that's daft. This is an amateurish home-grown nutcase, not an international celebrity terrorist nutcase though I've no doubt Bin Laden will claim responsibility and the FBI and CIA will back him up with proof. Those folks are in cahoots to divert the American taxpayer's money for worthless purposes. Mr. Bin Laden hopes to bring down the USA slowly but surely; the other two, like most people on the public payroll, are making hay while the sun

shines, which will eventually bring down the USA -- just slower than Bin Laden wanted.

Called dad. His veins are less painful today but he's been laid up all week. Gawain has done nothing to help, Dad says. Gawain says that's because he's sicker than Dad is; his discs were worse than ever. I unwisely told Gawain he should get out and exercise more like I'm doing. Gawain says he's in good shape for a man of his age. It's just his discs that aren't and exercise would make that worse -- then he hung up.

Lance played road hockey at his friend's house, not an officially sanctioned game so it doesn't count, and had a great time till he fell on his finger. Fortunately, he'd removed the splint and it didn't get damaged -- or we'd be out another $8. Lance can be thoughtful that way. Fortunately, Gwen was out when Lance came home so she wasn't able to scold me for my lack of parental discipline. Alys made up for Gwen's absence by scolding Lance for playing and me for letting him play, though I knew nothing about it.

Sunday 14:

Our Federal government has moved with commendable speed to punish Canadians for international terrorism. They've announced a bill allowing the police and spy agencies powers to do as they please with us wicked citizens. Opposition is limited to a few crackpot civil libertarians whom nobody has ever listened to and won't now.

Alys kindly offered to accompany me to the dry-cleaners this week when I said I didn't want to go. Then we discussed my reluctance and she called me a baby!! Foolishly I let this persuade me to go once again on my own to meet the She-Wolf of Whitebay. Our conversation at the store went something like this:

She-Wolf, sneering, "Those shirts have the sleeves rolled up."

Me, boldly going where no man has gone before, "But the collars are unbuttoned."

She-Wolf, "There's only one collar to a shirt, there are two sleeves. Do you think I've nothing better to do here but get your laundry ready for cleaning? This is our busy day, you know."

I unrolled the sleeves and slunk away. Even if Alys kills me, I am NOT coming back to this store. I'll find another one and pay the difference from my allowance. Missing lunch one workday won't do me any harm. It may even help me lose weight.

I noticed Lance didn't jump in with an example of how badly the world treats him so I think he's learned from his previous experiences with Alys. Those people who say pain isn't a good teacher should learn from this evidence.

Monday 15:
President Bush has rebuffed the Taliban's offer to negotiate and says they must hand over Bin Laden or else they'll be attacked. Shades of 1914 when the Austrians demanded that Serbia hands over the murderer of Austria's Archduke Ferdinand, thus beginning WW1. The only thing that will save us, this time, is the ugly little guy has no big ugly friends.

On my journey home, I pondered the idea of approaching Mr. Ogilvie with my plan to increase my section's productivity by hiring a clerical assistant. I asked Gerry's opinion and he said my section is a bunch of lazy jerks who should all be fired. Gerry and I have never agreed on the need for administrative procedures. Fortunately, I don't think Gerry will ever get into a position of power and be a threat.

Lance did basketball in gym today but it was only practice so it didn't hurt his finger. It also didn't bend the splint because he took it off to save it and, as he didn't hurt his finger, he didn't learn anything. Gwen was at work so I didn't hear about my lax discipline tonight, no doubt I will tomorrow when she finds out.

I told Alys about hiring an assistant and she thinks it will be a good idea. She added, "You should hire a woman, from what you've told me having one worker in your group can only help." I'm puzzled by her comment because I thought I'd always been fair to my staff in our discussions.

Tuesday 16:
I met the initiator of the ACR and asked him to describe the incident and the events leading up to it. I didn't tell him who I was but he'd read it on the front cover of the procedure and his manner was very unpleasant; he claimed I almost killed him. I assured him his boss signed off on the document so I knew it was right, at which point he had hysterics, raging, storming, and foaming at the mouth. Presuming it was delayed shock from his near-fatal accident; I got the company nurse to medicate him. When I returned in the afternoon, he was calmer. The nurse said I wasn't to upset him again so I kept off the subject of his boss.

His description of events, shorn of the colourful industrial language he used, suggests the procedure may not have covered all possible circumstances. This is very disappointing because this one has been three years in preparation and had 27 revisions before issue. I asked him how they have been operating the machine till now? He said till 'that day' they were using the Owner's Manual! Well, no wonder they had an accident. Changing procedures, like these people did, without a transition plan and a phased approach is very dangerous; it's like jumping between rail cars on trains moving in opposite directions.

I don't know how they hadn't had an accident before now because I remember looking at the Owner's Manual when we started; I'm sure it read well in the original Japanese but no one over here could have understood it. That's why we didn't use it when we wrote our procedure.

I had the initiator describe the events and tell me why the procedure was no good. I'm not going to ignore his views, after all, he is the eyewitness, and hopefully, will become a two-eyed witness again when the bandages are removed. However, my procedure on how to do root cause analysis says I've got to look further than the superficial reasons for the failure and dig deeper into the underlying reasons.

RCA is a useful tool for helping one be objective. Why, for instance, wasn't the operator's supervisor overseeing this first use of a new procedure? There has been a serious failure of management here. The operator, with his twenty-year's experience in machine tools and five on this particular machine, probably would have welcomed some oversight while using a new procedure for the first time. And why didn't he ask his supervisor for support? Clearly he was afraid of being thought inadequate and this points to a poor safety culture in this shop. The manager is probably one of those young people who, afraid for their own skins, behave like old-fashioned tyrants and browbeat their staff to improve production at the expense of safety.

I had interviewed the manager earlier, while the operator was resting in the nurse's station. He seemed a nice young man but that was probably just an act put on for my benefit. Now I think back on the interview, he seemed very uneasy and nervous. A guilty conscience there, I note, for my report. Everything I hear and see convinces me that the shop is so poorly run it's a miracle they haven't had a dozen such accidents before. Their safety record, the best in the corporation their figures claim, is either good luck or deliberate under-reporting. I'll suggest an auditor review their statistics as well. I can't completely exonerate the reviewers of the procedure (of which the shop manager was one), however, because it does need tweaking. I noticed two spelling errors (pages 71 and 245) and a syntax fault on page 193.

For my Public Speaking presentation, I decided against using the Extreme Orator methodology, concentrating instead on what I've learned from the course, Public Speaking not Root Cause (I've already said how much I learned from that). I did, however, find that experimenting (at home in front of the bathroom mirror) with the 'in-your-face' approach helped me to do the things I already do more confidently so I think there may be something in it. I won't tell Gerry; it will only make him more conceited.

My speech on Stress in the Workplace, with special emphasis on reorganisations and downsizing, was very well received and I'm beginning to feel I don't need this course because my public speaking is already good, apparently. Maybe, all along, it's been my lack of confidence holding me back. When I make a speech I sound unsure even when I know what I'm talking about; at least, that's what I've thought until tonight where I got rapturous applause. I'll give the course another couple of months and then quit.

I told my loving, supportive family of my successful presentation when I got home and they showered me with praise -- oh, no, that was just my daydream driving home. They were too busy watching a TV program called Temptation Island to notice I was home. That show is very vulgar; I'm disappointed in my family for watching it.

Wednesday 17:
I've written my PAP recommending an implementation plan for all new procedures and incorporating a transition phase from the old way of doing things to the new. I've also, cleverly, incorporated a lot of actions I know the MERD would have asked for if I hadn't included them. This way there's a chance I'll get my actions done, at the expense of everyone doing a few extra jobs they would have ended up doing anyway because the MERD would have tacked them on to some PAP sometime. Luckily, I'm too late for this week's MERD meeting so I've got two weeks to tweak the plan as I'm in the USA next week.

Lance and I visited his doctor. His finger has healed and it's fine, thanks to the quick work of our local GP and the magical metal splint that works without actually being on a finger.

Talked to Gwen about University next year on the way to soccer practice. I'm glad we have this time together without the rest of the family wanting their say. I can really listen to her and what she's trying to tell me. She wants to go to University in Britain or Australia or failing that, British Columbia or Newfoundland. It's great at that age, when the world is yours to command. In the end she'll go to Toronto the same as everyone else in this neighbourhood but just now she's dreaming.

I told Alys about Gwen's travel dreams. "She'll go where we can keep an eye on her and like it," Alys said and went off to browbeat Gwen into submission, despite my urging her not to. Alys doesn't understand the softly, softly approach any more than Gwen does. I turned the radio up while I wrote my diary so I couldn't hear them discussing Gwen's future.

Thursday 18:
Tweaked the PAP some more. Today's MERD identified a whole lot more actions senior management want to have done so I incorporated them too. When I present my PAP, they'll say, "Take those actions out because someone else is doing them." That will leave my actions to be carried out -- as Baldrick, Blackadder's sidekick on the TV show, would say, "a cunning plan."

At today's MERD I was forcibly reminded, by one of those idiots who thinks everything gobbledegook is gospel, of another American innovation to our glorious subsidiary company's madness -- the Phonetic Alphabet. This, like so many of their 'innovations', comes straight from the military and must, therefore, be efficient. Over a field radio during a battle I'm prepared to accept the phonetic alphabet may be a useful aid, over a table face-to-face in a quiet meeting room, it's asinine.

Alys and Gwen are speaking again tonight (they weren't on good terms at breakfast) because they've fallen out with Lance who offended them by saying something terrible about women; after last nights discussions he suggested they weren't all 'sugar and spice and all things nice'. Lance doesn't understand the concept of a 'polite fiction'.

Friday 19:
Tweaked the PAP again after overhearing a conversation between Mr. Ogilvie and his boss, Mr. Bustard. I now have 18 actions in the plan, 15 of which are things the MERD has told others to do.

All my staff told me today they'll need extra help if I'm going to be doing PAPs and can't support them on their deliverables. I began to think that maybe I should prepare, if only in my own mind, a justification for another member of staff, softening Mr. Ogilvie up in stages, so I can get some work accomplished before the year is gone.

Alys took Lance to soccer practice, leaving me to help Gwen with her homework, which I did by keeping out of her way. She had finished by the time Alys and Lance returned, as I knew she would, so Alys didn't learn the truth and we had a pleasant evening until bedtime.

Weight: minus 1 lb. Better.

Saturday 20:
After the constant bombing from their respective air forces, American Rangers and British SAS soldiers are inside Afghanistan.

Called Dad. He's not well, his varicose veins are very painful and he's resting on the couch watching TV. He had to get up to take my call so was grumpy. Gawain isn't well either, something he ate didn't agree with him and he didn't want to speak to me, Dad said, which means he hasn't forgiven my comment last week about exercising.

I told Dad that Lance's finger was healed and he said, "Lucky he broke it in Canada. Over here he'd still be waiting to see a doctor and when he did, the bugger wouldn't know what to do." Apparently, Dad's doctor didn't advise an operation on those varicose veins, which was Dad's diagnosis.

Lance had a friend over to play road hockey, so he said. What they actually played all day was video games. Gwen was at work, and then went out with the people from work in the evening, so Alys and I had some quality time together. It's such a long time since we had time together we didn't know what to do and just wasted it cleaning the house.

Sunday 21:
Back to the dry-cleaners. Today's witty repartee went as follows:
She-Wolf, "These shirts aren't cotton."

Me, "I didn't say they were."

She-Wolf, "What about these pants, this jacket? Are they linen or man-made?" She then proceeded to read out loudly, in excruciating detail, the labels of all my cleaning. For some reason I couldn't stop being embarrassed at the constituents. Is it my fault polyester wears well for work?

When I got home, I put my foot down with Alys. I said either we use different cleaners or she goes from now on. I think the message got through because Alys murmured "Yes, dear," in a very docile tone. Gwen could be right; I just need to be firmer sometimes.

I spent most of the rest of the day packing and unpacking my bag for the trip tomorrow.

October 22-26:
I'm in the flag waving, gun toting, and the tub-thumping USA.

I know this will sound unlikely after what I've written but, despite the American government, despite the armed soldiers everywhere we went, and despite the understandably heightened emotions of the populace, I am enjoying my stay in the US. As I've found on previous visits, the people are 'extreme'-ly nice, and this is the only place in my diary you will find the word 'extreme' written without sarcasm.

One day, we were lectured on the superiority of the American way-of-life over all others and I couldn't help thinking, as I listened, that the Americans wrote their Constitution too soon after the War of Independence. They were still angry with the British Government and wrote a constitution reflecting their belief that the biggest threat to a citizen's freedom was his, or her, own government; thus throwing out the lessons learned by Britons in the 1,000 years prior to 1776. What Britons had learned in that time was the greatest threat to a citizen's liberty comes from fellow citizens in the shape of churches and sects, robber barons, gangs of freebooters, and other special interest coalitions (lately known as lobbyists). America is free of 'government interference' or 'government support' (choose your own interpretation) but their citizens are at the mercy of each other and, consequently, are constrained at every turn. Unfortunately, America's success puts the rest of the western world in particular danger because, having stronger governments to balance personal liberties, they risk importing America's private constraints too and doubling the chilling effect of restraint.

Americans are in less danger because they won't be allowed to work for humane social policies through the government; their rich people and businesses are too strong to allow that.

Everywhere we go here in the US, there are armed and uniformed men on the streets, most of them teenagers. Am I the only person who thinks it strange that we give guns to the group of people we know to be the most unstable, teenage males, and then train them to kill people? Putting young men through this military process at such an impressionable age is why the top ranks of American industry are filled with men who don't understand life or living. They're all 'graduates' of the Vietnam War Management Academy. Maybe somebody should remind them they lost and that bringing the same techniques they used then to present day industry isn't necessarily a good thing. I'm afraid for the future of the USA; they're heading off on a militaristic track that leads nowhere good.

For example, the FBI says it's time to forget civil rights and start using torture again because terrorism suspects are refusing to talk. Fortunately, the basic decency of the American people is prevailing and the suggestion has not been picked up by anyone, even though two more postal workers died from Anthrax poisoning.

Another plane crashed in New York this week. This one looks like an accident but the passengers are just as dead. I think I'll walk home.

Saturday 27:
Arrived home after a short uneventful flight, disturbed only by my own fears. My family were so pleased to see me home they went out for the day, Alys and Gwen to the Mall and Lance to play road hockey at his friend's house. Silky stayed in to keep me company and have her tummy tickled.

With my faithful cat at my side, I called dad. His veins are better but his stomach is upset. It's a bug going round, he says. Gawain's tummy upset is over; since he stopped overeating, says dad. I tried to tell them about my trip, in between the medical reports, without success. They hear everything I say as insincere sympathy and got crankier as the call went on. I gave up before Dad talked me out of his Will.

Sunday 28:
Today I got a reprieve from my other weekly torment. There was a

young woman Assistant in the dry-cleaners and she was very friendly and helpful. Not that she had anything to complain about in my case, I'd unrolled the sleeves, unbuttoned the collars, and brushed off the cat fur. Alys had sneered at me as I did all this, asking if I was going to dry-clean the clothes too. I ignored her. She's the one who should be going to the store; men aren't equipped to deal with cranky female shop assistants.

Gwen was at work all day and Lance round at his buddy's house playing video games. I had more contact with them when I was in the USA. At least there they talked to me on the phone -- because Alys made them. Spent the day smoothing the kitchen floor ready for the tiles while Alys, who was supposed to be cooking, stared balefully at the breakfast bar. My resolution remains unaltered despite this mental arm-wrestling. I took Alys off to the Extreme Coffee Pub to keep her mind off it. This turned out to be not such a good idea as they were renovating, removing the bar that used to jut out from the counter. Alys said, "See, breakfast bars are right out of fashion."

My heart went out to the breakfast bar. I've been out of fashion all my life and I know how it feels.

Weight: plus 2 lbs. Not bad considering my week in a hotel and my lack of exercise during that time.

Monday 29:
Began planning my campaign to get someone to research documents for my procedure writers and file their work after they've finished. Those are the bits the men hate... other than the actual procedure writing I mean.

Toronto's basketball team, the Raptors, isn't having a good season, apparently. I don't mind. Watching Gwen and Lance on their school teams, I quickly realised basketball is dismal. Stung by the complaint his new game was pointless, basketball's inventor gave points for everything, standing up, falling down, or running for more than a second before the referee flaps his arms like a windmill in a hurricane. Who's the only person in basketball who breaks a sweat -- the referee, that's who?

Tuesday 30:
Today's paper had pictures of Canadian warships sailing out of British Columbia heading for Afghanistan. Everyone is feeling very

patriotic and macho at this; I am full of foreboding. I've no doubt our soldiers, sailors and airmen will do a fine job. I just can't see them ever getting out of the region. The US and Brits will pull out, leaving their lesser allies to be peacekeepers, probably for longer than Cyprus or Lebanon or any of the other places the UN has kept troops beyond when a proper victory on someone's part would have settled, rightly or wrongly, the question.

Today, at work, was our contribution to the pharmaceutical industry's recovery from recession -- flu shots! They used to be for the very old, very young, and those in poor health but that didn't do enough for the industry so now we all are encouraged to have them. At the end of the first winter season when we all took the shots our company announced that the average sick days for those who didn't have a shot was 1.5 and for those who did was 1.25. Despite the economic benefits of this difference (to the company, not the individual who still carries all the risks) being so small, they've taken to carrying out ever more aggressive marketing each year. Arthur Lakelady would rather have natural flu than the man-made stuff and, once again, I declined.

I mentioned my section's need for a researcher to Mr. Ogilvie today and explained how it would increase production. He asked if I was mad; to be asking for more people when we're fighting to hang onto the people we have? I let the issue drop. I've sown the seed.

Lance's hockey team had its first practice tonight so I took him to the arena, then Gwen to soccer, and then Alys and I went back to the Extreme Coffee Pub because it's handy. I had the 'Extreme' Rocky Road double chocolate Mississippi-mud Pie with extra whipped cream, chopped peanuts and a cherry. Alys had dry biscotti that she dunked in her 'Extreme' mountain-Columbian mesquite-roasted allspice-flavoured Latte. Alys really knows how to enjoy herself.

Wednesday 31:
Halloween
The first of our flu shot victims was off today with mild flu symptoms. She'll be back tomorrow, she says.

This year I didn't go out Trick or Treating with Lance. What a Treat! Year after year, since Gwen was three, I've been trudging around the neighbourhood with all the other Dads in the rain, snow, hail, wind and cold -- always cold. Of all North America's holidays, this is the worst. It's organised extortion in which the extortioner has all the discomfort. Tonight, I handed out candies to the kids who came to our door and found it surprisingly difficult and stressful. How many candies and what kind should each reveller get? In the end, I let them grab what they wanted from the bowl and we ran out early. Later in the evening, our carved pumpkins got smashed all over the patio, which hasn't happened before. Alys says she'll hand out the candies next year. I'm too relieved to be offended by the slur on my character.

November 2001:
Gathering Storm in a Teacup

Thursday 1:

Security is to be increased at work and everyone must re-submit a revised Security Clearance form for investigation. Again I put on my management face and support the initiative but I can't see what good this will do. I fill in my form and mail it at once; at least in this regard, I need have no fear of something strange happening because I've never done anything remotely subversive in my life.

Presented my PAP to the MERD. It went very badly. My Public Speaking course didn't cover what to do when attacked by mad dogs. The mad dogs say I have to do more research and present it again next week. Also, the only 'actions' they didn't want doing were my three. They have forgotten they gave all the other 'actions' to other people. This may work in my favour. If I'm quick, I could close out their actions on my PAP against their actions on other people's PAPs.

More flu shot victims were off work today, others hung around the water coolers discussing their fever, diarrhoea, and sundry symptoms. The main reason people who don't have the shot miss work is because they catch the disease from those who do but won't stay home in case it shows up the flu shot for the fraud it is.

After years of ignoring encouragement from her parents to do something other than soccer Gwen finally decided to do ice hockey this winter and tonight was her first game ever. It wasn't bad. Many of the girls were new to hockey, partly because girl's hockey is new in Whitebay and partly because girls seem to get more interested in the sport when they get interested in boys, so Gwen's lack of skating skills wasn't a big problem. She was the hardest competitor out there.

The campaign to get ice hockey for girls was bolstered by the familiar complaint of discrimination. Boys have had hockey in Whitebay since the town began but not girls, so the refrain went. As usual, ignoring the fact that the boys and their dads organised their own league and girls did not. As well, the cry was there weren't enough available arenas and the boys wouldn't give up any of their ice time, which kept the girls from playing. Ignoring the fact the girls had ice time for figure skating, synchronised skating, and ringette, which together added up to more time in the arena than the boys. Like the 'golden goal' in overtime, crying discrimination is always a game winner.

Friday 2:
Worked on revising my PAP but as I haven't really anything to add my work consisted of staring at my computer screen for about two hours.

The rest of the day I spent persuading my section to fill in the security forms and send them off. At first, I thought they were worried they might be deemed security risks but it turned out most people just thought the whole thing a waste of time. This is awful. If everyone has spotted it's pointless, confidence in our leaders will plummet and morale will suffer. However, I think I convinced them to take the initiative seriously.

Mr. Ogilvie shook his head at me in disbelief when we passed in the hall today so I know the assistant seed is germinating.

After last week's success, Alys took Lance to soccer practice again and I 'assisted' Gwen again. I think I'm on a winner here, so long as Gwen keeps her mouth shut. Unfortunately, she's already hinting at favours required in exchange.

Weight: plus 3 lbs., which is catch up on last week's trip, I hope.

Saturday 3:
As the tiles are now confirmed for next week, we booked the Tile Shoppe installation contractor (otherwise known as 'Cousin Nico') for the week beginning November 26; the earliest Cousin Nico could start. This leaves a week or so for late delivery and still leaves us plenty of time to have the house straight by Christmas. When she'd put the phone down on talking to the Tile Shoppe, Alys wandered around the empty kitchen muttering darkly about the unaltered breakfast bar. I'm holding fast onto this one, I feel somewhat King Arthur-ish in my determination to win this battle because I know trying to move that breakfast bar would be a disaster.

The new immigrants' ID card announced a week or so ago has already run into problems. Like a lot of this stuff, it will fade from sight along with the war. Politicians have to be seen starting initiatives but they don't have to finish them. Hopefully, the terrorist bill will fall into that category. On the same subject, the US says the 'noose is tightening' around Bin Laden. As they don't know where he is, this statement seems a little optimistic.

Lance's first ice hockey game and the team won, which is a good start to the season. It doesn't feel like hockey season because the rain is still pouring down, keeping everything green outside. Fortunately, with so much exercise these past two days, Lance should be able to finish the other half of the pillowcase full of Halloween candies he hasn't already eaten.

Called dad. His stomach bug has cleared up and Gawain's stomach problems are gone too. Unfortunately, Dad's ears are now giving him trouble. It started with an earache and now he's totally deaf, he says. I spoke up, thinking it would help, but he said to stop shouting because it hurt his ears. He's going to the doctors on Monday. Gawain has a headache and is lying on the couch with the lights off watching black and white movies because the colour ones hurt his eyes. Talking to Dad and Gawain is much the same as being at work because in neither case can I join in. At work, the talk is either sport or TV and I watch neither. With Dad it's illness and I'm always healthy. I may as well be deaf and dumb; writing is my only outlet to the world of communication.

Sunday 4:
In the evening, we all went with Gwen for her first game of the indoor soccer season. It was an easy win, as always. Unfortunately, the indoor season gives the team a false sense of security because the competition is weaker than outdoor. Lance, as usual, was bored and bought doughnuts and pop to pass the time, having now finished his Halloween candy, and complained he could have been playing the video game he's just rented. Alys and I watched the game and grumbled at the coach's decisions, a typical night at the game, in fact.

Didn't get to the dry cleaners so I missed meeting the She-Wolf.

Monday 5:
I lost weight this weekend! Weight: minus, say again, minus 1 lb. Finally, I've broken through the fat floor and I'm headed back to my proper weight. No change on the waistbands yet.

Most of my people still haven't returned their new security forms. I reminded them of the need, warning them of the possible consequences to the Western World if one of them should turn out to be a sleeping terrorist. Mohammed pointed out that if he was a sleeping terrorist, he would hardly write that on the form. An argument I found hard to refute, other than to say, lamely, "Well, if you were honest, you would."

Worked diligently on revising my PAP, honing the MERD's irrelevant actions to somehow cure the root causes I found. The fact the MERD's desired actions were to fix problems faced by their own departments and not my root causes made this a tricky task but I think I succeeded. I'm looking forward to Thursday and the MERD meeting with confidence. Question: would this be a good time to use Extreme Orator's methods? Answer: no, it would not.

Gwen went to ice hockey practice in the evening, which is good. I think it would have been better if they'd had a practice before their first game but you can't have everything.

I helped Lance with his homework for a time; then he decided Alys would be better. Judging by the discussion I participated in and the one I later listened to, I think both parents' support was about the same.

Tuesday 6:

Got an e-mail from security telling me who in my section was delinquent in sending in their forms. I reminded my people again and Padraig reminded me I was to get them more help. He says he can't possibly find the time to fill in this form and meet all his deadlines too. He wants to slip all his deadlines two weeks to cover off the additional work of the form. I told him I'd spent fifteen minutes on the form, at most. Padraig said, "Yes, but you've never done anything, or been anywhere, or thought anything, that security might want to look into. I wasn't so fortunate. I need time to properly present my home life in Northern Ireland or it might be misconstrued." This doesn't sound promising.

Continued tweaking my PAP.

In the evening, Alys and I helped Lance with his homework. We took turns sitting with him because if we leave him for a moment, he plays video games. Gwen did her own homework without any assistance, as usual.

Wednesday 7:

My department's people are all working on their security forms. How is it I have all the people who need to explain themselves to security?

One of our Canadian Directors, Juan Lostone, has fallen foul of the new order. He was escorted out today. My own nerves are stretched to breaking point whenever someone is walked out this way. I have to say it is a very effective management technique, much favoured by pirates and other sadistic brutes since time began. I've heard of the 'seagull manager', who makes a lot of noise, eats everything, shits on everything, and then flies off leaving the mess for someone else to clean up. We have a similar kind. The 'cuckoo manager', who sets up home in your nest, pushes the company fledglings out and eats all the food before flying off south to repeat the process at some other stupid corporation.

Continued tweaking my PAP. Not so confident today, on second reading some of the connections between causes and actions appear a bit tenuous.

Took Gwen to soccer practice and Lance to hockey practice. Gwen has applied for her full driving licence and will soon be able to drive herself to these events. I will feel quite lost.

Alys spent her free time in the kitchen, I think, hovering around that breakfast bar and plotting its demise. She had some new ideas on how to improve it when I got home but I'm proud to say I stood firm. Today Alys, tomorrow the MERD!

Thursday 8:

A New York woman has died of Anthrax poisoning and the US and allies are moving to cut off al-Qaeda's funds.

Speaking of terrorism, my presentation to the MERD did not go well at all. They spotted how thin the connection was between my causes and their actions. They have strongly advised me to re-write my causes to make the connection clearer and re-present my PAP next week.

My staff is still working on their security forms BUT I'm getting some short-term assistance in my section. Mr. Ogilvie agreed to me hiring a temp, to increase productivity. "The sooner you're finished, the better for everyone," he said. I'm glad he's coming around to seeing the value of my section's work. Pity it has taken four years to reach this point. We have to go to an outside agency for help because there are no clerical people left in our company; they were downsized in the last re-organisation.

What kind of qualifications does one need to manage documentation systems in a large, labyrinthine, now multinational, corporation? I contacted the local temporary help agencies and await their response.

Gwen's ice hockey team won tonight's game and they were very pleased with themselves. I knew practice was useful for something.

Friday 9:

Our local nuclear power company has announced that the station they closed down four years ago to 'focus on their newer units and return them to top performance' and which they had planned to return to service by December will not, in fact, be ready then. It will be ready for Electricity Market Opening on May 1st, 2002. In fact, we're told it must be running by then or the supply situation could be tight when the air-conditioning season starts. This station was to restart back in the summer and this is the second delay announcement; look out for more. I hope the delay is to ensure they get it right because we live between two of the utility's nuclear plants, one of which is the one being restarted.

Worked on revising my PAP to meet the MERD's needs. Will try to re-introduce my actions into the revision in the hope of salvaging something from this mess. I'm also working on a plan to ensure I never get picked as an SAP again.

I took Lance to soccer practice because Gwen didn't have any homework and she and Alys were going shopping. Then a bunch of Gwen's friends arrived and they went shopping, leaving Alys stuck at home. Now I have to go shopping with Alys tomorrow and I hate shopping! And Alys hates taking me because she said I sulk. For the record, I do not sulk. I simply try to encourage Alys to come home when she has bought what we came for and to buy it first rather than wandering around looking at other stuff.

Weight: plus 1 lb?? What is going on? Can the gym scales, which are the old-fashioned beam and weight kind, be unreliable?

Saturday 10:

FBI says the Anthrax campaign down there is likely the work of a young male loner. On this topic, I more or less agree with the FBI and if it isn't your average hormonally challenged young man I can suggest a better alternative. If I were 'crime profiler' I'd be looking for a middle-aged man, in a company being reorganised, who is beset by niggling little irritations brought about by rampant consumerism and self-important (other) people.

Lance's team won their second game of the hockey season. This is the best start Lance has ever had and reflects the inexperience of his first-time coach. He will lose his top players in the balancing (where the league tries to even out the teams), which happens after next week's game. I gave the coach the benefit of my insight and he says he's not worried. His son is the best player on the team and they can't take him away. Once again, foreboding overwhelms me. I'm like that Trojan woman, Cassandra, who was always predicting doom and no one would listen. I hope she got raped and pillaged to a good home after Troy fell, I should look it up. If she did, maybe I will too, when our Troy falls.

Called dad. His earache is gone and has been replaced by a sinus headache. After he'd described the state of his handkerchief when he blew his nose, I didn't feel well enough to continue our conversation and quickly rang off. Gawain is better -- but pretending not to be, to get out of work, Dad says.

Gwen was at work so I went to the Mall with Alys where I spent my time hanging around outside women's clothes shops. Men's lives are spent loitering, waiting to get into some women's pants, waiting for some woman to buy herself new pants, or waiting for them to come out of the toilet. No wonder most men take up sports. Alys doesn't approve of golf but would she let me do something quicker, like squash?

Sunday 11:
In the morning, Alys sent me out to pick up the dry cleaning (definitely my last trip!) and to do some shopping. I think Alys has been avoiding the dry cleaners. Maybe the She-Wolf is too much even for her. My lecture today went like this:

She-Wolf, on finding we hadn't picked up our cleaning last week, "Can't you see the signs?" She pointed to the three large hand-written signs around the shop exhorting customers to pick up their clothes early because it's a small store.

Me, apologetically, "We were away last Sunday."

She-Wolf, sarcastically, "Do you only come out on Sundays? We charge $10 if you go past a month, you know."

I fled, only to be victimised by a dove at a traffic light. While I waited for the lights to change, a dove walked out from under a car ahead of me in the outer lane. I just knew it would fly up when the cars moved and splatter its lifeblood over my windshield. Things weren't that bad. It flew up all right but landed on my front bumper. I braked. The tires on the eighteen-wheel rig behind me screeched, which frightened the dove and it flew up onto my hood. It stayed there while I drove gently through the junction. The eighteen-wheeler wasn't able to make it before the lights changed and the blast of his horn followed me all the way into a supermarket parking lot. I parked round the back so he couldn't see and come after me. The dove, its mission to bring peace to Ontario's roads completed, flew off when I got out of the car -- just before I could wring its neck.

This urge to kill a fellow sufferer on the planet Earth emboldened me and I decided I should go back to the dry cleaners and face down my demon. When I saw it in that light, I knew that Alys's docility on hearing my decision not to go again stemmed from disappointment and not respect. She'd seen at once that I'd never save her if a real dragon threatened. With this new stiffened resolve, I drove home and told Alys we were to continue using the She-Wolf's dry cleaners. She said, 'Yes, dear,' in what I'm sure was an awed whisper. Maybe there's something in this macho man thing after all; I feel I may have risen in her estimation.

Took Gwen to indoor soccer and another easy win. I'll be pleased when Gwen gets her licence, driving for an hour and a half to watch a fifty-minute game is pretty stupid, particularly when the team has a big squad and players only get fifteen minutes playing time.

Alys spent all day helping Lance with his homework. How come, when we were kids, we did our homework and now we're adults we're doing our kids homework? At the last school Open Day I saw projects, like fully functioning nuclear reactors and internal combustion engines, supposedly done by twelve-year-olds. Our support to Lance and Gwen is amateurish by comparison.

Monday 12:
Mohammed has handed in his security form; the others are still working on theirs.

I have to say employment agencies are fast. Resumes began arriving by fax and e-mail today and I'm going to interview the first candidate tomorrow. There are all sorts of people out there who want to do clerical work, BA's, MA's, Phd's, even some old ex-clerical people. Why are we grinding our children into library dust for an education when the result is a job they could have once gotten with a high school dropout's diploma? The answer is because nowadays you need a B.Sc. in Hospitality Technology to get a job flipping hamburgers.

I haven't thought of a way to get out of being an SAP. In the meantime, I prepared for Thursday's MERD again. I wish it were still summertime because then various members of the MERD go on vacation and often what is fought over one week is waved through the next. With the MERD, luck is an important element -- as it is with anything our senior management touches.

Drove Gwen to ice hockey practice again and we chatted guardedly about her plans for University. She doesn't trust me after our last chat. I did learn she has narrowed her sights to Canada; Newfoundland or BC are the front-runners. I said jokingly, her mum and I wouldn't be able to visit her there often and she was polite enough to say she was sorry about that but she wanted to see more of this great country.

When we got home, we found Alys and Lance had fallen out over his homework again so I was sent straight up to Lance's room to check it was done. Sat up till midnight watching Lance work and writing my diary.

Tuesday 13:
On coming down to breakfast this morning, I found the real reason I'd been sent to watch Lance work. The breakfast bar, which we never used for breakfast, was missing. Not all of it, just enough that it couldn't be replaced. Alys says I can finish tidying up the rest when I get home because it was too much for her. Easier said than done. It was an integral piece of the countertop with a cupboard and drawers underneath. I have two weeks to 'tidy up' before the tilers arrive and they won't bring enough tiles to do the additional floor space left behind when the bar is gone! Went to work in a depressed mood.

Renee has handed in her security form. She's very nervous about the whole process and says it's a government plot to round us all up and put us in camps; this is how it began back home. Is she right and, if so, am I going to find myself short-handed?

Worked some more on my PAP, with ever diminishing hopes. Thursday morning, early, would be a good day for the asteroid scientists are always worrying about to hit Earth. Wednesday night would be even better.

In the morning, I interviewed an excellent candidate for my records clerk position except he had a Ph.D. in Computer Science and was determined to rebuild our document system from the bottom up. I don't think Mr. Ogilvie would like that, nor would the Senior Vice-President of Information Systems Maintenance, Improvement and Excellence, who is quite protective of his turf.

In the afternoon, I met another candidate, a young woman with only one or two facial piercings and excellent qualifications, an Honours degree in Oral Communication. Unfortunately, while I'm sure her vocabulary and grammar would have been first-rate, the three ball-shaped studs in her tongue and the one in her lower lip made her tough to understand. On the plus side were her nipple rings and the chain connecting them, which her thin T-shirt entirely failed to hide. Still I decided against hiring her, much to the disappointment of the males in my section who saw her chest arriving for the interview. I hope it won't come back to haunt me. She may have gang connections, or worse, a lawyer.

Britain has announced plans to hold foreigners suspected of terrorism indefinitely without trial. Britons have short memories too. It was that policy in Northern Ireland that turned hundreds of IRA sympathisers into IRA terrorists.

Gwen offered to help with the breakfast bar when I got home but, fortunately, she had to go to work and I was able to start with only Lance's help. Alys had made herself scarce shopping for a new countertop. By the time she came home, the woodworking part was complete; i.e. I had cut off the ragged ends with my power saw. The gaping hole in the cupboards where the breakfast bar used to be will take more than one night to fix.

Wednesday 14:
The Taliban have lost Kabul and the north of Afghanistan to the Northern Alliance, the present bunch of mass murderers we favour.

Miguel has handed in his security form. He agrees with Renee; we're all going to be 'disappeared'. They all want me to give them a character reference, all except Padraig, who says he doesn't trust any Brit -- not even one who's been here as long as I have. Should I trust

Padraig who hasn't been here as long as me?

I have found the perfect candidate for my job. I don't know why I didn't think of it myself, a History graduate with a major in Byzantine bureaucracy! Lydia, the graduate I'm referring to, turned up for an interview today. She has no obvious tattoos or piercing, other than earrings, which everyone has nowadays (particularly boys), and she understands an organisation's need for reams of densely written documents. I hired her at once. I wish the Universities were turning out more students with useful knowledge instead of tradesmen's skills.

Alys drove Gwen to soccer and Lance to hockey practice so I could write my diary and practise presenting my PAP. I know the PAP by heart now so my presentation should be easy. Sadly, no asteroid had landed by 11 pm when I went to bed.

Thursday 15:

The MERD finally passed my PAP, without me saying a word, after removing my actions -- again. This is a relief, particularly as I plan to wait a week or so and close out all the actions they imposed on me to the other CRAPs from where I got them. Once I've done that, I will be able to do nothing. I spent most of the day inputting my CRAP into the ACR system. I made a note in my PC Planner schedule for next Thursday to close them all out. Some days, as I think I mentioned before, my genius just shines through.

The talk around the water coolers today was of the Victoria's Secret fashion show on TV last night. Some parts had to be blurred out by the networks and the discussion centres on this vital infringement of civil liberties. Our own government can throw us in jail for minor misdemeanours in the War on Terrorism but we get upset about not being able to see all or, if you are in the 'demeans women' camp, being able to see any of the ladies' private parts. It's good to know we haven't lost all sense of proportion in these sombre times.

All the Lakelady family went to Gwen's ice hockey game and, of course, they lost. Lance was very sarcastic about the quality of play, casually ignoring his eight years of formal and informal practice and play. No wonder women complain about men demeaning them.

Friday 16:

Bereft of any real news, the papers announce that the US is

tightening the noose around Bin Laden -- again. People-in-the-street, however, have stopped listening and moved on to more urgent matters like the Victoria's Secret debate, which still rages.

Weather is cold and wet, like every other day this fall. Of course, the weather brings out the ethnic 'British' jokes, 'it's all right for you with your waterproof skin,' or 'this must make you feel at home, eh?' and 'take this lot back with you when you go.' In our mad world, the Human Rights Commission would award me compensation if I complained to them. I could cash in with a big settlement and not have to go through another reorganisation, or worse, writing another PAP. I say that because Gerry says the MERD were so pleased with my performance writing the last PAP, they want me to do more! I think he's making it up. He's always claiming to know more about what's going on at the top than the rest of us.

Alys and Gwen went looking for a new countertop while Lance and I wandered round Home Terminal trying to find a reasonable solution to the gaping hole. It's too big for a door and Alys says she doesn't want a slab of board slapped on because that would look tacky. I wish stores had the sensible closing times they used to do. It would have been very pleasant to be kicked out at nine o' clock instead of being forced, by a lack of ideas, to haunt the aisles till midnight. Even Lance, who will normally even do homework to stay up beyond his bedtime, was tired of it by then.

Saturday 17:

Our Internet Provider (IP to those of us in the know) was using the Extreme Corporation service and Extreme is in financial trouble in the USA. In order to serve us customers better, and maintain service in the event of an Extreme collapse, our IP is moving to another service and they e-mailed instructions on how to convert to the new service -- starting with the e-mail service. I spent the best part of the day tinkering with the e-mail conversion, following the instructions religiously. I say religiously for a reason. It involved lots of incomprehensible mumbling, with a mountain of imagined sins cursed and -- at the end -- it all came down to faith. Now it doesn't work. I called their Help Line. It was busy.

Lance's hockey team won its third game. I told the coach he should have played his son in goal instead of letting him score three goals. He snorted derisively but he'll be sorry he didn't listen.

Gwen came home from work before we got back and removed the doors from the remaining kitchen cabinets. She says this way the hole isn't noticeable. Oddly enough, while it isn't a practical solution, it works; you don't notice the hole. I'm leaving it as it is because it gives me time to find a final solution. Alys, unfortunately, didn't think it funny and said so, loudly and often, and she and Gwen had a row but it serves Alys right. It was her taking unilateral action on the breakfast bar that got us into this mess. She can hardly complain about Gwen taking unilateral action on the hole where the breakfast bar used to be. Alys didn't like me taking Gwen's side so she isn't speaking to me either. No spoon-hugging tonight!

Called dad. His sinuses are better (thank God) and Gawain is better too. In fact, they are both fit and well ('relatively speaking, for men of their age and living where they do and in the times we live, etc.')! Unfortunately, Aunt Hester is very ill and so is my Cousin Peter.

Sunday 18:
After further tinkering with the e-mail, re-doing all the instructions again in case I missed something, it still didn't work and worse, the Internet side of the service didn't work either. Help Line still busy and I'm infuriated by their recorded message, which says e-mail them. If they wanted us to use e-mail them during the conversion, why did they choose to screw it up first!! More, increasingly frantic, efforts to make it work are of no avail and I call it quits, among other names not so printable.

Went to dry-cleaners in a macho frame of mind, determined to face down the She-Wolf. Our confrontation went something like this.

She-Wolf, staring at the hand written receipt I gave her, "What's this?"

New me, in a firm macho tone, "The machine was down when we brought our clothes in on Wednesday."

The She-Wolf sniffed and began punching into the computer the information from the slip of paper. For a moment, I felt quite proud.

She-Wolf, "This phone number isn't on the computer."

New me, still macho but puzzled, "It must be. I'm here every Sunday."

The She-Wolf read the number out slowly and I saw the problem right away. Wednesday's assistant had transposed two numbers. I told the She-Wolf the correct number.

She-Wolf, "That's not what it says here."

Me, exasperated, "The girl transposed two numbers. It's easily done."

She-Wolf, acting unconvinced, "And neither you nor your wife noticed? I can't give out Mrs. Lakelady's clothes to anyone who comes in here, you know. Security's important. People need to feel their clothes are safe with us."

Me, far past sane, "Do you think terrorists go about stealing people's clothes? What would they do with my wife's blouses and my pants?"

She-Wolf, "How should I know what terrorists do?" Then she added grimly, her beady eyes boring into my soul, "Or what they look like?"

I showed my driver's licence to satisfy her I wasn't planning world domination through stealing the Lakeladys' clothes and left. Reflecting on this exchange as I drove home, I was, at first, downcast by my lack of success but then I decided it wasn't so bad. At least I got our clothes, which didn't seem likely early on, and I did stand up for myself for once. So I look forward to next week's encounter with something like courage.

Most of the afternoon was spent looking for a countertop without success. We will have to have one made. And we will if we can find a colour and pattern 'we' like. It's harder than picking tiles. Lance and Gwen have developed strong opinions about what a kitchen should look like -- unfortunately they aren't similar opinions. I blame the plague of shows about home decorating on TV these days.

Gwen went to indoor soccer with Alys, who maintained a prim 'I'm only doing my motherly duty by being here' expression on the spectators' bench. It's a wonder the team didn't fold under her disapproving glare. However, they didn't and it was another comfortable win.

Monday 19:
Gerry says Web-Builder magazine recommends not using an IP at all. (I asked, very satirically, why it wasn't called Extreme Web Builder but Gerry failed to answer. I expect it's because the Web is too new and hasn't yet gone through the quite difficult, very difficult, and extra difficult stages.) Web-Builder recommends a wireless link to the Web via a geostationary US military satellite conveniently located over the Western Hemisphere. I've no doubt Web Builder's editor runs 'Extreme' Decathlons in his spare time.

People at work are back to discussing the War on Terrorism, it's quite overshadowed downsizing and Victoria's Secret as the chief topic around the water coolers. I'm not sure why the change because nothing much is happening in that war, certainly no more than in the Corporation's 'War on Employment' or the Victoria's Secret's 'War on Warm Flannel Underwear'. I'm glad I've got my Internet problem to keep me occupied otherwise the Restructuring Team might think I have as little to do like the rest of our staff. I spent all day waiting on the phone for an IP service representative to answer, without success. However, the time wasn't entirely wasted, I can now hum all Barry Manilow and Barry White's hits. Are all people called Barry sickly sentimentalists or is it just a coincidence with these two?

Lydia started today and quickly got into the swing of things. How right I was in my choice. What looks like a pointless and baffling series of different document repositories to the untrained eye is plain sailing to her. She's also the only person I've ever met who has an affinity to Portaluus, our document and work-tracking database. I doubt if even its unmarried programming parents (and there must have been many screwing up over a long period of time and in isolation from, if not at odds with, each other) showed the same intuitive understanding.

Apparently, Lydia has a tattoo. She offered to show me but I declined the invitation hastily. I continued to say no even after she assured me it is quite decent and only on her shoulder; I think she was a little hurt by my lack of interest. This revelation has shaken my good opinion but I think it's okay. Young people have to kick up the traces and a small, discreet tattoo is a fairly harmless way of doing it.

The evening was spent searching aimlessly through samples of the countertop. We bought a million samples home to compare to our kitchen woodwork (though we could have taken the woodwork to the store because most of it is piled in the basement) but none were quite right. Gwen said we needed to compare to the new tiles too -- not helpful.

Weight: no change. I've obviously stabilised things after my trip. It should start heading down now.

Tuesday 20:
No doubt as part of the noose tightening exercise, the US has

upped the bounty on Bin Laden to $25M.

Mohammed, who apparently left Egypt in a hurry after Sadat was assassinated, is the first of my staff to be cleared by security, which I put down to them looking at his papers first on account of his name.

Lydia has more than one tattoo and despite being pressed, I declined to see any of them. She also frequents basement clubs with names like The Cadaver Club and The Casket Club, where the patrons dress up like vampires. They call themselves Goths, I gather. Lydia and Alys share a common bond; they both believe in the superiority of the past over today, both believe in women being cosseted damsels protected and cherished by valiant heroes, and both would frighten the life out of Attila the Hun if he were unlucky enough to cross them. In fact, I'm coming to the opinion most marauding tribes, Huns, Goths, Vandals, and Vikings, were just a bunch of men escaping from their even more ferocious womenfolk -- a bit like modern men who order brides from Asia, in the hope of getting a wife who won't eat them alive. Some hope!

[Alys, who came into the room and read this over my shoulder while I was writing, says I have to take that last part out but I won't because she's gone now and this is an accurate record, not to be censored by anyone. We won't be spoon-hugging again and in a way I'm almost glad. Sex at our age! Sex is for babies.]

My Public Speaking speech this month was on the War and Security in the Western World and emphasised my opinion concerning the foolishness of all the heightened security everywhere. It wasn't as well received as my earlier speeches. At one point in the debate, I thought the teacher was going to have to wrestle some dissenters to the ground. The debate so unnerved me I could barely finish. Even my PAP experience of the past weeks didn't help. Next month, I'll do a less controversial topic.

Wednesday 21:
Gerry says Extreme Renovator recommends replacing the kitchen with a stainless steel, kettle-style barbecue surrounded by a light, airy open space. People who want to sit while they eat can use beanbags or sit cross-legged on the Sicilian marble floor. I asked where people who wanted to store their food before cooking put their groceries, but Gerry couldn't remember.

Speaking of home decoration, this year's tasteful Christmas outdoor ornaments are blow-up doll Santas and Snowmen lit from inside. Driving home in the dark, I saw a number of them on various lawns around the town. They make last year's 'in' ornament, icicle lights, look tastefully traditional.

Finally spoke to someone at the IP Help Line. They can't help me. I need to call someone else. Call 'someone else' and, some time after midnight, they put me back to the first person I spoke to and whose phone is once again busy. Today's telephone music is New Country. I prefer Old Country; at least, you could enjoy the joke -- even though it was on you, the listener. New Country sounds like Rock, is as smugly self-important as Rock, but unlike Rock has words you can hear, which is very annoying.

When I got back to the first person, they grudgingly parted with a string of letters and dots and, after rooting around in my computer from her office in Tulsa or Yellowknife or somewhere, she told me where to put them; the letters and dots, that is. I followed the instructions and, amazingly, my computer is cured. Now I wonder why the string of letters and dots wasn't included in the instructions or why she didn't put them in when she was rooting around inside. Does everyone get together behind my back and plan ways to annoy me?

While I was doing battle with the IP gods, Alys took Gwen and Lance to soccer and hockey practice respectively then she and one of the moms from Gwen's team went shopping, 'to let me have some peace and quiet while I played about with my computer'. It's only 'my' computer when it isn't working; the rest of the time I can't get on it for kids doing homework, or Hotmailing their friends and sexual deviants, or else it's Alys paying bills and looking up old school friends.

Thursday 22:
The US says Bin Laden is on the run and the noose is tightening. They say this to distract attention from the other announcement, which was the number of dead at the WTC, estimated at the time as being tens of thousands, is now less than 3,900. Where was everybody who should have been at work that day? Apparently, since that day most of them have been hiding in their basements while their spouses claimed the life insurance. Americans are a truly ingenious people.

DISASTER! I went into the ACR system to carry out my dastardly cunning plan of closing out my actions against all the previous actions, and I found all the owners of the previous actions had closed out their actions to mine!! I asked the DOLT if this was acceptable behaviour and Cec Hobbgobelin, Chief of the ACR system, said it was the usual thing to do!!! He then asked if I'd be the SAP for another 'documentation' ACR that has just arrived!!!! I said no and he replied, "It wasn't really a request. The MERD had already decided you're doing it." Two things upset me about this, one is I have to go through another round of root cause investigation and PAP writing and the other is, Gerry does seem to know more than I do about what's going on around here. Maybe he is 'in' with senior management.

Our bank has merged with another bank. Us users wouldn't even notice the difference after the merger, they said, and I didn't -- until I tried to use it. We wanted to make changes over the Internet to our savings portfolio, only to be told that service was no longer available on our particular parcel of funds. Undismayed, I went to our local bank branch and recognised no one behind the counter. When I asked them to make the financial adjustments, the pleasant young man I addressed asked, "Do you have any identification?"

I retorted, "I've been coming here for fifteen years and I've never seen you before. Have YOU any identification?" Finally, after much huffing and puffing, old Mavis was wheeled out from the vault, where they'd locked her, cryogenically frozen, for just these kinds of emergencies, and she confirmed I was who I said I was. They made the small adjustment I wanted and we parted on superficially amicable terms. I shall pull every one of my pennies out of their bank as soon as possible.

Gwen and her team winning at ice hockey brightened this awful day. Lance complained about the quality of the play, as usual, and technically he's correct. However, it's such a pleasure to see people having fun playing sports that I'm happy to settle for mediocrity on the stick handling. Now I look back on it, I've hardly enjoyed watching soccer or hockey since Lance was seven. Alys, for once, agrees with me.

Friday 23:
I began reading through the new ACR I've been assigned. Apparently our documentation management system is understaffed and has no space left since we closed down the old headquarters building. They are unable to keep pace with the company's

requirements, even with the superb new computerised system we installed after we got rid of all the people. I have to find the root cause of the problem and fix it. My guess is the root cause, our CEO, Mr. Genuflecten-Grovel, is already fixed and, even if he isn't, he's beyond the need for fixing. Maybe if we put out a contract on his grown children, who are already working their way up the ranks of the corporation, we could stop the problem from repeating itself in the future. Unfortunately, the world is full of Mr. Genuflecten-Grovels and short on sober, steady Arthur Lakeladys.

Lydia showed me the outfit she's wearing for tonight at the Casket Club. I advised her to dress after she'd left work, rather than in the company washroom as she planned. She assured me she had a long black cloak to cover up with and she'd wait till everyone had gone home. I hope she does; the Code of Business Conduct doesn't specifically forbid sexually explicit outfits on the premises but only because they never thought anyone would wear anything like that in the office. I found the outfit disturbing enough on the hanger and squeaked, "No" when Lydia offered to model it for me after everyone left. I believe no one should wear clothes, I've argued the point on many occasions, and this is exactly why we shouldn't. Clothes are far more stimulating than nudity. Everyone going nude would, I believe, have two important benefits for society; one, people would watch their weight, and two the population would fall steadily because sex would become extinct.

Lance's hockey team, what's left of it after the 'balancing', had a practice tonight with their new players; only one of whom could actually skate. All the solid workers are gone, much like our reorganisations at work to be honest.

Driving back from hockey, I noticed the strong wind we've had these past few days has blown down all the blow-up Santa and Snowmen dolls. On the lawns of Whitebay, it looks like Santa is doing push-ups, or, in one place, Santa is 'doing' a Snowman (or Snowwoman).

Saturday 24:
Lance's hockey team lost really badly even though the coach's son scored a goal. Three of the players that were 'traded' from our team showed up on the other team and took great delight in scoring and setting up goals for their new teammates. At the end of the game, the players started fighting and, when the riot cleared, the coach's son

was still lying on the ice. We heard later in the evening, his leg is broken and he is out for the rest of the season. This is going to be a long winter.

Called dad. He isn't very well. He had the flu shot and now he has the flu, complete with vomiting, diarrhoea, hot and cold flashes, and aches and pains in his joints. Gawain is no help because he's being pathetic about another trifling cold he's picked up from somewhere, or so Dad says. Aunt Hester is worse but Uncle Frank is better, which was a pleasant surprise because I didn't know he'd been ill. Cousin Peter has dropped from sight. Not literally, it's just no one has updated Dad on his condition.

Gwen says I've got to come to grips with the 'Lance problem' or he and I will end up like Dad and Gawain, emulating each other's illnesses. She says this because I've had a ticklish cough these past days and now Lance is coughing, discreetly so we 'don't know' he's ill. I reassured her the situations were completely different. It's just a phase Lance is going through and he'll grow out of it in no time. Gwen went purple, bit her lip, balled her fists and growled, "Wake up and smell the Java," whatever that means. Sometimes, I don't understand my kids at all.

After last night's wind and rain storm, the blow-up Santas that were all laying flat are now all ripped to shreds and it's the hard plastic 'free-standing' ones that are now doing push-ups on all the lawns in town.

Bought a piece of oak patterned chipboard that matches our kitchen cupboards and a whole new set of cupboard doors. I couldn't find a matching door so all the old cupboard doors will have to go to the dump. Gwen was right to remove them after all. Spent most of the day working and cursing in the kitchen. Alys, Gwen, and Lance helped me by going out. By the time I was finished, I'd bruised one fingernail so badly I'm sure it will fall off and my hands were scratched to pieces. They looked like Silky had slept on them. Unfortunately, this was after I'd called dad and they'll all be healed by next Saturday so, once again, I'll have nothing to talk about.

Sunday 25:
Met my nemesis at the OK Corral dry-cleaners and she was surprisingly civil. I'd screwed up all my dwindling reserves of courage for the meeting and I didn't need them. I think I'm accepted as a regular now, which is a good feeling. I don't frequent bars or

other watering holes so being a regular at the dry cleaners is as close as I get to community spirit.

I spent much of the day smoothing the floor where the breakfast bar had been, filling in holes and sanding. If the tilers arrive on Monday, I don't want them saying they can't work because the floor isn't properly prepared.

Gwen's indoor soccer team won. This time, I watched the game on my own because Alys and Lance didn't come. They stayed home to prepare Lance for a math test tomorrow.

Monday 26:
Cousin Nico and the boys failed to turn up; just as well we left ample time before Christmas or we might be eating out for the holidays. "They'll be there tomorrow," says Gina, the friendly lady at the Tile Shoppe.

Somehow, despite being tied up and imprisoned in an old fort, Taliban prisoners got hold of guns. Air strikes and western Special Forces killed them all, many with their hands still bound behind their backs.

I asked Lydia how her evening went at the Casket Club and she smiled dreamily. I didn't press the point. She suggests I come along and experience life without inhibitions myself. I pointed out I had no inhibitions; I grew up in the Sixties and Seventies. Lydia says I was too young and too far out of the scene in the Sixties and Seventies to understand about inhibitions. She has a point but I'm still not going with her. Alys would never allow it. Sadly, because I couldn't help saying 'I told you so' to Lydia, when her hoarse voice confirmed she has the cold in her chest I warned her about last Friday night when I saw her costume, she didn't speak to me for the rest of the day.

I have laid out my Terms of Reference for my new root cause analysis and begun alerting victims of my coming investigation.

Lance says he did well on the math test. I hope so or his mom will be down on those teachers like an avenging angel. Alys is joining the Parent School Council. She's decided the kids who have parents on the council do better than kids who don't and Lance is not going to miss out because of other people's manipulation of the system. She's going to keep them honest, or make sure Lance gets a share of the dishonesty as a bare minimum. Gwen says Lance should just do his schoolwork then it wouldn't be necessary for his mom to do anything. Alys said Gwen doesn't understand life and should keep her negative opinions to herself; Lance's confidence will be damaged by this kind of talk and he'll fail. What he needs is to be reassured to bolster his spirit. Gwen snorted and stomped off to her room to do her homework. Lance went back to his computer game.

Tuesday 27:
Cousin Nico didn't arrive again today, definitely tomorrow says Gina at the Tile Shoppe.

Continued on my Terms of Reference for the MERD on Thursday and, while twisting in my chair to reach a binder, put my back out. I left early and crawled into my bed at home to ease the pain, which is where Lance found me when he came back from school. Taking his cue from me, he leapt on the bed, landing flat beside me and bouncing me up toward the ceiling. I'm afraid I wasn't very understanding when I landed back on the mattress and Lance went off to his computer in a huff.

Gwen and Alys visited me when they too arrived home and were more sympathetic than Lance until Alys learned I'd yelled at Lance and then she wouldn't speak to me. She says she thought I was more of a man than to take out my frustrations on a small boy. As this 'small boy' is forever crowing about how he's taller than his mother and sister, I was so flabbergasted I couldn't speak. Alys took my stunned silence to mean I was ignoring her and stomped out of the room. It is now nearly eleven o'clock and she still hasn't reappeared, and nor has any supper appeared. Silky has appeared and is now sleeping on my stomach; I daren't move in case she becomes frightened and her claws ravage my private parts as she leaps off. Silky and I will spoon-hug tonight. She's the only one who really cares.

Wednesday 28:
Today it was reported that the US Defence Secretary, Donald Rumsfeld, commented about Taliban prisoners, "the President said dead or alive and I know which I prefer." Effectively, he has now given his murderous Afghan allies carte blanche to massacre their prisoners, as though they needed encouragement. Considering there's no proof any of the prisoners belong to the Al-Qaeda terrorist group or even that Al-Qaeda were responsible for the WTC attack, this is nothing more than cold-blooded murder, except in Texas where it's considered a citizens arrest.

I hobbled into work after getting my own breakfast; Alys hasn't forgiven me for raising my voice to 'her' little boy. I know it's the stereotypical thing to do but, on my way home, I'll pick up some flowers for her.

People at work are no more sympathetic than my family. A number, including Gerry, slapped me on the back and offered various remedies, most of which seemed to require lying on the floor and letting them walk on me.

Absolutely sure the tilers will be there tomorrow, says the woman at the tile store.

I finished the root cause analysis Terms of Reference and practiced presenting them.

My family eyed me coldly from the supper table as I limped in through the door bearing my peace offering. Alys accepted the gift and thawed enough to tell me which vase to put them in. Gwen and Lance seemed even colder than before, probably because they didn't get a present. I ate a chilly, lonely supper and crawled up to bed. At least Silky joined me again; she's such a comfort in my hour of need. We had a brief talk about my day, and then she went to sleep. We'll spoon-hug again tonight. At least Silky doesn't mind me writing my diary as we hug. Alys can get very strange about it. She says I should be massaging her back, not using it for a desk.

Alys took Gwen and Lance to soccer and hockey practice respectively so I could rest my back. This symptom of Alys's concern touched me, till she added, "Maybe then you'll stop play-acting and get on with some work."

Thursday 29:
The Lying B%#^* at the Tile Shoppe excuses her relatives with the following sweet words, "There's no point in them coming now because they don't work weekends so instead of a five-day job it would be a seven-day one."

I agree, through clenched teeth, and the date is reset for next Monday.

Our merged banks have followed up more quickly than I have after last week's confrontation. They sent us a letter saying we must close out the particular package of funds we have saved for years and replace them with newly approved ones. I am more than ever determined to remove my money from their bank. I can't believe the way this has gone; they merged and I'm supposed to put my affairs in their order so they can do what they want their way with my money.

The MERD didn't like my Terms of Reference. It seems that the corporation's removing all the documentation specialists and closing down the Corporate Library at the last reorganisation is not the problem. The problem is that the remaining handful of demoralised records management people aren't working smart enough and I have to find out why and suggest ways of curing them of their laziness.

Hobbled home, low of spirit and bent of back, to be greeted coldly by Alys and Gwen at the door. Lance has hurt his back in the gym today and somehow it's my fault. He is lying on his bed in terrible pain and I'm the only one strong enough to get him in the car and to the doctor. The doctor gave him some muscle relaxant and told him to lie down when we got home and on no account is he to do any chores. Alys says I'm to do them.

I took Gwen to her ice hockey game, mainly to get out of doing chores. They lost but watching was still fun and Gwen says playing is too. The game didn't end in a brawl and no one was sent off the ice. Can it really be considered hockey?

Friday 30:
Renee, who came to Canada as a refugee from the recent fighting in the Bosnia, is okay according to Security. Her look of relief and surprise, when I told her, is a secret just between us. I think Security should be on a need-to-know basis, in this case.

Began revising my Terms of Reference to incorporate the comments from yesterday's MERD. Is it too late for that asteroid?

Lydia had a different outfit for the club tonight. I wish I could say it was a better one. When I sardonically enquired why she felt it necessary to cover the few places it did cover, as there was no discernible value in covering them and no one else did, she said it was to preserve some mystery. I didn't think there was much mystery in the backs of people's hands and knees. I declined her offer to model again and I felt bad about it all day and all the way home. Constantly turning down offers to become closer to one's staff isn't a good thing; my training course said it's bad for employee morale. Lydia will think I don't like her and that's not the case. When we talk about history and literature, I find we have so much in common. She's read everything I have and thinks pretty much the same about them. I'm even glad she hasn't been interested, up to now, in the Medieval period, except out in Byzantium, because it means we can learn from each other.

Lydia doesn't go to these clubs alone, as I discovered today. I was working late (to avoid going home to those chores) when two girls with white faces and black hair, eyebrows, lipstick and clothes arrived to meet her. Lydia introduced us, after offering once again to model her outfit now that we were alone, and the couple examined me as though I was a museum specimen, which to them I probably am. When I declined Lydia's modelling opportunity, all three giggled and left for the ladies' washroom whispering and glancing back at me. Then, the other two returned and flashed open their coats at me before scampering off to re-join Lydia. Their outfits were also in contravention of our policy and very revealing so I tut-tutted, lecturing them like a stern but kindly schoolmaster and it was surprisingly sexy. Despite all appearances, and a lifetime of being trampled on, could it be that I'm really the kind of masterful domineering man that women fall for after all?

Lance is still unable to do chores so I had to do his when I got home. If I don't, I'll never be allowed back into the family. Maybe I should have gone to the Club and claimed I'd worked late.

This evening, on our Internet Provider's transition site homepage, is a dire warning of what will happen if I'm not 'transitioned' by December 31st. Attached to the warning is a button that says, 'check your settings NOW to see if you are ready' or words to that effect? I decided, as I'm up and running, I must be ready and, foolishly, pressed the button. I lost both my Internet and e-mail. Called the Help Line, which was busy answering calls from all the other people who pushed the button. I wish I'd kept the string of letters and dots I got from them last time.

Weight: minus 1 lb. I'm heading in the right direction, at last. I expect it's the stress. That's the secret to being skinny all your life, be twitchy nervous.

December 2001:
Merry Christmas -- Bah! Humbug.

Saturday 1:
Called dad. His flu is no better and the doctor has given him antibiotics to clear his congested lungs. He blames it on pollution -- and global warming for not killing the germs each winter. I suggested 60 years of smoking might have played a part. Dad says he could sue the cigarette companies and make a fortune. Despite the fact he smoked all his life knowing it was bad for him, the sad thing is I know he's right. Gawain's trifling cold isn't any better either and nor is Aunt Hester's bronchial pneumonia. I didn't tell them about my back or Lance's.

Lance's soccer team did fundraising outside a Liquor Store today. Half the team would be begging in the morning and half in the afternoon. I say begging because they were just standing outside the door in their uniforms asking for donations. It was all supposed to be arranged with the Liquor Control Board of Ontario management but something went wrong and the boys were driven off by an irate Salvation Army man who said outside the Liquor Store was their pitch all December. The store manager confirmed his story. However, he let the boys stand off his property to beg and the team raised $500 by the end of the day. The parents are so excited they want the kids to do it again next weekend. The boys aren't quite so keen.

Lance's panhandling shift was in the morning and I stayed to make sure the boys were safe then spent the afternoon trying to get a response from our IP. Late in the evening, I decided to look into their competitor's offerings but I found a huge line at their store in the Mall. I'll try again tomorrow.

Alys and Gwen went Christmas shopping and came home laden with bags. I asked if they'd left anything for the rest of Whitebay to buy. Gwen said, as she left to wrap the presents, "We left them all the man things."

Sunday 2:

Went to dry cleaners and found my old nemesis, the She-Wolf, missing. The pleasant young woman serving says the She-Wolf quit. No doubt it was the stress of correcting a town full of poor customers that got to her. Now I have to start becoming a regular all over again and the new assistant didn't even check my clothes for fur, collar buttons, cuffs, materials, etc. Next week I'll leave the collars buttoned and see what happens. If that works, I'll stop brushing off Silky's fur because that's the biggest chore. Silky has a thing about dark trousers, she only has to see someone wearing them and she rubs herself lovingly across both legs, inside and out. Visitors say, somewhat angrily, we should brush her. We do. Every week we brush enough fur from Silky to knit ourselves another cat but it doesn't make any difference.

I took Alys and Gwen Christmas shopping when I went to the Mall to get information from the competing IP service and they came back with even more bags than yesterday. I asked if this time they'd bought up all the 'man things' and they said no. Apparently, heartless men who shout at small boys and then moan about doing the said small sick boy's chores don't get Christmas presents.

The young man in the Internet store says they've been really busy this past week. He's so well up on industry trends he puts the blame on Christmas. Back home, I continued trying to get a response from my present InP (Internet non-Provider).

Alys and I went to Gwen's indoor soccer. Lance stayed home and played video games.

Monday 3:

Unsurprised to find tile layers failed to arrive. Definitely tomorrow says the Lying Bitch at the Tile store.

Finished Terms of Reference and issued them to DOLT for approval. Called more and different victims to prepare for my investigation, which is now based on their inadequacy rather than the Company management's reckless behaviour.

I didn't ask Lydia about her evening at the Club but she told me anyway, in vivid, not to say sweaty, detail. Despite what she says, I'm sure I wouldn't like it. I find just shaking hands with strangers a trial and even as a Boy Scout I couldn't do knots. I'd always believed Scouts learned knots as an environmental thing for when sailing ships come back after the coal and oil run out. Do the Scouts and Guides know what use their graduates are putting knots too? I changed the subject back to work!

After midnight I got through to our IP, who gave me the string of letters and numbers again, which miraculously make the whole thing work. The helpful assistant tells me not to press the 'check your settings' button again or his personal warranty is revoked. I trust him more than I trust the company he works for so I'll take his advice.

Weight: no change. This is it, downward to washboard abs from here.

Tuesday 4:

Interviewed first PAP victim, who was understandably upset by my Terms of Reference. The victim was the person who initiated the ACR and he'd innocently expected the investigation to provide support to his contention a terrible management error had been made in the last reorganisation. Generally speaking, I agree and will try to make some of that come across in my findings. I doubt if any such actions will survive MERD review, though.

We met Gwen and Lance's teachers in the evening and was pleasantly surprised to find that Lance's were normal human beings and surprisingly young, despite Lance's lurid descriptions. They're extremely pleased with his performance this year. He is working quite well and beginning to show promise after so many years of bumping along at the bottom of every class. If he only applies himself more and tries harder, he may actually become educated. I pride myself it is because of the help I've been giving him, and Alys has too, but the teachers all feel it is their support and that Lance is maturing. This makes me a bit miffed because they insisted I get involved and then when I do, they don't even give me any praise. I can't help thinking the teachers have become jaded dealing with all those parents who just don't care. I told Alys, somewhat light-heartedly, that mothers might carry children for nine months but fathers carry them for eighteen years. We won't spoon hug in bed -- again. Sometimes, Alys can be quite sensitive.

Gwen's teachers were suitably chastened and promised to try harder to keep up with Gwen for the rest of the semester. I hope they do for their sake; Gwen has very old-fashioned ideas about discipline.

Tilers will definitely begin tomorrow, says L.B. at rip-off mart known as Olde Worlde Tile Shoppe. They've been held up on another job, which is complete now so there's nothing to stop them.

Wednesday 5:
On the GO, I told Gerry about Lance's good progress this year pointing to my, and Alys's, additional help. He, at least, didn't say it was Lance maturing. No, he said, "Teachers have to pass them at Grade 8 or the teachers have to go back to school and take refresher courses." There isn't a lot of support for good parenting anywhere in our society nowadays.

Incredibly the tilers failed to arrive again. It is now two weeks since we've been able to use our stove (because it's in the 'good' dining room) or our breakfast-room table and chairs (because they're in the family room). The fridge is in the hall, which is a real nuisance for the kids; they've nowhere to dump their shoes, bags, and jackets when they come home from school. If this goes on much longer, they will have grown into the habit of putting their things in the closet and then what? My children and I will have nothing to talk about, that's what.

Canada and the US have frozen the assets of Middle Eastern groups suspected of being terrorists. Can our Government retrieve the money they had given to the Taliban before all this began?

Our Internet connection has stopped working again and even entering the magical string of gobbledegook doesn't fix it. I'm being driven mad by this particular innovation. Perhaps that's the purpose; computers are planning to take over the planet by driving humans mad. Needless to say, the IP phone number is busy.

Alys took Gwen and Lance to soccer and hockey practice leaving me to fix 'my' computer -- again.

Thursday 6:
Tile layers still not here and there's no point them coming now because they don't work Saturdays and Sundays. When I call, they agree to come next Monday, 'Contractor's Honour.' That's like Scouts Honour only without the concept of a promise behind it.

Lydia has a new tattoo. She got it at the Club last Friday. I declined her offer to let me see it, partly because I'm sure the Code of Business Conduct doesn't permit such intimacies and partly because she said she'd have to smuggle me into the ladies washroom to see it. I hope the fashion for Body Piercing and Art passes soon before we sink back to binding feet and heads. We're already back at the shuffling, head-bobbing toneless chanting stage where music is concerned. I find it ironic that the more technologically advanced we become, the more culturally backward we go.

The IP providers phone number is still busy. I'm glad it's an 800 number and free to me on my phone bill. I read recently that much of the world's software is done in India via satellite and frankly I wouldn't be surprised based on my experience to date.

We all went to Gwen's ice hockey game, even though it meant me missing the 'please hold while a representative laughs at you' message on the IP's Service Centre telephone.

Friday 7:
President Bush says he will not make deals regarding the surrender of Kandahar, the last city in Taliban hands. He believes Al Qaeda people are hiding out there.

Lydia's outfit for tonight at the Casket Club covered all the usual parts of the body, which should have been a relief. However, she modelled it for me in the afternoon, before putting her work clothes over the top of it so no one else would see it, and I think it was the most lewd outfit yet! It was made of a thin shiny material that insinuated itself like a second skin into every crevice and cranny of her body, with vivid designs that directed your eyes to the salient features of the female form. I don't understand the need in women to be stared at by crowds of lecherous onlookers. I needed an hour's quiet time and a strong cup of tea to recover my composure. Question: Would Alys mind if I went, just once, to the Club? Answer: Yes.

This question came back to me in the afternoon when a friend from a company I used to work for, called and suggested we meet for a drink. We agreed to meet at the local Exotic Dance bar and I couldn't help feeling Alys wouldn't approve of even this brief foray into the seamier side of the entertainment industry. I decided to break the news to her after I'd been -- and put all the blame on Seth; after all, they're never likely to meet.

I did learn Seth has been working away from Toronto for a few years, he left right after I left the old company, and he's only just returned. That information took all of two minutes and the rest of the time we watched young women pretending to have sex on stage while more young women pretended to have sex on a large screen TV above the stage. How did we get from 'women don't have orgasms' to women having orgasms everywhere you look in only a hundred years? We decided to meet again for a drink next week to catch up some more on old times.

Still no answer at the IP provider's technical centre, perhaps it's a Hindu festival.

Weight: minus 1 lb. Now I'm getting somewhere.

Saturday 8:

The school's theory about Lance maturing isn't holding up too well at home, he sulked all the way to hockey. And his team lost again today but not without a fight. In fact, there were several fights and one of our team was kicked out of the game.

Called Dad. His chest didn't get better so he got new medicine and it seems to be working. Gawain was working this week but it turned out he went back too soon and had to go off sick again. He now has the same medication as Dad. Aunt Hester is better and so is Cousin Paul, who has mysteriously reappeared.

The number of people confirmed killed in the WTC is now down to 2,800 as more people emerge from hiding. How much longer before they announce there was actually a population explosion in the building?

Lance's team spent the day begging again and I spent the morning waiting in the car, reading my paper and praying for his shift to end without some irate drunk laying into the boys. I realise the Liquor Store is where people's defences are down and where appealing for funds for a sports team is likely to be most effective but it is also the scariest. Men in plaid shirts and work boots trundled out carts full of cases of beer and spirits while wizened old women bought shot-sized bottles of spirits.

At first, I left the radio on Lance's favourite station, 92.5 FM, the Voice of the Ghetto but then the two DJ's, Big Dog and Willy, started discussing a program from the previous evening about boobs. They replayed some of the phone-in messages and to cap it all, Willy said to Big Dog, "And talk to me as if I have boobs." As Willy is a girl, and you have to risk a jail term mentioning anything about a woman's body publicly nowadays, Big Dog seemed, at first, taken aback and very apologetic for never mentioning her boobs on air before. From then on he never stopped mentioning them and I switched them, Big Dog, Willy and both her boobs, off. I'm glad Lance was out panhandling when this was going on. Somehow, seventeen years ago, when Alys broached the idea of having children, I never imagined it would lead to begging on street corners while listening to immature adults titter about women's breasts on public radio.

The Internet's still not working, nor is the phone line to the IP's Technical Centre.

Sunday 9:

Kandahar fell and sure as shooting in an American downtown neighbourhood, there were no terrorists hiding there, or, at least, none Western soldiers could see. By now, they're more likely to be living in Kansas than Kandahar. Terrorists aren't caught so easily, not successful ones anyhow.

All the stores, newspapers, and radio stations have their Christmas charity drives in full force. Humans are incredibly stupid. First, we sucker ourselves into this ugly seasonal layering of greed on top of gluttony with a solid basis of avarice; then we rush around saving folks from the worst aspects of our folly. The way to stop poor children feeling left out at Christmas is to drop this binge buying of unwanted, unasked-for, unneeded gifts by people with too much money and not enough sense.

But the burning question of the Lakelady day is, will the tilers arrive tomorrow? The kids hope not because we're either eating out or getting food delivered, which they think is the coolest thing since the last Ice Age. The adults hope the tilers will arrive because we can't afford to live off prepared foods, either financially or healthily.

Alys and I went to Gwen's indoor soccer and watched another easy win. Lance stayed home and played video games. Really, I don't think this item is worth repeating; please take it as read from now on that Gwen's team has won its Sunday game and Alys and I watched it.

Monday 10:

We are laying tiles! That's like saying the Pharaohs built the pyramids. I mean we, the Lakeladys, prepared the ground and caused it to happen not that we were doing the work though it came close to that. The important thing is -- tiles are finally being laid in our kitchen and bathrooms.

Miguel, whose family fled Chile when Pinochet lost power, is accepted by Security. Gerry says he's been cleared and I'm just a formality; i.e. I'll soon be formally kicked out of Canada.

Interviewed more victims for my PAP. I should be disgusted with myself for subjecting people who are drowning in an ocean of work to this charade, trying to make up for our management's blunder, but I don't because I'm just as much a victim as they are so they can lump it. If they hadn't initiated this dumb ACR, I wouldn't be doing this dumb PAP and they wouldn't be looking at a year's extremely hard labour working on the actions the MERD and I will inflict on them. The reward for initiating an ACR is an 'attaboy' and as much extra work as you can fit into your dwindling amount of time away from work.

One of today's victims was particularly bitter about my PAP. He said he'd told the initiator not to do it but the man was always a simpleton. The initiator's been with us fifteen years and he still doesn't understand how things work around here, the victim said. I nodded in agreement but I felt some discomfort because until the last reorganisation left me stranded, I too had been a bit simple. I too had imagined our management knew what they were doing and that I should be helping them.

Alys supervised the tilers today. She says Nico, the foreman, is really nice in an Italian kind of way. When I pressed her to explain the phrase, she went pink and said, "You know."

I didn't but Gwen told me he is young, muscular with dark wavy hair and few clothes. 'All T-shirt and tight pants' was her actual description. Gwen says Alys was giggling like a five-year-old and plying the men with coffee when she got back from school. Gwen thinks I should take a few days off work because she doesn't want to become part of a broken home while she's trying to study for her Ontario Academic Certificate.

I was so shocked by Gwen's story, I asked Alys about the giggling and coffee. She said she'd made them afternoon coffee and Nico had told her a joke -- that's all. I asked what the joke was and she couldn't remember! Maybe I will take a day off.

Weight: plus 3 lbs. It's just catch up on the weeks of eating in restaurants waiting for tilers, I expect, and nothing to worry about.

Tuesday 11:

I took the day off work to observe the Alys and Nico situation and found it as Alys said. Gwen overdoes things sometimes. I'll go back to work tomorrow.

Wednesday 12:

A mistress is something between a mister and a mattress.

Last weekend was our company's Executive Christmas Party and today we saw the fallout from it. MaryBeth, the CEO's personal assistant, was fired. MaryBeth had too much to drink at the party and lambasted one of the Senior Vice-Presidents with whom she's been having an affair. Apparently, the SVP has moved on to another personal assistant and she isn't happy about that. Gerry says the SVP never cared for her at all; he only wanted easy access to the CEO's calendar and office. I wouldn't believe anyone could act that way -- except that the personal assistant the SVP's moved on to has just been announced as the CEO's new PA, replacing MaryBeth, which means the SVP already knew MaryBeth was out of favour and who the in-favour one was. Judging from this sequence of events, our CEO comes after me on the rumour grapevine; I didn't think anyone did. What's truly frightening is that the SVP in question is an elderly man who came to our company with a protégé who is also rumoured to be his mistress -- and he's married to someone else! This level of performance from a man of his age demoralises me. I will never have enough energy to be an SVP. Or does our executive health plan include unlimited supplies of Viagra?

I asked Lydia, who was drinking in this evidence of life in the mainstream if she thought the club scene so free now she'd witnessed everyday life in the raw. She shrugged and replied, "If MaryBeth had gone to a club and had two or three lovers in a night she wouldn't be so uptight about losing this one." Listening to Lydia, I felt my hair go a paler shade of grey, otherwise known as white. Fortunately, I know she wouldn't behave that way because she's too nicely brought up, even if what she says is true, which I doubt. Of course, I doubted MaryBeth and the SVP too, when I first heard the rumour.

I met with more victims today and heard their sad tales. My PAP will probably be the straw that breaks their backs and, really, I think it's a kindness to put them out of their misery. Some still hope I will bring them aid, I could see in their eyes a hopeful longing for peace, order, and sense. The sooner such flickering remnants are extinguished forever, the better for all of us. We are doomed to serfdom by modern business practices and we should accept it. Until the present crop of power-mad sociopaths that have been leading the Western business world for a decade are locked up, and their disciples with them, any kind of humanity is pointless.

I took Gwen and Lance to soccer and hockey practice and used the time I spent watching them to catch up on this diary. On the way back, Gwen and Lance were talking about what they'd found when they got back from school. What they found was Alys and Nico having coffee in the best room and laughing together. Gwen and Lance are very young in the ways of the world and get their views from TV. Naturally they imagine the worst and are fearful of losing their mother. I tried to reassure them and only succeeded in sounding lame. They see me as a blind cuckold.

Thursday 13:

Today, our all-news radio station was announcing more Christmas sales. It seems the continual downpour we've been enjoying since September, and the lack of snow is inhibiting Christmas shoppers. I'm sure Jesus is disappointed about that and I felt badly for him so I went out at lunchtime to buy some gifts. This is two weeks early for me. I hope he feels better up there in heaven knowing I was willing to make the effort for his birthday.

I didn't attend the MERD meeting because I was putting together my PAP based on the interviews and research I finished yesterday. As a sop to what's left of my conscience, I have tentatively suggested an action saying the documentation people could get more staff. I know, in yesterday's diary, I said I shouldn't do this but I'm going to try. Maybe I'll become a martyr and be remembered fondly in the happier times to come when the human race finally matures.

The tilers are almost finished. The tiles are laid and we are waiting for the glue to dry. Tomorrow, they will grout between the tiles and twenty-four hours after that we can walk on the kitchen floor. By next Monday, the heavy appliances can go back. The kids are pleased to get another weekend without home cooking. When they're older, they'll understand how bad for them the past month has been. For some reason, the school's health classes and our droning on and on about the quality of fresh food has failed to make an impression.

Took Gwen to her ice hockey game. Alys stayed to help Lance with his homework. Gwen again advised me to stay home while the tilers were in the house. She asked if I hadn't noticed how much makeup Alys is wearing this week? Or how short her skirt was when I got home tonight? I couldn't say I had noticed, because I hadn't, but when I thought about it, I realised Gwen was right. Alys did look surprisingly well turned out this evening.

Later, when Gwen was in bed, I asked Alys, very casually, what she was doing tomorrow. She replied, "Shopping like I usually do on Friday. As I have done for the past twenty years, or haven't you noticed that either?"

I protested at this slur on my character but Alys continued, quite violently, to list another set of faults I never knew I had. She'd never mentioned them before. She ended the list by saying, "You wouldn't notice if I were stark naked hanging by my legs from the dining room chandelier screwing Nico."

Why, when they want to make a point, do women always bring nudity into it? Don't like war? Undress. Don't like fur? Undress. Don't like welfare cuts? Undress. They're obsessed with their own bodies. I fled to the safety of the retreat to write my diary. Universal nudity is one thing, personal nudity is quite another and I'm not cut out to deal with it. Her speech does show how her mind is working, however. I shall be more watchful tomorrow night when I get home.

Friday 14:
I removed the suggestion of giving the documentation department more staff from my PAP. I don't want to be a martyr.

Went for a drink with Seth to catch up on old times. I discovered he left the old company right after I did and he's only just returned to the neighbourhood. After that, the dancers distracted us so we agreed to meet again next Friday and catch up on old times.

When I got home from work and Alys from shopping, we found the tilers gone, which would have been cause for celebration -- if they'd cleaned the walls or put back the beading around the skirting board. At Alys's bidding, I left a forceful message on the Tile Shoppe's answering machine. Alys wants them back immediately.

I noticed Alys was wearing regular clothes tonight. Was it just for shopping or has she fallen out with Nico? I couldn't ask Gwen because she was at work and Lance had been playing road hockey after school so he didn't see them together, as he told me when I took him to soccer practice.

Weight: plus 2 lbs. Still suffering from a surfeit of restaurant food. Next week will see a big improvement.

Saturday 15:

The tilers returned early, (very early out of spite, I thought), then, when they were sure the whole Lakelady family was up, set to work. They claimed they were always returning to finish but I felt it was my strongly worded message and mentally patted myself on the back. At ten o'clock, the Tile Shoppe woman called with apologies and promises to get the tilers back asap. When I said they were already here, she asked to speak to them and I handed Nico the phone but he didn't want it. Eventually, Paolo, the apprentice took it. I could hear Gina from the other side of the kitchen when the phone was pressed to Paolo's ear, which it wasn't for long because he wasn't wearing hearing protection and her decibels were extremely sharp. When Paolo hung up the phone, they all glared bitterly at me. I went out, recommending Alys to watch them for the rest of their stay in case an accident should happen to our furnishings. By lunchtime, the tilers were finished and cleaned up to Alys's satisfaction. I'm relieved we're almost back to normal because, if we'd gone on much longer, my credit card bill for food was going to be larger than the bill for tiles, which was impossible. Also, my weight was going to be a larger number than either of them.

Thanks to the breakfast bar removal, the bill for tiles went up by one whole box. According to Nico, they would have only been two tiles short but had to buy another box of a hundred. I glared at Alys, who pretended not to notice. I noticed she was very pretty today and the kid's suspicions became mine.

Lance's hockey team lost again today. This time there were no fights but we did rack up what must be a record number of penalty points for a single game in all of hockey's history.

Called dad. He and Gawain are both better from their illnesses but Gawain went back to work last Monday and his back flared up again. He had to take the rest of the week off.

In an effort to get off the subject of sickness, I tried to tell Dad about the tiles but he misheard and now thinks I have piles. I was going to correct him but he was so interested and sympathetic, I just wallowed in the attention. So long as he doesn't tell everyone over there my 'problem' it will be a harmless enough misunderstanding.

Alys and I went to the movies after the hockey game, leaving Lance to play video games while Gwen was at work.

Sunday 16:
Internet and e-mail are working again and I never did get to speak to the Technical Centre. They are going to give all their customers 10% off their top-of-the-line service as a reward for our loyalty and patience. I don't have the top-of-the-line service and it would cost me money to get the discount so my loyalty goes unrewarded -- as always.

Unfortunately, I've lost all the useful Internet connections I was connected to. In particular, BillBuddy, an Internet service for paying bills and transferring money. I re-found their site, using Search, and tried to re-connect but my e-mail address is different and the site won't accept my efforts. They have an on-line re-connection form to fill in and I sent it off. It isn't a big deal -- only they owe me a $45.

Surprisingly, we still have connections to innumerable webcam girls who will show me everything they've got for a very modest outlay. I have to say the one thing the Internet has finally proven is that women don't sell their bodies out of necessity -- mostly it's for the fun of it. I never believed it was a necessity; I just wish I had the magic something that brought out the naughty side of them, instead of being terrified whenever one looks at me.

Lance was at a sleepover with his friends last night and they played video games all night. Consequently, he slept most of today. After her work, we took Gwen to indoor soccer and Alys and I cheered on her team to another easy win.

Monday 17:
Padraig being cleared pleases me, particularly after his concern on filling out the security form. His unnatural cheerfulness at the news makes me deeply suspicious; this is another need-to-know moment, I decide. On balance, it's more important for our Company, and hence Ontario, and so Canada, and on to the Western World, that the Vacation Request Form procedure be completed rather than our Security people also becoming suspicious.

When I got home I found my fears about the kids and me having nothing to talk about was misplaced. According to behavioural experts, if you do something for three weeks it becomes a habit that you can't get out of for the rest of your life. I can confirm this does not apply to teenagers; all their school things were on the floor in the hall again tonight. I've no doubt it was a relief for them, psychologically speaking, to get back to normal. Putting their clothes and bags in the closet these past weeks has probably traumatised them and they'll become serial killers.

When I pointed out this teenage phenomenon to Alys, she said I was to stop bullying the kids. They had a lot on their minds when they came back from school. Like what, I asked. Like homework, Alys replied. Lance must finish his homework quickly because he's sprawled in front of the TV every night when I get home. I didn't say this to Alys because she seemed very low this evening. Missing Nico, Gwen said when I dropped her off at work.

BillBuddy's computer replied to my e-mail saying they would send a new password in a separate message. E-mail is amazing, these people are out there in Colorado or Montana or somewhere, and yet they reply in minutes.

Tuesday 18:
Worked on my PAP, preparing for the MERD meeting and presentation. I've put the one honest action back, buried deeply among the other actions, all of which were on my last PAP. My plan is to close out the CRAP actions on my last PAP to these actions and put longer dates on these actions, so gaining myself additional time or even, if I can continue this dastardly plan until the re-organisation sweeps me away, never do their 'actions' at all.

Our leaders have finally admitted the truth. The re-organisation, now called the 'Transformation', will not happen this year. February 1st is the new date. Lydia says if I get fired she and I can start a mobile brothel business. She will be the Madam and I can be the driver and interviewer of the staff. Lydia has an unhealthy interest in matters sexual, I fear. Poor girl, like all young people, she longs for an adventure and Canadians don't like adventures.

This month's speech to my fellow Public Speakers, on the horrors awaiting us if we don't do something about Rap music, was much better received than last month's presentation. The secret of good public speaking is to say only what the audience wants to hear.

Right after my speech, I began to cough and haven't stopped since. My throat and chest feel like they're on fire. I can't believe it. This is the second year running I'll have been ill over the Christmas holidays.

Alys says I'm not to pass on my cough to Lance because, as we know, he's susceptible to everything going. Lance meanwhile decided tonight was a good night to wrestle with his aged parent, thus ensuring he gets days off school with Alys to look after him. When Gwen came home from work, she was angry with me for giving Lance the opportunity to pretend to be ill. I protested Lance was wrestling with me, not the other way round but Gwen stomped off to her room to study muttering 'Uncle Gawain' under her breath.

BillBuddy still has not sent the password, so I filled in their form again. One day soon I will be deluged by passwords, none of which will work because they will cancel each other out.

Wednesday 19:

Finished my new PAP and sent it to DOLT for tomorrow's presentation. Lydia and I worked on some research items together for a procedure Padraig was to have started a year ago. In the end, it seemed more sensible for Lydia to write the procedure too and she began writing immediately. I think it may be ready for first review tomorrow. Padraig will be angry because he was saving it for after he finishes the Vacation Request Form procedure, but it can't be helped. The competition from Lydia will be good for them all.

My cough continued all day though at a lower intensity. Maybe it was just someone's perfume or after-shave in the classroom last night. Lance has started coughing today. Have we caught a cold or is he just being his usual self?

Alys took Gwen and Lance to soccer and hockey practice so I couldn't infect them. However, when Lance came home he wrestled with me again to be sure of catching it. Gwen says Alys didn't come back to watch her practice like she usually does. She said this in a meaningful way. What am I to make of it? Alys probably went shopping.

BillBuddy's computer acknowledged my form by saying they'll send me a password in a separate snail mail. Why can't they send me one with this e-mail?

Thursday 20:

As prophesied, the MERD did not like the suggestion of getting more people into the document department. That action lasted about two minutes. Nor did they like the fact most of my actions were the same as my last PAP's actions. The PAP now has a whole raft of 'suggestions' I'm to 'review' and incorporate 'if they seem reasonable'. Maybe the disappointment they've experienced at my efforts on this occasion will convince them to give the next PAP to someone else. Gerry perhaps, he's always loud in these meetings when his boss lets him attend, which is too often. I think his comments today on my PAP were intended in jest but they didn't help.

I took my concern about the documentation system to Mr. Ogilvie, suggesting he talk to his fellow Directors because they didn't seem to value good recordkeeping. He was quite sharp with me. It seems our Company is very concerned with recordkeeping because, in these litigious times when everyone sues everyone, good records are the first line of legal defence. I apologised for my doubts and left very unsatisfied; martyrdom looms. By keeping our documents in such a mess, are our senior managers hoping to supplement their pensions through litigation, or stave off firing with their tribal knowledge?

As also predicted, Lydia has the first draft of her procedure ready for internal review. Padraig is horribly angry and wants the Employee Association, our union, to do something about my giving 'his' work to temporary staff. He feels she should have been researching for the procedure he's writing now rather than 'scabbing' for management. I pointed out she'd given him the research he needed on her first day here. That only made him madder. No wonder they're always fighting in Northern Ireland.

My cough continues unabated and so does Lance's. Still, mine isn't bad and provided it doesn't get worse, I'll be okay for Christmas this year.

No answer yet from BillBuddy so I phoned them. They say the password has been sent by mail; I have to be patient.

Gwen's team won another ice hockey game but I wasn't there to see it. Alys says I have to get better and stop infecting the kids.

Friday 21:
Revised my PAP and sent it to DOLT for approval. As all the new actions consist of seconding documentation staff to our MERD Managers' departments, it is sure to be approved. This won't help the rest of the Corporation get their documents filed but that's not my concern now. I just want to be off this and all PAPs.

Right after Lydia prepared for her night out at the Club, I went for a drink with Seth to catch up on old times. I discovered he left the old company just after I did and he's only just returned to the neighbourhood. After that, the dancers distracted us so we agreed to meet again next Friday and catch up on old times. It was exactly like last week. In fact, if I'm ever going to find out what he's been doing these past years, and vice versa, we're going to have to meet somewhere else. The sight of naked young women writhing around on stage in front of us is sensory overload. On the other hand, this may get me ready for attending the Club with Lydia. Putting it like that, it's practically a duty to see old Seth and catch up on old times. Despite seeing lots of naked girls, I'm strangely disappointed I didn't see Lydia's outfit.

My cough, which continues day and night, was completely cured while I was in the bar with Seth. Is beer a cough cure or have I contracted Legionnaire's Disease from my home and office heating systems?

Saturday 22:
Called dad. He has told everyone about my piles and they send their best wishes for my recovery. Aunt Sophie had an operation on hers and it helped a lot, Dad says. All my elderly relatives have sent recipes for homemade remedies I should use to ease the pain. Dad says, "With luck, this won't be the start of the long decline to where his health is." Gawain says it serves me right for over-taxing my body with exercise at my age. I felt like I'd grown up and joined a prestigious club that, until now, has been closed to me -- the Embarrassing Ailments Club. On the whole (if you'll pardon the pun), I preferred listening to their aches and pains -- even though I know they're as imaginary as mine. Maybe I won't visit them next year like I promised.

I tried to tell them about my cough, which remains a constant irritation, but it wasn't in the same league as piles so they pretended not to hear. On the other hand, I heard all about their coughs and sniffles that are incipient asthmatic bronchitis (in Dad's case) and a piffling cold (in Gawain's case) according to dad.

Took the now desperately coughing Lance to his hockey. His team lost again today and it ended in another brawl. Fortunately, Lance wasn't on the ice when the fighting started so we walked off scot-free. I will, however, soon have to acknowledge his cough. He'll hurt himself bringing it to my attention if I don't. After his bath, Alys rubbed Vick into Lance's chest and back while glaring daggers at me.

Sunday 23:

Finished my Christmas shopping. Jesus should be happier now because today the stores were full of shoppers all exhibiting goodwill toward each other. My bruises will fade by New Year. I think anthropologists, or whatever scientist it is that studies these things, have got women completely wrong. We're told they are the conciliators, the glue that holds society together, the collaborators not competitors; these qualities don't manifest themselves much at intense shopping times.

Lance's cough is now much louder than mine so Alys took him to the doctor. It seems he's actually ill. I felt a bit guilty and spent the afternoon bringing him drinks and cookies to keep his strength up.

Alys took Gwen to indoor soccer so I could 'look after Lance to make up for making him ill.' Personally, I feel that if I'd gone to the doctor, he'd have said I was ill too. Who would have looked after me? Silky, that's who. She kept me company on the couch while I watched Lance and TV.

Monday 24:

Christmas Eve.

Alys and Gwen wrapped the presents they've been buying for weeks now and I went Christmas shopping. The trouble with going early, like I did this year, is that you begin to have second thoughts -- your confidence over that 'perfect' gift sags as the adverts and radio interviews slowly, but surely, drips poison into your brain. From now on, I stick to my tradition of shop once, on Christmas Eve, and I'm done with it. The other good thing about going on Christmas Eve is the shops are full of men so there's no bruising and the shop assistants gift wrap everything, knowing we helpless males will make a pig's ear from their silk purse if left to do it ourselves.

In the evening, we Lakeladys went to a Carol Service with friends and without Lance, who stayed home, watching semi-naked women cavort to music on MuchMusic, so our friends wouldn't catch his cold. If the doctor hadn't pronounced him ill, I'd have been very suspicious. I couldn't sing very well on account of my sore throat and headache; however, I like carols, church choirs, hymns with a good tune, and stained glass windows. If the church would stick to these basics and not dabble in superstition, I'd go more often. Still, it is better than our new religion of gluttony.

Tuesday 25:

Christmas Day

Speaking of gluttony, I also like Christmas Dinner, Christmas Pudding, and Christmas Cake. They're comfort food in a world where comfort, psychologically speaking, has been missing for some time. Watched the Queen's Message to the Commonwealth and found it too modern for my taste. Alys liked it but then, like all most women (mustn't stereotype, Margaret Thatcher would probably agree with me) she goes in for that wussy, touchy-feely stuff. I prefer a rousing call-to-arms accompanied by the stirring sounds of the Highland Regiments' massed pipe bands.

Gwen & Lance retired to their rooms with their presents right after breakfast and were hardly seen again.

Called dad. He and Gawain are having a quiet Christmas. They did watch some Christmas movies, Christmas on Elm Street, Psycho Christmas, Die Harder at Christmas III, and the Christmas Terminator, but otherwise, they hardly noticed the day. The weather is too cold and wet to go outside and everywhere is shut except the video store. Christmas in the UK is a drag, apparently. I decided against a discussion on the spiritless nature of the modern consumer Christmas. Promised Dad we'd definitely visit in the summertime.

I felt so ill by suppertime I went to bed and listened to my family laughing at their new movies. Even Lance seemed well enough to be downstairs eating candies, while I lay, sweating and coughing, dreaming of Lord Marchmain's death in Brideshead Revisited. Actually, I've noticed in movies, anyone who has a steady dry cough is doomed; from wayward old peers to consumptive showgirls, the dry cough is a killer. Particularly if they say they're going to get well 'when the warmer weather comes'! In case this is the last entry in my die-ary, Silky, who is spoon-hugging with me through my passing-over, gets everything!

Wednesday 26:

Boxing Day

I love cold turkey with all the trimmings. We kept a Christmas pudding for today too so I'm suitably comforted. My cold seemed a lot better today and I got up and lay on the couch, much to Lance's disgust. Mine too, the couch is littered with candy wrappers and toffee and chocolate crumbs after his day on it yesterday.

There was nothing on TV so we watched Lance and Gwen's

Christmas videos and DVDs -- Pearl Harbor, Live and Let Die, Armageddon, and Gone in Sixty Seconds. I despair of the human race and wonder if maybe I'm an alien.

Alys thawed enough to bring me drinks whenever she was making one for Lance, so it didn't turn out too bad.

Thursday 27:
Vacation
Nothing from BillBuddy yet. If the North American economies have a poor season it will be because my funds are stuck in this electronic Fort Knox.

I stayed late in bed again, recovering my strength. Looking back on my Christmas Day entry, I've postulated a new medical law; if you think you're going to die, you're not. The reverse is also true. One thing, however, remains unchanged; Silky still gets everything! I was ill last Christmas too. It's finally happened; I've become allergic to false bonhomie and greed.

When I did get up, it was to help Alys prepare for our traditional Lakelady Christmas buffet. I pointed out having a sick person (me) making food wasn't a good idea. Alys said I was right, I shouldn't do the food -- I should vacuum, clean the bathrooms, tidy the kids' (and her!) coats and shoes away from the hall, and generally make the place tidy.

As it turned out, most of our usual guests were ill too so we were a very depleted group. I hope the small group means I've only begun a minor epidemic and Ontario's production isn't affected next week. Our conversation centred mainly on Universities, the Ontario Health System, and our worst fear -- that our sons never leave home. That truly is today's epidemic. Once, one daughter selflessly stayed on to look after her aging parents. Today, thanks to the changes we've made to our society, we've an unmarried son in every home being looked after by his aging parents. Our ancestors were right, boys need to be driven, beaten, and ruthlessly drilled to be of any value. Without frontiers to explore, borders to defend, or empires to conquer, men are worthless. It's time to roll up our tents and march silently into history's long night with the Greeks, Romans, Vikings, Crusaders, Navigators, the Thin Red Line, the Old Contemptibles, the Few, and all the others who built this modern world but weren't equipped to enjoy it.

No hockey because it's Christmas. Lance is playing with his new video Gamebox and games. He and Gawain discussed their respective Christmas video games. Gawain bought himself a Gamebox for Christmas, now he and Lance have something in common, other than a predilection for copying their father's illnesses I mean.

Gwen, after discovering I wasn't about to install her new CD burner in the computer, went off to visit her friends and wasn't seen again till after our guests had gone.

Friday 28:

Alys and I rose early so we could clear up from the party. Gwen and Lance exercised their rights as teenagers and lay in bed till noon.

By midday, I had to go to the doctor; Alys ordered me to. He said there was nothing wrong with me and wrote me a prescription for a host of cures. I'm glad I wasn't ill. After that, I spent the afternoon (and evening) lying on the couch with my armoury of puffer, codeine, and couch medicines before me on the coffee table. I let Alys, Gwen or Lance change the movies because, if I'd stirred, Lance would have been horizontal in my place and it's my turn for the couch. Why does visiting a doctor always make me feel ill?

Still nothing from BillBuddy; the North American economy is tottering.

Saturday 29:

Called dad. He and Gawain aren't well. Gawain ate too much over the holidays and Dad ate something that didn't agree with him, he says. I commiserated as best I could, considering how little I cared and tried to change the subject in case they got on about my piles again.

No hockey because of the holidays and the season of goodwill.

Gwen was at work all day, making money for her running-away-to-university fund. She and Alys have come to an understanding on Universities. In public, they will both say Gwen is going to Toronto.

I stayed in to keep warm, Alys went shopping but couldn't find anything she liked, or so she said when she got home.

Sunday 30:

Today I installed Gwen's CD burner in our computer; I couldn't put it off any longer or Gwen would have done it herself. It turned out to be ridiculously easy. If I don't make it through the

'Transformation', I'm going to become a computer accessory installer. I clearly have an aptitude for this; it worked first time!

Gwen showed me how to use it. She downloaded songs from the Internet using a file swap service called Wazoo and then copied them to the CDs. The music wasn't quite to my taste. Young ladies singing about masturbating while their shirts go up over their heads and their skirts drop to their feet may be exciting at seventeen but they're terrifying to a seventeen-year old's parents.

I even burned a CD of my own featuring George Formby, Peggy Lee, Jo Stafford, Burl Ives, Gracie Fields, Glenn Miller, Doris Day, and Debbie Reynolds. All before my time and all great, though George Formby can be a bit risque. Strangely enough, Lance and Gwen liked my CD as much as I liked Gwen's; just playing it can now get me a room to myself whenever I need to write my diary.

Alys went to see if her friend (one of the sick ones at our Christmas buffet) was better. Gwen muttered darkly that mom was oddly dressed for visiting the sick. Gwen has always been suspicious of Alys's motives but it's become very noticeable lately.

No soccer or hockey so Gwen and I watched movies. Lance played video games.

Monday 31:
New Years Eve.
After years of watching over our young children, we are finally able to go out for New Year again. Unfortunately, all our usual New Year friends are recovering from operations or illnesses (maturity isn't all it's cracked up to be). Gwen was going to parties with friends so we decided to take Lance and head downtown for Toronto's New Year Bash. Lance would enjoy the pop groups and we'd enjoy the feeling of oneness with our fellow Canadians. The feeling of oneness was hard to achieve because Alys and I were the oldest people in Nathan Phillips Square. However, all the pushing and shoving to get near the stage and the general discomfort of it all was quite like old times at Rock concerts when we were seventeen. I'd never heard of any of the performers, and one or two could hardly be described as performers they were so obviously terrified of performing in public; one group of singer-dancers kept so far back on stage, and were so covered in hoods and dark glasses, they were invisible. I hope, for their sakes, they grow out of it soon. Also, constantly being asked to pretend it was midnight, for the cameras,

was irritating, but at least, we were there. Gwen watched it on TV at her party. When she told me this on New Year's Day, I said jokingly, 'It can't have been much of a party if you were all watching TV'. Gwen said it was the TV in the host's parents' bedroom and every partygoer was in bed. Kids love to shock their parents so I'm not concerned; however if she starts going to the clubs downtown, I shall put my foot down.

January 2002:
Happy New Year -- I hope.

Tuesday 1:
While the Lakelady family slept late after our revelry of last night, eleven of the fifteen European Union countries adopted a new currency today, the Euro, and did away with their own currencies. This common currency will bring them a million benefits and no drawbacks if you believe the pro-Euro camp, and a million drawbacks and no benefits if you believe the anti-. I'm explaining this for future readers of my diary because, like all such currency unions of the past (most of them in Europe where they don't let previous bad experiences get in the way of another bad idea), it will be gone when posterity rolls around.

New Year's Day is a quiet day for most of us, watching movies, reading Christmas gift books, and eating and drinking too much. I'll be glad when it's over and I'm back at work because there I can watch my calories better. Alys went to see her friend again.

Wednesday 2:
With his Christmas gift money Lance bought new trousers in the Boxing Week Sales. I expect it was a man who decided women should only have enough cloth to cover the top half, the bottom half, or the middle half of their bodies, without ever covering the whole thing, but who decided the excess material should go to make teenage boy's pants? In the event of a strong wind, Lance will never be seen again in Ontario. And, with all that material, why wasn't it possible to cover his boxer shorts?

Is Jesus happy with Boxing Week Sales or does he only want us to shop before His birthday? Why doesn't the church speak out on important questions like this?

No soccer or hockey practice. Alys and Gwen went shopping and came back loaded with bags. I asked how this could be when they had emptied the stores before Christmas? They rolled their eyes in despair and then modelled their new items for me. This is why wise men never buy women clothes. Who would have guessed anyone would wear any of those things?

Thursday 3:
There was no MERD meeting today because not everyone is back. DOLT, however, met and grudgingly passed my plan. I'm free -- until the next one comes along.

I called BillBuddy and the woman I spoke to said she 'pressed the button again' to send out another letter. Where are BillBuddy's letters going? I would feel surer of success with a quill, parchment, and the Pony Express.

I learned from Lydia that she was going to return to college last year and do an MA in History but chose instead to keep 'Temping'. This won't do. I will make it my mission for 2002 to see she goes back to University this summer without any further procrastination. I don't think she realises women are the 'coming thing' (they always are, as any reading of history will show. They are always more rebellious today than they were yesterday and always about to take over the world. Men are so insecure.) She must get an MA so she can get a job in our mailroom.

No practices because of the holidays but Gwen's soccer team had a parent's meeting, which I attended because Alys doesn't like that sort of thing -- democracy that is. She's all in favour of coaches doing what the parents tell them but she doesn't like what the other parents tell the coaches. I have considerable sympathy for that point of view after every parent's meeting I attend. I'm not a fan of democracy either. The only reason we'd go to all the trouble of voting is to get a better class of leader, but a quick review of the large western countries and economies in my lifetime suggests countries would do just as well using primogeniture. Bring back the King, say I.

Friday 4:
Allowing for the working of Fate, I'd assumed I'd get my first letter from BillBuddy today because I called and asked them to send another one yesterday. However, Fate knew I was expecting that outcome and double-crossed me -- no letter came from BillBuddy.

Lydia was off to a different Club tonight, one where they dress in skimpy but normal clothes. I was very relieved when she showed me tonight's outfit. Compared with the others this one is practically fit for a Convent though perhaps one run by Mariah Carey (who makes a living as a singer but dresses and acts like an exotic dancer). Unfortunately, I reminded Lydia of her ambition to do an MA. She didn't speak to me for the rest of the day and I didn't get the opportunity to have this barely legal outfit modelled, which means I missed a chance to bond with my staff without shattering the Code of Business Conduct.

Alys visited another sick friend in the evening. As she says, now the kids are older we can do this sort of thing where we couldn't before. I agree but Gwen, when she came back from work and found her mom absent, was upset. She demanded I do something before it's too late. Kids are like that; they spend all their time doing their own thing but if their parents aren't where they left them, they get annoyed. I told Gwen she should be proud of her mom for helping the sick. Gwen stormed off to her room and slammed the door so loud Lance heard it down in the basement, where he was playing video games. He complained we'd spoiled his concentration at a critical moment and now he was dropped down a level -- whatever that means.

Saturday 5:
Called dad. Really I don't know why I bother. They don't even have the courtesy to ask about my piles now. It's just one long whine about their symptoms; they're so self-centered. Today, they've got colds. Somehow, on one of Gawain's brief forays to work or the video store he picked up a cold germ and now they're both sick.

Here in Ontario, the rain has changed to falling slush that may yet become snow. Fate is playing games with our local ski resort's livelihoods. A uselessly thin covering of snow fell overnight but the temperature remains stubbornly above zero so they can't even add to it with their own snow.

The morning rush hour, however, was snarled up by the 1 cm of snow and every ditch was filled with 4-wheel drives. The drivers of these things believe that because they can go faster in poor road conditions, it follows they must be able to stop faster too. But while four-wheel drive is new, four-wheel braking has been standard from the start. In bad weather, four-wheel drive cars are little more than unguided missiles.

Lance and his friends had another foray to the Mall. Now, they are 'hoodies' and wear a hood over their baseball caps. This, with the dark glasses and baggy jackets and pants, completes the average North American teenage male's transformation from gangster to harem woman. Why they don't go straight for the veil, I don't know. The role reversal you see all around is leading to some strange sights; half dressed girls swaggering down the street with a posse of muffled boys shambling along a few paces behind. North America has always had a problem with male nudity and sexuality, witness the yards of cloth the men here wear to go swimming, but lately, it's become quite bizarre. My Gran would be pleased to find headscarves back in fashion though she'd be surprised to find them on boys. Gran and her friends only wore them to hide their curlers; teenage boys wear them to keep their shaved heads warm. The saddest part of this fashion is that, when the boys are fifty and really bald, they will have hair implants on their heads -- their despotic wives will make them.

Lance's hockey team lost again today but Lance no longer cares about hockey. I'm glad because once again the teams had a fight on the ice; this time, two referees had to pull the combatants apart and got caught up in it with sadly comical results. Gwen came to Lance's game and complained about the lack of skill, saying all they care about is hitting each other. Alys tried to agree but Gwen is being very snappish where her mom is concerned so they fell into silence, one each side of me. Gwen held my arm, and then Alys did the same. Now I know how the rope feels in a tug o' war.

Sunday 6:

This year's ski season isn't going to happen for Arthur Lakelady. Today we had more snow that melted by lunchtime. The resort owners must be tearing their hair out. It isn't that there's no snow up there, Lance says the runs are in good shape on ski club night, it's just no one wants to go skiing when it's wet.

I took Gwen to indoor soccer because Alys said she wanted to help Lance with his homework. I think she just didn't want to spend an hour and a half in the car with Gwen, who is still being mean to her. As it turns out, Alys didn't help Lance with his homework either. Apparently, soon after Gwen and I left, she had a call from one of the ailing friends and left Lance to play video games. I helped Lance with his homework when I got back. Gwen, on hearing the story, went to her room and stayed there. Gwen's determination on the subject of Alys's imagined misbehaviour is beginning to shake my confidence. Should I be checking up on Alys? Should I call the sick friends? I'll start locking this diary away as a precaution. One day Gwen and Alys will be friends again and these ugly suspicions are best forgotten.

Monday 7:
Went to the gym today and was surprised to see Lydia there. She's joined the gym to get back in shape, she says; it's her New Year Resolution. Her shape looks pretty good to most of us around the office but of course, being men, we don't know anything about what looks good on a female. Still it's excellent news; young people should take care of themselves from the start. Like saving for your retirement, it's too late when you reach 40. I had fun showing Lydia how to use the treadmill. It's surprising how difficult treadmills are when you first try one.

Our bread-making machine, which is only a year old, needs a new paddle because the non-slip coating on the original one is wearing off. I called the appliance manufacturer's service department and I was told, 'Janice is off sick. She'll call you back.' I like the informality of our local suppliers. I doubt if I'd get to hear of staff health problems if I called some other global appliance giant.

Nothing from BillBuddy, so I called again. This time, I was quite sharp with Sean, who said he'd have a Supervisor call me to get the problem sorted out. No Supervisor called.

After waiting for BillBuddy, I waited for Gwen. Then she called asking to be picked up from work so I went to the pool where she works. I waited and waited before getting out of the car and wandering the empty halls of the Recreation Centre until I found a cleaner who said everyone had gone hours ago. My growing panic quickly turned to anger when Gwen answered the phone at home; I was quite sharp with her. In return, she was quite sharp with me! She claims she told me last night she was at Whitebay's other pool but I don't remember such a conversation and I'm not convinced it was entirely my fault.

Tuesday 8:
No call from breadmaker, Janice, yet.
Transformation is delayed -- again. We are going to be transformed by March 31; a 'challenging' schedule says senior management in the buzzword of the week. 'Impossible' says everyone else. I've heard of companies where the employees play

Buzzword Bingo, a game you win by collecting management clichés. That would be no good here; no game would last more than one announcement and everyone would win -- except communication and the English language, of course.

Lydia joined me in the gym again today and I have to say I have never caused such a stir in the gym before; all eyes were on me -- well, us. Lydia's tight spandex shorts and sports bra (left breast and thigh checked and approved by Nike) may have had something to do with it. (Why didn't Nike like the right ones? They appear equally exquisite to me.)

Women are always complaining about men staring at them and I got a sense of that today. However, I can't help feeling this is a two-way conversation. Even in my own modest experience, I find whenever I look at a woman in the street, or wherever, she's invariably looking right back at me. Lydia may not have actually spoken words to the men in the gym but her message was loud enough for them all to hear.

Took Lance to Ski Club. Normal kids who join the school Ski Club travel with the rest of the club on the bus. Lance, however, despite prompting from us to join didn't and now needs a ride there and back. He says they told him it was to be Wednesday night, which was his hockey night, so he didn't join. Then, when they changed it to Tuesday night, they said it was for older kids only. Then, when they didn't get enough older kids and opened it up to everyone, he didn't hear about it till too late. In previous years, Lance had complained about the buses and the ski lessons, both of which he misses with this arrangement, so I'm very suspicious.

Alys and Gwen are friends again, joined in sisterly indignation against the wickedness of callous men, otherwise known as me. Gwen has decided I don't care what happens to her, I only care about Lance. Alys is sure I don't care about any of my family and they went off to shop their hurt away.

No call from BillBuddy's Supervisor yet either.

Wednesday 9:
No call from Janice yet ...nor BillBuddy.
Lydia joined me at the gym today, her third time. We did the treadmills and weight machines together. She's never been to a gym before so I had to spend time showing her how the weight machines work. She's a surprisingly slow learner for someone so bright. She

says she's 'gyminally challenged' and I think she must be right. I spent the hour catching her, supporting her, putting her feet back onto the pedals and bum back onto seats, etc. I was a bit shaky on that last part. I was even shakier on 'spotting' for her on free weights, particularly when she lay on a bench and did chest presses while my hands hovered inches above her breasts ready to catch the weights if they should fall.

I was still in a dream when I took Gwen and Lance to soccer and hockey practice, which was just as well because neither of them is speaking to me. Lance has taken his mom's side and thinks I don't care about him either. The good news is I didn't have to listen to their suspicions about Alys. Now they probably think Alys would be better off with Nico anyway.

Thursday 10:
Still no call from poor Janice. She must be seriously ill.

Lydia came to the gym again but she was too stiff after yesterday's efforts to do anything other than watch me. I must say it is nice to be appreciated. Not only does she think I'm strong and fit, she thinks I move beautifully too. I took the opportunity to ask Lydia if she had applied for a place at the University of Toronto and she said no. I warned her I shall keep asking every day till she does. Her reply was not in the spirit of our company's Code of Business Conduct. I was shocked because she seems such a nicely brought up young lady. She was noticeably colder after this brief exchange and went off to watch an elderly man do press-ups.

Before our estrangement, Lydia told me why she particularly started coming to the gym. She had been doing an Extreme Weight Loss Clinic at a local plaza, where they measured every part of your body every week while you followed their diet plan. Lydia wasn't planning on losing weight, just maintaining it so it was a surprise when, after the first week, they told her she'd lost an inch, made up of an eighth of an inch off her right calf, an eighth off her left thigh, an eighth off her left biceps, and five-eighths off her bust. When this happened for a second week, she decided to leave before she became flat-chested. The gym seemed to offer a way of sculpting her body without losing the important and interesting bits. The 'interesting bits' didn't seem in any danger to me -- or any of the other men in the gym, I noticed.

Called BillBuddy. Candace says she'll get a Supervisor to call me back as soon as a Supervisor is free. This doesn't sound too good. It sounds like the Supervisors are all busy sorting out problems caused by their own system's incompetence. No Supervisor called.

BillBuddy's management is built on the same fallacy as all modern management; i.e. activity equals achievement. The ideal all companies should be working toward is where their top-notch products flow effortlessly from the factory or office while the few staff all snooze gently at their desks, available if needed for the rare glitch but otherwise unemployed. Whenever people are actively meddling with things, you have problems, problems that show up in your products as defects, which loses you customers. Modern managers don't feel they are getting their money's worth if the workers aren't running around in a panic all day long. That's why managers are forever re-organising, to maintain the panic. Even though almost all the work done by employees nowadays is pointless. It's the Twenty-first Century equivalent of counting paper clips or polishing brasses.

Gwen's ice hockey team lost its game tonight and they were laughing as they came off the ice! What kind of sport is this? The coach should give them a sound tongue-lashing till they got focused.

Friday 11:
I called the breadmaker factory and spoke to Janice who has been at work since Tuesday! Apparently, they no longer make breadmaking appliances and haven't for a year now. Janice is all out of parts and quite annoyed that she's been left to tell the customers -- again. It's no wonder these people are only local manufacturers. With this kind of service, that's all they'll ever be.

Called BillBuddy. The supervisor will call, says Ryan. No Supervisor called. Reckoning now -- BillBuddy owes me $45, I owe the phone company $10.

Lydia has gone back to the Cadaver Club tonight because last week's Club was too boring. As she is speaking to me again, she offered to model her 'dress' for tonight. Once again, seeing it on the hangar, I declined the opportunity -- and her suggestion to go to the club with her. She says there are other 'mature' people and I wouldn't be alone. She also says I look good and I worry too much about my appearance! Perhaps she's right. Maybe, if a young woman thinks I look good, I should give the gym a rest. Today's physical effort was much the same as always anyway, grim, with one bright spot:

Weight: minus 1 lb. It's a new start for the new year.

Perhaps, next week, I should go to the Club. Just to see what it's really like.

Saturday 12:

Called dad. He isn't very well. It's so cold and wet over there he doesn't feel like doing anything. With gritted teeth, I forbore from saying that he doesn't want to do anything even when the weather is fine. Dad hasn't been out and wouldn't let anyone in, to prevent infection, so now he's got nothing to do but contemplate his own deteriorating health. He's going to the doctor next week to get a prescription for his depression -- and not before time! Gawain is well enough to go back to work next week.

In place of our local Canadian breadmaker (parts from China, assembled in Canada) we bought a Japanese made one (Japan parts and assembly), another blow to patriotism. Somebody should do something about it -- our inability to manufacture appliances, that is, not my buying foreign ones.

Lance's hockey team had a practice today instead of a game so they didn't lose. They did have a fight, however, because the kid who got kicked out three weeks ago got into an argument with one of the coaches. The coach, unable to clip the stupid beggar's ear, as any right-thinking adult would have done only thirty years ago, stomped off -- never to return, he says.

Gwen was at work all day and Alys went to see her friends. I expect they went shopping. Is it still 'shopping' when they don't buy anything? It was called 'window shopping' when our mothers did it but I haven't heard a modern equivalent. Gwen said I needed my head seen to when she got home and found that Alys had been out all afternoon. Now she's not a friend to either of her parents. Being a teenager is such a trial in the modern world; without hunger, imminent war or pestilence to occupy their active minds, life is a struggle.

Sunday 13:

Taking advantage of the warm weather, I cycled and Lance rollerbladed along the waterfront trail where it wasn't as warm as it appeared and we came home with rosy cheeks. Normally we'd have skied (me) and snowboarded (Lance) but there isn't the incentive this year. Both Gwen and Lance had indoor soccer games today and they both won, which, for Lance, made up for his father dragging him out earlier into the icy blast of the waterfront trail.

Alys and I cheered on both teams in our usual way; i.e. silently gnawing our fingernails to the quick.

Monday 14:
The warmest day on record for this part of the world and I begin to think the Greens may be right. Global warming is a reality, at least in southern Ontario.

I asked Lydia about the Club. Apparently she didn't get home until Sunday!! I couldn't help being annoyed and spoke sharply to her about the dangers of such behaviour. She pouted, the way young people do when they know you're right, and said her apartment was so horrible she never wanted to go back to it. Then she put her arm through mine and said, "She needed a good man to look after her."

I replied, pretending to be a stern parent, "Keep you in line more like," only it came out squeaky and un-stern.

"Well, you know what to do," Lydia purred. "Come with me on Friday and keep me in line."

We seemed to have strayed from the Supervisor and staff relationship so I fled back to my office at this point. Lydia was still chuckling at lunchtime when we went out for our walk.

BillBuddy's letter hasn't yet arrived so I called them again in the evening. This time, it was a man who 'pushed the button'. Let's see if the sex of the finger on the button makes a difference. They owe me $45 and now I owe the phone company $15.

Weight: no change. Wait: no progress!

Tuesday 15:
Ndabe, who came to Canada when the Rwandan peacekeeping force came home, is cleared by security. My speech on New Year Resolutions is well received.

At the gym, Lydia and I walked and talked on the treadmills together. There was no repeat of yesterday's conversation and I'm satisfied it was just a one of those innuendo jokes women are always playing on we unfortunate men -- or me, anyway -- because they know I can't answer back. However, when we went for our lunchtime walk it was cold and she slipped her hand through my arm and snuggled into my shoulder to shelter from the wind. I hope no one saw us because...

A whole lot of our Canadian executives were escorted out today and, as usual, we survivors only heard of this through rumours. Nothing is announced so the stories grow exponentially concerning the reasons for their dismissal. You can be sure another flock of American vultures will arrive in a day or so, bringing their psychotic, sociopathic behaviour with them. If they rebuild the World Trade Center down there in the USA, I hope this time they'll be honest and call it the Global Rip-Off Center. Maybe then we out here in the ripped-off rest of the world wouldn't feel so bitter about their hypocritical pretence that they want to be our friends and partners.

Alys took Lance to ski club so I could have a rest, she said. Gwen was at work so I was able to work on this diary till they came back. Gwen's first act on coming home was to take Lance aside and grill him for information. Her second act was to shake her head thunderously at me and retire to her room for the night. How much mischief does Gwen think her mother could get up to in two hours?

Nothing from BillBuddy yet. I'm still confident one of the later button pusher's efforts will have done the trick and I'll get the letter or a call tomorrow.

Wednesday 16:
Security asked for a copy of my birth certificate. On hearing this, Gerry joked, "Just a matter of time" but I'm relieved. Clearly Security has been working on the difficult cases and is only now starting on mine. Seeing their plan makes me feel much better. It all makes sense, only I feel a little hurt that Lydia, who isn't even an employee, has been cleared ahead of me.

Lydia is really getting the hang of the gym now and today ran with me for 20 minutes on the treadmill. Oh to be young again. She was barely glowing when we finished while I was sweating and gasping like an asthmatic in a sauna. If she hadn't helped me with the Pectoral Fly machine, I don't think I could have done it today I was so winded. Some of my weakness was due to her straddling my legs with hers and holding my hands to help me move the arms of the pecs machine, which naturally thrust her breasts into my face. I was too weak to move the bars even with help so Lydia lowered the weights by bending over and around my side to get at them. This caused her exercise shorts to slide down her back and reveal the head of the dragon I presume is tattooed on her tailbone. At this point, I decided to go for a cold shower.

Speaking of cold water, the Walkerton Inquiry report is out, leaked to the press. It blames two incompetent and dishonest brothers and the Ontario government for cutting spending -- no surprises there.

I insisted on taking Gwen to soccer practice and Lance to the ski club, that way Gwen can have no suspicions about her mother roaming the night on her own. It didn't work as well as I thought, Gwen was just as suspicious when we got home and found Alys showered and reading a book. She never showers at night, only in the morning, was Gwen's comment to me when she got me alone. I was very sharp with Gwen because this is going too far. Alys probably had a relaxing spa bath when she could be sure of having some hot water, a fact she confirmed when later I asked her what she'd done all evening. Now Alys is speaking to me and Gwen isn't.

Thursday 17:
Asking around, I can't find anyone who hasn't been cleared by Security, which is puzzling. However, it proves my theory, I was too safe and got checked last. I feel quite proud actually. I sent Security my birth certificate.

Gwen went to ice hockey right after work and we all attended the game so she had no opportunity to lecture me on my failure as a husband. Her team won, which made for a relaxing drive home.

Nothing came from BillBuddy so I called them again and asked for a Supervisor. They were all busy but will call me back as soon as they are free. Waited until midnight and gave up. BillBuddy owes me $45 and I owe Bell Telephone $20.

Friday 18:
Lydia still has not applied to the University of Toronto -- but she is getting very annoyed at being nagged. This is a good sign; it means I'm wearing her down. After I had raised the matter with her, she snapped at me and stormed off back to her cubicle. Young people are so emotional, up one minute, down the next. I'm glad I've left all that behind. She didn't join me in the gym today or show me her outfit for the Club tonight because of the above, which was very disappointing. From now on, I must remind her of her future after we've been to the gym and never on a Friday. Her outfits, deplorable though they are, set me up for the weekend. I hope Alys never learns

of the benefit that she gets from them.

Speaking of secret benefits, I met Seth at the bar again to discuss old times but I know no more now than when I went the first time. The combination of naked girls on stage, on TV, and lap dancing on the tables all around, is too much for our vocal and social abilities. However, on balance, I find I don't much care what Seth has been doing and I suspect he doesn't care what I've been doing these past years; the girls are infinitely more compelling in every respect. I'll give up on old times and concentrate on meeting Seth for these new times hereafter.

Alys took Lance to soccer practice, which, with Gwen at work, was safe -- for me. Provided Gwen doesn't find out.

Weight: minus 1lb. All Right!!

Saturday 19:

Call dad. His depression is better since he started taking the tablets. Gawain has been at work all week and that helped too, Dad said. Dad visited everyone and everyone has been to see him; it was just like old times. I feel very uneasy. When my aged relatives get together, they talk of nothing but aches and pains. It's like a doctor's surgery without a doctor. My 'health problem' seems to have gone clean out of their aged minds. Thank God for senility, how soon can we make Alzheimer's disease mandatory?

Lance's hockey team lost again today and the game ended in a brawl. The season is going downhill fast. Fortunately, to counter-balance the horror, Lance's soccer team had a practice and it went amicably.

Gwen was at work all day and never found out about Alys being out with the car on her own last night. She did discover Alys was out shopping with a friend in the afternoon and that made her suspicious enough. The emotional extremes of teenagers are hard to take sometimes. The whole thing is ridiculous; Alys is nearly forty and Nico can't be more than twenty-five and twenty-five-year-old men look for twenty-three-year-old girls -- usually.

Sunday 20:

Apparently, there were about 400 incidents of bad water in Ontario last year. The newspaper report doesn't say how many is normal.

Gwen went to work followed by indoor soccer practice and never learned that Alys was out visiting her friends this afternoon. Lance went to his friend's house to play video games and, as I'd still received nothing from BillBuddy so because it was a cold, wet day and I'd nothing better to do, I called them again. Another male button-pusher has told the computer to send me the letter. They could have written me a letter in hieroglyphics on papyrus and sent it by hippopotamus in the time taken by their computer to wing me a password by modern mail. BillBuddy owes me $45, I owe the phone company $25. When the numbers match, I'm going to ask Bell telephone to get their money from BillBuddy.

Monday 21:
Lydia is speaking to me again; I'm pleased to say. It would have been tough if she didn't. I explained my motives for nagging her and she took it in good part; she says she knows I have her best interests at heart. But I'm still worried for Lydia. Young people get so caught up in the excitement of the changes that come between 17 and 27; they don't realise it doesn't last. One moment you're taking exams and leaving school, then you're at University taking exams and leaving, then a first 'real' job, then marriage, then babies, then late Twenties and then nothing -- just the pleasantly tedious round of domestic life we call family. The problem is, you miss one of those steps and you don't get to the tedious round of life we call family, you get the even more tedious and destructive life people nowadays call 'singleton' and hype to the heavens. Usually followed by jumping off a bridge.
Lydia says it's sweet I worry so much about her but I needn't because she has a plan. She won't say what it is and I suspect it's the one all young women have, dreaming of a complaisant, faithful Mr. Right who just happens to be a billionaire. She held my hand on our lunchtime walk, which was disconcerting at first but later, after consulting the company's Code of Business Conduct, I decided was sweet.

Tuesday 22:
Lydia and I spent a lot of time in the gym today because nothing much is happening at our desks. The Transformation has everyone avoiding doing anything and the main thing they are avoiding is reviewing our procedures, even the one Lydia sent out. We lifted weights and helped each other on the Gravitron, which was a good laugh. The Gravitron requires you to kneel on a couple of pads about

waist height and pull yourself up and down on bars above your head. We weren't very good at it but the view of Lydia's bottom right before my eyes was worth the embarrassment of being incompetent. Lydia called me a dirty old man for commenting on her elevated posterior position. We understand each other perfectly. She sees me as an easily teased older man and I see her as a somewhat naughty daughter, I think. Only I feel strange when we touch, which I didn't remember with Gwen when she held my hand. Lydia held my hand again today during our lunchtime walk. We weren't holding hands all the time, most of the time she just had her arm through mine, and her head on my shoulder.

To take my mind off life's pleasantnesses, BillBuddy's letter still had not arrived so when I got home I called and demanded to speak to a Manager. I was put on hold for twenty minutes and then mysteriously lost the connection. I called right back and got the 'all our representatives are busy, please hold and we'll get to you right after coffee' message. Finally, an hour later, a Supervisor pushed the button. Perhaps that will get some action. Reckoning now is BillBuddy owes me $45, I owe Bell $35.

Alys took Gwen to work and Lance to the ski club. Gwen glared meaningfully at me again as she went out the door, which suggests my plan of comparing 'hand holding' with my daughter isn't likely to happen soon.

Wednesday 23:
More gym time with Lydia. For someone who never exercises, she's surprisingly fit -- all over. I couldn't help noticing how taut and firm her breasts were when we bumped into one another while stretching. I must be growing very clumsy because we bumped quite a lot and I was trying not to. I'm not sure the competition from Lydia at the gym is doing me any good because, after stretching, we did the stationary bicycles. Lydia pedalled furiously for 15 minutes and jumped off looking like she just started. I got off at the same time, creaking and groaning in every joint. At least, the bikes allowed us to talk, or more accurately in my case gasp, about life as we exercised, which the treadmills didn't when we were running. I can't help thinking Lydia and I are soul mates, we have so much in common. I wish I could talk to Alys this way but she just isn't interested in history anymore.

Gwen was at work when I got home so no 'hand holding'

comparison test. No matter, I already know the answer. Every time Lydia and I bumped today, my heart pounded like it would burst. I definitely don't see her as a naughty daughter. Took Lance to ski club to give myself time to think. Driving back, I decided I shouldn't think. It isn't good for me. I also decided I should be more suspicious about Nico because looking back on these past weeks, I can't help feeling that Alys, like Lydia, may not fully understand her own feelings. And if she doesn't, Nico too may be confused about where his interests lie. It's hard for us mature people to be wise for ourselves and for those who are still young.

Thursday 24:

We heard rumours today that one of our senior vice-presidents has been suspended for sexual harassment. Not because the lady he was 'harassing' minded, they were lovers. Unfortunately for them, another lady observed them, who did mind. Lydia says it was jealousy that did it. She may be right. What frightened me is not the lovers, however inappropriately they may have behaved, but the fact we have entered the world of dictatorships where informers spy on us all, turning us into the authorities for harmless things based on foolish laws meant to catch real wrongdoers. I must be very cautious with Lydia; someone may misconstrue our love of history and books for the other sort.

Lydia and I didn't get a lot of exercising done at the gym today because she got a cramp in her calf after only a few minutes on the bikes and I had to stretch and massage it out. While I was working on her calf, kneading and stroking, Lydia told me, with some gentle prodding on my part, that her plan is indeed to marry a rich man. She says when she's done that she's going to move out to the country and breed Llamas. I lectured her on the importance of taking life seriously and having a proper life plan in place early so you can be ready for retirement. She said contritely, it wasn't her only plan; she had a Plan B. But I know she only said that to shut me up because she could tell I was disappointed in her naiveté. I'm beginning to think she was right when she said she needed me to keep her in line.

Gwen was at work, Alys was out in the car and Lance was playing video games in the basement this evening. I'm not sure I shouldn't be out too.

Friday 25:
Lydia's outfit for the club was up to her usual standard; does she make them herself or are we paying her too much? I asked her this and she says she gets them from a shop on Yonge Street, where a friend of hers has an interest. I didn't have the nerve to ask what sort of interest or agree to have it modelled but I was tempted to go with Lydia tonight. My courage failed me there too and I went with Alys to Lance's soccer practice. Gwen was at work but even she couldn't have faulted Alys tonight.

Saturday 26:
Lance had hockey practice instead of a game, thank God, and, because the coach who was willing to stand up to 14-year-old bullies is no longer there, they didn't have a fight either. We did lose a few players to injuries as the bullies mowed down their own teammates but no fights. Alys went shopping while I did the hockey run and she didn't come back till quite late and she'd forgotten most of the things she went for so she's going again tomorrow.

Gwen was at work all day so she didn't get to grumble about Alys being out most of the day.

Called dad. His answering machine said he was out spending his kids' inheritance. I didn't know he had anything to leave? I left him something, a message asking him to call me but he didn't.

Sunday 27:
Gwen was at work all day, so no lectures or dagger-ish looks, and afterwards I took her straight to soccer practice. We didn't get a lot of quality time in this brief trip because she is still acting strangely. Apart from suggesting old people like Alys and I should be spending what little time we have left together, she hadn't much to say.

Lance's hockey game was another disaster. We played the top team and, by the time we were five goals down and the first period wasn't over, our players were so humiliated even the wussy ones were prepared to have a go and the fights started. Our leading penalty points champion was kicked out of the game after nine minutes, our only serious player went thirty seconds later and the game went downhill from there. All in all, we lost three players and the coach before the game was over. We lost that too.

Fortunately, Lance's team won at soccer. Lance got a brilliant goal; I only wish Alys had been there to see it. Gwen has a point, you never know which day could be your last and spending it shopping seems a terrible waste. I resolved, during the soccer game, that Alys and I shall have more sex.

Monday 28:
Asked Lydia about the Club and immediately wished I hadn't. Jealousy is a terrible thing; it eats you from the inside out. I'm not just jealous of the people Lydia 'plays' with at the Club. I'm jealous of everyone whose youth is lived today. They have so many ways of having fun, so many ways of meeting and greeting, that I can't see how anyone from now on will have any difficulty with sex. It's practically abnormal.

Lydia and I went out for lunch and held hands right through the meal, which made it difficult to eat but we weren't really hungry so it didn't matter. She told me how much she wants a friendly understanding man with her at the Club; the young men there are so crude and rough. I became angry at the thought of young men treating her, or any young woman, roughly and ended up promising to save her from them by accompanying her there next time she goes. Lydia kissed me as we were leaving; she said it was for the way I made her feel. It's nothing to the way her kiss made me feel. Later, of course, I realised Alys may not understand my motives and would certainly forbid me to go to the Club.

Alys and I attended Lance's school parent's meeting most of the evening so I didn't have to decide on how to broach the subject of my chivalrous defence of Lydia. We met Lance's teachers, again, and got the same lecture. Alys was very strange. Normally she's defensively aggressive in these encounters; tonight we sailed through in a rosy glow of good will.

Tuesday 29:
I didn't tell Lydia that I haven't yet arranged Friday night. She assumes it is a given because I said I would. The practical difficulties of such a step are, however, insurmountable. Consequently, though we did the gym and had our now usual lunchtime walk, I was unable to enjoy the time, as I should. Even Lydia murmuring sweet nothings in my ear when she brought me a draft updated procedure, didn't settle my queasy stomach.

Lydia and I have interesting conversations about things that matter, like history and philosophy. Things I can't talk to Alys about anymore, though she seemed to be interested when we were courting. It's a bit like our sex life; we seem to have grown apart. I noticed this again today when Lydia and I were reviewing some documents she'd discovered in our system that were incorrectly filed (we wrote an ACR on the error and left it for someone else to fix). Then we discussed her future and particularly her plan to marry a rich man. I'd always been sceptical because I assumed she meant a billionaire but it turns out she only meant someone established with a good standard of living compared to her own. Put in that light, even I would qualify so it isn't such a foolish plan after all, her own circumstances being so difficult. She's been temping since leaving university two years ago, an Honours degree in Byzantine History (a major in Byzantine Library Procedures isn't enough anymore for this shallow, material world), and lives in a small bachelorette, in an old house, in a run-down part of town, with an elderly landlady. I wonder if Alys would mind Lydia taking Gwen's room when Gwen goes to university?

Alys insisted on taking Lance to ski club; she said I looked tired and needed to rest. Gwen was at work so she didn't scold me for giving Alys another night out with the car -- until she came home. I was pleased when she retired to her room to do homework.

11 pm (in bed): A strange thing happened when Alys and I came to bed. She snuggled up to me and said she 'might' be going out Friday night 'with the girls'. I don't know what to make of it. Is it a trap? Does she know about my promise to Lydia and is waiting to catch me out?

Wednesday 30:
Spent all day mulling over the strange coincidence of Alys wanting to go out Friday. It cheered me up so much I was able to enjoy my walk and gym time with Lydia. Maybe I won't have to upset either lady, which is just as well. They may not be my fighting weight but they would undoubtedly win any fight.

In the gym we did all the machines I like to see Lydia on, the Gravitron, the Glutemaster, the chest press bench, and the 'birthing machines'. Those last ones are the leg exercise machines only ladies do, where their legs get opened wide and the watching men struggle not to dive into that Valley of the Little Death. I grew steadily weaker as the hour passed and Lydia helped me on the Pecs machine again. This time, she sat on my lap, crotch-to-crotch, and hauled on my arms. It was no use; by this time all my strength had gone to parts where Pecs machines can't reach. My cold shower at the end was almost a relief. Lydia, I know, would be horrified to think someone my age was contemplating 'that' with a young woman like her. Young people are always disgusted to find old people still have sex.

I took Lance to ski club and watched, for a while, the future generation at play. I must save harder for my retirement because these kids will never amount to enough to pay me a pension. When they're not sitting on the hillside doing up their snowboard bindings and talking inanities, they're sitting in the snack bar talking inanities.

When I got home from dropping Lance off, Alys confirmed she is going out with the girls on Friday night. She doesn't know what time she'll be back. Very late, she says. I wonder what time the Club closes?

Thursday 31:
I asked Mr. Ogilvie about calling Security to check if they got my birth certificate. I'd hate to think it hadn't arrived and they were patiently waiting. Mr. Ogilvie said, "No. They have it." He offers no other information and I'm speechless.

The Club, Lydia says, doesn't really close. People just come and go as they please. I told her I needed to be back by midnight and she asked if I changed into a pumpkin after that. She isn't pleased but she's less displeased than she would have been if I hadn't kept my promise so I was happy enough to enjoy our walk and gym time. Lydia sat on my lap a lot today, on the gym machines and again at lunchtime, which was odd because the restaurant wasn't that busy. I tried to make a joke of it at lunchtime, saying I felt safer than when she sat on my lap in the gym because now she had more clothes on. I was very embarrassed to learn she had fewer clothes on because she'd left her panties and hose off. Maybe this Club trip isn't a good idea; I'm intellectually in favour of nudity, as I've said, but the practical aspects of it are unsettling.

At home, I found Lance downloading songs from Wazoo and burning a CD, which I made the mistake of listening to it. All the songs are by 'artists' who yell in time to a drumbeat, mistake repetition for rhyme and think 'fucking' is the English language's only adjective. I wish we were still at the Sharon, Lois and Bram stage, or Raffi perhaps. Sesame Street was good too, particularly Oscar the Grouch, who probably got that way dealing with BillBuddy.

Nothing has arrived from BillBuddy -- neither the Supervisor call nor the long-awaited letter. I despair of ever getting my money out of them. I had one last go tonight but I know it's pointless. Their mission statement is obviously to make a profit by keeping any money sent to them.

Actually, I don't blame the young men of today for preferring rap music when you hear the alternatives. Britney Spears, Celine Dion, Mariah Carey and all those indistinguishable boy bands are nothing more than elevator muzak. We, way back in the Sixties, did our children a bad service by putting music in supermarkets and other public places. All we've done is raise a generation of kids who think that aural wallpaper is music. And why do they all sound like they're whining? It's as bad as Blues or Jazz in its constant, self-centred, self-pity.

Still, Gilbert and Sullivan would be pleased to know that patter songs are all the rage, more than a hundred years after they made them popular. I can't help thinking they'd be disappointed in the quality of the writing, though.

Alys took Gwen to work and shopped until she took Gwen to ice hockey. I helped Lance with his homework for as long as either of us could stand, then I went to brood on what I'm to wear at the Club. Lydia says wear nothing; I'm sure she's just teasing. I looked through my wardrobe trying to imagine what went with any of Lydia's outfits and came to the same conclusion she did. I've nothing to wear. Decided on a sweatshirt and jeans.

February 2002:
Love is in the air.

Friday 1:

I no longer understand what's going on. Mohammed has been 're-cleared' by Security. Leaving aside there isn't such a word, why has he been cleared twice before I've been cleared once? Mr. Ogilvie says not to worry; they'll get to me in good time. Good time for what?

I called home and told Lance and Gwen to shift for themselves this evening, saying I'd be back late. Gwen was going to work anyway and Lance said he'd go to Brent's house 'and do homework' so there was no difficulty with them. Alys was already gone.

Lydia's outfit for the Club was more daring than any I've seen to date. And this time, I got to see it on; I use the term loosely as it wasn't 'on' very much. Certainly it was only just 'on' those parts that are usually covered. The good news is that, after my initial embarrassment of partnering an attractive, almost naked female, into a gloomy cellar, I found everyone else also almost naked. I was the most dressed person in the place.

I can't describe the evening except to say it was everything I'd imagined -- and a whole lot of things I couldn't have imagined. The puzzling thing is, despite all the leather and instruments of torture, I've never met a more polite group of people, certainly much nicer than the ones I meet at work every day, so why did Lydia think they were rough? We left earlier than necessary and went back to Lydia's place, which also wasn't as bad as portrayed. I felt young again just creeping surreptitiously through the old house to her room because Lydia's landlady doesn't like her entertaining visitors.

Weight: minus 1 lb. I think it might be due to stress.

Saturday 2:

Near to our modest detached dwelling sub-division is a sub-division of larger homes that Lance called 'mansions' when he was younger. Today's edition of our local newspaper reports that six of those mansions are pot-growing factories. Charged with various offences are large numbers of Vietnamese people who came here as refugees. They were probably led astray back in Vietnam by American servicemen boasting of the western world's free enterprise system, as all Americans do because they're brainwashed from an early age by the robber barons who run that country. Fortunately for us, we in the West don't have a 'free enterprise system'. We have a closely regulated, fairly expensive enterprise system, even in the USA; otherwise, we'd be living in the same poverty as the rest of the world.

Speaking of the USA and the free enterprise system, I had another go at BillBuddy today and was left hanging forever before they promised to have a Supervisor call me and send me a new password. I think the Phone Company has told them to stop messing about and take all my remaining money in one go. BillBuddy owes me $45 and now I owe Bell Telephone $50. I give up. If I'd got a lawyer's letter right from the start, I might have got somewhere but now it would cost me as much to get a letter as I've already thrown away on this bunch of sharks. They can keep my money, which was what they wanted all along. BillBuddy's management should be the next against the wall when the revolution comes, right after lawyers and politicians.

The way to grow pot, so the newspapers helpfully tell us, is hydroponically. Also, you bypass the electricity meter so you can run dozens of 'grow lamps' 24 hours a day. It seems pot needs lots of heat and light. No wonder it makes people happy; it's dried summer. Over 200 'pot houses' have been found in Toronto in the past days. You'd think the government would be pleased with this 'growing' industry, which cuts down on the smuggling trade and boosts the local economy but apparently they're not. What disturbs me is that Alys and I, on our evening strolls last summer and fall, regularly walked past two of the houses without noticing anything amiss. Should things go badly wrong with the Transformation and I'm forced to look for a new job, I won't go into the police force; Sherlock Holmes I'm not.

Called dad. Gawain answered and my worst fear, concerning the silence over my health, was confirmed when he made a very coarse crack about my 'problem'. He confirmed the whole family has made a host of homemade remedies to give me when I'm over in the summer. Dad and Gawain are both fabulously well, now that Gawain is sharing Dad's anti-depressants, and Dad was out visiting a lonely widow up the street.

Today is Groundhog Day. For those of you who don't live in North America I'll explain. If a large furry rodent comes out of its hole today and sees its shadow, we are destined for another 6 weeks of winter -- so the story goes. I can tell you Arthur Lakelady's prediction, if the groundhog doesn't see his shadow, we will have another month and a half of winter.

Lance's hockey team lost again today. It was a very tame affair because all our true-blue hockey players are suspended.

Gwen was at work and only glared at me when she came home and found Alys had been out all afternoon visiting. I went shopping with her in the morning -- to allay Gwen's fears. I tried to tell Gwen, but she locked herself in her room. She is becoming a little strange. Alys says it's the exams.

Sunday 3:

Today is the pinnacle of the radio-controlled Robot Rugby season, otherwise known as American Football. It bears an uncanny resemblance to the Battlebot program on TV where teams build robots and use them to crash into the opposing team's robot to win prizes. You don't need a degree in Psychology to know that inside those huge male bodies is a tiny man trying not to be seen. Of all the perversions of sport (and all professional sports are perversions), this one is the worst. Sport is supposed to make us fit and healthy but in this one a tiny number of steroid-built people damage their long-term health daily for the pleasure of millions of obese couch potatoes.

I skied this afternoon; Lance snowboarded because skiing is only for old people now. A gaggle of teenage girls and I watched the teenage boys doing tricks in the half-pipe. Last year, the girls were skiers but not anymore. This year they are 'boarding' (not really. Girls buy skis and boards then stand on or beside them to watch the boys ski or board). As in all things, they have followed the boys in their historic 'me-too' role. Girls have gone to school for the past 100+ years but the reality is it has made no difference. Boys invent new things to do and girls come trailing after, crying it isn't fair that the boys are doing it (whatever 'it' is) and they aren't. The education system says girls have overtaken boys in all areas of education. It will take more than that to stop them walking one step behind. The thing is, I really can't fathom what women see in men?

It didn't take long for Lance to meet some of his school friends and dump his dad. I skied on my own for a time before bumping into Lydia, or to be precise Lydia bumped into me. It seems she decided to come out today with a friend who then went off with a male friend, which gets back to my earlier point, why would anyone leave Lydia for a man? A lucky break for me as I got company; skiing on your own at our small local hills is a bit tedious. Lydia isn't a great skier and kept knocking me down at the worst possible places, around blind corners or on narrow trails away from the main slopes where we could have waited forever for help if we'd been injured. Then she got cramp because of the cold and it took a lot of massaging to get it out. Lydia suggested she could remove her ski pants so I could get at the stiff parts but I declined. Even though there were very few people about where we were I know someone would have come by and misunderstood. Girls nowadays are not careful enough with their reputations.

When I got home, I found Alys was home too and unhappy with our computer. Lately, we've started to get some embarrassing advertisements popping up for no reason at all. They feature lots of beautiful young women called Jennifer (statistically speaking a far higher sample than in the population as a whole) who have installed webcams in their bedroom. I'm glad we didn't nickname Guinevere 'Jenny'. She already seems too interested in the ads and might have been led into making what I think is a poor career choice. I can't help noticing that a lot of the webcam girls claim to be college students. I hope this isn't the result of trying to encourage women into technical subjects. Alys wants the computer fixed. I said I'd get right on it and spent a happy hour watching 'Jennifers' encourage me to buy memberships of their websites. The computer isn't yet fixed because I've no idea why this is happening.

Fortunately, Gwen was at work and went to indoor soccer right after; Alys took her, which is why the Jennifers and I had such a happy hour together.

Lance missed hockey (hurrah!) because he was 'boarding but in the evening went to soccer. His team won so it was a good day all round in the Lakelady house.

Monday 4:
Lydia and I went to the gym. She's tenacious, I'll say that for her, most kids give up after a few days and go onto something else. After

our skiing and bumping yesterday, Lydia was a bit unsteady and I had to assist a number of times. That's the effect of coming back to exercise after missing it for only a few years. I've no doubt that when she left school she was as fit as a fiddle, now she needs all the help she can get from me.

Speaking of school, Lydia tells me she went to a Catholic school and is proud to say she can still get into her uniform of a short tartan kilt, white knee socks and blouse, and a blue tie and blazer. I said I was impressed and then had to hurriedly decline to have it proved to me here in the office. She told me her local Catholic school is considering doing away with skirts because the girls are wearing thongs underneath and then bending over to give the boys a show. I left quickly. Really, the things young people say these days. I don't know what Mr. Ogilvie would say if I told him. However, we returned to the subject on our lunchtime walk and I learned a lot about schoolgirls. I also learned a lot about the quiet places around our office building. Even though we're in a bustling city, there are places where you can be alone.

President Bush announced his budget today and confirmed his plan for a new internal Homeland Security force to combat terrorism. The big question must be, will their uniforms be black shirts or brown?

I spent the evening trying to rid our computer of the pop-up sex ads. Alys says either the ads go or the computer goes, so I tried my best. There are a lot of exciting services out there, not just webcam girls. I can get Viagra, a pump to enlarge my penis, and some creams guaranteed to keep it hard for as long as I want, all from various companies in the US. American men must be in a bad way; perhaps it's just the effect of having to match up to those plastic-perfect American women. By the end of the evening, I had screens full of ads and could barely find the desktop. Tomorrow I'll be more successful. I shut it down before Alys came to inspect it on her way to bed so she didn't see what my efforts had achieved. So long as I start it up in the morning, and close down the ads before Alys sees them, the computer and I will be quite safe.

While I worked on the computer, Gwen and Lance had to do their homework by hand with Alys helping them. They thought this was stupid because the ads were just 'part of life', which makes me wonder what they all get up to at school. I'll ask at the next Parent's Night.

Weight: plus 1 lb. I expect that's due to the stress I'm under fixing ads.

Tuesday 5:

Mr. Ogilvie asked about Lydia today, how she was settling in and if she was working out. I said she was 'working out really well and twice over,' meaning the gym and in the office. He looked at me strangely and suggested she could help him on a project he'd wanted to start for some time but hadn't had the resources; it wouldn't take much of her time. Mr. Ogilvie being impressed by my choice of staff was so flattering, I agreed at once. Lydia wasn't as pleased; apparently Mr. Ogilvie leers at her in the hallway and elevators. I told her he wasn't leering, just appreciative of having such an attractive young woman about the place. Lydia went quite pink with pleasure. I don't think she gets enough compliments.

After this exchange, I learned that her Plan B is to win the lottery. I replied sharply that, if that were the case, she'd better make Plan B into Plan A because winning the lottery was more likely than marrying a billionaire, particularly in Ontario. She threw a hissy fit and went back to her researching.

Alys inspected the computer while I was at work and was not impressed. She says it is worse than ever. If I don't fix it soon, it is going in the garbage where that kind of thing belongs. I'm sorry she can't be more generous, all the girls in the ads look like nice girls to me and most of them claim to be the girl who lives next door. Fortunately, that isn't true because our neighbours are a very nice family whose daughter, Carmelita Rosa Maria, would be in serious trouble if she did anything like this.

My efforts with disk maintenance and options did seem to improve matters so, by midnight, Alys granted the computer a reprieve, provided I finish the job tomorrow. I think it's very unfortunate these ads should start when Alys seems to have stopped visiting her friends; I hope she hasn't fallen out with them. This is the second night she's stayed in and it's making her cranky.

Gwen was at work all evening so when she got home, thinking to allay her fears, I told her Alys had been in all evening. She didn't seem impressed.

Lance and his mom worked on a school project before and after ski club, until they fell out and Alys had to finish it herself. I hope she gets a good mark -- for the teacher's sake.

Wednesday 6:

Lydia and I had a long talk today about her future and we mapped out a sensible plan for getting her a job or going back to college for a more commercial degree. She listened very attentively, gazing at me with such a steadfast look of interest that I'm sure she's beginning to settle down. Unfortunately, we were in her office, which is quite small, and we kept bumping knees and hands. I humoured Lydia by letting her call this new plan, Plan C, partly because even serious things need some humour to lighten the load and partly because our touching was making me feel very disturbed. I couldn't help noticing Lydia wasn't in the least bit bothered by our touching; young people nowadays haven't been brought up the way we were and that can lead to us more mature people getting inappropriate ideas. I also discovered not all young people think it disgusting when old people have sex.

Went to the doctor for my annual check-up, which I take every third year. He wants me to have a blood test, which is why I go as rarely as I do. Last time (the first time), I fainted and hit my face and head on the desk-chair-thing I was sitting in. That took longer to heal than any disease I might have been suffering from.

Spent the evening downing pop-ups and I think I've done it. Not one popped up between 9 pm and midnight. Alys says the computer can stay provided it remains house-trained and if I want that sort of thing on my computer I should do it at work, like other men. I knew she blamed me for this and I vehemently protested my innocence. I blame Gwen and Lance and their horrible 'Hotmail', where grubby spotty teenage phonetic spellers demonstrate why the phonetic spelling method of teaching English is not a good idea.

Alys took Gwen to work then soccer practice and Lance to the ski club. She didn't come back between dropping them off and picking them up but I lied to Gwen when she asked so she was happy -- and so was Alys?

Thursday 7:

Helping Lydia with her draft procedures was as disturbing as yesterday in her office and it got worse when we got onto the subject of the Victorian period, an era where Lydia feels very much at home. She thinks the Victorians concept of enjoying your love life discreetly, while maintaining the dignity of your marriage partner is very much something we could learn from today, and I have to say I agree. Monogamy is a straitjacket when stretched over 60 years of adult life. It was fine when people wed at twenty and only lived to forty but it's completely wrong now.

I couldn't help thinking that, if she really believes her own professed views, we might become more than just friends. For a moment, visions of apartments, done out in lurid red, and a voluptuous Lydia lying on a chaise longue filled my mind -- till I gave my head a shake. Lydia may be a wonderful young woman but she is still a woman, with all the list of demands that entails, and steering a course between Alys and Lydia would be like being the Ping-Pong ball at an Olympic table tennis finals.

A week or so ago, Alys and I discussed the TV. My suggestion was we get rid of it because, apart from Lance, no one watches it enough to justify the cable charges. Alys's suggestion had been we get digital TV because there was a special offer on, three months free and a free set up. Naturally, 'we' chose the digital TV and the service man, a husky young fellow in jeans and a tight T-shirt, was installing it when I got home from work. Lance watched the new picture carefully to see it didn't falter as the man left. I watched Alys carefully to see if there were any symptoms as she walked the man to the door. Nothing unusual took place. Gwen has got me as daft as she is. Fortunately, she was at work right after school and never got to see the installer. I can't help thinking the green-eyed god, jealousy, might be playing with Gwen too.

No pop-ups today, only an ad for a software package that prevents unwanted pop-up ads from appearing on your computer. Where were they last week when I needed them?

Finally had time to view the new digital TV channels. We went from 75 channels with nothing to watch to over 900 channels with nothing to watch. In fact the last 300 channels don't have pictures, they're just music and very selective music at that. There's a channel devoted to 'thirty years of number one country music hits' for example. Bad luck if your favourite country song only made it to number two. The channel I was most excited about, when I saw the name, was SexTV; however, it was showing the European Male Stripper Championships and I didn't watch it.

Friday 8:
Today, a waterfall of rain poured down melting all but the largest piles of snow. No one was out at lunchtime except Lydia and me

cuddling and laughing under her umbrella as we walked the empty streets. Our noses and cheeks were red with cold but every bit else of me was hot as can be. We had to keep walking because anywhere dry was filled with homeless people. I can't believe this is the Toronto I emigrated to. Then we were a prosperous, if somewhat dull, place. Now we look like a vibrant, multicultural, honorary member of the Third World. According to economists, who obviously use a different definition to the rest of us, we're richer today than we were twenty years ago. Do economists ever leave their offices?

One explanation for this apparent paradox is reorganisations. My working day was spent trying to get people to review our procedures when all they wanted to do was discuss the state of our union, as though they were all Presidents of the United States. We are well paid for producing nothing, which is nice but probably unsustainable. Today's homeless were the bottom end of the pyramid yesterday and were just the first to become un-sustained.

I didn't go to the Club with Lydia because Alys wanted to go shopping and needed me to carry. I did get to see Lydia's and her friends' outfits for tonight before I left and they looked very fetching. I don't see now what I saw wrong with them only a few weeks ago. Lydia was right, I had too many inhibitions before and, despite my beliefs about nudity, I attached too much significance to clothes. Now I don't mind that the three girls combined weren't wearing enough material to attach a brooch too, let alone significance.

I felt jealous of Lydia all evening as I trailed the Mall after Alys and Lance. Lance takes after his mother when it comes to shopping, they love the hunt, the chase and the final kill of a new clothing item, or hair care product, or piece of jewellery. When I asked why I was needed, there was nothing bought they couldn't have carried themselves, Alys said, "I only said that to get you here. I need you to restrain Lance from getting tattooed or pierced."

I actually felt my hair go another shade paler at the thought of a public scene in a busy Mall. In the end, it wasn't so bad because Lance settled for temporary tattoos and stud earrings. There's hope for him yet. I have none for his contemporaries and consequently my pension, which relies on them turning out to be productive workers.

SexTV was showing male strippers again and I feel cheated. What's the point of a sex channel that only caters to women and gay males?

Saturday 9:
Called dad. He was out and so was Gawain. I left a message on their answering machine but they didn't call back. I wasn't surprised because the message on the machine was Dad and Gawain singing The Indian Love Song ('when I'm calling you-o-o-oo') in falsetto and a cracked baritone. I wish I knew their doctor's number.

Lance and I skied and boarded again today (Lance has given up on hockey and missed his team's game. They still didn't win) and Lydia bumped into me again. Her skiing is much better now but she hadn't come out dressed for the weather, which was rather cold, so when Lance went off with his friends, we retired to the tacky snack bar the ski hill calls a 'chalet'. Lydia didn't come with a friend today; she came hoping she'd run into me!

The snack bar was busy but we found a quiet corner and spent an enjoyable afternoon sharing fries and giggling at the other customers. We had to sit very close because of the crush and I was glad of my one-piece ski suit, which kept us both from accidentally doing something we shouldn't -- in public.

Sunday 10:
I invited Alys to come skiing but she had to get the rest of the shopping, she said. If Gwen had been about (fortunately she was at work), she would have pointed to Alys's smart haircut and clothes as evidence of imminent wrongdoing. I, however, felt so guilty about being pleased, when Alys declined to ski, I let my suspicions pass unspoken.

Another whole day in Lydia's company and I feel younger every time. We skied till lunch time then, seeing Lance and his friends heading to the snowboard park, we put our skis in the back of my car and left, returning in time for Lydia to jump into her car and disappear before I found Lance and we drove home.

Alys was home when we arrived and in such a good temper, considering we'd left her to do the grocery shopping alone, I was immediately suspicious again. Gwen too said, "I told you so," in a very gloomy voice after Alys had welcomed her into the house like a long lost princess.

Monday 11:

Work remains a frustrating place because nobody wants to do anything in case it's wasted effort, made obsolete by the coming Transformation.

After this gloomy start, my day got brighter as I sat with Lydia and chatted. At first we talked about the new procedure she's writing, then we moved on to more interesting subjects like books and movies. Lydia looks at me in a way that no one else does, as though I was someone to look up to and not just another middle-aged man in a middle management position in a middle-sized company in a middling-sized country. I shouldn't feel flattered I know, but I do. It's great. To be young, all you need is love. Being old is just the final stage of dwindling love, your parent's love is gently withdrawn, your partner's love grows cool, your children's love is coldly switched to others, and then you're old. Everybody should be given a Lydia in the middle of his or her life to make the end bittersweet, like a great novel. You know it can't be -- but you so much want it to last. The gym was not bittersweet; it was agony. Helping Lydia, who dresses in little more than bra and knickers, with her exercises is more than I can bear. Of course, gymnasium means 'the place for being naked' so Lydia is actually over-dressed. When I told her this, she said she'd strip off -- right after I did.

Tuesday 12:

The pop-up ads are back and Alys is angrier than ever. I fear for the computer's life. Once again I Scandisked and Defragged the hard drive, ran the anti-virus programs, ran the QuickClean and 'ExtremeClean with Shredding' programs but nothing killed the ads. The Jennifers and I had a fine old time of it, wrestling with our respective needs.

Alys took Lance to soccer practice (he's now fallen out with his ski club friends) so I could concentrate on the computer and Gwen was at work. When Alys brought Gwen home, Gwen took me aside and asked if I thought Alys's outfit of a thin blouse and short loose skirt was normal wear for mothers dropping kids off at soccer practice in February? As I had been too busy to notice what Alys was wearing when she left, I couldn't sensibly reply. I just said, "At least her coat was warm enough." Gwen snorted and stomped off to her room. Gwen's suspicions are making me doubtful too.

Wednesday 13:

Our gym has a 'personal trainer' service, though, until today, I've never seen anyone use it and now I know why. The job of the personal trainer is the nearest you can get to S&M practices in public without being arrested. While Lydia and I were running on the treadmill, the personal trainer led her victim, a pleasingly plump lady, to the centre of the floor and had her lie face down over a large ball, which left her bottom high in the air. Then the poor woman had to lift her right arm and left leg off the ground for ten seconds, followed by the same with her opposite limbs. She was engaged in doing this, very red in the face, when the trainer began chatting to someone. The unfortunate woman was left repeating her embarrassing exercises for what must have seemed like an eternity.

I worked on pop-up ads while Alys helped Lance with his homework. Gwen is acting strangely again, locking herself in her room. The ads and I had a pleasant evening. I studied each carefully to find clues about how they are arriving and what might send them away. Nothing useful was revealed by my examination other than learning I liked to look at the female form and I knew that already. By midnight, the ads had stopped coming and I went to bed.

Thursday 14:

On the 'world's only radio station for rednecks' were a couple, who happen to be sexologists, giving Valentine's Day advice. They practiced Tantric (I believe it's the Oriental word for Extreme) Sex, along with such famous stars as Sting apparently, and all I have to do to be able to have sex for 5 hours at a time is practice Kegels, three hundred times a day. I remember Kegels because Alys did them after, or before, or during (I can't quite remember which) her pregnancies. Kegels are exercises for the 'floor of the pelvis' as the suddenly coy experts described them. The way you do them is to pretend you are preventing yourself wetting your pants and it's not as easy as it sounds, which makes me wonder why more of us aren't walking around in diapers. I resolve to start immediately and reach twenty before feeling so nauseous that I have to stop. I'm determined to do thirty today and work up to three hundred in thirty days time. You can do them anywhere, in your car, at your desk, at the dinner table, anywhere, provided you don't grimace as you clench.

But who has a spare 5 hours for sex? I don't think Alys would be pleased if I start taking that long. I didn't discuss the subject with

Lydia because young women can't be expected to understand about these things. They're still at the 'isn't it all wonderful' stage, rather than the 'isn't it wonderful it still works' stage.

I had my blood pressure tested and gave a blood sample at the clinic before work. They remembered me from last time and let me lie down for the sample -- results next week.

Lydia and I celebrated Valentine's Day, and my good blood pressure results, with a walk in the park and a bubble tea from one of the local Chinese restaurants. Bubble tea is a cold drink with large frogspawn sized black tapioca balls floating in it; they should sell it to teenagers as 'frog spawn coke'. It would do well because kids will do anything to gross out their parents. The park was empty, this being early February, and we had a bench to ourselves. Snuggled up against the grey misty wind, Lydia and I looked like a couple of illicit lovers from an old black-and-white spy movie. It was very erotic.

I took Gwen to work and then ice hockey while Alys helped Lance with his homework. Fortunately, there were no pop-up ads tonight so the computer survived its near-death experience again. Unfortunately, Alys now thinks I know how to get rid of them and is more than ever convinced I'm the one who brought them in the first place.

Friday15:
Spent the day at work dreaming about Lydia and jealous I can't go with her to the Club tonight. My jealousy grew significantly worse when she showed me her outfit, one she'd worn earlier and I'd said I liked. Her two friends joined her later and teased me with their versions of nudity patched with leather and lace. Somehow I must get back to the Club.

Arriving home in a sad state of mind, I was greeted by an irate Alys telling me there was another one of those pop-up ads on my computer. I checked and found Alys hadn't read it properly; it was a very lurid window offering us a software program that prevents unpleasant pop-up ads. Thanks to keeping this diary, I know this happened after the last plague of pop-ups. My diary has unexpected benefits because, in the past, I've been slow spotting conspiracies. Now I see where the problem is coming from and how I can fix it -- just pay the cyber-protection-money. Decided not to fix it. I like my quality time with the Jennifers too much.

As Gwen was at work and I'd taken Lance to soccer practice, I suggested to Alys we spend a quiet two hours celebrating Valentine's Day in bed. I was amazed when she agreed. Unfortunately, I haven't had time to do the Kegels so the two hours wasn't fully used but I couldn't help thinking those pop-up ads may have influenced Alys too.

Weight: minus 1 lb. Probably due to having no appetite all day and the unexpected exercise in bed this evening.

Saturday 16:

I tried to do twice as many Kegels today to make up for forgetting them yesterday but by twenty I felt so ill, I stopped.

Went skiing with Lydia, leaving Alys to do the grocery shopping alone because Lance was also at the ski hill and Gwen was at work.

Lydia and I skied all day when we weren't giggling like teenagers over silly jokes or holding hands surreptitiously during breaks. Breaks are a tricky time at ski hills because the snack bar is full of teenagers spending their lift pass money on pop and fries. Lydia's skiing is much better now so when she knocks me down on a quiet trail among the trees, I don't help her up as quickly as I used to do. Ski suits are surprisingly sexy on women; they emphasise their bottoms nicely. I decided not to tell Alys about my day out with Lydia. I'm not sure she'd understand.

When I got home, I wasn't altogether surprised to find Alys had missed most of the groceries, too heavy she claimed, and she has to go again tomorrow. Gwen's suspicions have truly taken hold and I see sinister motives in all Alys's behaviour now.

Called dad. He is laid up after a heavy fall -- from a tree! Gawain is laid up with a sore back after trying to lift Dad up from his fall. The doctor has changed Dad's anti-depressant prescription because he felt the previous pills may have contributed to Dad's sudden decision to climb an old tree at the age of eighty-one. Dad says the doctor's just jealous because he could never climb that tree when he was a lad and Dad could -- and still can. In the olden days, presumably, he climbed down too.

In the evening, we went out to dinner followed by the local theatre, our Valentine's Day treat. The play was 'Shirley Valentine' and Alys thought the story of a middle-aged housewife meeting a sexy Mediterranean young man so wonderful she was in raptures. Gwen nudged me as we left and said, "See!" Maybe I should have Alys or

Nico watched. After all, Alys has lots of free time on her hands.

Sunday 17:
Skied with Lydia all day while Lance 'boarded with his buddies. It is wonderfully energising to be in the company of younger people. They are so enthusiastic, so willing to learn, and eager to explore ideas. We discussed Byzantium, Rome, Greece, and the medieval periods, before moving on, or back, to the Victorian Era. We retired to the chalet again after a particularly heavy fall had bruised Lydia's bum and thigh, or so she thought. We were very cosy till Lance and his friends came in and Lydia had to get off my knee. I explained to Lance that Lydia's behind was too sore to sit on the hard bench and he seemed to understand. He said he'd have to be sure he didn't accidentally tell Mom and could he have his allowance now, please.

When we got home, Alys asked about skiing and I told her of my day and how lucky I'd been to run into Lydia again. She said it sounded so good she'd come next time. I'm glad. She'll see Lydia and I are just friends and she has no reason to be concerned. Can't help thinking the competition between the ladies may work in my favour, though, and to be ready I did thirty Kegels today.

Gwen spent the day at work and the evening at indoor soccer. Really, she's little more than a lodger now.

Monday 18:
Lydia and I went to the gym and helped each other with weights and stretches. After our skiing yesterday, Lydia felt we needed to loosen up. Her buns, calves and thighs were particularly tight, she said, and suggested I massage them to remove the stiffness. I declined. My massaging Lydia's buns and thighs wouldn't have removed the stiffness; it would just have moved it. The way young folks are brought up today is so free and easy; they just don't realise what touching them means to us older men. Fortunately, I understand these things and can watch out for both of us. I'd hate to think what an unscrupulous man could get up to if given the opportunity.

Alys didn't go out this evening, a fact I made known to Gwen when she came back from work. Gwen said, "She didn't need to. She's been out all day, only getting back home when we kids came in from school."

I couldn't help noticing, as Alys and I helped Lance with his new school art project ('replicate one of Michelangelo's paintings or statues using common household waste'), that Alys was looking particularly attractive tonight. Maybe I could hire a private detective like they do on TV?

Weight: plus 1 lb. Probably from sharing Lydia's fries in the chalet on the weekend.

Tuesday 19:

Realised I forgot to do my Kegels yesterday. Manage thirty before feeling ill and stopping. Do I really want to have sex for five hours? How important is that ambition in my life? A month ago I would have said it wasn't important at all but lately it's becoming an important one again.

My Public Speaking speech on the merits of skiing versus snowboarding was well received. Of course, if there had been anyone below the age of thirty in my class, I'd have said it the other way round. I don't need any more 'debates' around my speeches.

Lydia began working with Mr. Ogilvie for an hour today. She says she hated it. I think she'll soon get to see his good qualities and settle down. It's an opportunity for her to stop 'temping' and get taken on full time, as I told her. She gave me a strange look by way of reply. I often get strange looks when I say something and I wonder at times if I'm not too clever for my acquaintances, or is it I'm too honest?

I've wondered a lot about honesty and integrity lately because our new American masters have written them into our 'values' statement and our Code of Business Conduct. It prompted me to invent a new law -- the Arthur Lakelady law of opposites. When someone writes values you have always believed everyone held into their Mission and Values Statement, it's because they're foreign and new concepts to the writer -- who has, however, just discovered they are good for his image.

In the evening, after Lance's soccer practice, while reaching for the TV remote from my prone position as Silky's evening bed, I put my back out and had to lie still for a long time before I felt recovered enough to get up. Silky helped me stay prone by staying put on my lap, snoring gently. Alys helped by changing the TV to the History channel, and bringing my night-time tea. Lance helped by going downstairs to play his Nintendo game. I feel a bit guilty about Gawain who has never had my sympathy with his back troubles and I see now with his lifestyle he is likely to suffer just this kind of injury. I will try to be more understanding this Saturday when I call. When it was time for bed, Alys lifted Silky off my lap and helped me upstairs. We won't be spoon hugging tonight, I'm sorry to say because our Valentine's night bash was great and Alys is looking exceptional again tonight.

Gwen, the lodger, was at work till late.

Wednesday 20:
I wish I'd listened longer to that radio interview. If I only manage 150 Kegels per day, can I have sex for 2.5 hours?

Woke up with a stiff back, which was better than the pain I was in when I went to bed, and Alys fussed about me at breakfast and everything. It was like a second honeymoon only without the sex. [A bit like our first one really, where I'd severely injured my hands by slamming the car hood down on them after removing a fish from the exhaust manifold.]

Lydia was too busy to help me today; she and Mr. Ogilvie were working together on his project and they stayed on after we all went home. I hope once she gets past this learning stage, she'll be back because there's so much researching to be done and she's the best there is for that. I also miss our lunchtime walk.

Today's date reads the same forwards and backwards, 20-02/2002, and at two minutes past ten, it was 20-02/2002/20:02, which won't happen again till I forget when. It was clearly a slow news day in the Western world because I've remembered now, it won't happen again for thirteen months -- 20-03/2003/20:03.

Went to doctors to hear results of blood test and explained about my back. He says sit and lie straight and the back will get better and take two aspirins if it's painful. My blood tests were fine except he thinks my cholesterol is creeping up. He gave me a sheet of paper outlining things to eat and things to avoid and said, "Do this and we'll re-test you in 6 months."

This is not good news but there's no point telling him it will be bad for me so I agree to give it a go. I reason that, if God had wanted me to eat salad He wouldn't have made it of raw leaves and He'd have made it taste like roast beef.

After I'd left the surgery and was gloomily driving away, cursing the weakness of old age, I saw the doctor running after me waving his brown folder. Gloom changed instantly to terror as I braked and wound down the window. He leaned in, gasping for breath (he's terribly out of shape for someone in the health field) and said, "I forgot to tell you..."

"What?" I asked timidly.

"Your PSA test..."

"Yes?" I squeaked.

"It was fine too."

At that moment, I had a mental picture of a newspaper headline saying, 'Man kills doctor then dies of heart attack.' This image saved the doctor's life because I know Alys wouldn't like us to be in the news that way and I drove off. On the way home, I celebrated this good medical news with an 'Extreme' burger at the local 'homemade taste' global burger joint. The Extreme is the one with layers of bacon fat slopped on cheesy dairy fat slapped over a patty of beef fat on a processed white bun-- yummy.

I took Gwen to work and later to soccer after dropping Lance at ski club; Alys says I'm fit enough now and she needed a rest after pandering to my whims all weekend. Gwen said... Well, I won't record what she insinuated.

Thursday 21:

Today was Lance's school picture day and Alys, as usual, took pains to ensure he was turned out smartly for the event. I don't know why she still bothers. The photos all record that Lance somehow manages to re-dress into what he wants to wear between Merlin Crescent and school.

Alys took Gwen to work and I picked her up much later. Gwen says Alys was late getting home and that made Gwen late for work. She also said grimly, "You may not care what your wife gets up to but I can't be late for work or I'll lose my job." She wants me to speak to Alys! This after I'd been to the dentist and was not yet fully recovered!

I went to the dentist for my annual check up. The dentist would prefer I go twice yearly so he can afford more of life's goodies. I prefer to go once a year to avoid Helga, the Hygienist from Hell. It's always a different Helga; tonight's was Sonia, She-Wolf of the SS. First, they X-ray my teeth, which involves placing hard pieces of card in my mouth and zapping me with radiation. The hygienist hides behind a lead bunker while doing this to be sure she is safe. The radiation is followed by the gum pick, a sharpened spike the hygienist stabs into your gums till they bleed. When she knows how easily you bleed, the hygienist uses this information in the next phase where she takes sharpened hooks and hacks away at your teeth and gums until the few undamaged areas are all bleeding equally. Having cut your mouth to ribbons, Helga finally grinds the mess to a pulp by polishing it with an abrasive paste. At this point, the dentist comes in, pokes at your teeth for twenty seconds with another sharpened hook and pronounces you fit to leave. The receptionist brightly suggests another appointment in six months and I say no. We agree on twelve months and I totter out into the snow, safe at last -- until I met Gwen.

Friday 22:
Voluntary Leaving Buyout (VLB) applications are issued.
In common with everyone at work I received my VLB application and an invitation to request a pension calculation, which I decided to do. I can't afford to leave but it will be nice to see how much I'm worth. The corridors are alive with people speculating if VLB also stands for 'Very Large (leaving) Bonus.'

Lydia visited for a short while this morning because Mr. Ogilvie was out at a meeting. Lydia says she still doesn't like Mr. Ogilvie but she can see I was right about him appreciating having a young woman about the place. Mr. Ogilvie particularly liked her tattoos. A red mist seemed to fall between Lydia and me at this point and I was glad there were no sharp objects nearby. How dare he see her tattoos? How could she show a man like him something so precious to us? Despite this small betrayal of our affection, we arranged to ski together tomorrow because I can't get to the Club tonight.

I also notice Seth hasn't called in weeks. I wonder where he's gone? The exotic dance bar would be a fair replacement for the Club, and easier to achieve. I wish I'd got Seth's phone number when we met instead of staring open-mouthed at naked girls.

After school, Lance went boarding with some friends and was later carried back into the house by a friend and friend's dad. He'd fallen and hurt his back. We laid him out on the couch and the friends fled -- probably frightened we'd sue them for negligence. Lance lay, wrapped in a blanket, watching all his favourite shows and sipping hot chocolate supplied by Alys till bedtime when he was just strong enough to hobble upstairs. Silky and I weren't pleased because I couldn't get on the couch and she couldn't get on my lap. Lance's lap was a very poor substitute, I think, for she only catnapped when she usually sleeps soundly. Gwen was out at work as usual so didn't participate in, or comment on, this disgraceful exhibition of copycat illness.

Saturday 23:
Last night, Alys and I had a long discussion concerning Kegels and their effect on our sex life. My doubts were justified. Alys does not want five hours of sex or even 2.5 hours. We agree this isn't a goal 'we' want to pursue. It may be one I want to pursue, however.

My back was well enough to go skiing today so I went and met Lydia. I was still stiff so we retired to the chalet earlier than usual and there, where and when it was quiet Lydia showed me her new tattoo. Seeing it seemed to unlock some last barrier of reserve between us because we held hands and talked nonsense for hours until it was time to go home. We are meeting again tomorrow. Lydia says she thinks Mr. Ogilvie is jealous of me and that's why he won't let her go back to working in my group. She says she may have made things worse by telling Mr. Ogilvie how happy she was to be under me and how wonderful a boss I was. She'd said all this, thinking to further my career before realising Mr. Ogilvie fancied her like crazy and would hate any man who stood between them. She begged my forgiveness and it took some time before I was able to soothe away her fears. Fortunately, Lance didn't come in while this was going on.

I shared my fears for her well being with Lydia, asking her if 'Mr. Ogilvie fancies her like crazy' should she be working with him and staying late? She reassured me by saying she knew how to handle men, especially old ones like Mr. Ogilvie. How does she know how to handle old men like Mr. Ogilvie? I decided not to tell Lydia that Mr. Ogilvie and I are the same age. We just don't look it because I keep myself in shape.

Called dad. He's still in bed and very grumpy. The new pills aren't nearly as good as the old ones. Gawain is too infirm to help, so they have a nurse coming in to look after them again. She refuses to move the TV up to Dad or Gawain's bedrooms and the stairs are too steep for them to come down. She did, however, take the cordless phone up to their rooms so I could listen to them complain. I much preferred old technology. With a corded phone, I could have only passed on my good wishes. Remembering my back ailment of last week, I tried to be sympathetic but they thought I was being sarcastic and we parted on bad terms.

Gwen's running away fund must be in good shape by now; she was working again all day today. After snowboarding, Lance went to hockey practice and tried to keep out of the way of the rest of his team. For the most part, he was successful, unlike one of the smaller players who was carried off injured after a particularly heavy challenge. The rules concerning dangerous play aren't enforced during practice so you get to see what a game is like without those biased, blind buffoons called referees.

Alys had a quiet day to herself, she said, while glowing with beauty and satisfaction. I will hire a private detective.

Sunday 24:

Squirrels mustn't like snowdrops because, unlike the crocuses, the snowdrops come back every year. (We never see crocuses twice, only a lot of plump squirrels.) Unfortunately, it's always the same six snowdrops -- never any more. In England, they would have multiplied until there was an army of them under our apple tree. Here they just soldier on, a brave platoon of green and white that will shrivel the moment the sun gets hot.

I secretly continue with the Kegels. If I ever get to be a senior manager of the company, I don't want to be found wanting when we get across the boardroom table, or wherever it is they play naughty boss and secretary.

Alys didn't come skiing today because she and Gwen were shopping for a Prom dress. Lance's buddies went to a different hill so I dropped him off there and Lydia and I spent the afternoon on 'our' hill catching up on our history discussions that have been so curtailed by Mr. Ogilvie monopolising her time at work. We revisited the Victorian period again; agreeing that couples should have secret lovers again and that the Victorian love of over-dressing revealed they were sex mad -- again. We discussed the book on Victorian erotica Lydia is reading for ideas to take to her Friday evening club scene. I feel we are kindred spirits. We can talk about these things with such honesty and in a spirit of intellectual enquiry that leaves me quite breathless at times. At lunchtime Lydia and I packed up our skis and left to carry on our intellectual enquiry at a more fundamental level in the back of my car along a quiet lane.

When I told Alys she should have come skiing because she could have met Lydia, she went very pale and muttered something under her breath. She assures me she'll be with me next week; she's looking forward to having a good chat with Lydia. Next weekend may need careful handling.

Later in bed, I was surprised to find Alys snuggling in to me; competition is an amazing thing. And I think the Kegels helped my performance; I will continue practising them.

Monday 25:

After the weekend, when people had time to contemplate the VLB, the 'halls are alive with the sound of musing' again, if you'll pardon the Sound of Music pun. No one wants to work. They only want to talk. I kept to my office, hoping not to be noticed.

However, I couldn't help noticing Lydia is helping Mr. Ogilvie with his project again. I feel I should complain; an hour a day was what he and I discussed. And I can't help wondering about Lydia's tattoos. I saw them in my own time when tattoo watching is legal. Did Mr. Ogilvie violate our Code of Business Conduct when he agreed to see them? The Code is quite explicit, we can't do anything enjoyable but it's mandatory we have fun at work.

I left my office briefly, a foray to the gym intending to raise my spirits but without Lydia's company it's dismal too. I may quit.

Alys was out when I got home. She'd taken Gwen to work and then gone shopping, her note said. I helped Lance with his new school project, 'build a fully functional astronomical radio telescope using only old household electronics' parts'. Too depressed to care if Alys was misbehaving but Silky didn't notice or care that her 'bed' was upset.

Tuesday 26:

I have decided not to apply for a pension and buyout package. With my luck, I'd be accepted without a chance to withdraw. Lydia worked with Mr. Ogilvie again all day today. I shall have to say something because my section is running out of the research items they need and the new procedures aren't getting formatted as they should. Some of the older men are becoming peaky and muttering about my lack of backbone. I heard Padraig remark to Miguel, as they he passed my cubicle, "Lydia is our support, not Ogilvie's." Miguel said something coarse about Lydia supporting Mr. Ogilvie, which I won't repeat here, and I was tempted to be sharp with him. In the end, I decided I'd just warn Mr. Ogilvie that his keeping Lydia late at night was causing gossip. Unfortunately, when I saw Mr. Ogilvie later, Lydia was with him. I'll tell him tomorrow.

I was more fortunate than my workers, for Lydia and I went to lunch again and held hands -- again. When I told her Alys didn't understand me anymore, her eyes filled with tears. Lydia is so sensitive to the pain of others.

Took Lance to ski club because he is friendly again with the ski club crowd and this is their last night. Alys visited some friends because, she said, the house is so empty with Lance and Gwen, who was at work, gone. I pointed out I would be home and she said, "Yes! Writing that *%#ing diary as usual." It's true, my diary is taking a lot more of my time than I anticipated but I was shocked. It isn't like Alys to swear.

Wednesday 27:
Gerry was filling in his application for the buyout package and persuaded me to do the same. "What can go wrong when half the company are applying?" he said. "It's only a request. It doesn't bind you to anything," he said. I just know something will go wrong. Like me, Gerry is too young to go. He just wants to know what he's worth.

Lydia came to see me at lunchtime. I complained about her lack of support to my section and she said she doesn't enjoy working with Mr. Ogilvie but he seems pleased with her so what can she do? As a temp, she has to give satisfaction or 'she'll be out on her ass'. I deplore the language but can't fault her logic. She agreed to try and get back to help us for a few minutes each day. She also agreed to lunch and we went to a small restaurant far away from the office where we held hands under the table. After, we walked through the park, stopping at those few quiet places where we could be alone. Lydia asked me to accompany her to the Club again. She misses me. I promised to find a way.

I dropped Gwen at her practice and watched Lance's soccer practice. Lance's team had an exhibition game against an older girls' team and won handily. I couldn't believe it, nor could Lance. When you watch the girls play each other, as we do every week, they look sharp, skilful, and confident. Matched against even much younger boys, however, you see the gulf between the sexes. Boys are all round quicker and more aggressive and the girls' confidence drains away, leaving them floundering.

Alys went shopping.

Thursday 28:
Lydia was as good as her word. She spent, at least, thirty minutes with my section this morning and it cheered them up enormously -- old Mohammed, who is a devout Muslim and doesn't approve of women working (Muslim women anyway), was sweating profusely when Lydia bent down to get the folders on his desk. I must tell her, for the future, that Muslims are sensitive about things like low-cut T-shirts and he may take the matter to the company's Appropriate Behaviour and Dress Ombudswoman. Still, I think it was all right this time because he seemed so pleased to see her back in our section. He was also pleased to see her back... view, for her T-shirt, had only criss-cross strings on it, which revealed, if revelation was needed (which it wasn't) that she wasn't wearing a bra. Nevertheless, I felt it my duty to confirm this fact on our lunchtime walk and lecture her on appropriate workplace dress. She looked so contrite and pouty that I had to spend most of our time together soothing her. We were both content by the time we returned to work.

Lydia spent the rest of the day in Mr. Ogilvie's office. My section became very grumpy and no matter how I tried to raise their spirits they stayed depressed and unproductive. Miguel said unless we get the kind of support Lydia gives we won't get any procedures out this year.

Gwen played her last game of ice hockey this evening and it ended in a tie, which sums up the season. Alys and I cheered her on while Lance mooched around the snack bar with the other hockey brothers. Next season, Gwen will be at University and she'll never become an NHL star.

March 2002:
Goodbye is such sweet sorrow.

Friday 1:
After our 'discussions' (read nagging) on what she is to do after her contract with us expires, Lydia walked over to University Admissions office today. She made the long lunchtime hike only to be told she couldn't be given an application form; she had to get it off the University's website. Lydia pointed out she was a poor graduate who didn't have the Internet and they said, 'Tough, we don't let people just walk in off the street and apply; we prefer them sight unseen.' So she came away empty-handed and she and I spent the afternoon surfing through cyberspace trying to locate the form. I'm considering a strong letter to the Dean because his surly staff unnerved Lydia and almost ruined six weeks of constant effort (read nagging) on my part.

I spoke to Mr. Ogilvie about Lydia today. It seems his project was much more involved than he imagined and he will need to keep Lydia full-time, especially the night shift he joked. He should be more careful, that's the sort of talk that gets you fired under our new Puritan regime.

In the afternoon, I called home to tell Alys I was working late and then going to a 'leaving do' I'd just heard about. Alys wasn't home so I left a message on the answering machine. Helped Lydia dress for the Club, then I helped her friends, Anna and Gina, dress too. My life has become a lot more exciting since Lydia arrived. Lydia and I left the Club early and retired to her apartment, more tiptoeing in darkened houses. A feat I had all to do again when I got home. Luckily, Alys wasn't back so I was able to take the moral high ground when she woke me by tiptoeing into her dressing table.

Saturday 2:
Called dad. He still isn't well; an ingrown toenail has gone septic. He needs an operation and he's on antibiotics, which are upsetting his stomach. Gawain isn't well either. He got up to move the TV and

dropped the video player on his foot and broke it, his foot that is. The VCR is fine, which is just as well because they can't get about and there's nothing worth watching on TV. They're both in Gawain's room watching videos. I no longer try to find illnesses of my own to discuss, particularly after the 'piles' episode, so I sympathised as feelingly as I could.

Went skiing with Alys and Lance. Lydia didn't show up but I wasn't surprised. Right after I'd told her about Alys coming out, Lydia told me she'd have to work the weekend on Mr. Ogilvie's project. How Mr. Ogilvie could have estimated an hour a day last week and now needs weekends as well as long days, I don't know.

Gwen was adding to her running away fund by working and Lance 'boarded with his friends so it was a quiet, un-contentious, day.

Sunday 3:

Went skiing with Alys; Lydia must still be working with Mr. Ogilvie. I was glad during the day because I thought they might have words if the two had met but when we went to bed, Alys went to sleep. Exhausted from all that skiing, she said. I wonder if this weekend has set her suspicions at rest and she thinks I've been making it up? This could be a downside to competition.

Gwen was at work all day and indoor soccer in the evening. Lance 'boarded with us at the ski hills and sulked because none of his friends could come.

Monday 4:

In the half-hour she spent with us today, Lydia told me about a 'spinning' class she has started attending in the evenings because she can't get to the gym with me anymore. For those of you who aren't into fitness, spinners aren't related in any way to Quakers or Shakers (other than all being religious maniacs). This is something you do on a stationary bike. I decided spinning would be a pleasant change at the gym and hopped on a bike. The bike was programmable and because I'm not handy with electronics, it took me a few tetchy moments to choose a routine that began gently and worked up to a crescendo. I started well, then after a few minutes, it went faster and faster, my legs flew around like propellers until, for one brief glorious moment, I thought I'd developed buns and calves of steel, like on the videos. It turned out to be cramp and "Extreme"-ly painful. I wish I'd had Lydia there to massage the cramp out. That's the other thing wrong with kids today; they're never about when you need them.

Lance went tubing with the ski club to make up for the night they missed when the snow had melted. Gwen was shut up in her bedroom studying and Alys went out shopping with a friend, she said. Gwen, who appeared at 11 pm to hunt for food, reminded me the Mall shuts at ten before returning to her lair and slamming the door behind her, which caused Silky to leap off my legs and lacerate me.

Tuesday 5:
Told Lydia of my spinning experience and she laughed! Young people are so callous. She can't get to the gym now because Mr. Ogilvie won't give her the time off. Otherwise, she would have come today to show me how it's done, she said, before leaving for Mr. Ogilvie's office. She seemed differently dressed today, more tailored cut and colours but less of everything else, which is strange after her complaints about Mr. Ogilvie ogling her. When I got home, I told Alys about this, hoping to get a woman's view, and she snorted (and snorted is the only word for it), 'Slut!' Obviously, I didn't describe Lydia's situation properly because that wasn't the response I was expecting.

However, I'm pleased to say Alys wasn't upset with me; she surprised me by snuggling into me at bedtime. I must work harder on those Kegels.

Gwen studied all evening and Lance did homework with Alys's help. I don't know how Gwen can study with all that noise going on in the next room.

Wednesday 6:
Eunice, Mr. Ogilvie's secretary, has announced she's applying for the VLB. I'm surprised because she and Mr. Ogilvie have been together for years, through at least four reorganisations. I don't know what she'll do when she goes; her aged Mother died last year and she's never married because she's been too busy looking after the 'old woman', she says. When I asked what she'll do, Eunice said, 'Travel, to see if human nature is any better anywhere else.' I think she'll be disappointed.

Met Lydia for lunch but we weren't very hungry so we went for a walk instead. Lydia said she missed me and I comforted her. Then

THE DIARY OF A CANADIAN NOBODY

things got out of hand. Luckily we were in a secluded part of the park and no one saw us. We were so shocked by what happened, we met right after work to talk about it. I meant to say it mustn't happen again, or at least not in such a public spot, but before I'd got the thought properly expressed it had happened again. I spent my journey home imagining everyone staring at me accusingly.

To add to my guilty feelings, our renewed relationship of last night seems to have fired Alys up and she was very loving again in bed tonight. Jealousy may be one of the seven deadly sins in some people's eyes but not mine. I tried not to let my mind dwell on where she'd been all evening spoil the fun.

Gwen was again at work and soccer practice. Hockey practice has ended so Lance and I played squash.

Thursday 7:
Once again I received only two days pay and Alys is upset. It seems our finances are thrown out of kilter if a regular deposit isn't made, which puzzles me because I'm not badly paid. It turns out that, when I applied for a pension calculation, Payroll assumed I was leaving and terminated me. I don't seem to have any luck at all; hundreds of other people applied and no one else had this happen. I raced down to Payroll, to have them fix the problem before Alys did.

Lydia and I met for lunch and agreed that what happened yesterday mustn't happen again. It was too public. Unfortunately, on the way back to the office we stumbled into a secluded spot in the park and our good intentions fell away like most of Lydia's clothes. I thought I could get a grip on myself -- but I already had one on Lydia and she on me so the moment of rationality passed. Luckily, once again no one saw us and we escaped unseen. We agreed from now on it would be best if we went to Lydia's apartment at lunchtime. Misbehaving is one thing, but being caught is quite another.

Gwen had a hockey game and then work and was so late home that I didn't get the benefit of learning where Alys was after she dropped Gwen off. I stayed home to help Lance with his homework though I feel it would be better for all of us if I didn't. All this is doing is ensuring he runs away to sea, or the modern equivalent -- the streets of downtown Toronto.

Alys's problem with my pay didn't seem to spill over into our personal life. Perhaps it helped her see how much she needs me because she was very loving in bed tonight. Satisfying two women today means I won't have strength for Kegels tomorrow.

Friday 8:
The VLB window closed today and now we just have to wait and see who won the jackpot. Who has applied and kept it secret? Who has applied and been turned down so senior management can torture them daily for disloyalty? Answers will be revealed next week.

Helped Lydia dress for the Club tonight, in the women's washroom after everyone had gone for the day. She made me dress her so I'd be miserable all weekend knowing what I'd missed. Her friends were meeting her elsewhere so I didn't get the full force of this weekly ritual. Nor did Seth call. I've no idea what happened to him.

When I got home tonight, Alys said to Lance, "Show your Dad what you've done," in that awful voice she reserves for the truly evil wrongdoer. Lance showed me the broken vacuum hose, which he claims went like that spontaneously without him doing anything. I visited the store where we bought the vacuum cleaner but they don't do hoses, only filters and such. I have to contact the factory and, after an extensive search of the basement and office, I can't find the Owner's Manual. I muttered dark comments about overly efficient tidying up just outside, I thought, Alys's hearing but apparently it wasn't. We won't be spoon hugging tonight. Lucky I didn't do those Kegels because I won't need them. Part of the reason for my dark comments is the knowledge Lydia is in a basement Club having fun while I'm in our basement looking for dumb vacuum manuals.

Gwen was at work raising money for college, and Alys took Lance to soccer practice. She didn't come home during the practice, which made me wonder if she too was having fun while I was searching our basement. Silky, however, had a good evening's rest without interruption – hallelujah.

Saturday 9:
It appears the vacuum cleaner was so new I hadn't actually filed the manual anywhere. It was on my bedside table, under a lot of other very important papers. It wasn't THAT easy to spot -- or not as easy as Alys makes out, anyhow. We're in luck; the manual gives an address, e-mail address, and phone number. I phoned and got an answering machine because the factory is closed on weekends. Globalisation hasn't spoiled life for all the world's factory workers,

thank goodness. They have a voice mailbox and I left a message.

Called Dad. He and Gawain are both able to get about again and their full-time nurse has left them. I said I was sure they were sorry about that but it seems she was very strict about things, 'always bossing us about and in our own house,' says dad, so they're not sorry she's gone. Dad's toenail operation is next week, provided the antibiotics have cleared up the infection.

Alys has forgiven me and we enjoyed another night of passion. Must get back to those Kegels; they are vital to our love life's continued good health. Alys even went so far as to say 'a little longer would be nice.' I wish I'd been more self-disciplined these past weeks and been able to impress Alys with my prowess.

The snow is so poor that the local ski resorts have only a few runs open. Lance was disgusted with their reduced offering and went to hockey, the last game of the regular season, where his team lost again. Some of the parents are saying we're going to be a 'playoff team'; i.e. one that comes good for the end-of-season playoffs. Hope really does spring eternal in the human breast. This is the worst team Lance has ever played on; they couldn't win a lottery (neither can I actually).

Alys went to Lance's soccer team parents' meeting and didn't come home till late. She said some of the parents just kept on talking and wouldn't shut up. Gwen snorted contemptuously at this explanation when she heard it. Gwen says I've got to remember that children from broken homes don't do well at school or in life.

Sunday 10:
An actress I've always fancied, Elizabeth Hurley, is having a baby and claimed an American from the movie world, Steven Bing, as the baby's father. Mr. Bing, somewhat ungallantly, has demanded a paternity test. I understand his actions. In the past few years, judges have ruled that men who were later discovered not to be the father still had to pay child support because 'paternity' is more than just being the biological father. At the same time, the government and courts hunt down 'deadbeat dads' who are the biological fathers of children they've never even met. These determinations to make some man somewhere pay for every unmarried woman's child has become a serious problem for men, particularly rich ones.

Gwen was at work and later indoor soccer. Lance just did indoor soccer. Alys came to Lance's game but had to go visiting an ailing friend and wasn't able to watch Gwen's game. Gwen says I have to put my foot down or her academic prowess will suffer.

Alys was very loving again tonight but I'm exhausted; two women are too much. I wonder if Viagra would help? The question is, have I the nerve to ask the doctor?

Monday 11:
No visit from Lydia today; no happy thoughts from me.

The war in Afghanistan that raged so hotly across our TV and newspapers all winter has now disappeared from view, leaving only the poor GIs and Tommys out there to moulder on, a bit like my snowdrops. The good news is no more barroom bravado from people who were never likely to meet a Taliban fighter. The bad news is we will get to watch it all over again in ten or twenty year's time, like in Palestine. I believe today is the day when the official number of Americans charged with looting and fraud at Ground Zero exceeds the dwindling number of officially dead. It's also the day we learned the Homeland Security's uniform will be black shirts – have our leaders no knowledge of history at all?

Crocuses are coming out. Fortunately, the weather is still cold so they might actually last a few days this year.

Alys went out with 'the girls' most of the afternoon while Gwen went to work with many dark looks in my direction. This would have been a chance to follow Alys to see where she went, only Lance and I played squash again because I've taken time off to stop him watching TV or playing video games all day. The good news is that, even after twenty years of not playing, I can still beat someone thirty years my junior. Of course, it helps that Lance has never played and I used to take lessons. I see it as striking a blow for seniors, something like the way Billie Jean King's victory over a man twenty-five years older than she was 'proved' women could beat men at tennis.

Tuesday 12:
The days are slow at work. There's nothing to do and no Lydia to do it with.

Obviously, the phone link to the vacuum factory wasn't the best method because they haven't responded. Now I've e-mailed my request to the factory, let's see if modern technology holds the key. Spent much of my day off trying to get in touch with the vacuum factory. I'd have more success with my 'inner self.'

Alys took Gwen and Lance shopping today to buy summer clothes and stuff. She also bought me new shorts and tee shirts, which is why I never go shopping. Left to my own devices, I'd have worn last year's models or even those from the year before. Being under Gwen's watchful eye all day kept Alys above suspicion.

It also tired her out, she said, when we went to bed. Last week I was exhausted trying to keep up with the women in my life, this week I'm raring to go and no one is interested. It's hard to get the right balance in relationships.

Wednesday 13:
No Transformation news, no work, no Lydia, no fair.

In the evening, I took the opportunity of Gwen being at work, Lance at his friend's house, and Alys out with the girls, to visit an out-of-town walk-in clinic. The doctor was very understanding when I told him of my wife's insatiable demands. He winked and said it was a problem lots of us suffer from. Picked up my prescription from an out-of-town drug store where I didn't think I'd be recognised. Unfortunately, our neighbour Ben was picking up a prescription too. Why on earth would he use such an inconvenient store?

Alys wasn't home all evening so Lance and I played squash again and then ate out. Eating out with the kids has been much more complex since they grew out of McDonalds. Gwen only eats pizza or Caesar salad and Lance only eats meat from a bone. Today we ate at The Extreme Greek and Lance and I had lamb shank on rice. We left the rice.

Thursday 14:
Maybe I should have taken the VLB. Without Lydia, it all seems so pointless.

I took Gwen to soccer practice leaving Lance to watch TV. Gwen said nothing about her mother's absence, which was a relief. Actually, she said nothing at all, just sighed forcefully there and back. She's reached the age where I'm a great disappointment to her. Once, not so long ago in my life (but an age in hers), I could do no wrong.

Friday 15:

Our company has given a free blanket to everyone who didn't have a sick day last year. I checked my time sheets and find I missed only one day, which I think very unfair. If I'd known there was to be a free company blanket I'm sure I'd have come in that day, though I can't remember what I was sick with. Am determined this year I will come in whatever I've got. Not only will it guarantee me a prize, if I'm infectious it will reduce everyone else's chances. I handed out the blankets to my staff and I must say they weren't as grateful as I'd have been if I'd received one.

Eunice was approved for the VLB and is leaving on April 1, the first leaving date. I've no idea how Mr. Ogilvie is going to manage without her; she did everything for him.

I took a Viagra tablet last night, in case Alys wanted to continue working out her jealousy on me but she didn't. Too tired from shopping, she said. Unfortunately, without the expected release, I was embarrassed all day at my 'appearance' -- particularly when I met Lydia in the hall and she hugged me. Next time, I'll take half a tablet. Mr. Ogilvie didn't seem pleased at Lydia's spontaneous burst of affection and I think they were arguing after I left. Jealousy can be a curse as well as a blessing.

Fortunately, Mr. Ogilvie wasn't too close when she hugged me or he'd have heard her tell me to meet her for lunch, which I did. We went to her apartment, the Landlady was out and played Naughty Secretary, something Lydia had been longing to do since she'd seen a couple do this at the Club. I wasn't there that night, and I'm hopeless at acting, so my performance of the Stern Boss, who delivers a sound spanking before having his way with said secretary was probably a bit of a disappointment for her. It saddens me that I'm letting down all the women in my life. Thanks to the Viagra, however, I didn't let Lydia down on the last bit.

I still have no reply from the vacuum factory, so I phoned and e-mailed again. I did, however, hear from Seth. He's taken a job on the East Coast in the growing Hibernia offshore oilfield industry and he'll call next time he's home, though, he says, that may not be soon. I suspect oil workers have plenty of attention from lots of attractive young strippers. Young men only make money to get the attention of better-looking girls; the world may have changed but the original male (and female) programming hasn't.

Saturday 16:

I called Dad. He is unwell. The operation on his toe has left him very poorly. He thinks elderly people should just be left to die in peace. His new happy pills aren't working either. I feel guilty about my continuing good health. It's ironic that I never have any illness to tell Dad about yet I missed getting the 'good health' blanket.

Didn't go skiing because we were waiting for the heating contractor to come and service our system. Afterwards, Alys insisted we go shopping though we didn't buy anything. She says I'm hopeless because I don't like anything. Being disappointed at not getting skiing, and depressed at watching hundreds of foolish people aimlessly staring in windows at things they don't need, can't afford, but want desperately, I was a bit short in my response. I don't think I'll need a Viagra pill tonight.

Lance's hockey team played its first game of the playoffs and won!!!! The parents are going wild with visions of winning the 'A' final. For those of you who aren't hockey people, I'll explain how playoffs work. The regular season ends with all the teams occupying a place from first to last in the league but real hockey fans don't care about that. It's the playoffs that they live for when the top team plays the bottom, second plays second bottom, and so on, in a round robin to come up with another ranking. This playoff ranking is what counts because the first and second in the round robin play each other for the 'A' final, third and fourth play in the 'B' final and so on depending on how many teams were in the league this year. Unbelievably, and admittedly after only one game, we're up near the top of the playoff ranking. They'll never hold on to it, of course.

Sunday 17:

Half a Viagra is perfect though I think the Kegels helped too. We made up after we went to bed and Alys was pleased with my performance last night and I was pleased to find myself appropriately 'dressed' today, no embarrassing bulges for people to see.

We went skiing and didn't see Lydia, which, I'm sad to say, pleased Alys but didn't please me. Soon Alys will be sure I've made Lydia up in order to entrap her into having extra-marital sex (i.e. any sex you get after you've given your wife the exact number of kids she wanted).

I took Gwen to indoor soccer later while Alys took Lance to his second playoff game. Gwen's team won, as always, but the real shock was getting home to find Lance's team had also won. They have now won more games in the playoffs than they have all season!!! And they're in second place in the ranking!!!

Monday 18:
Lydia has been announced as Mr. Ogilvie's new Secretary! I'm pleased for Lydia. She won't need to temp or go back to University now. I congratulated her warmly, when she came to tell me she wouldn't be able to support my group in future, and she looked at me in a strange way, as though expecting me to say something different. I noticed she was wearing a conventional, though rather short-skirted, business suit. Her blouse was surprisingly thin too. Is Mr. Ogilvie an unscrupulous man? Should I warn him about the free-and-easy ways of young people and how he, as a more mature person, needs to be on guard for both of them? I decided not to, even though I can't bear the thought of him touching Lydia.

Lydia and me played Naughty Secretary again at lunchtime to celebrate her new status. The game is a lot realer when she is a Secretary and wearing a business suit. Also, I now see why Secretaries invariably have such short skirts. There must be many more Stern Bosses out there than I imagined.

I didn't tell Alys about Lydia's promotion because Alys has been very unkind lately about Lydia and if she thinks the danger has passed, she may not be so loving toward me. Then what would I do with the other six Viagra tablets? How long would they keep?

Gwen was in her room studying all evening so she didn't intrude on my blissful, lustful reverie or Silky's rest. Lance, however, had nothing to do and continually wandered by, punching or karate kicking me, hoping for a wrestling match. Alys was visiting friends, she said -- and that's good enough for me.

Tuesday 19:
My speech on Retirement Options was well received. I'm having doubts about the usefulness of this course when everything is well received. Can it be, that despite all evidence to the contrary, I have a knack for public speaking? Should I become a politician if the Transformation throws me out of honest work? Or are the rest of my Public Speaking classmates being nice so I will be nice to them when it's their turn? It's terrible to always have doubts about

yourself. Confident, but often less capable, people soar and the rest of us plod. Knowing that confidence is the key doesn't help either. You can't fake confidence convincingly, or I can't anyway.

Speaking of confidence, today, Lydia and I played Stern Boss and Naughty Secretary again at lunchtime, only this time she was the boss. She assures me it's only temporary. It's part of her self-training for the next step up the corporate ladder. She needs to build up her confidence to order people about, she says. I can't help feeling she already has the confidence. I also can't help feeling sore because all that time lifting weights in the gym has made her arm surprisingly strong.

Alys helped Lance with his homework while I was out at my course and I know she did because they were at opposite ends of the house when I got home. The indoor temperature was ten degrees colder than the outdoor one. Gwen had nothing to complain about when she got home from work. The family was as closely united (and divided) as even her strict views could wish.

Wednesday 20:

Global warming apparently also causes cold weather and we are suffering accordingly. It's the first day of spring and the coldest one on record. This wasn't so good for Lydia and I. Her Landlady hadn't gone out and we had to retire to a cold bench in the park. At least we had the park to ourselves but it was too cold for anything other than cuddling.

I still have no answer from the vacuum factory, so when I got home, I called and left another message. Gwen was at work followed by soccer practice and Lance was at a friend's house doing homework, so his phone message said. More likely playing video games and Hotmailing girls with rude names. Alys was out with her friends, so the note on the table said. I no longer want to know what friends she's seeing; I have my own secrets to keep though I share them with Silky while she sleeps.

Went to the gym today because tonight is the night, the six-month anniversary of my new strategy. The results are as follows:

Height -- 5 ft 9.5 ins. Damn! Now I'm approaching the forbidden zone on the Body Mass Index chart from two directions -- my weight is going up and thanks to all the pounding on my joints and their discs, my height is going down.

Weight -- +3 lbs

Waist -- 36 ins., no change
BMI -- 28, up from 27.5
Abs -- no sign of any
Chest -- 42 ins., no change.
Folds of flab on stomach -- no change.
General 'blurring' around edges -- no change.

A new strategy is called for. One that produces results -- like hypnotism or herbal remedies, both of which are heavily advertised in my free paper and are guaranteed to work.

Later, while I was glumly surveying myself in the mirror, Alys admired my 'new' torso, as she called it, purring seductively as she ran her hands over my buns of steel. Maybe the gym is working, or maybe it's still just competition. Who cares, I have only five and a half Viagra tablets to worry about now.

Thursday 21:
First full day of spring and also the coldest on record.
The good news is it's too cold for snow, ha-ha.

I have a new member of staff, Tammy; she's fresh out of University and very energetic. She's been transferred to my group partly to compensate for losing Lydia and partly to continue her exposure to all the different sides of our business, says Mr. Ogilvie. Tammy and I had a welcome-to-the-group talk and she seemed somewhat bitter about being transferred. I didn't press the matter. I just told her when she saw the work we did, she'd gain a new understanding of the foundations that support the whole enterprise, and we're the people who maintain those foundations. Tammy didn't seem to be impressed.

I called the vacuum factory and e-mailed them again. I'm getting concerned that I never get a Service Representative on the line.

It was Gwen's last hockey game and we all went to see it after Lance and I played squash again. Our games are getting harder for me; all his soccer and hockey makes Lance very fit.

Friday 22:
It snows heavily.

Gerry and I walked from the station to work through inches of slush, arriving cold and wet at the office. I now have a ticklish cough that I think may develop into something interesting to discuss with Dad tomorrow. This Global Warming is getting out of hand. If, as the newspapers say, Polar Bears are losing their habitat up north, they can come to Toronto.

Our Transformation is delayed again though it's sold as an opportunity to improve on the already improved organisation. We will now become super-competitors on May 1st.

Lydia was too busy at lunchtime to go out. Actually, I think she just didn't want to go out in the sleet storm.

In the evening Lance had a soccer game, which I watched; Gwen was at work. Who knows where Alys was?

Saturday 23:

I called Dad. He is still not well. His foot is healed but now he has a lung infection. Aunt Hester is in hospital, intensive care no less, with pneumonia and has had a tracheotomy to help her breathe. Gawain is laid up with bronchitis. I didn't mention my ticklish cough.

After our lack of success with the vacuum factory, I visited Whitebay's own vacuum centre -- The Vacuum Lady. This small old building (complete with a small old lady) is a one-storey wooden cabin on a large lot that was once on the edge of town but, thanks to our lunatic Council and urban sprawl, is now downtown. It is stuffed full of bits of old vacuums and spares for new ones. The lady tells me my vacuum manufacturer went out of business last October, a month or so after I bought the appliance and no she doesn't have a spare hose. That's what you get for buying Canadian! I've a good mind to write to the Prime Minister about this.

Lance's hockey team won again today and is firmly on top of the playoff standings. They have one more game tomorrow; even if they lose it they are still going to be in the 'A' final so the parents' old-fashioned math tell us. The amazing thing is, they are just as incompetent as they have been all season, only now the puck goes in the net for them and before it didn't. It's as if every opposing goalkeeper has decided to even things out by letting us win.

Alys came to the hockey game but disappeared afterwards. If she really is having an affair, as Gwen would have me believe, she is remarkably indiscreet about it.

Sunday 24:

As there isn't a Canadian vacuum manufacturer left, we bought a new Asian built vacuum cleaner. I've no doubt it will last forever, a permanent memento of western industrial decline and my lack of patriotism.

Gwen was at work all day, returning only to go to indoor soccer. Alys, who took her to work, was absent all day. I took Lance to indoor soccer at lunchtime, we lost, and hockey at suppertime, we won!! I say 'we' won because the kids were their usual selves and only my nail-biting, feverish support scraped us home. We are in the 'A' final on the Saturday and Sunday after Easter!! Watching Gwen's soccer game was a breeze; they won easily.

Alys looked very pretty when we got home. She was showered, perfumed and ready for bed, hurrying me along when it looked like I might dawdle in front of the TV. I'll need another Viagra prescription soon if I'm to keep this up.

Monday 25:

I have decided to sign up for the hypnotism course of treatment. It offers miraculous cures without eating anything unusual or not eating anything at all. It sounds perfect. I will continue going to the gym so when the unsightly rolls of flab leave my midriff, my toned abs will stand out like rippling sandbars on a tide-swept beach.

Tammy isn't proving to be a replacement for Lydia, in any sense of the word. She refuses to use all that youthful energy for supporting the others. She only wants to write procedures and says she needs an Assistant to do research for her. She also says she wants my job in five years, max. I think it's great the way we teach young women to be assertive (as though they needed it) but they need to learn the old wartime adage too -- don't believe your own propaganda. Men aren't as useless as they sometimes appear.

Speaking of Lydia, she and I spent lunchtime together at her place. Unfortunately, the stress of being discreet at work and the fear her Landlady might return at a crucial point in our tryst is too much for me. I will take a whole Viagra tomorrow and phone the doctor for another prescription. Lydia said she didn't mind my failure to stay hard; she likes oral sex. I think going from being a once or twice a week man to becoming a five and six times a week man is straining my libido. Is this what it means to grow old?

Lance had no hockey, soccer or homework tonight and we were all left without anything to do, except Alys. She scooted out for the evening. Gwen, who had homework, started on at me as soon as Alys left but after I'd pointed out that Nico couldn't possibly be available every time Alys goes out, she seemed somewhat pacified. Silky and I kept the couch warm; she dozed and I wrote this diary.

Tuesday 26:
Lydia and I sneaked off to her place again today and, thanks to the whole Viagra tablet, I was able to keep my end up in our lusty sexual gymnastics. If humans had sex every day, they wouldn't need gyms or diets. This thought, which came to me in the post-coital cool down period when I was lying with my head between Lydia's breasts, led me to another -- maybe this is how Alys keeps so thin?

Work is even quieter now. The only activity for the past weeks has been the organising of leaving parties for those fortunate enough to escape from the corporate madhouse in the VLB lottery. Our department's 'do' is tomorrow.

The evening was quiet too. Gwen was studying, Lance was at a friend's house doing homework and Alys was out keeping herself slim, says Gwen, though that isn't what she really said. Gwen got an acceptance letter from Western University today. She isn't even pleased because it's the out-of-province ones she's interested in.

Wednesday 27:
We had a leaving 'do' today for everyone leaving and I made a speech. So did Mr. Ogilvie. Then I handed out the cards and gifts to the lucky leavers. I was surprised how many of them went out of their way to thank Mr. Ogilvie for all his help to them. Can you believe it? Here they are going out the door and still they're sucking up to the boss's boss!

Lydia and I enjoyed another lunchtime romp where we acted out scenes from the Club. Somehow, I've got to get there again. Still, now Lydia is staying at work it isn't such a pressing problem.

I decided not to sign up for the hypnosis treatment. Eating something weird is better than having someone messing around with your mind. I'll sign up for Herbal Remedy instead.

I took Gwen to soccer practice and Lance to his soccer game because Alys was out. 'Shopping' she said. I hope she really is being unfaithful because that would be fair and I'd like Alys to feel as I do with Lydia at least once more in her life.

Thursday 28:
March came in like a lion and is leaving as one -- one with

toothache. Gerry, who has contemptuously ignored my oft-repeated Grandma's advice 'not to cast a clout 'til May is out', is rewarded by having his ears frozen off on our walk to the office. As my Gran lived in the north of England where they spent a millennium fighting the Scots, I wonder if the 'clout' is really clothes or that other northern meaning of a slap or punch; i.e. does the saying mean don't take off winter clothes till June, or don't attack the Scots till June? And is May the month or the blossom? I suppose it doesn't matter much either way -- now I live in Canada -- but this is the kind of intellectual problem I could have sorted out with Lydia before we took to being lovers. Lovers have other things to think about, like where shall we meet, when can we meet, and how can we keep it secret? Not that we did any of that today!

At the office, we had some bitter laughter at senior management's latest announcement. Today is the last day for hundreds of people who believed they were leaving to save the company's cash flow. They may have believed that yesterday but today we learn the company has just hired three more American-dollar Senior Executive-Vice-Presidents. Announcing these highly-paid-with-stock-options appointments is a particularly good joke that is appreciated by leavers and survivors alike. No doubt the deep cuts to the Public Relations department played a part in the timing of the release.

Along with the announcement of the new appointments came the announcement that the Transformation will not now be complete until June 30, the 'challenging' schedule turned out to be impossible as everyone but our leaders knew. The Transformation is almost six months late at this stage and running true to form.

After sampling a work colleague's herbal remedy breakfast shake, I decided to just eat less and I haven't signed up for the course. My new eating regime (I don't do diets, they're faddish and dangerous) starts tomorrow.

Friday 29:
Good Friday.
I woke with a nasty sore throat, ticklish ears and a stuffed up runny nose. Alys insists I visit the doctor and refuses to take 'all closed on Good Friday' as an answer. Go to Walk-in Clinic where I find the doctor has walked-out. Read interesting articles on Vikings, Ford Focuses, attic insulation, and what to put in your Retirement Savings

Plan this year. 'This year' was actually last year but I'm certain the advice is still good, though I'm a little unsure about the Enron shares. I don't take much notice of the business world, fiction isn't really my thing, but I'm certain I read somewhere they weren't doing well.

After the doctor assured me I don't have Asian flu, strep throat, consumption, cholera or anything other than a head cold, I decide to rest and let nature take its course. Lance wants to wrestle and Alys pulls him off. I thank her profusely; pleased she understands the needs of an invalid. However, she only needs me to help clean up for our guests tomorrow. Lance goes off to play Mephisto III on the computer and I am put to work. Final insult is when Mrs. Lakelady says, 'if you have enough energy to roughhouse with Lance, you've plenty to help me clear up the garden when you've finished in here.' I hope I'm never seriously ill in this house because I'd be found dead in my bed by a policeman investigating my disappearance, before this family recognised I was ill.

Gwen, who didn't need to study and didn't have any homework, went out and left the household chores to her parents. When I was a lad, we had to help. Kids nowadays are spoilt.

Delayed my new eating regime because this is a holiday and I'm too sick to starve myself at this time. Will start next Tuesday.

Saturday 30:
Easter Saturday.
I called home to see how Dad is doing. His lung infection isn't cured and he's on a new medication. The 'miserable so-and-so who has the gall to call himself a doctor' refuses to give Dad his original happy pills back because he says, the present ones are much safer. Aunt Hester has had her tracheotomy re-inserted and is back in intensive care. My sister-in-law, Joan, has the worst kind of Asian flu you can get. I decide not to mention my head cold.

On my way home, the radio informs me the Queen Mother has died. I'm saddened by the news because I have a brief connection to the Queen Mum. She taught me that, no matter what adults say, there is a point to the Royal Family.

A long time ago, when I was in elementary school, we were all marched out of class to the side of the Great North Road where we were to stand and wave as she went by. It felt like we stood all afternoon, kicking stones and waving to the non-regal traffic until a big, black car, with its royal pennants flying, drove sedately past and the Queen Mum waved at us. To this small boy, anything that missed you an afternoon of school was a 'good thing' and the Queen Mum was.

Sunday 31:

It is 5:30 in the evening and our guests have been and gone to get their daughter back to University. Considering how I was pulled from my sickbed to clean up for their arrival, I'm grieved. I doubt if they had time to notice my special efforts with the new vacuum cleaner around the back of the love seat where it was always hard to reach with the old one.

Without soccer, Gwen and Lance were forced to flee the house after the traditional Easter morning Lakelady Egg Hunt otherwise they might have been forced into vacuuming or dusting or setting the table. As it was, they avoided all that, arriving back only just in time for dinner.

April 2002:
Starts and ends with a fool

Monday 1:

Easter Monday and All Fools Day.

Lance and I did his Art and English homework. English is a book report on 'The Outsiders' (a sad bunch of juvenile delinquents who should be in prison). The Art report is on Henry Moore's life and requires us to complete a reproduction of one of his sculptures in a suitable medium. In our case, we've done 'Three Points' in papier-mâché and I learned that Lance is never going to be a sculptor. I'm not sure Lance learned anything.

Gwen was studying in her room, pausing only to eat the pile of chocolate eggs she found yesterday in the Egg Hunt. Being diligent, persistent, and hardworking, she finds twice as many eggs as Lance, who is none of those things.

Tuesday 2:

I return to work today thankful I've not had to take time off being ill. Maybe I'll get blanket this year.

It's a sad day with so many empty offices. However, the Senior Executive Vice-President of Facilities Improvement and Excellence Department said today they're going to make Senior Executive offices on our floor. I'm pleased because we'll have a chance to network with some senior executives and perhaps influence their input during the rest of the Transformation.

The new American executives started today, joining the others who've been 'helping' us change since we became a subsidiary. The good news is they fight among themselves like ravenous beasts, thus negating each other's efforts; the new ones will be no different. Hardly anything they start gets finished and the few things that are finished won't last their leaving, except the excessive bonuses paid out for easily manipulated performance figures; for some reason our remaining Canadian executives like those too.

With our US executives came a flock of carrion birds, aptly termed high-flyers. These self-employed consultants don't creep in the door like their lowly workaday colleagues. These parasites fly over the continent searching for their next victim. When they find a wounded corporation, they circle it emitting their raucous cries of 'EBITDA, EBITDA' before swooping down to plunge their heads and beaks right through the great gashes in the company's purse to slake their hunger on the raw cash inside. Then they fly away to build ever-bigger eyries in the Rockies. It isn't clear whether these creatures come from the Rockies or only head to the mountains when they're rich enough. If they'd left enough money for my salary, I could take a vacation down there and investigate.

Lydia was too busy organizing the new executives' arrival to come to lunch.

Alys took Gwen to her soccer game while I 'helped' Lance with his homework. With Gwen, the best way to help is to stay out of the way till she asks for assistance. With Lance, it's more a case of supervising his time. He finds it impossible to sit still for more than two minutes -- unless he's on Hotmail or playing a computer video game.

Wednesday 3:

There's now no doubt I was left until last because they had such faith in me. Everyone else passed the Security checks weeks ago but I finally heard today that I'm cleared. Gerry says they checked with the UK before deciding and added, sarcastically, "You know how long they take to do things over there." I don't believe that and take offence at his sneering at my heritage and me.

I saw Lydia today and admired her new clothes, very chic, very expensive, but exactly right for her new role with Mr. Ogilvie where she will be meeting all kinds of important people. At lunchtime, the chic new clothes came off even easier than her regular ones. Is this why senior executives have doors on their offices?

Another blizzard today, global warming has gone mad.

Couldn't start my new eating regime, we have too much food left over from the weekend and Alys won't let it go to waste. I protested that's exactly where it would go, to my waist, but Alys was adamant -- I can start eating less as soon as I've eaten more. Gwen and Lance are no help in things like this. They won't eat leftovers unless it's pizza, which they will happily consume cold for breakfast if the opportunity arises.

Alys took Gwen to soccer practice, much to Gwen's disgust because she was late picking Gwen up at the end of the practice. 'And,' Gwen said to me later, 'she looked all crumpled and dreamy when she arrived. You've got to do something, Dad, before Lance and I are abandoned.'

Thursday 4:
Global warming is temporarily delayed while we dig out from another storm.

My hopes of networking with senior management were dampened today. The Facilities people are erecting a wall across half the floor, after evicting the remaining 'ordinary' staff. It seems there will be an access-restricted door to the new offices. Still, we'll meet them in the elevators.

We have a new Premier in Ontario, a fellow who resigned from politics less than a year ago. After the old provincial premier had resigned, the governing party held an internal party selection where the 'party' rallied around to stab our local boy in the back. Now the new fellow just has to get back into the Provincial Parliament. There's a nastiness to democratic politics, with its shifting alliances and shifty dealing, which makes your average dictator look decent by comparison. What's worse, I no longer believe any of it gets us where we want to be. Like they used to say about television, people watch on the LOP principle; i.e. they watch the Least Offensive Program. That's what democracy does; it gives you the least offensive choice.

I began my new eating regime today by missing out toast at breakfast. This was not a good idea because I was so hungry by mid-morning I bought a muffin. Now I'm not only over my limit, but I'm also a dollar poorer.

Lydia's new clothes are even better for playing Naughty Boss and Secretary. They're so thin you hardly know they're there. Unfortunately, they became a bit crumpled and she had to change before we went back to work. Mr. Ogilvie noticed the change and Lydia made up a story to explain. We have to be more careful in future.

Friday 5:
Yesterday, I missed out dessert at my evening meal. A much better option, I thought until I had a slice of toast with peanut butter and

jam before bed, which led to terrible heartburn all night and no rest.

When I rose this morning, I found last night's April shower, the one drumming on the roof and windows so hard I couldn't sleep even when the heartburn let up, has cleared the snow. Global warming has finally arrived though it's late this year. The shower destroyed the crocuses; they're slimy smears on the grass. Snowdrops are still standing.

Missed out apple at lunchtime yesterday and this was successful!! I've cracked it. My weight problems have been that apple all along. It was a very successful day for my new eating regime.

Saturday 6:

I try to avoid the fantasy world of current affairs because, as my Grandma used to say, "The news is always the same, only the names change." Still, I bet even Gran never heard of a gay youth suing the local Catholic school system for not allowing him to take his boyfriend to the prom. Whatever the outcome, his place at law school is secured, as are the places for the two young women from Maine (I feel a Limerick coming on) who were recently found not guilty of indecently exposing themselves while jogging in the nude. They were not guilty because in Maine the law says 'displaying genitals' and women don't have visible external genitals, at least not while jogging. You have to go to become a gynaecologist or become very friendly with them before they show those. I think these cases are so new that they're worth recording here. Posterity can make what it likes of my report; its judgement will be as nutty as ours has been.

I was in a quandary today (re: eating regime) because I don't usually have an apple at lunchtime on the weekend. Missed out breakfast toast because I reasoned we get up later so there won't be time to get hungry before lunch. This proved to be the case and I'm now confident I've got my eating under control. Will power's all you need.

Called dad. He's a little better but Aunt Hester is still very ill in intensive care. I listened to a long list of gruesome symptoms till my own stomach revolted and I had to ring off. Dad called back a few minutes later to check on my health. I assured him I was quite well. He wasn't convinced and is talking of coming over to nurse me.

Today was the first round of Lance's hockey team in the 'A' final. We were up against it from the start. The run of good luck that got us to this point ran out over Easter and today they were their usual selves, incompetent and confused, only this time the opposing team didn't give us a chance. The game ended 6-0. Now our team's only hope is to win tomorrow and get into overtime where the first goal wins. I'm really disgusted with the team's supporters. Every game all winter, there's been just a handful of us watching, willing them to stop being themselves and win a game. Now it's the Finals and the place is packed with parents, grandparents, aunts and uncles, cousins and second cousins, are all out cheering the kids on. Where were these people on cold January nights? Home watching TV; that's where. Now I've personally willed the team into the 'A' Final and they're all here stealing my thunder!!

As Alys was with me throughout the evening, Gwen could only glower portentously at us when we returned because she had nothing to point to about her suspicions.

Sunday 7:

To celebrate my great start on the new eating regime and Alys's demand to go out somewhere, we went to the new Coffee Pub nearby. I had the Extreme Caffe Latte, the one with double sugar and double cream, and a Rocky Road cheesecake. Alys had Extreme Expresso and nibbled the edge of my cheesecake until I told her to get her own. At that, she turned sulky and we came home, so much for a romantic afternoon without the kids. We won't be spoon hugging again tonight and I've still got 4 Viagra tablets left.

Our nuclear power company has announced that the laid-up station won't be ready for Market Opening on May 1st -- what a surprise. It will be running this year, they say. Remembering that this station was not closed down because there was anything wrong with it, and it was laid-up ready for a quick return to service (they said), a year's delay on start-up isn't a good performance. At least, they are maintaining Canada's enviable record for excellence in comedy. Will we now have black- and brown- outs in Ontario? No, say the experts. Unfortunately, they're the same experts who are failing to re-start that laid up station.

When Gwen wasn't at work, she was with Alys at her indoor soccer for playoff games so no new suspicions were aroused. If the kids' soccer teams have a long run in the playoffs, all Gwen's suspicions may disappear. I hope so anyhow.

What can I say about Lance's hockey team? The team played just as badly today in the second leg of the final as they played yesterday in the first -- and won! So we went into overtime and nobody scored. We played 5 on 5 and nobody scored. We played 4 on 4 and nobody scored. We played 3 on 3 and nobody scored. We were now down to the weakest players on our bench and all hope gone. We played 2 on 2 and we scored. We are the 'A' Champions!! I wrestled Lance's trophy from him and put it on my bedside table. I deserve it, none of the players do.

Monday 8:
Nothing happened today; the Lakeladys are all too stunned by our hockey triumphs and Lydia is still helping out the new American interlopers.

Tuesday 9:
The TV was funereal today. Every channel carried the Royal Funeral, except for the news items where the Israelis and Palestinians are killing each other in record numbers -- record numbers for peacetime that is. Obviously, they do better in wartime.
My mood was funereal too, no Lydia to lighten the gloom.
Lance's school, along with many others in the region worked together to do the world's biggest Hokey-Pokey (or Hokey-Cokey, if you're from England) and think they made it to the Guinness Book of World Records. On balance, I prefer the kids getting a 'world record' to giving them an education. I'll be saved from paying another set of University fees and hence boost my retirement fund. It's too late to save Gwen; she's doomed to follow the treadmill her parents have trod. Lance and his contemporaries can live off the taxes she will be paying.

Wednesday 10:
Work continues not to happen and Lydia continues to support the new executives.
Tonight, with Ontario Academic Credit exams looming, Gwen's living in her bedroom took on a new dimension -- her lunch dishes and cutlery were left on the landing outside her bedroom door. I mentioned this to Alys, hoping she would have a woman-to-woman chat with Gwen, but Alys just said, 'Ontario Academic Credits' and then added, 'and the least you could do to help is pick up her dishes instead of leaving them lying around at the top of the stairs for

someone to trip over.' We won't be spoon-hugging in bed again tonight!

The cold, wet weather is taking the snowdrops to dizzy heights; i.e. they're still with us.

Gwen too busy studying for soccer practice while Lance had a soccer game. Enough said about that. Alys visited friends but Gwen no longer seems to care – results and university fill her mind now, to the exclusion of everything else.

Thursday 11:

The newspaper says scientists have shown that women whose partners are uncircumcised have a higher incidence of cervical cancer and this leads the scientists to suggest circumcision is a good thing because men don't wash adequately under their foreskins. Presumably, they would also advocate removing children's ears because they never wash behind them, or their fingernails because they don't clean under them. How about removing toes to prevent Athlete's Foot? Or removing brains to prevent meningitis -- and truly dumb research conclusions?

Like our nuclear power company, we too are going to miss the May 1st date 'we' set for Transformation. Already senior management's words are changing. Originally, 'they' were 'driving' business change to 'renewed excellence', now 'we' are missing 'our' dates. June 1st is the new date. The new executives quickly joined the chorus, exhorting us to greater efforts to achieve targets they have no understanding of. If I could see Lydia, I could ask her to give them an inkling of sense but instead, I nod approvingly with all the other managers who want to remain employed.

Friday 12:

Too busy preparing for the weekend to care what happened at work today and because we set off for Quebec immediately we were all home there was no opportunity for Gwen to doubt Alys or me to go to the Club.

Saturday 13: The Lakeladys have a skiing weekend at Mt. Tremblant in Quebec.

Sunday 14:

Cheap skiing is wet skiing because it's practically summer.

Normal service continues with Gwen saying this weekend of not studying right before her exams will crush her chances of good results and she'll end up at a second-rate university followed by a lifetime of unemployment, alcoholism, and drug addiction. I hope she isn't right about that because who will support my pension if not the Gwen's of this world?

Monday 15:
Last night's April showers were so violent we have dirt from the deck plant-stands all over the deck and a thick fog making the day dank and gloomy. Three snowdrops are still standing and four daffodils are almost out. If they'd seen any sun this past week, I think they might have been.

Our new Premier was sworn in today and from now until he leaves office, he'll be sworn at.

Gerry has been promoted. It was announced this morning and he was very smug about it on the train home because this makes him an 'executive', he's no longer a mere manager. I tell him to be careful; executives can be fired, not like us managerial professionals with our Association. He pooh-poohs my advice and is very caustic about the Employees Association. He says I'm just jealous and I agree. He says, condescendingly, I shouldn't be because steady people like myself are the backbone of any organisation. I can't help feeling he almost said donkey rather than backbone and that's how I feel most days, plodding dumbly to retirement or redundancy while others ride on my back waving loftily to the sullen crowds.

Tammy, my youngest, newest member of staff, is angry at Gerry's promotion. She says he demeans women. I tell her he doesn't discriminate; he's rude to everyone, not just women. At which point she says, "she might have guessed I'd side with him because he's a man and my buddy." She makes 'buddy' sound so suggestive it unnerves me. I try to reassure her but she storms off before I stammer out anything. What am I to do? I call Human Resources who tell me to follow the 'inappropriate language or behaviour' procedure. I do though I'm not sure which of the two has used the inappropriate language. I filled out the forms, in triplicate, and arranged a meeting with the protagonists. Although normally I'd hate all this man-woman, black-white stuff, (to me, a raised consciousness is just hypersensitivity combined with self-importance), in this case, some good has come of it. The

Inappropriate Language procedure is long, involved and needs revision, so I add it to the list of outstanding work my section has. I wonder if it would be very unwise to ask Tammy to update it?

I also wonder if I haven't been very unwise in confiding my doubts about my staff to Gerry these past months. He's now in a position to do them some serious damage and me with them.

Gwen's first exams were today and she says she did okay but would have done better if she'd had the weekend to study instead of being forced to slide down mountains in the pouring rain -- she doesn't like the cold. However, her indoor soccer team played the last of its playoff games and won, as usual. Somehow, playing in a nice warm indoors on the evening before exams doesn't lead to incipient alcoholism. And, as we were all together at the game, there were no dark thoughts to spoil my evening.

Tuesday 16:

Today, our Senior Chief Executive Officer and Head President decided to make an announcement about the future, stressing the need for us all to work harder and smarter. Considering he's just got rid of hundreds of our colleagues without reducing the workload, this seems a little obvious. What we wanted to hear was suggestions on how we might do that, without each of us losing our spouses -- or three spouses as he has. The tone of his address was vaguely menacing, dwelling on the dire consequences for individuals who fail to measure up to expectations (it's called accountability in the managerial world, when applied to subordinates, ass-licking by everyone else, particularly when applied to management) and for the corporation if we worker bees fail to carry out our management's clever plans successfully -- this time. Listening, I got a strong impression the failure of the last four re-organisations was somehow my fault, which might explain why we have to keep having these upheavals. I'm not doing something right.

Our first heart attack of this reorganisation followed in the afternoon. The last re-organisation produced three heart attacks, one fatal.

The new buzzword, brought by the new American SVPs is 'ladders' and we have to succeed 'rung by rung.' I keep the thought that, on the board game, every ladder comes with a snake (and it's head is always near the top) to myself. It doesn't do to be openly cynical in transition times.

Gerry flew out to the US last night on a training course. He's gone for a week so I have some quiet train rides to look forward to. Working over next weekend should take some of the gloss of his shiny executive smirk because he won't get overtime.

Global warming is back. Today set records for this part of the world, 25 C, and the heat wave looks set for another 3 days at least. Calgary got 25 cm of snow to maintain the balance.

Gwen's exams went okay today and she was too busy studying tonight to notice anything.

Wednesday 17:

I woke up this morning with one eye swollen and gummed shut. Could I have caught pinkeye from talking to Dad on the phone? Alys says, 'at least you'll have something to talk to your Dad about next Saturday.' I agree glumly because, if past history is anything to go by, Dad is sure to have something far worse wrong with him when I call. Sometimes I think he has our house bugged, he times his illnesses so well. Or is it another one of God's practical jokes? The doctor at the Walk-in clinic says I have conjunctivitis. I say terminal cancer and he laughs. He'll be sorry when I sue him from my deathbed. I take his drops anyhow. Who knows, they may work.

We had 25 C temperatures and a severe thunderstorm while I waited at the doctors. Up north at Haliburton, not so far away, they had 20 cm of snow. The sudden heat in our neighbourhood killed off our 3 remaining snowdrops and opened up about a dozen daffodils. Unless the temperature falls soon, they too will be gone by the weekend. The weather report says cooler tomorrow so, with luck, they'll be all right.

Gwen had exams ('okay, I guess') and studying all evening, of course, (I don't know why I keep repeating that), and Lance played soccer. Alys took him there and he says she was late picking him up afterwards. I'm glad Gwen is too busy now to notice.

Thursday 18:

When I began to write this journal, I realised early on I'd never remember everything that happened in a day unless I wrote it down while it was happening. One of the things this simple act has confirmed is a suspicion I'd long held about my evening subway train. It seemed to me that every evening when I got to the bottom of the escalator, the train I wanted was leaving the station. Keeping a diary confirmed this. I've tried leaving at different times to see if I can change the sequence of events, without any success. The train still leaves just as I arrive. Tonight, however, I found the workings of fate are much more sinister than even I'd suspected. Tonight I wasn't taking my usual southbound train and when I got to the platform, the southbound train was there, mockingly waiting for me. The lights of the northbound train, the one I wanted, could be seen disappearing into the tunnel. Is this why Mussolini and Hitler made the trains run on time and why Stalin executed all those Engineers? Is fate driving me to be the world's next mad tyrant?

The newspapers say 4 Canadians were killed when an American plane accidentally dropped a bomb on them. This was a repeat of an incident a year or so ago when some Aussies and New Zealanders were killed in an American bombing accident. I could have warned the Canadian Department of Defence before they sent people out to Afghanistan because my Uncle Albert was with the British 8th Army during the invasion of Italy in WW2 and he always said the Americans were more dangerous to their Allies than the enemy ever was.

Last night was so hot we slept under a sheet with the window open; it's too soon to start the air conditioner. Today is another hot day, 25 C. Our daffodils are drooping but the weather report says cooler tomorrow. I have my fingers crossed. My swollen eye continues and I continue to have high hopes for my talk with Dad on Saturday.

Friday 19:
Gwen's birthday.
Our heat wave continues. Overnight heavy thunderstorms and torrential rain kept me awake and battered our daffodils to the ground. No matter, today was 25 C again and they wouldn't have survived that anyway. People like to joke we should have left North America to the native peoples (the native peoples say it too but they aren't joking. Fortunately we didn't leave enough of them alive to be a problem. Palestine won't be repeated here, thank heaven). Still, I'm beginning to think the native people weren't as dumb as we conquistadors imagined. Beads and blankets for this land look like a fair deal some days.

A drug-dealing father and stepmother, the Dooleys, have been found guilty of battering his son to death over a period of months.

Unbelievably, they brought the boy from his Grandmother's care in Jamaica so he could be with his 'family.' The events should remind us of essential truth in the stories of Snow-white, Sleeping Beauty and their wicked stepmothers because, in this case, it was the stepmother who was primarily to blame. Tony Dooley is another small victim of our current willful refusal to understand the importance of the old rules. Like it or not, marriage is for at least the length of time it takes to raise children and the children are of the couple, not someone else. Our biology has primed us to that and we move away from it at the peril of our children.

Gwen left her bedroom today long enough to come out for dinner with her family on the occasion of her birthday. Now she's finished High School, her last exams were today, we might see more of her. Afterwards, Lance was at soccer practice with me and Alys was at home so no worrying suggestions about Alys from Gwen.

Saturday 20:
Dad isn't very well, nor is Gawain. Dad's got lumbago and Gawain's herniated disc needs surgery. Aunt Hester is in a coma and unlikely to survive. Uncle Jonas has a strep throat that is threatening to become meningitis. I didn't mention my swollen eye.

The daffodils died without regaining consciousness. It's a shame because the weather forecast finally came true; today is cooler.

I looked up what happened to Cassandra and I shouldn't have. Agamemnon took her to Greece as part of his booty and she was murdered, when he was, by his stay-at-home wife and her lover. This revelation gives me a worrisome feeling of doom.

Alys and I watched Lance play soccer while Gwen stayed in her room reading. We won't actually notice when she's gone to university.

Sunday 21:
On the way to soccer, Lance says he wants to work in the WWF. I say I'm pleased because I've always liked animals, and we have an intellectual discussion on the morality of abusing and displaying animals, wearing skins (leather and fur), masked faces, ritual grooming, dominance displays, and so on. This went quite well until I discover Lance is talking about the World Wrestling Federation and I'm talking about the World Wildlife Fund. Looking at the focus of the two organizations, I can see where the confusion arose.

Tonight Alys took Gwen to her soccer game. When they both returned, Gwen muttered to me out of her mother's hearing, 'she didn't stay to watch.' Maybe Gwen stays in her room to avoid this apparently continual worry?

Monday 22:
Global Warming continues to amaze
I didn't have to bury the daffodils because overnight we had a new carpet of clean, white snow, which was flying sideways in a howling gale as I walked to work. It was still snowing lightly when I came home.

I no longer work for Mr. Ogilvie, or won't soon. He has been given a new department in the Transformation and my section isn't in it. He will continue to 'cover' until my section is found a place on the org chart.

Speaking of Mr. Ogilvie reminds me of my meeting with Tammy today. I decided to meet her and Gerry separately first to get a picture of where each stands in the great 'he demeans women' controversy. Tammy seemed calmer on the subject -- until I asked her if she wanted me to speak to Mr. Ogilvie about her concerns. She grew agitated again and said, "Mr. Ogilvie leers at her and stares at her breasts". My heart sank. Now I have two investigations to carry out. My task wasn't made easier by her wearing one of her famous blouses that barely conceals anything. I think I'll get Lydia to speak to Tammy; that may help. We don't see Lydia much these days; she's so busy. Not only is she supporting Mr. Ogilvie, now she's helping out one of the new executives, a Mr. Schoeppenfrauen. She told me recently, she has to do most of Mr. S.'s work at night because Mr. Ogilvie is so jealous of her helping out that he doesn't give her anytime during the day. I sympathised because I know how difficult Mr. Ogilvie can be when he's not satisfied.

Today, the American Secretary of State for Defence, Rumsfeld, continued his foolish utterances by saying the American pilot who bombed the Canadian troops had 'every right to fire on them' when asked why the man dropped his bombs against clear orders not to. No one doubts that in wartime people will be killed accidentally but the hopeless language and body language of Bush and Rumsfeld has lost them many friends in Canada.

My eye is much better though still gummy. Did the drops do it or just time and my body's normal healing mechanism? My Grandma used to say 'a cold lasted 7 days if you took medicine and a week if you didn't' and I wonder about that. Do drug companies and doctors simply tell you to take their potions for the length of time your body needs to get better naturally?

Tuesday 23:
St. George's Day
Gerry has come back from his training course in the US. He says everything is expensive down there on account of the exchange rate. He feels we should use the US dollar then we won't have that problem. I point out our salaries would just be proportionately lower so shopping in the US would be equally as expensive as it is now. He grumped a bit then said, 'his friend Ryan had come back from the UK and everything there was horrendously expensive. It was a real rip-off.' At this new dig at my birthplace, and on this day of all days, I snapped and said, "Finding everywhere expensive is Capitalism's way of telling you you're poor," which I thought a pretty good riposte for me. He looked angry and we changed the subject. I think the Transformation may not be so bad if it sends us in different directions.

Didn't see Lydia so no help on the Tammy front, if you'll pardon the pun.

I rarely watch TV but tonight we're between winter and summer sports seasons so I did, just for research. Posterity requires me to report on 'entertainment' in the early 21st Century. Here goes. Reality shows are all the rage, as they have been since the quiz show fad faded about a year ago. People remain fascinated by muddy sadomasochists treacherously doing each other down for cash. As I watch one bunch of slimy rats plotting to oust someone who was their 'friend' an episode ago, I'm struck by the thought that the reason people like this sad stuff is because it's how they behave every day, especially at work. And that's why I'm always at risk in every re-organisation or upheaval. I'm not in the golfing gang, the curling clique, the scuba diving sect (yes, really), or the smoking corner. Smoking is my best hope. For one thing, I can do it (the others are iffy) and for another, all the experts and zealots say smoking is dangerous so I feel I'd be pretty safe taking it up. It's an axiom of modern life that, if everyone (particularly experts) says something is so, it isn't -- the exact opposite is true.

We had a hard frost overnight that caught our clump of tulips just coming out at the end of the path near the garage doors. They weren't out, only their leaves and unopened heads were in evidence, and now most of them are lying flat on the ground.

Gwen still in her bedroom and yet somehow able to know her Mom is misbehaving. Alys went shopping this afternoon and wasn't home when the kids got back from school, though why Gwen still needs to go to school when everything is finished, I don't know.

Wednesday,
April 24: Our Anniversary
Early in the 1990's, across the English-speaking world, we had real old-fashioned witch-hunts where children accused their daycare workers and parents of being witches. We watched as the full majesty of the law ground the unfortunate victims into pulp before the whole thing was recognised for what it was, bunches of over-imaginative children and manipulative, self-serving investigators acting out petty jealousies. It took me a while to realise I'd stood by watching throughout it all doing and saying nothing, thinking no doubt that the means justified the end (preventing child abuse). My inertia was probably the same as those of 17th Century folks who stood by while their fellow citizens were hanged or burned. I will never join a witch-hunt or a crusade because they're one and the same thing; it's just a question of whether you approve of the quarry or not. My disgust has returned, redoubled, with recent events where the Afghans have become responsible for all the world's ills and are hunted to their deaths, despite the carnage everywhere else. A non-Afghan bomb exploded in Madrid yesterday, which didn't make it onto the front page of any North American newspaper.

American sports fans have taken to booing the Canadian National Anthem at sports events, no doubt they blame our soldiers for being in the way of their misguided missiles.

Today is the Anniversary of the Lakeladys' marriage and we celebrated in true Lakelady style -- quietly. It will probably become an international day of celebration after this diary's publication so I'm asking you all now to keep it dignified, no street parties or marches with bands and floats. That isn't the Lakelady way.

Still no sign of Lydia so no help on the Tammy front.

Tonight on the subway I saw an advertisement for 'Practical Philosophy' and I shook my head in disbelief. Is nothing to be left 'unimproved'? Surely the point about philosophy is that it isn't practical, it's impractical and, therefore, the basis of almost every war since time began. This improvement, if it catches on, and the recent demands for compensation for victims could put an end to war and then where would we be? Getting rid of the philosophy and the United Nations, that other well-meaning (I think?) source of armed conflict could end the modern strife. Without the UN, for example, there'd be no Israel and no continual Middle East crisis.

Back to spring-like temperatures and the tulips are reviving. I have hopes of getting a decent show from them -- we sometimes do.

Gwen and Lance are now at outdoor soccer practice as their respective teams gear up for the coming season, which means more worry for me because Alys used to take Gwen to her practice but Gwen now can drive herself. I took Lance to his practice, which left Alys at home to do what?

Thursday 25:
Today a corporate auditor interviewed me on our departmental role and I was surprised to learn the auditor didn't understand the importance of the work we do. I told him straight, without our procedures, no one in the corporation could work because they wouldn't know what to do or how to do it. As I don't have Mr. Ogilvie to stand between these folks and me now, I had the pleasure of enlightening him. I think he understood.

Lydia appears to be lost.

Israel's leader, Mr. Sharon, has decided not to let the UN investigate the actions of the Israeli Army at Jenin because some of the investigators may be prejudiced against Israel. The Israeli government's prevarication has pretty well declared them and their army as guilty.

It's sad that 2,000 years of persecution, and the knowledge that their persecutors rarely ended happily, didn't teach the Jewish people anything. If at the start of their new State, they could have come to an accommodation with the area's original inhabitants, it might have endured. As it is, I can't see it lasting much longer than the Crusader State it so resembles. When the West is eclipsed, Israel will be destroyed and all for the want of a little understanding.

Friday 26:
It was snowing hard when we got up and a slushy layer of the stuff is lying across the garden. How tough are tulips?

The Transformation is almost complete for now -- but I'm sure the re-engineering process will go on to doomsday; these days the tacky souvenirs last longer than the organisations they're supposed to promote. I still have the mugs and baseball caps from the first two re-organisations.

Gerry visited my office and was telling me in a loud voice, which I couldn't repress, how useless our present management team is when Mr. Ogilvie walked in. I tried to laugh it off as a joke but Gerry persisted because he's no longer happy with the promotion he got. He wanted a more prestigious post but today it went to a rival, an undeserving rival according to Gerry. I tried to soften his wildest ranting but I could tell Mr. Ogilvie wasn't pleased. I feared I was making things worse, and even worse, was beginning to sound like I agreed with Gerry as I tried to soothe him. When Gerry finally took himself off, I distanced myself from his views very forcefully and think I persuaded Mr. Ogilvie of my loyalty. It's all right for Gerry; like most others, he's got a new job. I'm still waiting to hear where I might be. My small group, there are only three left, and I continue working without knowing if we're part of the organisation or not. We're supposed to report to a new manager but the position hasn't been filled. Miguel, my most senior procedure writer, says I'm bound to get the job but I know I won't. I would have had a call by now if it were mine.

Speaking of senior management, Mr. Schoeppenfrauen is going home and I'm dumbfounded to hear Lydia is going with him as his personal assistant. She must have made quite an impression. I obviously have a talent for picking staff.

Hearing that Lydia was leaving us, I zipped along to her office to ask if she'd talk to Tammy for me. I've been putting this off because I don't like passing the Security Guards who frisk you at the entrance to our leaders' bunker. Lydia invited me up to the 35th floor and got me past the Imperial Guards without too much fuss. We had a long reminisce about the good old days before I spoiled everything by bringing Tammy into the conversation.

It seems Tammy has been a nuisance in every department she's worked since we hired her and she's been moved on after every incident. Lydia says she's just looking to screw money out of the company with a settlement for some contrived sexism case. I sarcastically said, "Well, thanks for putting her in my section. I really need a money-grubbing opportunist trying to get me too. I suppose you folks at the top of the tree considered the possibility she could be a genuinely demure maiden?"

"We put her in your section because yours were the safest hands we knew." Lydia said after a moment, "and we did think she might be genuine at first, some kind of religious upbringing, perhaps, one that teaches girls to wear skimpy, see-through clothes and then accuse men of staring at them. In the end, we decided she's just an ordinary mischief-making feminist weirdo, the sort who plays politics everywhere they go."

Knowing the company trusted me with this sensitive role (though not enough to tell me I was on a suicide mission) made me quite proud at the time Lydia spoke but now I wonder if it wasn't a way of getting rid of me as well as Tammy. However, what all this really means is Lydia will not help with my Tammy problem. She did, however, say I must get my section on the anti-harassment training course the Company offers. It doesn't stop harassment or complaints but it does keep away the lawyers; it's like garlic is to vampires.

I told Gerry on the train he should be more careful when talking to Mr. Ogilvie and he says I'm too timid. Directors, like him and Mr. Ogilvie, are always joshing and arguing. That's how they get things done. He may have a point. His booming voice and wild opinions on everything have got him a promotion to the Executive ranks while I languish, un-regarded, down among the mere professionals.

However, my own training in the US suggests he should be more careful. They have a cavalier attitude to employment that is alien to our culture. In the 'land of the free and the home of the brave' they expect military-style obedience to the boss and treat dissent as disloyal. The concept of a 'loyal opposition' isn't something they're familiar with. You'd imagine that being so proud of their dissenting past would engender a culture that thrived on listening to other viewpoints. But the only reason those dissenters, the Pilgrim Fathers and the rest, left their countries is because at home they weren't in charge of the oppressing. It's true Americans 'encourage' discussion, in fact, they're as likely to fire you for being a 'yes' man as they are for not being a team player. But they're suspicious of people who hold contrary views after the boss has spoken and they act with their normal Wild West shoot-first ask questions later mentality. The quickest way to 'freedom' down there is to be brave.

I was particularly struck by a dilemma posed during our training course by one of our American colleagues. He wanted to know how he could save one of his best workers in the next annual 'cull' when the worker persisted in not wearing the company shirt on the (voluntary) 'Company Shirt Day'. Nor would he wear a Hawaiian shirt on the (voluntary) 'Hawaiian Shirt Day' or take part in the (voluntary) after-hours public speaking training the company provided. This supervisor was advised by his American counterparts to give up; the worker was obviously doomed by his lack of corporate team spirit and the supervisor would only fall under suspicion himself if he persisted in trying to save him. McCarthyism, Stalinism and Maoism haven't died; they just went into American business.

I took Lance to soccer tonight, the team looks pretty good and we should have a successful season I think. My happiness lasted until I got home and found that Alys had been out having coffee with friends, she says. Gwen suggested I get a lawyer.

Saturday 27:
Spring in this part of Ontario brings sobering surprises when you see what your local council and their friends, the developers, have been up to during the long dark winter days. Lanes that were unpaved last fall are now four-lane highways and fields that enclosed cows or horses munching the autumn grass now sprout a thousand densely packed homes, in estates called Kingsmead Hollow, or Queen's Walk. Cynics may sneer at the Monarchy but those who understand what drives people (like advertisers and marketing types) know that Royalty strikes a chord in humans that plodding logic can't erase.

After witnessing the devastation progress is having on this once green and pleasant countryside, I returned from dropping Lance at his soccer team's practice in a sombre mood. My drive home reminded me of the scene from 'Lord of The Rings' where Frodo returns to Bag End to find the Goblins and their human counterparts have taken over. Tolkien knew what he was talking about; humans are three parts Goblin and one part Troll.

On a more positive note, even without their star and captain, the Maple Leafs won game 5 of their seven-game playoff series against the New York Islanders. (Why do they stop at seven? Why not 9, or 11? Why stop at all?) The celebrations from a house directly across the park behind us, quarter a mile away from our bedroom, kept us 'entertained' till 2 a.m.

The daytime weather is cool and sunny, which brought our Forsythia into flower. This is its best year ever; I've never seen such a profusion of golden flowers. The tulips are upright again, their brewer's droop gone. It's a wonderful spring show. I wish human sex were as clean and pretty! I've seen films, from the Fifties, when it looked like it might be. The Fifties were the peak of human development, since then it has been a steady slide back into primeval slime.

Called dad. He and Gawain are a little better, though still not well enough to go out and pick up new video cassettes. From the conversation, I got the distinct impression a sensitive and caring son and brother would fly over and get some movies for them. Also, Aunt Hester is out of intensive care and Uncle Jonas is better. Miraculously, despite the alleged incompetence of the medical system over there, his strep throat became a sore throat and not meningitis.

We had a family meal out tonight to celebrate the end of school and Gwen's accession to university-hood. She hasn't got her results yet, of course, and she says we should hold off celebrating because being forced to stand out on a mountain in the freezing rain will have certainly spoiled everything. Even this pessimistic pronouncement doesn't faze me because being all together meant there were no disturbing thoughts mentioned.

Sunday 28:
The weather report said we could expect 30mm of rain and strong winds overnight. Forecasters like to err on the bright side. Howling wind buffeted the house and battered the tulips, which don't get much shelter where they grow and they were just on the point of opening. This morning they are still on their feet, but groggy; in boxing, it's called a Technical Knock Out. The weather stayed much the same during the day, flattening the weaker flowers and scattering thousands of Forsythia blossoms across the lawn. The bush is almost bare, much like other years. The few remaining blossoms hang from the branches like a small child's snot.

I've decided not to continue with the Public Speaking course because I've discovered my problem isn't the speaking in public, it's the fear of being attacked by the listeners. My writing will be my testimony and influence the future more successfully than my speaking ever could. Perhaps I should do a writing course next year instead?

Monday 29:
Despite my Grandma's weather-wise advice, I have decided to change to my spring jacket. This was okay for the walk up from the station and not so good when I discovered I'd forgotten my building access card, my desk keys and my subway tokens for the ride back down. This was also the day I discovered we don't have a spare key for my desk. Transitions, it seems, are tough to manage, even simple ones like winter to spring jackets.

I signed my section up for anti-harassment training today through a grim, battle-axe of a woman whose expression made clear she understood why perverts like my section and me should be on such training. I think the main reason North Americans have such a problem with this is they pronounce 'harass' as though they were talking about a certain part of a woman's body. It gets them all excited and they can't stop thinking or talking about it.

The newspapers are full of eminent people suggesting we use the US dollar as currency instead of our own. This has become a popular topic since the Europeans adopted the Euro. Listening to the pro-US dollar and pro-Euro camps, I'm once again struck by how exactly Tolkien described his treacherous advisor, Wormtongue. The same honeyed words of defeat and despair drip from their tongues, urging us all to imagine the other side as all-powerful, and always will be, and our only hope is to become their puppets. Like all such advisors, they ignore history and its constant cycles. Up today will be down tomorrow, like Japan. In the Eighties, we were all 'turning Japanese.' Today, Japan is a stagnant economy in permanent recession and has been for the past decade. Nothing succeeds forever, not even Germany or the USA. Jane Austen's Mr. Darcy said, 'there is a meanness to all the arts women use to allure men.' It's nothing to the arts politicians (amateur and professional) use; their arts are truly disgusting and I think our present crop of so-called leaders in the English-speaking world must be the creepy-crawliest ever.

Went to the gym to continue the brilliant strategy. The abs machine was in use so I decided to get a mat and do sit-ups instead. I did thirty before I had to stop, my head was spinning and my stomach was twitching like crazy. It could have been the abs beginning to ripple but it felt more like a cramp. As I lay recovering, a reddish haze came across my eyes and it seemed to me there was a bright light far away; someone was calling me to it. I may be overdoing this gym thing.

Discussed the 'demeans women' incident with Tammy and she is incensed I've done nothing about it. She says I'm encouraging a 'poisoned work atmosphere' and she can get me for that. I mollified her by saying I'd been gathering evidence. It would be truer to say I'd been gathering my thoughts but as the few I've gathered aren't kind it's best I don't mention them.

I met Gerry next and he said the whole thing was garbage. Plain speaking is his hallmark and it's what we need more of nowadays, not less. I suggested it was possible to speak plainly without being unpleasant about people. He said, "Not in this company it isn't." And so it went on for another half-hour. Bringing Tammy and Gerry together will not help matters. They are both so keen on 'honest' speaking it will end in a fight. I tried to see Mr. Ogilvie about my dilemma but made the mistake of telling his temporary Secretary, Dianna, what it was about. Now he's fully booked until the day after I retire.

The Lakelady family, mother and children anyhow, were home alone all day today so they could watch each other in mutual suspicion and not disturb me with their fears. Or so I thought until Gwen told me in significant tones that 'her mother went shopping.' I suggested that, as Gwen didn't need to study now, she could go shopping with her mother and that would allay her fears. She shut her bedroom door too sharply -- but I expect I'll be able to fix it when she goes to university.

Tuesday 30:
Gran was right; I shouldn't have cast my clout. Today I walked up to work in cold rain, then the day brightened, only to end with flurries and overnight frost. Our gallant troop of tulips is still struggling on, despite overwhelming odds.

Work is tedious because Mr. Ogilvie has his new job and he's waiting to hear what is to become of my section and me. He no longer asks for updates etc. I'm in org chart limbo, or is it purgatory? Being a non-practising Protestant, I'm not clear which it is. I got to the gym again. In fact getting to the gym is easier now Mr. Ogilvie doesn't care what I do.

Talked to Tammy again, informally, this time, updating her on my 'progress' to date. She was very sarcastic, suggesting I was part of the 'glass ceiling' keeping her locked at her junior level. With her degree and talents, she should have made Director by now, she feels. As she is only 23 and has been here less than a year, this seems unlikely to me but I didn't say so. We 'glass ceilings' are unresponsive anyway.

The Lakelady children are in mourning; Manchester Utd is out of the Champions League after two ties with Bayer Leverkuesen of Germany. I'm happy enough, 'my' soccer team back home, Blackburn Rovers, have managed to stay in the Premier League and they are in Europe next year. This is heady stuff for us Rovers fans. Last time we were in Europe, our team fought fiercely to uphold their honour -- but not with the opposition. Blackburn Rovers is probably the only team ever to literally knock themselves out of a tournament.

This evening, I got a nail in my car's tire, too late in the day for any shop to fix it. I was lucky enough to find a WallyMart Tire service place. I know from their advertising they 'go that extra mile for their customers' so it was a shock to be told they closed in 30 minutes and, as the repair would take 45 minutes, they wouldn't do it. I was left out in the cold to put on the 'doughnut' spare and limp home. Yet another reason to dislike developers, as I'm sure the nail fell off the back of one of their trucks.

May 2002:
May blossom – yet

Wednesday 1:

The Ontario electrical energy market opened today for everyone to enjoy. It has been de-regulated so any rich person or corporation can provide electricity to us Ontarians. Marketers selling various kinds of schemes for providing us with electricity have approached the Lakeladys but we haven't succumbed to any. I wish I could say it was on principle. Unfortunately, it's because we got burned in the gas deregulation and don't want to repeat the experience -- once burned, twice shy. Recently, a Judge ruled that, while the government 'owns' the province's electrical grid, it doesn't have the right to sell it, so the Provincial Government is working overtime to change the law. Needless to say, the shutdown station that 'had' to be running by today isn't. It will be ready for the air-conditioning season in July and August, says the power corporation.

Today's really sickening blow is that Lydia has gone to the US with Mr. S. and she didn't even say goodbye. I'm pleased with her success but her promotion and move is disastrous for me. Who will I talk to about history now?

Heavy frost overnight leaves our tulips still standing and still not out.

Whenever the Lakeladys go on holiday (which isn't as often as it should be) the locals at whatever spot we've chosen to visit say, 'you should have been here last week. The weather was great.' That luck continues with the news today that the Canadian book industry is in serious trouble; General and Stoddart are going into bankruptcy protection. I didn't really have a lot of hope for my diary but the little I had has faded more than just a tad. That Supreme Deity is having one of its jokes again. Considering all the serious problems of the world, teasing Arthur Lakelady appears childish. Or is it the pagans had the right idea? Rather than one omnipotent God, are there lots of little malicious spirits that go around hexing cattle, curdling milk, and being a nuisance to me?

The Maple Leafs won the last game of their first playoff round last night. Celebrations are muted, partly because getting through is an anti-climax compared to the effort needed on the fans part to get them through. The other reason is they haven't a fit player left and the first game of the second round of seven is tomorrow night.

The Blue Jays, Toronto's baseball team, are not having a good pre-season say the newspapers. Baseball hasn't had a good season since the players went on strike for more money a few years back. The spectacle of millionaires' striking for better wages turned people off and attendance has been low at games ever since. Last year was better than previous so commentators think the game has turned the corner. I don't care. If grown men want to play children's games in their pyjamas, I say they should do it in private. I'm not encouraging that kind of behaviour.

When I got home, Alys said she would go out for some grocery items she'd forgotten on her expedition earlier today. Gwen glared at me as I said 'sure, no problem'. Once Alys was gone, Gwen pointed out there was no sense in her keeping tabs on her mom by day if I was going to let her wander off alone by night! And, she added darkly, did I think Alys was appropriately dressed for shopping? As I hadn't noticed what Alys was wearing, I couldn't adequately answer so Gwen flounced back to her bedroom. I may have to repair the bedroom door before university starts.

Thursday 2:

I read today the British and Spanish governments are negotiating the future of Gibraltar. Spain wants it back and will probably get it because modern British leaders have an underlying and erroneous sense of guilt that makes them spineless, Margaret Thatcher being the only exception. She wasn't just the only man in the government; she was the last one in that benighted country. Lots of places have similar Gibraltar-like oddities. France, for instance, continues holding two small islands off Newfoundland (St. Pierre and Miquelon) without anyone feeling the need to correct this awful historical 'wrong.' Spain itself holds a similarly Gibraltar-sized piece of North Africa called Ceuta without anyone, least of all the Spanish, thinking it wicked.

I feel sorry for Britons as a whole, not just the Gibraltarian ones who're about to be sacrificed. Revisionist, politically motivated historians, are rewriting and denigrating Britain's past and American filmmakers are stealing any remaining glory by dubbing Americans as the heroes into past British events. The rapacious Europeans won't leave Britons a vestige of their culture, having already stolen Britain's future through a series of one-sided treaties. John Major, the last Prime Minister (or should that be Ministraitor), came back from Maastricht, his Munich, and said Britons would be allowed to keep cricket, warm beer, and hedgerows – and that's all. He didn't get it in writing but it wouldn't have made a difference if he had. The Europeans reneged on the written guarantees he did get within days of him signing the deal and he hadn't the balls to renege on what he'd given away. Britain's present is just a transition from a soon-to-be footnote in history to final oblivion, and all this in a country whose armed forces are strong enough to stand up to any external aggression. Armed forces, however, aren't a match for leaders whose eyes are set on the honours to be had from handing over their fellow citizens for ritual humiliation by their neighbours. Americans are badly led, in my opinion, but at least, they are proud people with a belief in themselves and their country. Reading the British press, with its personal and national self-abasement, is like peering into a jar of slithery worms.

Torrential rain and gusty winds overnight have battered the tulips. They still aren't out and I for one don't blame them. If I'd had my way I wouldn't have been out today either.

Bought lottery tickets for the first time in more than a decade because the jackpot is now over twenty million dollars. It's worth investing two dollars for a chance to get that. Not that buying a ticket increases my chances by much; the odds are so great (1 in 21 million), that they're almost the same as your chance if you don't buy a ticket.

Our new Provincial Premier has turned 180 degrees on selling the provincial electricity grid. Last week he said it would be sold by summer, and then it was lease by summer maybe, now the whole thing is 'off the table'.

I can't help noticing that now Lydia is gone, Alys isn't so cuddly any more. Spoon hugging has once again become a thing of the past now the competition is safely down in the States or am I just getting caught up in Gwen's forebodings? Would telling Alys I'm becoming friendly with another female colleague help?

Friday 3:

Our fearless new Premier has today settled with the public service union, which has been on strike for about six weeks. I can't help thinking that either Ontario's left-wing party, the NDP, has been infiltrating the winning Progressive Conservative Party (it would be easier for the NDP than winning another election in Ontario), or we're on the way to another election. Next week I predict the Premier announces more money for Health Care and a tax increase!

Tammy has handed in her resignation!! And before I'd done anything about Gerry or Mr. Ogilvie!! She said, in her letter, it was because we are a bunch of sexist fascists who hate women. However, as everyone knew within minutes of her telling her buddy Dianna, it's because she's going to Europe with her boyfriend who is a professional ice hockey player. She isn't planning to work over there because she doesn't speak German. She's going to keep his house and bed warm for him.

When we men finally do roll up our tents and wander off into the sunset, we'll have a host of female camp followers trudging alongside moaning about the way we treat them and another host of females left behind moaning about how we're never about when we're wanted. The three constants in the life of men since time began are death, taxes, and women whinging about us.

On the way home, 'our train hit a pedestrian' as the announcement said. What the guard meant was somebody jumped in front of it. I would have thought a wet Monday morning in November was the time to go, rather than a sunny Friday in May. As it was, the suicidee got to go and we didn't. It took four hours to get home. Watching and listening to my fellow passengers as their horrified sympathy turned to frustrated anger was a sobering lesson in human psychology. Had the man not been killed, most of the passengers would have happily killed him.

The weather was cold and sunny so our tulips are looking good for the weekend.

Saturday 4:

May the Fourth: be with you.

If George Lucas, the film producer, is as smart as everybody says why didn't he release the fifth instalment of Star Wars, his re-enactment of the American War of Independence in a 'galaxy long ago and far away', today? How could he miss such an opportunity?

If things don't go well for me in our Transformation, I'll go out and get a job in product promotion; I've got an eye and ear for these things!

Today is the first day of Lance's soccer team's first tournament of the season. The rain poured down all day and I watched the games from the car. At first, I sat in the back with the rear door up. Then, when it got too cold even for that, I sat in the front with the engine running and watched through the flip-flopping wipers. It brought back memories of last year at this tournament when the whole Lakelady family huddled in the back of the wagon beneath one blanket. I wish I'd brought the blanket this year. I suspect Alys took it to Gwen's tournament. Lance and I spent a soggy night in the hotel. Lance in the pool with his teammates and me in the bar with the other dads, watching the Maple Leafs win the second game, this time after double overtime. The series with the Ottawa Senators is now 1-1, the Maple Leafs having lost the first game on Thursday.

Couldn't call Dad because we are away – it's a relief not to hear what's ailing them both if I'm honest.

Sunday 5:
The weather continues spring-like; i.e. the grey clouds continued pouring down a solid grey wall of icy rain and sleet. When we got home I found I was right, Alys did have the blanket. She and Gwen sat on it for their lunchtime picnic. The weather was beautiful, said Alys.

Lance's team lost in the tournament semi-finals, which was still a good start to the season. Winning would have been better but we're up there.

The tulips enjoyed the same weather I'd seen and they look further away from coming out than they did a week ago.

Britain's Foreign Secretary, Jack Straw, told Gibraltarians who were booing him on his visit to their until now safe home, that no deal was better than a bad deal. Somebody should have told him no deal is better than any deal; there's nothing to discuss. Look out Channel Islanders; you're next in this dismemberment of a great country.

Monday 6:
As I'm still being undirected at work, I went to the gym again and spent more time observing my fellow sufferers. You can learn a lot

about people in the gym. For example, I've always thought the human race crazy for putting clothes on to go swimming but in the gym, I find that there are people who put clothes on to shower.

Other observations from the gym are, a woman who arrives every day in a skirt that's shorter than the tee shirt she exercises in (and it isn't long) and a young man who, before beginning his exercises, turns on or up the gym radio then puts on his own headphones and Walkman. Presumably he wants to hear the radio above the noise of his CD.

When I left for work this morning, I noticed colour on the tulip flowers and, as today was as warm as the weather report claimed, I expected them to be out when I got home. Possibly they would have been. Unfortunately, the fine sunny day encouraged Lance and his friends to play basketball at the hoop above our garage doors. Lance assures me they were careful but a stray bouncing ball (and, from the footprints, some stray bounding feet) crushed the tulips before I saw them. There goes the last of our spring flowers. The good news is the periwinkle at the side of the house, quiet and unnoticed, like me, is in full bloom and has been for days.

I finally checked my lottery ticket and I've won a free ticket. Good old Beginner's Luck. It reminds me of when Lance was very young and he wanted to play slot machines at the seaside. Alys and I cautioned him against it, warning him he would lose all his holiday money. He played anyway and won a small amount. Since then, because he's convinced he is lucky, he has played slot machines and lost. Beginner's luck is Dame Fortune's way of suckering in new recruits. I won't buy any more tickets; I'm done with dreams of avarice.

Yesterday, the French people voted overwhelmingly for the 'conservative' presidential candidate, Chirac, even though he's been deluged with allegations of receiving bribes, etc. They did this in order to stop the 'far right' candidate, Le Pen, from winning. Mr. Le Pen's failing is he doesn't accept immigration or crime, both of which everyone else wants to accept, apparently. Mr. Chirac, the winner, has said he has listened to the people and will be tough on immigration and crime. I don't feel any comment from me can explain the democratic system.

Tuesday 7:
The USA didn't ratify the International Criminal Court yesterday

and all the rest of the civilised world did. The Americans' concern is for their soldiers who will be at risk during international duties. This is a poor argument with which to defend a good decision. This court, like so many of our modern laws and kangaroo tribunals, is just another way for special interest groups to undermine national security. Call me cynical but you can be sure the only people tried in this court will be those on the 'right' of the political landscape.

Speaking of the right, the leader of the 'far right' in Holland was murdered yesterday. Fortuyn was a strange populist in that he was gay. Most vocal gay people come from the 'left' of the spectrum. British newspapers report that 'far right' candidates have won seats on the council in Barnsley, UK. I've no doubt Britain's Labour Party will announce a new crime prevention policy and tougher immigration laws to ensure the 'right' doesn't grow much further. Ordinary people will soon become so frustrated at the mainstream parties' unwillingness to act on anything but their own interests, that the eventual backlash will be more severe than it need have been. All that's required to keep extremists out of power is for politicians to work on the behalf of the people who elected them and not for some other cause, however noble and grand they may imagine it to be.

We will no longer be confused between the WWF and the WWF. The cute animals won against the un-cute ones and the wrestlers are changing their name to the WWE. The cheering sight of 300-lb men in their undies being bested by a small furry marsupial makes today worthwhile.

We received an e-mail today announcing Lydia as the new Director of Administrative and Recordkeeping Excellence Services down in Head Office, USA. It seems the outgoing Director, a young American woman, had a falling-out with Mr. Schoeppenfrauen so the rumour goes. I think I have quite a talent for hiring; no one else has risen through the ranks as quickly as Lydia.

Senators won game three so the series is now 2-1 against the Leafs.

With Gwen at work, while she awaits final results and university acceptances, I'm spared her concerns regarding her mother. This reprieve is another reason why people must always be busy doing something; our brains simply can't cope with time to think. I took Lance to soccer practice while Alys went out with friends, which I think is sensible because our kids will soon be gone and she will need a social life of her own instead of theirs.

Wednesday 8:

Nothing happened today so the papers are once again full of interesting and meaningless statistics. Here are some examples:

The average life expectancy of Canadian men is slowly closing in on Canadian women. Many Americans think Canada is a state (thanks to the wimpy Canadian education system and the effect of American TV beamed right into our homes, most Canadian children think the same), and reported child abuse cases have increased in Ontario since the law was changed to make reporting mandatory – what a surprise.

At the gym, I discovered the young woman who arrives in the skirt shorter than her gym clothes is called Cassie and works in a department we are re-writing a procedure for. In fact, she's the person Padraig has to liaise with; she's our 'customer' in modern management-speak. She and I had a good chat about work and procedures while pedalling sedately side-by-side on exercise bikes. Cassie seems a sensible woman and I don't understand why Padraig keeps telling me she isn't supporting his re-write of the Stationery Supplies Inventory Management procedure. Maybe I should take a more active role in that procedure's progress. Maybe this is my opportunity to re-ignite Alys's interest?

Speaking of the Irish, Sinn Fein has declined an invitation to speak to the House of Representatives committee looking at the links between the Irish Republican Army (IRA) and the Colombian terrorist group FARC. They weren't so coy a few years ago when their leader dined at the White House with President Clinton. Is it too much to hope a connection between the IRA, FARC, the Taliban and Al Qaeda will be found?

The Maple Leafs won game four so the series is now 2-2. Why not best of five?

Gwen is still working diligently so her university fund must be growing nicely for she rarely spends any of her earnings. Gwen has the first dollar she made, Lance, on the other hand, has already spent the next ones he might earn. After work, I took Gwen to soccer practice while Alys and Lance stayed home -- I think.

Thursday 9:

Today's news is that levels of obesity and fitness are rising in Canada. More people are overweight and more people are exercising. This confirms my own case, I haven't been so fit since I was eighteen and yet my weight is leaving the 'green' area of the Body Mass Index and entering the 'yellow' part on its way to 'red'. Here in Canada, everyone perpetually walks and talks sports, while the number of obese people grows daily and organisations that require fitness in their members, like the Army, are forced to lower their standards to get recruits. Obviously, sport is dangerous and unhealthy.

I suggested to Padraig that, now we'd lost all our Assistants, I could help him with the Stationery Supplies Inventory Management procedure. His reply was uncomplimentary; I think he rather likes 'locking horns' with Cassie and doesn't want another man spoiling the fun. Men are so very possessive about women. Nevertheless, I insisted that in the future I will accompany him to meetings with our customer so I can get a sense of the problems we are faced with here. If I could show some success, maybe the department will be seen to be the valuable corporate asset it undoubtedly is.

Friday 10:
Cynicism got an additional boost today when our new Premier announced more money for schools, hospitals, and municipalities. I checked back in my diary and found it was last Friday I predicted he would. Maybe I'll become a political pundit when the company throws me out. Politicians, like all beggars, are so predictable when they want your patronage. Their indifference when they are in office is like a satisfied panhandler's too; they both think your average Joe is a sucker -- and they're right. Truth is, the only difference between a politician and a panhandler is in their ambition.

Spent another happy hour at the gym chatting to Cassie. She may not know much about medieval history like Lydia did but she loves Leonard Cohen and has all his albums. She's going to make me a CD of some of his live tracks that I don't have and I'm lending her one of his books. She didn't know he'd written books so we have lots to talk about.

My determination not to buy another lottery ticket lasted till going home time when I passed the booth. The prize is now $24 million so I bought more to supplement my winning ticket from last week.

The Ottawa Senators won game 5 so it's 3-2. Good thing for Torontonians it wasn't best of five.

Gwen spends every waking hour at work now she's free of school. I can't help feeling she has a little too much of the Lakelady perseverance and thrift. Still, it does mean Alys can go out looking nice without comments being made. I casually asked Alys where my copy of Leonard Cohen's book had gone. She pointed to the bookcase without a word but, as she was heading out the door, paused and asked, 'Why do you want that old thing?' I told her it was to loan to a colleague at work and she seemed satisfied. I have sown the seed. I think I'm getting quite adept at this political chicanery.

Saturday 11:
Called Dad. He and Gawain are well enough to get new movies but there aren't any good ones out there that they haven't seen. Hollywood doesn't make enough war, gangster, or other mayhem movies to fill every waking moment. I agreed it was a disgrace and someone should do something about it. Everybody is well, with the exception of Aunt Sylvia, who has fallen and broken her hip. Fortunately, it isn't serious; i.e. it didn't happen to Dad or Gawain.

It was sunny and warm at Lance's first soccer game of the summer season. It was only an exhibition friendly so I'm not recording the score. (I will if they win one!)

'The little paper that grew -- tedious but not serious' is all about the Maple Leafs and how they would win everything if only the newspaper writers were allowed to buy the players with an unlimited budget, pick the team, and set the strategy. I don't know why anyone reads or listens to this stuff in any media outlet. For some reason, we've been getting this particular newspaper delivered every Saturday for the past month and we didn't ask for it.

Needless to say, I didn't win anything on the lottery. I won't buy any more tickets.

Sunday 12:
Mother's day.
Lance cooked breakfast for Mother's Day and bought flowers. Gwen gave a card and gift certificate. I hope the retail industry has a happy day. The Supreme Deity doesn't think much of Mother's Day either because the weather has taken a turn for the worse with heavy rain and wind overnight followed by rain during the day.

Lance went to the hockey club banquet and had his usual bad time, so he says while Gwen went to outdoor soccer practice. Even she can't work all day on Sunday.

The Leafs won game 6 so its 3-3 in the series; maybe this is the year they win the Stanley Cup again. Lord Stanley, I'm sure, would be pleased to see Canadians (who he gave it to) winning it, rather than those folks in the republic over the border.

Monday 13:
My section's summer student arrived today and he's somewhat grumpy to find he has to take our 'orientation' course, right after he'd done the college's course telling him how to behave in the world of work. Apparently, they now train students to help them adjust from college to the work force, and in particular teaching them how to deal with technologically challenged people like me. I think the problem lies not with the kids but with us -- their parents and soon-to-be co-workers. We Baby Boomers think we're so important, we can't believe that one day we won't be here and our kids will manage just fine, probably with a huge sigh of relief. If being our parents was a chore (and it was, according to dad), being our children is definitely a bore.

This rant has been brought to you by a dark, brooding Lydia-free malevolence toward my peers and the hope of a brighter tomorrow, maybe with Cassie.

I gave Cassie my Leonard Cohen book and she gave me the CD she 'burned' for me. I'm not sure I like the phrase 'burned' but for those of you in posterity who aren't familiar with the term it just means copied. It also occurs to me that posterity may not know what a CD is so I'll explain that too. It is a plastic disk on which music (or speech) has been recorded so it can be played back at a future time – a replacement for the vinyl disks of yesteryear and touted as a more permanent means of capturing sounds. Ours are already far less permanent than my old vinyl disks but that could just be me.

The weather remains cold and wet; naturally, because Gwen had a soccer practice (after a full day at work) and Lance had Track and Field at school today. Our hallway is awash, knee-deep in mud; our Mud Room, needless to say, is a mud free zone. Alys, however, was spotlessly clean as she watched Gwen's practice and didn't stray from the comfort of the car. I felt this was a good time to tell her more about my new colleague at work, Cassie.

Tuesday 14:
Cold and wet with wet snow in the northern part of the region. Today's paper says that another lump has fallen off the Antarctic Ice

Shelf, taking it back to where it was in 1911 when Shackleton first mapped it. Global Warming has only taken us back to 1911. Politics and economics have taken us back to the Middle Ages.

At work, I did 'observation' training (otherwise known as 'rat on your colleagues' training) where I learn the techniques that made living in the Soviet Union such a pleasure. This, like so many of our recent advances in behaviour, comes via the USA. Considering they have been boycotting Cuba for 40 years on the principle that it isn't a 'free' country, I'm amazed at what they get up to in their own backyard.

I mention Cuba because Jimmy Carter, ex-President of the USA, is to visit Fidel Castro, the President-for-life-and-beyond of the People's Glorious Republic of Democratic Cuba, to set the stage for future normalising of relations. For my readers in posterity, the US has been boycotting Cuba for over forty years to the detriment of the Cuban and American peoples but the eternal gratitude of Fidel Castro, who is proven a hero in his people's eyes, and not a sad old revolutionary failure whose day has long gone. I wonder which members of the US government Castro pays for this guaranteed vote winner on both sides of the Caribbean Sea?

At my own undemocratic republic, known as work, this week has been designated 'employee week' by our CEO to focus us on the importance of employees to the company, as if we employees didn't know. (Perhaps it's to focus our executives on the importance of employees though it seems late for that.) I've no doubt it is meant well, a brave attempt to remind the survivors of the latest cull they are wanted (as in 'dead or alive'). However, the hollow laughter the announcement engendered suggests this program will need a lot of effort to be successful. The CEO says he's putting our employees first because they are our most important assets and, presumably, now there are fewer of them, they're even more valuable.

After my observation training, I noticed many of our VPs I passed in the elevators and hallways were all grim and uncommunicative, not at all their usual insincerely cheery selves. This is a glaring change in mood and character for some of them and my training says I should probably do something about it. I won't because I think it's because things are not going well at the top of the house. Now that I've grown used to not getting any 'direction' I think I can say the middle of the house is doing just fine. Conditions at work have almost returned to the easy-going Sixties and Seventies when we had time to think and work. Who knows, it may percolate up to the top and they might start thinking too -- and not about another pointless re-organisation. Perhaps they could think about our products, assuming any of them remembers or even knows what we make.

Lance's soccer team won its first league game, 10-1, in freezing cold, blustery conditions. At least, the rain had stopped. The field could have had more water on it -- but only if it had been a swimming pool. Water polo would have been more appropriate. Alys attended the game with me so no suspicions were aroused tonight in Gwen's bosom but she was too busy at work to care.

Wednesday 15:
The Leafs won game seven last night and go through to the Conference Final against Carolina starting Thursday. The Senators, who lost last night, led the series 1-0, 2-1, 3-2, but because the Leafs were leading the series at 4-3, the Leafs go through, weird or what? It's good for the Leafs because they are playing without seven of their injured 'stars.' If they can hang on long enough, some of the 'stars' could be back, fully rested, for the final parts of the Stanley Cup games.

Cassie and I discussed our recent exchange of gifts when we were at the gym today while we assisted each other to lift weights, stretch limbs and other supportive acts that only a regular gym-goer would understand. I find I'm enjoying the gym again almost as much as I did with Lydia. Even Cassie's comments on the sexual precociousness of the younger Leonard, as recorded in his book, didn't unnerve me like it once would have done. I'm more worldly-wise for having known Lydia.

Gwen is now able to drive herself to soccer practice and tonight did so for the second time. Now we may never meet her again as the only time we did see her was when we drove her somewhere. I told Alys about my conversations with Cassie on Leonard Cohen, laying emphasis on how much Cassie and I have in common with respect to music and literature. And that is true. Cassie is the only one I've ever heard mention the humour in many of Leonard's songs.

Now that Gwen can drive herself, Silky gets a full evening's sleep on my lap and my sensitive bits are safe. Another of life's concerns has gone for good and I suddenly realised that when they're all gone, I likely will be too. It was not a comforting thought.

Thursday 16:

Britain's present Prime Minister (another Ministraitor), Tony Blair, has announced he will hold a referendum soon on joining the Euro. He is buoyed up by his past referendums where less than half the voters turned out and those that did were the zealots for different States. Their majority vote on the day allowed him to do what he wanted to do, which was to hand over power to separatists. England was promised its own Parliament too but it never materialised, which also plays into the separatists' hands; they can now claim the London Parliament is England's and turn even loyal people against it. The alternative idea, where the British Government returns to being meaningful to British people wasn't voted on. 'What a parcel of rogues in a Nation.'

Coincidentally, Mr. Blair's announcement came at the same time as TVO was showing An Englishman Abroad, an account of a 1960s meeting in Moscow between the actress Carole Brown and the traitor Guy Burgess. In those far off days, traitors worked clandestinely to hand over their countries to a foreign power; nowadays, they infiltrate·the political parties and work together from a 'democratic' base. The same has happened here in Canada. The Conservatives signed an unpopular agreement, NAFTA, with the Americans. The opposition said they would repeal it if we voted them in -- then, when we did, they didn't. And they've worked tirelessly with the Americans to expand NAFTA ever since, despite the USA's continual attacks on our industries through the various legal avenues open to them. If Mr. Blair gets his way, he too will become famous -- just like Burgess, Philby, and Maclean.

The murdered Dutch politician's 'far right' party came second in yesterday's vote over in Holland, a result they wouldn't have got if he'd been alive. With luck, this will catch on and we'll see more party leaders being murdered before they can do any serious damage. From all accounts, Mr. Fortuyn simply believed what everyone believed until the Nazis made honesty and patriotism dirty words, unlike France's M. Le Pen, who sounds like a truly 'nazti' man.

There's a new rumour at work today, one that has driven the Transformation off the sounding board. One of our Senior Head Director's and a Senior Vice-Director from HR are supposedly having an affair. I don't know if it's true (I never do) but I've started doing Kegels again. Promotion has its price and I must be ready to pay it if the opportunity arises.

Cassie, it seems is a gardener. She tells me her Queen of the Night tulips may be out today, thanks to the watery sun we've seen, and her Oscar Wilde tulips have been out for a few days, which isn't like Oscar at all, to be out and about early.

Friday 17:

The newspapers are full of droughts all over Asia while we in Ontario suffer day after day of rain. Last night was no exception and Lance came home from his school soccer games caked in mud. Reminds me of my school soccer games, in fact.

The watercooler chat at work has given up on the 'affair' and is back to the Transformation, I'm pleased to say. Affairs are a one-day wonder in our company. Our Head Chief President and Operating Officer issued a message today stating that next week, the second week of his drive for greater focus, would be on the customers because *customers come right after* employees and -- *our success depends on putting customers first*. The italics are all mine but I feel a further comment on my part is superfluous.

Cassie and I enjoyed more interesting discussions about music and sexual precociousness today at the gym. I discovered she's a friend of Lydia's too, which hasn't come up before in our conversations. It seems she frequents the Cadaver Club and, outside of work, is also a Goth. She's going tonight and suggested I escort her, as she knows I've been there before. We went for coffee right afterward to expand on these revelations and whiled away most of the afternoon pleasantly. Long may the Transformation continue, I say.

The Leafs won the first of their series against the Carolina Hurricanes 2-1 and now lead the series 1-0. I didn't hear any revellers during the night. I think we've passed the point most of them had paced themselves for. It is years since the Leafs got this far and our fans had only trained for a short campaign.

Once again, at the last minute, my nerve failed me, or greed overcame me, and I bought more lottery tickets; the prize is now $34 Million.

Mentioned to Alys how much I'm enjoying working directly with Cassie. I can now confidently confirm that competition is good for humans, whatever Socialists might argue in opposition. Got to get some more Viagra.

Saturday 18:
Called Dad. He's fine but Gawain has stomach problems; the same as the soldiers in Afghanistan, Dad says. Also Uncle Joe has the same thing but not as serious as Gawain, naturally.

I'm sure I don't need to tell you that I didn't win the lottery. Six people did so the big prize has gone. I'm glad. It stops me throwing away more money on useless hopes.

Taking Lance to soccer practice, we passed more fields being turned into sub-divisions with giant machines scraping and gouging the land, destroying everything in their path. I don't know why we imagine aliens coming to destroy the planet; we're already here. Movies and books dwell on humans meeting destructive aliens when we go out to the stars but my guess is the reason we've never made contact with any aliens is because we're the monsters their writers have warned them about.

Sunday 19:
Gwen was in a soccer tournament and her first game was at 9 am on the other side of Toronto so we got to enjoy both the frosty morning and hail of this May holiday.

Victoria Day fireworks in the evening and the Leafs, with all their stars back, lost the second game in overtime. The series is now 1-1.

Gwen's soccer team lost in the tournament semi-finals after extra time and in penalty shoot-outs. With them out of the tournament, I can get some work done tomorrow in the garden. Victoria Day is traditionally the day to plant in Ontario because there's never any frost after the last weekend in May -- says tradition.

Monday 20:
Victoria Day.
Lance barbecued hot dogs for lunch in a hailstorm. He wasn't amused but kept at it because this was the first time we've let him use the barbecue on his own. If the weather doesn't improve soon, barbecuing will be back to me.

Despite the temperature, Alys insisted on planting our herbs and annuals this weekend. I planted them reluctantly and with good reason as it turned out. The radio says this was the coldest Victoria Day weekend in twenty years and much too cold for planting.

Tuesday 21:

Back to work after the long weekend and Gerry tells me I should read Extreme Gardener, another magazine to which he subscribes. They say the average Canadian garden can produce pineapples by June and persimmons by July, provided the gardener uses raised beds fitted with 'Extreme' underground heating and an 'Extreme' underground integrated irrigation and fertilising drip-feed system -- in combination with 'Extreme' Natural Sun Light and Heat ornamental garden lamps. These small modifications expand the growing season to 24/7 and 52 weeks per year. I'm pleased to report nature isn't entirely thwarted in her efforts to teach the human race sense; you have to install the 'Extreme' hothouse to get ripe bananas for Christmas. I can't help wondering if Extreme Gardener ran a series about growing 'exotic grasses' some time back. The similarities to those pot houses the police found some weeks back is creepy.

Work is so tedious now. My section and I plod on writing procedures but no one reviews them or responds to our questions. We've become invisible and my troops are growing despondent. I would feel like Paddington Bear, unwanted on the voyage if I didn't have an enthusiastic customer in Cassie. And she is my customer now because Padraig has decided he's too busy to continue work on Cassie's procedure. My staff may be down but my 'staff' is up and definitely feels wanted on the voyage. I made an appointment to meet Mr. Ogilvie to see if I can get some work direction for my troops and me. Unfortunately, he couldn't see me today. Tomorrow afternoon is the earliest.

In contrast to the gloom of work, my time at the gym is a glorious interlude of earnest discussion and flirtation. After twenty years of being a mere 'house husband', I seem to have become a chick magnet. First Lydia and now Cassie appear to find me interesting? Speaking of Lydia...

Renee, my Admin Assistant, told me she saw Lydia at the weekend, in Toronto, in a Mall. When I said Lydia wasn't the Mall kind, Renee said meaningfully, 'she wasn't alone.' I knew Lydia had a boyfriend though he never seemed to be anywhere about, so I asked, 'What's the boyfriend like?' Not so much a boyfriend, according to Renee, more of a Sugar Daddy. Lydia was out shopping with Mr. Schoeppenfrauen. I was a bit nonplussed by this revelation until I realised what must have happened. Mr. S. is back in Canada to confer with his fellow Conquistadores. He's come without his wife and Lydia came back with him to visit her family. She was probably just showing him the sights or maybe they were buying things for Mrs. S. and the little S.'s. I told Renee not to make more of it than it warranted. I hope Lydia makes time to visit me.

Today's newspaper had an article describing recent research showing that companies who downsize don't prosper. This isn't the first time it's been demonstrated, though why it takes researchers to come up with an answer any employee this past ten years could have answered for free, I don't know. I've no doubt our senior management will pick up on this research in about 11 years time, the day after they've finally convinced me to take the hint and leave.

Lance's soccer team won their second game 4-0. We are on a roll. Lance also won the 1000-metre race on his school's track and field day so he was pretty darn pleased with himself. Gwen was also playing soccer tonight and scored a goal, which as a defender she doesn't often do, but as she drove herself there we missed it!

The Maple Leafs lost another game in overtime and now trail Carolina 1-2. They should bring back the understudies who worked to get them this far and drop the stars. Their coach, however, is in the heart unit at the hospital -- really.

Wednesday 22:

Heavy frost overnight, apparently Global Warming doesn't know that Victoria Day is the start of the frost-free season. Our herbs are still standing; our annuals are not. I didn't say 'I told you so' to Alys because that wouldn't be nice -- for me. On the walk to work from the train Station in Toronto, dusky claret and cream apple blossoms and white lilac blossoms hung heavily over regimented rows of tulips and grape hyacinth -- but not so the ones in the Lakelady garden. Our rhododendron, apples and lilac remain stubbornly in bud. In most of the Southern Ontario, it's a glorious year for spring flowers, the British-style spring rain has seen to that. The Lakelady garden is setting a different fashion.

When I mentioned the blossoms to Gerry, he remarked he'd been reading a book recently on how Japanese kamikaze pilots were likened in wartime poems to cherry blossoms, flowering briefly and brilliantly. I have to say it made me see the Japanese people in a new light. I'd always assigned the title of world's top warriors to my own heritage, the British, because 1500 years of continuous warfare on every ocean and continent and against every people on the face of the globe is an impressive record. However, a nation who can get suicidally homicidal after listening to poems about the glories of cherry blossoms are in a league of their own. We, wussy westerners, have to imagine ourselves as lions, or eagles, or some other ferocious predator, before we can get seriously violent. Maybe I need a whole new category for the Japanese because, clearly, sitting on a Chrysanthemum Throne dreaming of flower petals is an amazing route to murderous mayhem.

Mr. Ogilvie put off our meeting till tomorrow but my time wasn't wasted. Cassie and I talked procedures most of the day and then retired to the gym to explore more interesting subjects, like music, literature and performance art of the kind you get at the Cadaver Club.

Gwen is still driving herself to soccer practice. It seems she doesn't miss our quality time together as much as I do.

Thursday 23:
Today is bright and sunny, with cold weather arriving later – in time for the weekend.

Lydia is still in Toronto and came to see me today. We talked about Byzantine history and her new job. I asked if she was still going to do her MA. She says now she has a senior position, she's pulled her application because she'll be too busy. I'm disappointed but not surprised. She also tells me she spends most of her time with Mr. Schoeppenfrauen these days and he's a fascinating man. His wife doesn't understand him, which is why Mrs. S. isn't up here with him. I asked Lydia about Mr. S. and find I was right. She was assisting Mr. S. shop for his wife's upcoming birthday when spotted by Renee the other day.

The Maple Leafs lost 3-0 last night and now trail the Hurricanes 1-3 in the series. Like I said, they should have stuck with the workers and left the stars to lose in the Final. The Leafs manager remains in hospital.

Ontario claims to have driven an Al Qaeda cell from the Province and I've no doubt more covens, sorry cells, will be found all over the world. Where is the Witchfinder-General when you need him?

India and Pakistan get closer to war. In the olden days (say 1990) we didn't much care what they did. Now they are both armed with nuclear bombs and have the missiles to deliver them, we're a bit more concerned. Britain has pulled its diplomats out. On the other hand, a heat wave is killing thousands of people in both countries so maybe a war won't be necessary. They'll get their murderous kicks the natural way.

Mr. Ogilvie again put off our meeting until tomorrow.

To get Lance up to maturity soon, Alys has signed him up for a camp counsellor leadership course. Lance isn't so sure. Gwen, however, says the Camp Counsellor Trainer is none other than our tiler -- Nico!!

Friday 24:

We got a Communication presentation from the company's newly appointed 'Senior Directors' today who told us of our future. They were pretty clear about everything except my section and me. It didn't appear on the org chart they used and, when I asked, were unable or unwilling to provide an answer. This wouldn't seem so personally directed at me if it wasn't for the fact I counted the bodies on the chart and it adds up to the numbers of staff less one. From this, I infer my section is buried in the chart somewhere but I'm not because the one person missing is a Section Manager. Gerry's theory about me not taking hints looks remarkably accurate today.

The other firm piece of information they were able to provide is that 'we' have missed the date again. July 1st is the revised date, which 'we' must meet. Considering 'we' have had no say in any of this, I'm puzzled as to how 'we' can help -- other than marching into the cannons, as always.

I tried to get my meeting with Mr. Ogilvie but again he says tomorrow or, in this case, Monday. I find I mind this evasion less and less every day because being Friday it's my gym day and it's Cassie's too. She described her costume for the Club tonight as we jogged together on treadmills. Somehow, I've got to find a way of going there again.

The final report on the Walkerton disaster was released today. The report says ensuring we don't get poisoned from our drinking water in future will cost an additional $280 million. The judge who chaired the investigation has also called for a Safe Water Act to be put in place.

My call for a Witchfinder-General appears to have been answered. Today's paper reports a high-ranking police officer as saying 'they've still got people here.'

Chasing other 'terrorists', Toronto Parks and Gardens is going after the cells of Canada geese who make a mess of the city's grassy spaces. People in the Western world really are hypocrites. They will happily kill harmless birds for 'making a mess' on the grass but demand third-world people live with lions and tigers roaming their backyards.

Saturday 25:
Leafs win game 5, series 2-3
We went to the local dinner theatre in the evening and the cast worked the Leafs game score into the script, which I thought pretty neat for amateur dramatics. We also used the Internet to book tickets for a theatre play in England when we're over there. This is a first for us and I hope (and pray) it will turn out well.

Lance's soccer team lost in the first round of the cup against a strong team from a higher division. They led throughout most of the game only to slip up late on and then lose it in the second period of overtime. Like the Leafs, who lost two games against Carolina that way, they're not good at overtime.

Called dad. He isn't very well. He caught Gawain's bug. Gawain is recovering slowly, too slowly to nurse Dad. Uncle Jonas has recovered completely -- because he was hardly ill, apparently.

Sunday 26:
A closer examination of our blossom trees reveals they don't actually have any buds on them. I made this observation because only a handful of blossoms appeared on our 4 in 1-dwarf apple tree and our flowering crab. A frost must have nipped them earlier.

We paid for a boat we are renting on the Norfolk Broads in England over the Internet. Aren't modern communications wonderful? From the comfort of our home in Ontario, Canada we can book activities in England and give ourselves weeks of anxiety worrying if they will have things for us when we arrive, whether some hacker has made off with our credit card details, or whether the US government is stalking us as terrorists.

Gwen took herself to her outdoor soccer practice in Alys's car and I took Lance to his outdoor soccer practice in my car, which would have allayed any of Gwen's fears -- if her mom had been at home when we all got back.

Monday 27:

Warm and bright, naturally -- we're at work.

If we had buds on our trees they would have come out today. I mention this because the apple blossoms on the walk to work were gone; that is, there weren't any.

Mr. Ogilvie can't see me today; he's in important meetings. I heard some more about my old protégé Lydia today, if I may call her so. It seems Mr. Schoeppenfrauen is divorcing his present wife, a young woman who used to be his Personal Assistant, and he's going to marry Lydia. I don't think this is a wise thing for Lydia to do. Mr. S. appears to be a very fickle kind of man and the marriage won't last. I fear someone sensitive like Lydia could be seriously hurt. I'm also hurt she didn't mention this development when we spoke last week.

My hurt evaporated when Cassie and I went to the gym together. She told me everything I'd missed by not being at the Club on Friday and I suggested I'd make an effort to escort her one night soon, though I've no idea how that might happen.

With my mind running now on happier lines, the train ride home was also a delight with the spring flowers on the trackside, wild phlox carpet the ground in mauve and white this week.

Tuesday 28:

Lance's team won their third league game 6-2. I missed it because I was in Hamilton with Gwen's team for their first game of the season. Gwen's team won 1-0. A good start to the season because Hamilton is always a strong team and this game was no exception to our annual struggle with them. Even better, Alys stayed to watch Lance's game so no uneasiness when we got home.

Many of our parents, and the trainer, at Gwen's game huddled around a portable TV watching the Leafs game finish regular time tied at 1-1. Sadly, the Leafs don't do overtime and, for the third time against Carolina, lost on a sudden death goal. They are out of the Stanley Cup as Carolina has won 4 games to the Leafs 2. I'm not a big fan of professional hockey (or any other professional sport) but I'm sorry the Leafs are out. They've given the city a real boost these past weeks with cars and homes sporting Maple Leaf flags and children at street corners waving cards saying 'Honk if you love the Leafs.' It's been fun.

We must expect 8 million people in the Greater Toronto Area by 2031, says the new urban plan, up from the just over 5 million today.

I can hardly wait. I was only saying to Alys the other day, how I wish we had 3 million new neighbours because I'm bored with the present bunch.

Mr. Ogilvie can't see me today. Tomorrow afternoon, his new secretary says.

Wednesday 29:
Wednesday is gym day so, after we spent most of the morning reviewing the infamous and underdeveloped procedure, Cassie and I went to the gym. It's amazing to me how much help fit, strong young women need when faced with gym equipment. It's less amazing to me how much I enjoy helping them. I shall restart the Kegels and make a doctor's appointment. If Viagra should be needed, I'll need a prescription. Maybe they could add it to the water supply while they're fixing those inadequate water treatment plants?

Our Ontario government, suddenly on the side of the little people, has told the privatising electricity companies that they have to cut the size of their Senior Manager's golden parachutes and if they don't, the government will step in and do it for them. Our new Premier is a marvel, like Spiderman whose movie has recently broken all box office records. The election can't be far away.

Overnight, a thunderstorm rolled through the area turning our bedroom curtains into x-rays photos and our roof into a steel drum. By morning, the few apple blossoms we had were lying on the ground beneath the trees.

Mr. Ogilvie still can't see me (nobody can now I'm not on anybody's org chart, I'm a disembodied spirit wandering the halls and haunting my office), maybe tomorrow afternoon.

Thursday 30:
Mr. Ogilvie called me to his office this morning well before our appointed time. He received a draft copy of the auditor's report on my procedure writing section and he isn't very happy, with the report or me. He seems to think I said too much, or too little, and definitely lots wrong. He asked me if I realised how hard he's working to save us all from extinction in the Transformation and how unhelpful this audit will be? As I wasn't aware of saying anything that could lead to his outburst, I kept silent. I can only assume the auditor was either from a competing department and wants to destroy us, or was even dumber than I thought and failed to

understand my explanations. I left Mr. Ogilvie's office without seeing the report. He thinks I've done enough damage and he'll fix it himself. There was something about the way he said 'fix it' I didn't like. Is he too seeking to destroy my section? Am I becoming paranoid? The worst thing about paranoia is you could be in terrible danger and not know it because you think you're sick.

This didn't seem to be the moment to discuss the lack of direction my work is suffering from so I'll wait to next week and try again.

The commuter train service is threatened with problems because its maintenance workers have gone on strike. The train company says we can last about two weeks, provided there are no major problems.

The Toronto School Board has rejected the government's budget cuts and will run a deficit if the funding tap stays off. I think they're pretty safe. Our new Premier is in his pre-election announcement mood and a deal will be arranged. What voters everywhere should remember is that the same leader who gives you everything you ask for is also the leader negotiating on your behalf with outsiders. The chances are he'll give the outsiders all they ask for too and you'll end up with less than if you'd had a strong leader in charge. Beware of electing wussy leaders!

The FBI is to divert more of its agents to the war on terrorism and away from the war on crime and the war on drugs. That's where the US government wants it to go and, as every politician knows, you have to be up-to-speed on trends if you want to keep your budget. The Toronto School Board should have asked for money to combat terrorism.

Friday 31:
Finally, at work, we all got letters confirming us as incumbents in our jobs and we can relax --everyone but me that is. My letter says I'm unmatched and I'll be placed somewhere soon. All my section reports to Mr. Ogilvie again -- only doing something different, he says. He doesn't know what my 'unmatched' letter means, he says, but will find out, he says. My section now has the direction it needed; I don't. Is this the hint I should take?

Later we learned, although everybody (but me) got 'incumbent' letters, not everyone was incumbent in the job they've been doing for the past years. Two people I know were made incumbents in each other's jobs -- and neither knows anything about the other job. There's a stately lunacy to the way management and unions apply rules in these situations, as if they were well-to-do Alzheimer patients.

Despite the worry about work, Cassie and I had a great time at the gym. She is safe and keeps her own job, the best of both worlds. I'm not safe and haven't a job but I do have an attractive young woman to be with who likes me so I don't care. Explaining the work situation to Alys later, however, was a different affair and only the fact tomorrow is the weekend stopped her going straight to Head Office to 'have it out with them'. I hope she's cooled off by Monday.

June 2002:
World Cup runneth
over and over and...

Saturday 1:
World Cup begins.
I love soccer and hate the World Cup, which is a ritualised, sterilised version of the game where professionals go through the motions of playing and consequently turn off everyone who wants to see a sport full of speed and passion. I think FIFA should be charged with bringing the game into disrepute for staging this travesty.

Lance's team is in another tournament this weekend. The weather was good, bright, sunny, cool and windy, just the kind of summer's day I like. The team did okay but not good enough to go on, two ties against so-so opponents. Still, all the games were more exciting than the bits of World Cup I watched.

Called dad. Dad and Gawain have got over the Afghan bug and would be quite well if it wasn't for the general dreariness of the weather getting them down. I didn't remind them that they never leave the house anyway so the weather isn't a problem. Those new happy pills aren't doing the job; I think they're sugar placebos.

Sunday 2:
I watched ten minutes of the World Cup game between England and Sweden. The commentator, trying to inject life into an especially dull point, described the teams as 'locking horns.' He must have been thinking of a snail's horns. England achieved another great victory with this tie.

Monday 3:
The headlines today are all about our own Canadian Prime Minister's firing his Chancellor and chief rival, Paul Martin. Most people thought Martin was the only good thing about this government so it will be interesting to see how things develop.

Also today, we were reminded it is ten years since Sunday

shopping arrived in Ontario and what a success that has been. Sunday is now the second busiest shopping day after Saturday. I used to be disgusted at the way the average human in the Western world spent the time our productivity and wealth have given us in doing nothing more than shopping and watching TV. Now I see the average human being has the mind of a grazing animal and they may as well do the Mall and TV thing while they wait to die. Nature would have kindly put them out of their misery early, by way of a wolf pack or lion.

Well on their way to joining the grazers, are the kids in Lance's class and school who haven't been doing regular lessons for a week now and we're still almost a month from the end of the school year.

An improvement our local education board is introducing soon is to do with exams. In particular, they're doing away with them, says Lance, because modern kids can't stand the pressure. From now on, progress at school will be based on work in class and at home. Considering most parents do their kids homework nowadays, this should ensure future generations are even less equipped to face the future than we were but no one will fail school unless their parents are illiterates. It will also prevent the offensive cases of brilliant people who hardly do any work but pass anyway. From now on, only dull drudges with educated parents will succeed. I don't know why we don't just admit we hate remarkable people, except in sports, and declare ourselves a Socialist Republic. This rant has been brought to you by courtesy of the fact Cassie didn't come in today – she's sick. I warned her the outfit she described to me on Friday wasn't suitable for Canada's climate, not even in June.

Apparently the video of Lydia's wedding in Las Vegas is available. It seems to have been a very quick affair. I can only assume Mr. S. was already in the process of divorcing his previous wife because I can't see how a divorce could happen so fast in the Western world. Maybe Americans are like Muslims in this, as in so many other things; perhaps saying 'I divorce thee' three times while clicking your heels is how you do it in California. I declined to watch the video when offered.

Today's colour from the GO train as I went home was blue. The ground was as covered in blue flowers as my mood was buried in blue thoughts.

Tuesday 4:

Our Federal Liberal government has reached the point all such gangs reach when they've got away with it for too long; they've taken to fighting among themselves. After firing Mr. Martin at the weekend, the party is splitting into two camps prior to a leadership convention early next year.

Lance's team lost 1-0 in their fourth league game. I hope this isn't the beginning of the end.

Mr. S. and Lydia are back for a big meeting with our SVPs. I saw Lydia briefly, admired the matching engagement and wedding rings and asked if she's happy. She tells me she is. So much so she's quitting work to lie by the pool reading books, after walking the dog and attending a spinning class at the same gym as some pop singer I'd never heard of. I asked her if that was what she really wanted and, to my surprise, she said yes. It was always her ambition and now she'd almost achieved it. I was going to ask what achievement she had left for her life when Mr. S. joined us and they left.

The good news is Cassie was back at work. It was a slight cold, she said, to which I smugly replied, 'I told you so.' She smiled, hugged me and walked off wiggling voluptuously. Thankfully, there was no one in the corridor but me at the time.

Wednesday 5:

Made an appointment to meet Mr. Ogilvie tomorrow

Not to be outdone by the Federal Government, our Provincial government has been diligently working to cause mayhem in the name of politics. Last night, the whole Board of Hydro One, the Province's electricity distribution company, resigned. They did this because the Provincial Government is going to pass a law allowing the government to roll back the severance packages Hydro One's senior management had negotiated with the Board. The Chairman of the Board complained the government has known of the packages since 1999 but he's wasting his breath. We have a new kinder, gentler Premier who doesn't hold with capitalism that's red in tooth, claw, and pocket book because he knows there's an election coming soon.

India and Pakistan march closer to nuclear war over Kashmir. The Indians are taking the George Bush line against terrorism and blaming it on Pakistan. The Pakistanis blame the problem on India's occupation of part of Kashmir. I blame it on human nature and curse all our houses.

Human nature, however, wasn't so very bad at the gym where Cassie and I worked on our abs and pecs. I'm not sure you can actually see a woman's pecs but Cassie's will now be providing a strong foundation for her charms, or so she claimed. I had to take her word for it because the gym was too busy to allow closer examination; Transformation is leading a lot of people to re-evaluate their lives and priorities.

Thursday 6:
Appointment with Mr. Ogilvie cancelled and re-booked.

Hydro One has a new Board and, according to the papers, it's to be led by the only left wing Premier the province has ever had, Bob Rae. My infiltration theory is looking better all the time.

The federal NDP leader has stepped down. This was a surprise because it's the first time most of us knew she existed.

Mr. Ogilvie was too busy today. He'll see me tomorrow. To be honest, I no longer want to see him now, only, if I say so, he'll think I'm being unpleasant and be angry. Cassie wasn't too busy to see me and we spent a happy hour in the gym followed by more happy hours in the nearby park earnestly discussing music and life.

Friday 7:
Re-booked meeting re-cancelled.

The commuter train service is still running despite a strike by maintenance staff, which is more than can be said for Amtrak, the U.S. railway, which will close down next week if the government doesn't give them money. President Bush has been too busy overhauling his security and intelligence services to notice the trains aren't running on time.

Ontario's auditor says the cost of rehabilitating the old mothballed station our nuclear operator is trying to restart may end up driving up the cost of electricity – he was obviously under the impression thousands of people were going to work for free.

The Economist magazine did another of its mean-spirited summaries of the Royal Family, this one for the Queen's Jubilee. The last one was at the Queen Mother's death. To quote Gilbert and Sullivan, the Economist is 'the idiot who praises every country but his own'.

Mr. Ogilvie is too busy. We'll get together next week Mr.

Ogilvie's new Secretary, Francine, says.

It's bright and sunny and just as well because today is the day for Gwen's soccer team's car wash where the girls get to play wet T-shirt competitions to raise cash. I find this as tacky as Lance's begging outside the liquor store.

All that talking to Cassie at the gym nowadays has worked – my weight is minus 1 lb. Knowing how life is, it's probably the coffee with double cream and date square I have afterward that's doing the trick. Cassie has taken my advice regarding costumes for the Club and today's was something she could wear on the street anywhere in North America. Indeed, girls do wear Catholic schoolgirl outfits all year round, even when the temperature is -10 C and the uniform includes an alternative of grey slacks -- but who am I to judge. I'm only an adult after all, possibly the last one on the continent.

Saturday 8:

The weather is now warm enough and our first seeds have sprouted. Alys says the pathetic little clumps of green need thinning. Poor things. They've struggled so hard to get even this far and I'm supposed to cull them. I can't help comparing their situation to my own in the workplace 'garden' so I pulled them out gently and replanted them in other parts of the garden, hoping that will not upset them too much. Maybe some 'gardener' at work in our corporation's upper ranks will deal kindly with me because I was kind to these seedlings.

England beat Argentina 1-0 in the World Cup. Go team go!

Called dad. The general dreariness of last week has made him rundown so he's got a tonic from the doctor. Gawain has to get by without. They're both too tired to do anything except watch movies, which is fortunate because that's all they do anyhow. I told Dad we've booked our flights for July-August. He says he hopes we bring some good weather with us because otherwise we'll have a bad time of it. I wonder if I should ask his doctor to give him the original happy pills. Even if he breaks his neck climbing trees, he'll be better off than he is now.

Sunday 9:

Five years ago, against my better judgement, we bought an above ground pool, which the kids swore to help maintain. Of course, they didn't and still never do. Today I opened the pool for summer. Lance had provided momentary assistance before his bored fiddling encouraged me to let him escape back to the Mephisto game he plays against his friends, each sitting in their own houses and communicating by way of the Internet. If they didn't actually meet at school, they wouldn't recognise each other in the street. The code names they use for their messages show the differences between the sexes. Boys have names like hockeyjock or footballnut. Girls' code names are all sex related, sexeee, sexkitten, sexyblonde, sugababe, hottie, hotpants, or Dcup. Our ancestors knew what they were doing when they oppressed women!

While I struggled with pool covers and cleaning, Gwen's team won their first cup game 2-1 in extra time.

Lennox Lewis defeated that horrible man Mike Tyson for the title of World Heavyweight Boxing Champion. I'd hoped the human race would have grown up and jailed these people for assault and their fans for incitement to commit assault but, of course, the opposite happened. Kickboxing and cage fighting make boxing seem tame.

Monday 10:

Items in the news today: It's hot! Mick Jagger is to be knighted in next week's Queen's Birthday Honours List. The World Youth Day cross arrives in Toronto. It's called WYD but it's really W Catholic YD and the Pope is coming to visit. Quebec now recognises gay civil unions. India and Pakistan appear to be going off the idea of nuclear war. Russians rioted when their team lost in the World Cup, only one dead; the passion is going out of soccer.

The flowers outside the GO train this week are purple; maybe it's in celebration of the Papal visit.

Today at work it was announced Padraig had won our company's draw for not having a sick day in May. This is a new program in place of the blanket we handed out last year. The rest of my staff visited me throughout the afternoon to complain that Padraig has already had more sick days than they have this year. I said it was 'the luck of the Irish' and sympathised with them. However, as they have all had more sick days than I have (none) and I haven't won a prize, my sympathy was wafer thin. No matter what scheme you put in place to encourage people, it always leaves more unhappy than happy.

I was happy when Cassie and I met in the gym and talked about her weekend, starting with the Club. Somehow I have to get there again but Alys, despite Gwen's suspicions, seems to be more of a home body these days and is also much more attentive to me. I wonder if she'd like to try the Club?

Tuesday 11:
Thankfully for my mood, Lance's soccer team won 3-0 and sit atop their division. Promotion beckons if they can hang on to September or have they just been playing all the easy teams to date?

France is out of the World Cup; the first time since 1966 that the holders have gone out in the opening round and the first time a holder has gone out without scoring a goal. I love sports statistics -- the duller the game the more the mental arithmetic, like baseball, American Football or cricket.

More news: The Pentagon is finally rebuilt. A gang of teenagers has carried out four car-jackings in Toronto this past week.

Gwen took herself to her soccer practice and I drove Lance his. As I watched the kids running about, I couldn't help wishing Club night were Tuesday between 7 and 9 pm.

Wednesday 12:
The Americans claim to have foiled a plot by Al Qaeda to set off a 'dirty nuclear bomb'. It was only at the planning stage, you understand; Al Qaeda hadn't any explosives or nuclear material or anything like that but the plot was foiled anyway. An American once said 'nobody ever went broke underestimating the intelligence of the American people'. Yet another example of the American Government failing to understand we aren't all American people.

England scored another great World Cup victory, tying Nigeria 0-0. Thanks to Sweden and Argentina tying also, England goes through. They have scored 2 more goals than France did -- so far. I predict another World Cup where England goes out without losing a game.

The federal government unveiled its new immigration rules including the new Maple Leaf identity card. Five teens have been arrested for the spate of car-jackings; our education system doesn't even make them smart enough for a life of crime apparently.

Scientists, after years of research, have shown that to live to be a hundred you need to come from families where longevity is the norm -- so much for the gym and healthy eating. I'm reduced to giving you all banal trash from the fantasy world of politics and current affairs because absolutely nothing is happening at work. The Transformation has brought us to a standstill, which is good for me because it means I can meet with Cassie almost every day to talk about that procedure without having to produce any tangible results. And we can spend more than just lunchtime in the gym because no one else is doing anything either. I predict a baby boom in Toronto if this goes on much longer.

Thursday 13:
Our new Premier has said the provincial government won't sell Hydro One; they will look at other options. The various newspapers lead with this or other concerns, such as a water quality lab in London, Ontario, that isn't up to standard and more people in southwest Ontario may have been exposed to E. Coli. Walkerton didn't teach us much apparently or maybe $280 million doesn't buy a lot in the water industry.

A Russian newspaper says Bin Laden is still alive and living in Afghanistan. Frankly, I think that's to put the Americans off the scent, not that they've got close enough to get a scent.

Bishops and priests of the world's largest Christian sect, the Roman Catholic Church, have almost agreed that from now on interfering with choirboys is a firing offence. For such a traditional church, this is a huge step. Personally, I hate to see all the old verities cast aside for modern political correctness.

Cubans rallied with Fidel Castro against the Bush administration's push for change in Cuba. I've no time for Castro but I think he has a point. President Bush should focus on the USA sometimes, after all, that's the country he was elected to govern. His mandate in Cuba is no different to Castro's – they were neither of them voted in by the Cuban people.

Sweden and England go on to the next stage of the World Cup when Sweden beat Argentina today.

Cassie and I moved on to the next stage too. I can safely record she is an old-fashioned girl without tattoos or piercings; at least, not in the places you can safely see in a secluded part of a park. I said I didn't like tattoos and she showed me she didn't have any. I would have stopped her if I could have moved or spoken. I'm glad I couldn't.

Friday 14:
Lance and the school band went on their annual pilgrimage to Canada's Wonderland Theme Park, where they play music for half an hour and then ride the amusements for free for the rest of the day.

Cassie came by after everyone had gone (no one is hanging around when they don't even know if the work they're doing is of any value to the transformed company) and modelled tonight's outfit for her trip to the Club. It was every bit as good as the ones Lydia and her friends wore all those months ago and quite beyond the pale for our Workplace Dress Code, I'm happy to say. Why is everyone having fun except me? I didn't warn Cassie she'd freeze to death in the weather we're having, mainly because, once again, I found it hard to articulate actual words.

Saturday 15:
It's cold and wet again. Called Dad again. The cold, wet weather over in England has brought on bronchitis and he has some new medication. It upsets his stomach so he's going back to the doctor's on Monday for a different prescription. Gawain too is ill. He hurt his back on his first day back at work and it got steadily worse until he had to go off sick again. He's thinking of suing his employer to get onto long term disability.

An old school friend and his wife are visiting Toronto so we met them in town and took them on a tour of the sites, starting with the world's tallest free- and up-standing dildo, the CN Tower, and followed by its near neighbour, the world's largest free-laying mechanical pussy, the SkyDome.

Sunday 16:
Cold and wet again. The World Cup drones on; Ireland lost to Spain on penalty kicks after extra time and Sweden lost to Senegal in extra time.

Gwen worked all day and took herself off to soccer practice afterward. It's like having Caspar the Friendly Ghost living with us. I took Lance to soccer practice and sat in the car catching up on the week's events for this Diary. You are the fortunate recipients of my gloomy thoughts; I hope the weather changes soon!

Monday 17:
Today was sunny and almost warm with showers; is this the

Global Warming we've heard so much about?

It was budget day in Ontario today and the true conservative voters' rout was completed. The conservative government put up taxes and spending and we're off to the next, as yet unannounced, election.

In France, the crook beat the crank. Chirac's party beat both the left and the far right to win a comfortable majority in Parliament. It says a lot about democracy that, with so much at stake, only 38% of voters turned out. I don't know why people bothered fighting to get the vote.

The huge forest fires threatening much of Colorado looks like it was started by a Fire Prevention Officer burning a letter from her estranged husband. I don't make this stuff up; I'm reporting from the newspapers.

In the World Cup Brazil beat Belgium so it's Brazil versus England on Friday. The USA beat Mexico and go on to meet Germany. Posterity will thank me for reporting this non-event if the sporting media is to be believed.

My own drive for enhanced fitness was made all the more sweet today – Cassie kissed me. Just a peck on the cheek while I was helping her with some weights but I feel my life is again becoming meaningful – or do I just mean complicated? The coffee shop after the gym was crowded with 'transformees', confirming what I have long suspected; our company could go months without half of its staff working. However, it meant Cassie and I had to squeeze together to sit and the heat of her thigh, hip and arm against mine was electric. It seems I'm not as old as I sometimes think I am. Sadly, unlike Lydia, Cassie doesn't live near work.

Tuesday 18:
Global Warming is struggling in Ontario. Today was bright and cold at first, and then bright and lukewarm later. Still, only three more days to summer! The weather didn't stop Cassie and I enjoying the warmth of a secluded suntrap in the park at lunchtime. I'd like to report this downtime was reducing the stress caused by the Transformation but it seems to be adding to it.

Here in Canada, the Parti Quebecois is doing badly in bye-elections. This would be good news normally because they're separatists who want to destroy the country, but in this case, it's not. They are losing to an even more nationalist bunch.

In Cuba, the Communist Party has announced the result of a petition demanding the perpetuation of the socialist worker's state. Fidel himself started the petition so you know the whole thing was an honest public response to the American government's pressure for reform. Who says satire is dead.

Another Ontario school board has been securing a World Record. This time kids from Toronto schools took part in the world's biggest hug. My pension, which depends on these little beggars being productive in twenty years, isn't looking too safe at this crucial stage of my life.

Gwen and Lance both had soccer games but we're not invited to Gwen's games anymore so we watched Lance's.

Wednesday 19:
Today was pleasantly bright and cool at first, then later hot and muggy – summer is definitely coming in. At the best of times, Ontario's weather can't decide whether to be Arctic or Tropical so it flips spitefully between both for weeks on end. At the worst of times, it does it all in one day.

Lance left for Ottawa today on his school Graduation trip. Only a year ago, on their trip to Quebec to ski and improve their French, the kids all took a tearful farewell of their parents. This time, the too grown-up kids all hurried onto the buses to escape the embraces of their anxious mothers.

In sporting news, South Korea beat Italy and Turkey beat Japan in the World Cup and the US is to probe the use of steroids in baseball – there hasn't been enough, I guess.

This week's GO train trackside colour is golden-orange from great clumps of tall lily-like flowers. It's a joyous color for a joyous day – gym day. I can't believe I thought of dropping the gym when Lydia stopped going. Today, Cassie and I helped each other with stretches to reduce our work-related stress. The views I had of Cassie's body from unusual angles, even though lightly clothed, took my non-work-related stress to wonderfully new levels.

When I shared my thoughts with Alys on how wonderful it is to have a companion at the gym, she suggested I start using a local gym in the evening and she would join too to keep me company. It's nice she feels that way but I'm much wiser now than I was only a year ago. I suggested that we explore the idea when my current work gym membership runs out. The important thing about competition is those competing must think they can win.

Thursday 20:
Lance is on his graduation trip and the house is silent. Gwen is working or holed up in her room, it could be either.

One of our few remaining Canadian SVP's, Rich Fallguy, has been 'let go'. It sounds like the management team was hanging on to him and just couldn't 'Klingon' anymore, which may be true. That's the comfort of being a merely 'professional' grade, you aren't singled out for special treatment at difficult times. You go with whole swathes of others, executed in job lots as it were.

Mr. Bing has been confirmed as the father of Elizabeth Hurley's child. I'm glad we got that sorted out; it's been worrying me a lot. This is fast becoming the new family; a woman finds a wealthy man, gets pregnant and brings up the child alone on the support payments. They don't even have to find a rich man these days; the courts will do that for them. We seem to be moving back to a time when most men were not part of the everyday life of the community. The result will be as it was before, mayhem as rival gangs of men who have no stake in their country fighting it out in the streets and regular people, that is women and children, cower behind their closed doors hoping the least murderous will win.

Suicide bombers struck Israel – 19 and 6 dead in separate incidents. Hearing the news from the Middle East is like reading the Old Testament -- over and over again.

The funeral for the trucking family killed in Grimsby recently attracted truckers from all over the continent because the murdered father of the murdered family was a famous trucker and is an inductee to the Towing Hall of Fame.

A pop star named Brandy had her baby on Father's Day, which reminds me of the joke we used to tell at school; Mother's Day is nine months after Father's Night. I record this so posterity will know their kids' jokes really are as old as they think they are. Lance once told me a joke from school that my Dad had told me as a joke from his schooldays.

Friday 21:
The Transformation, which was set for July 1st, is delayed again. Now it will happen 'in July'. Those folks who have been assigned new positions in the organisation are full of frustrated excitement.

THE DIARY OF A CANADIAN NOBODY

For those who haven't, like me, it's another few weeks of naked fear. The symptoms are the same, wide eyes, an inability to concentrate and an overwhelming urge to pee.

I'm considering suing the gym. They have put a chart on the wall alongside 'my' treadmill showing the heart rate for levels of activity by age. When I was jogging nicely at my usual 6.5 mph, I decided to take my pulse and compare it to the chart. I couldn't find a pulse in my wrists so I tried my throat and, by placing my right fingertips on the left side of my neck, I got a result. Unfortunately, to compare to the chart I had to look back over my right shoulder and this upset my balance. My head bounced off the padded bar as I fell on the conveyor, which promptly shot me off the back and into another wall, like a case of beer at a Brewer's Retail store. My injuries appear slight but who knows, there may be a fortune in them thar bruises. Even if there isn't, it got me a lot of Cassie's attention; she massaged and stroked every aching limb long after the limbs had stopped aching. After, in a quiet spot on our walk to the coffee shop, she kissed some more bruises better. I think I'll check my pulse again on Monday – it may be normal by then. It had returned to only twice normal when Cassie modelled her outfit for tonight's clubbing and is still thumping like a diesel engine as I write this.

My above analogy to beer cases came to me in the evening when I participated in one of the worst experiences of Ontario life, the Brewers Retail store. For those of you who don't live in Ontario and haven't had the pleasure of the North American attitude to alcohol in all its glory, I'll explain. To buy beer here, and most other Canadian places aren't too much different, you enter a pre-fabricated garage-like affair where rows of empty bottles cover one wall and a steel-topped counter faces you. You deposit your cases of empties at one end of the counter where an assistant counts them and gives you your bottle deposit back, without speaking. You choose your brew by examining the empty bottles on the wall and join the queue on the 'exit' side of the store. When it's your turn, you order from a second assistant who barks your choice into a microphone, making sure to let everyone in the store know what kind of cissy drink you want. A few seconds later your case of beer comes flying out of a hole in the wall, like a fire-phobic coffin at a crematorium, and thuds against the stops at the end of the conveyor rollers, rattling the beer bottles and threatening to splash your purchase all over you. You leave the store without having spoken a word to anyone and nor does anyone speak to you. This experience is so unpleasant I usually buy beer at the Liquor Board stores (which sells wine and spirits to a much nicer class of customers) because they leapt into Twentieth Century – right after the 21st Century started.

Lance came back from Ottawa today after soaking up the cultural delights of such things as the Hershey chocolate factory and the Nation's Capital shopping mall. My school trips were to the Roman Wall or to a local Norman castle or other vaguely meaningful places. Now that children are only being trained as consumers, shopping malls are indeed more important.

Saturday 22:
I went with Lance and his team to a soccer tournament on a hot, sultry weekend – summer starts abruptly in Ontario.

Pop star Britney Spears tops the list of most powerful celebrities. It's perhaps a comment on the 'powerfulness' of these folks that last year's top celebrity didn't get in the top ten this year.

In Sweden, a sperm donor must pay child support for three children conceived with sperm he donated to a lesbian couple for artificial insemination. The lesbian couple has since broken up and the mother and the Swedish state have found a sucker.

The Americans are talking about partial privatisation and route cuts to save their railway company, Amtrak. Also in the US, a judge says they have to stop executing mentally retarded people; what will they think of next in that big-hearted country?

British troops are pulling out of Afghanistan after handing over control of the multi-national force to Turkey. The good news is the war in Afghanistan appears to have taken fewer lives than are lost in Washington DC in any given year -- if you don't count the Afghani dead but who does?

England lost to Brazil, 2-1, Senegal lost to Turkey, and Germany beat the USA. I'm supporting Korea (who beat Spain) now, anything to stop the Brazilians or Germans winning again.

Called dad. He got new medicine and is feeling a 'little' better. Not enough to do anything but enough to watch action films again. Last week they were too exciting for him. Gawain is still off work and he's going for tests on his back this week.

Sunday 23:
Lance's team won the soccer tournament's Consolation Final so

ended third. Later, in the afternoon, Lance and I played basketball in our pool, which has reached 79 degrees warm. Colder than I like to get into but not bad when you're actually in it and the air temperature is in the 90's.

Gwen was at work and later soccer practice. I'm not sure I'd recognize her now if we met.

Monday 24:

Hot and humid, global warming has done its stuff and Ontario is back to normal. I'm probably the only person in the world who doesn't care for summer -- it itches.

Today's paper had an interesting advertisement for a new service for married women with boring husbands. They put the women in touch with gigolos; only they don't call them that nowadays, and these 'escorts' satisfy the women's needs. Now it isn't well known, and I don't advertise, but I, Arthur Lakelady, provide a similar service. Women who love to bake old-fashioned pastries have only to get in touch and I provide the satisfaction they can't get in this age of dieting and heart worrying fat- and cholesterol-free eating. Only yesterday I met a woman in an empty parking lot for a furtive exchange of favours, I got date squares and she got pleasure from knowing they went to a good home. It's sad 'this love that dares not speak its name' but I hope one day we can come out of the pantry and be seen for what we are, normal human beings with a tiny harmless pastry kink.

Israeli tanks are back parked on Yasser Arafat's lawn – tanks may win them the battles but until the Israelis change their behaviour they will not win the war.

Arizona is the next place in the US to be hit by bushfires. Has Arizona checked its firefighters one wonders? Meanwhile, floods in Russia have killed 24 people and 222 people died in an earthquake in Iran.

Bin Laden is alive and well, says an Al Qaeda spokesman.

At work, our Head Senior Vice-President of Organisational Effectiveness and Excellence put out an e-mail confirming the 'transformation' will happen in July. This 'confirmation' delays the date from the 'first' to sometime in July. As I haven't yet heard where I'll be, I gather a little hope from this; maybe they're wrestling with the problem of how to appropriately reward a loyal, long-serving, hard-working, competent employee like me? Or maybe not.

I didn't check my pulse on the treadmill today, not all my bruises from Friday have healed. It didn't matter anyhow; Cassie and I continued massaging aching limbs without the need for such violent action because we were both cramped from our weekend activities – my stressful pacing on the side of soccer fields and Cassie from the Club and after. Why doesn't Gwen's team go to a tournament for a Friday game with Alys as family representative? Because I want it to happen, that's why.

Instead, I went with Gwen to her game on the other side of Toronto and watched the coaches throw away the win. If I were a team manager or media pundit, I would say it was the referee's fault because apparently everyone involved with professional sports does absolutely nothing and referees do everything and they do it all wrong. Sport is the only Western industry left that the world has an interest in so this daily scene of grown men crying is acutely embarrassing.

Tuesday 25:
Today is hot and muggy and there was a smog warning issued. When the remnants of our industries are gone, and we've become too poor to afford cars, this smog problem will also be gone. There wasn't any smog in the park where Cassie and I whiled away the hours.

WorldCom, the world's largest telecoms company, has admitted to a $4.5 billion fraud. This is part of the ongoing Enron and Arthur Anderson scandal that's rocking the USA business community. Many people are worried that investors will lose confidence in the US and pull their money out. Any investor who has confidence in the parcel of rogues who run that country is a fool anyway and deserves to be parted from his money. Talk about a Third World country with missiles!

President Bush has presented a new peace plan for the Middle East that requires the Palestinian people to find another leader -- so much for popular democracy. Their elected leader, Yasser Arafat, is no longer popular with the President of the USA and his overwhelmingly unelected Cabinet.

Gay Pride week begins in Toronto and attendees at the events can drink in Toronto bars until the wee hours, unlike soccer fans who were denied the opportunity to drink 'after hours' while watching World Cup games in pubs.

Lance graduated to High School today and can look forward to four more years of social engineering education. He had a soccer game in the evening to round out his busy day.

Wednesday 26:
Germany beat Korea and Brazil beat Turkey so it's back to the past for the World Cup.

In other trivia (you'll thank me for this if trivia games come back into fashion in your time): Toronto's workers began striking today and the G8 leaders arrived in Calgary for the start of their summit. Amtrak is still running even though the US government has not come up with any cash; it's to be hoped President Bush doesn't go home from the summit by train. In Arizona, those bush fires are still blazing.

Today at work, one of our junior lady executives was 'escorted' out, which was appropriate because apparently she'd been running her Escort Service, taking bookings and managing her 'team', from her cubicle. This is definitely against our Code of Conduct, unlike paying yourself obscene bonuses with company money.

Cassie and I went through her procedure word for word, line by line, throughout the day, except when we went to the gym. I was ready to miss out the gym but Cassie kept me honest by reminding me she could hardly massage my aching muscles in a meeting room even if it had no windows. Put in that light, it was clear where my duty lay and we spent an hour ensuring we were fit and rested enough to wrestle with the problems of maintaining adequate Office Supplies again in the afternoon.

Thursday 27:
They got Gerry
It is with mixed feelings I record the fact they got Gerry. My sombre warning about what I'd learned on my training trip to the USA went unheeded and he paid the price. The trouble is, when you tell people up here in Canada of how they behave 'down there' in the US, people like Gerry always say 'we need that kind of accountability' because they think they're working hard and other people aren't. People never realise that the people they think are 'lazing about' are saying the same 'lazing about' thing about them.

Still I am sorry about Gerry's departure even though we've never been close since the unfortunate words over the security checks. He was involuntarily separated and, as an Executive, got nothing except the pleasure of being escorted from the building by Security.

The Transformation date, whenever it is, is growing closer and there's still nothing for me. I didn't get a package and I haven't been terminated, so what is happening? There's still no news and I'm growing even more despondent. My only hope is I haven't been promoted to that first step onto the scaffold, Gerry's executive position.

Our new corporate leaders talk a lot about 'leadership' because it's the latest thing south of the border. They assume because they're at the top they are leaders, not understanding that leadership is something that flows up from the bottom. A leader is someone that other people choose to follow; it's an honour bestowed by the people, not an appointment from the top. No one in their right mind would follow the folks forced on us everywhere in the Western world so we just take their orders. And like serving staff everywhere, we favour those who we choose and we drag our heels for those we don't, which is why founders of companies get the best staff and mere managers get people who can just turn up sober for an interview.

My prediction was correct. An Arizona firefighter has been charged with setting those wildfires. Writing a diary is convincing me I'm psychic. Perhaps I can become Mystic Arthur (or maybe Mystic Merlin) when the company kicks me out for either being a security risk or being too set in my ways for the new super-competitive age.

I believe Gwen had a soccer game after work today. Unfortunately, with this arrangement, she doesn't see that Alys is home every night now and has a renewed affection for me that borders on indecent. Fortunately, I did visit the doctor and the out-of-town drugstore again so I'm equipped to meet all eventualities. I love competition (except at work for jobs, of course).

Friday 28:
I'm reprieved again. Transformation will now happen on the July 18th, all being well -- or not. I think this date may be real because finally our new American management has cottoned on to the fact our company's week begins on a Thursday and ends on Wednesday and to 'transform' on any other day would send the computers into chaos.

One of our Canadian Directors was let go today. He just didn't understand that being a team player means total subservience to the boss. I've no doubt that, like Gerry, he actually believed the bit in our US training where they said they 'welcomed' contrary views. An American is flying up here to replace him.

I tentatively asked Mr. Ogilvie what happened to Gerry and he said, 'don't ask.' He then proceeded to tell me it was all Mr. Bustard's doing. Mr. Bustard, the Senior-Executive-Vice-President of Administrative Excellence and Mr.Ogilvie's boss, recently took an Extreme Management course at the Rotweiller School of Management and Gerry was the guinea pig he used to see if the course had taken. It had. I see now why Mr. Ogilvie looks so worn and nervous all the time.

I, on the other hand, am amazingly cool and relaxed because I go to the gym. It's true; going to the gym does cure anxiety and reduce stress. I recommend attending a gym three times a week in the company of a young, attractive person of the appropriate sex (appropriate to you, that is) and working out vigorously. If I could get to the Club as well, life would be perfect. Though just seeing what Cassie (or Lydia and her friends) wears when she attends is maybe as much as my worn-down-by-worry middle-aged frame should risk at this time.

Saturday 29:
Lance's team is in the Robbie soccer tournament and won both games today. The Robbie is the 'big one' for youth soccer in our part of the world.

Couldn't call Dad because we were away, which makes me feel better already.

Sunday 30:
Unfortunately, Lance's team lost today's first game so they are out. Only one team went through from each group. In significantly less important soccer action, Brazil won the World Cup 2-0.

Gay Pride parade is uncensored this year, so the radio says, and all sorts of sights will be seen. They were expecting about a million visitors before this announcement and it will be interesting to see if the numbers go up or down in anticipation of streets full of lewdness. How will the police be able to arrest heterosexual exhibitionism in future when they've allowed the gay variety? Or will we have the strange situation where heterosexual relations continue to be constrained by law but homosexual ones don't? Perhaps, it's fitting that, after centuries of persecuting left-handed people, people with warts and black cats, people of the wrong religion, black, brown, red, white or yellow people, and gay people, your average man in the street is left with only himself to persecute.

July 2002:
Canada Day and the
last Lakelady family day out

Monday 1:
This being the last summer Gwen may be home, the Lakeladys attended Toronto's Canada Day celebrations together one last time as a family. At one event, on the Toronto Islands, I was amazed to meet a work colleague dressed in Morris Dancing clothes. It seems he's been a Morris Dancer for many years and regularly dances in events such as these. I can see why he's kept it quiet. It occurs to me that, if England wants to be taken seriously again as a world power, they should eradicate Morris Dancing from the record, like the Soviets used to do with heretics. I know everyone is ethnic nowadays but Morris Dancing is going too far. I wonder if other people wish their ethnic events weren't quite so embarrassing?

I read in Natural History of the Senses of a people who celebrated life and death by putting a young virgin girl in a hut made of heavy logs and having the young virgin boys go in one at a time and learn the wonders of sex. When the last young man was 'on the nest', the tribal elders pulled a rope and collapsed the hut, crushing the couple. That's the kind of manly ethnic event we should be reviving, not these excruciating dancing affairs. Whenever I read about human history or hear the daily news, I get nostalgic for earlier, nicer times -- like the Jurassic period. Tyrannosaurus may have had big teeth but at least they had small brains and couldn't think or act anything like humans, which has to be an improvement.

In the evening, Alys took Gwen to her soccer game and Lance and I went to the local fireworks. The Lakelady's seem to be on an even keel right now, which hopefully the Transformation won't overturn.

No work, no gym, no fun! Just a vacation,

Tuesday 2:
The paper says the police arrested some nude males at the Gay Pride parade so they obviously spotted the danger I saw the other

237

day and moved to nip it in the butt before it got out of hand. I'm not impressed because, as I said earlier, I can't see why people shouldn't be allowed to walk around naked if they want to.

We didn't walk around naked but Cassie and I tested the possible new freedom in brief glimpses at the Park. I hope Toronto's outside workers stay on strike so they can't trim the bushes.

Another hot, humid, hazy day, just like all the other Ontario summers. Some Toronto pools are opened up even though the workers are on strike.

American planes bombed a wedding in Afghanistan killing more than 30 people. Add these to the small numbers of isolated killings by the Americans in their raids on villages to catch 'terrorists' and we're heading for another Vietnam.

Another loopy 'world' organisation came into being today, the International Criminal Court. The Americans, Russians, and Chinese aren't playing and rightly so. Not that their objections are high-minded but neither are those of the nations who approved.

George Michael, a British pop star in past years, has released a controversial CD describing Prime Minister Blair, as George Bush's poodle. It seems I'm not the only one disgusted with Mr. Blair's efforts to end the life of a fine country.

I heard that Gwen's team won 1-0 and are in a solid second place in their division. I think Gwen still plays on it but I have no solid evidence.

Wednesday 3:
Toronto's inside workers are set to go on strike too. Meanwhile garbage piles higher in Toronto's parks where emergency dumps have been established. In this heat, the city is beginning to smell, as I notice when I walk through it in the mornings.

Fortunately, our Park remains garbage-free or Cassie and I would have to rent a hotel room. Work was non-existent again today.

The Americans say it wasn't a bomb that killed that wedding party in Afghanistan. It was most likely gunfire from one of their anti-tank planes. I'm not sure how this is better.

Two American airline pilots were stopped from taking an airliner into the air when they were found to be drunk. Maybe the US could also check their Air Force pilots before they fly.

An Afghan government minister says Bin Laden and his second-in-command are still alive.

The American millionaire, Steve Fossett, finally went round the world in a balloon. It's a back to the future moment that returns us to the Georgian era. Moving right along to the Victorians, he's going to try for the highest glider (sailplane) flight next. He may be American but somewhere in his genes, he's British. They're the only people I know who think archaeology is a modern industry.

Our newest American executive's first order was to cut the 'goddamn wasteland' at the side of one of our factories. Because we've learned it's always best to follow these people's orders, this was done, and now we have to give back the prestigious environmental award we won for promoting a natural butterfly habitat. I don't think the Canadian in charge of Facilities Maintenance and Excellence at the factory, and who should have warned the new SVP, will survive much longer than the homeless butterflies.

A huge crash on the 401 burned two people to death and closed the road in one direction for most of the afternoon and evening. This is the third accident I've been caught up in the past three weeks of driving to and from soccer. Is this a coincidence or do harassed sports parents cause these accidents?

Thursday 4:
Our weather is still hot and muggy, with showers and cooler air in the afternoon. Fortunately, the showers were after Cassie and I returned to work.

In world trivia, President Bush, who has had strong words about corporate wrongdoing in the US, has now been accused of insider trading, which ties in pretty well with my earlier statements regarding the political system in the US. Despite all the harsh words and the unemployed, pension-less people they have in the U.S, no one will go to jail and no mass movement will come forward to correct the imbalance between rich and the rest. The oligarchy will circle around, protecting each other's behinds, and say what a wonderful thing democracy is – and so it is for keeping the obedient masses impotent (though personally I suspect that's a good thing when I look at the world and see what the masses have done elsewhere).

Sir Elton John has received an Honorary Doctor of Music from Britain's Royal Academy of Music and Michael Jackson, the American entertainment superstar, has become an honorary director of Exeter City Football Club in England's southwest. When I'm world famous, about a month after this diary hits the astonished streets, I'm going to be an honorary director of Blackburn Rovers FC -- or else!

Relative to the US, Canada's birth rate fell during the 1990's so our population is growing more slowly than theirs; economic reasons are preventing people having children, says the report; reorganisations and downsizings, says I. Just as well we Lakelady's had our kids in the Eighties. The report fails to mention the native populations of all the Western countries' birthrate is falling – only immigration, and the fact immigrants have more children is keeping our countries' population numbers growing.

Our MERD meeting had a new executive attendee who was astounded to learn we are not using the phonetic alphabet at every opportunity. He is writing an ACR to say how dangerous we've all been until the moment he arrived and discovered our problem. Our home-grown Phonetic Freak didn't know whether to look smug at playing the game before the rest of us or ashamed he hadn't thought of the ACR option before the new guy did. For my future readers, who I hope are wondering what I'm talking about, the phonetic alphabet works by replacing perfectly good English letters with incomprehensible words to ensure civilians can't understand what military folk are talking about, as follows:

A = Allies, who are Accidentally killed

B = British, see Allies (see Gulf War)

C = Canadian, see Allies (see Afghanistan War)

D = Dead, see Allies

E = Enemy, who I've never seen since I got here. (See Afghan War.)

F = Friendly fire, see Allies.

G = Gun, which no military man should be without, preferably unloaded.

H = Heck, wrong ones again (see Allies)

I = India, who are likely to be the next Ally to be accidentally bombed.

J = Juvenile, see war movies.

K = KILL, KILL, KILL, see Allies

L = Look out, incoming!! See Allies.

M = Military Coding (see psychiatrist)

N = New Zealander, see Allies (see post-Gulf War)

O = Ozzie, Australian, see Allies (see post-Gulf War)

P = Procedure, which I happily ignore. See Allies.

Q = Quandary, which I'm not in. (see macho leadership manual)

R = Raid, see Wedding, see Allies.

S = Surprise, you're dead! See Allies.

T = Tora! Tora! Tora! See Allies.

U = U-boat, submarine. See Japanese trawlers, an accidental sinking of. See Allies.

V = Vengeance is mine saith the Lord but He didn't really mean it. (See any Christian, Jewish, or Muslim war)

W = Wedding, for anti-tank cannon shooting practice, see Allies.

X = XTERMINATE, XTERMINATE, XTERMINATE, see Allies.

Y = YES, direct hit!!! See Allies.

Z = Zealot, our enemy. Not me, I couldn't care less. I just kill whomever I'm told to.

Friday 5:

As Enron's bosses head for court, the Women of Enron headed for Playboy magazine and the issue came out this month. Some of the Enron women were signing magazines in Toronto today. This is a new way for ex-employees to get their separation pay. If it becomes the new paradigm, I need to do better at the gym. Sadly, the picture that accompanies the advertisement in our free paper suggests the women of Enron have been plasticized just like all the other Playboy women and most of Hollywood's starlets. It isn't surprising that men are afraid to commit like another article claims when women are so nakedly reptilian in their expectations of themselves or their partners.

Alys has caught the bug too and spent a good part of today in a beauty parlour, where she was manicured, pedicured, hair styled, massaged, and thoroughly plasticized. Fortunately, thanks to Viagra, we put all that right in bed later.

City dwellers live longer than country people, a report on Canada's health system says; so much for fresh air and locally grown organic food. Trying to correct that finding, people are illegally dumping garbage all over Toronto during the strike; the director of water supply says the water will stay as safe as it was before. After Walkerton, no one is sure how safe that was so it isn't reassuring.

The report on the American bombing of Canadian troops says a new electronic system to prevent 'friendly-fire' deaths could be in place in about 15 years. Great, however, I'm going to go on record now and state quite frankly and openly that, should I ever be called on to fight for Queen and Country, and I see guns being fired in my direction, I will shoot first and ask questions later. It's the American way and, on balance, I think it's also the Arthur Lakelady way.

Toronto's inside workers are now on strike too. People who live in the Greater Toronto Area are among the healthiest in the country, says the paper, quoting from the report I mentioned yesterday. Unfortunately, those who live in the Durham Region, where Whitebay is, are no better than average, probably because we breathe in too much pollution from Toronto. The brown haze hanging over the city and blown our way on most days of the year is frightening.

The court says the government can't sell Hydro One again. The government says the court didn't stop them selling a minority stake in the ex-Crown Corporation last time so that's what they'll do again.

I was right about the Canadian SVP for Facilities Excellence etc. He was marched out today for failing to disclose that the 'goddamn wasteland' was a butterfly sanctuary. I doubt if he was asked about it at the time but he paid the price for his staff's obedience, as he also would if they had disobeyed.

Sometimes, the gremlins slip up and the world becomes right for me. At the last minute, Alys decided to join Gwen at her soccer tournament in Sarnia and they left in the afternoon. I phoned Lance and told him I would be late home from work tonight. I was deliriously happy until I called Cassie to tell her I would join her at the Club and that's when I discovered the evil spirits were eviler than I imagined they could be. Cassie can't go to the Club tonight, she's going with her mom on a girls' weekend!

Saturday 6:
Called dad. Dad is fit, though depressed. After yesterday's disappointment, I can finally sympathize properly. Gawain is incensed, though apparently fit because the tests on his back showed nothing wrong and the specialist recommended exercises for his muscles. Gawain is thinking of suing the specialist for malpractice and defamation of character. He hasn't started the exercises he was given, in case he injures his back.

Lance and I went to his team's practice and exhibition game. Then, as the weather was hot, we got the pool ready for use -- again. After skimming, vacuuming and shocking the pool (mainly by my language) for the whole afternoon, it was ready for use.

Sunday 7:
Gwen's team is out of the tournament because they lost a game and one other team didn't. Alys and Gwen were home by suppertime and very disgruntled. Even the sight of a sparkling pool didn't make them happy.

Monday 8:
David Bowie, the rock star, says he will never live in Britain again because of the way the media there treats celebrities. I agree with him. The British media is disgusting in its treatment of people in general, never mind celebrities. Poor John Lennon was driven to living in the USA by celebrity-mad fans and media and was promptly assassinated by an American fan. The worst of it is their press holds Britain back. Who is willing to try for glory in any sphere with those media vultures hovering? When I become a great literary star, I'm going to boycott the British media too.

Talks to end the city workers strike are going nowhere and union worker pickets prevent contractors from removing piles of rotting garbage. Walkerton taught these people nothing.

Multi-millionaire singing star, Michael Jackson, is claiming the record industry rip-off black artists. Considering how much he's made from the industry, and how few record companies survive for any length of time, this is a strange accusation.

Over the weekend, the Deputy President of Afghanistan was assassinated or maybe just murdered. The distinction is probably lost on him. He was buried next to his brother who was executed by the Taliban last year.

It was hot again today but not at the gym where the air-conditioning kept my sweaty body cool enough to prevent me passing out. It wasn't so much the exercise causing me to perspire; it was more Cassie's new gym clothes bought on her weekend away with her mother. I do feel mothers should restrain their daughters but I'm glad they can't. Who knew gym knickers would come back into fashion, and in such a body-hugging way – it almost makes up for my missing the Club on Friday though I know that was my last chance. The evil sprites that plague my existence wouldn't have carried me so high before dropping me so hard if there was to be any new opportunity in my future.

Tuesday 9:
Cold and wet in the morning, hot and dry in the afternoon.
Cassie and I reviewed her procedure for much of our time at the office, which wasn't long as we took an early lunch that became a late lunch. It seems Cassie and Lydia attended the same school so I got to see their old uniform, again. Do all Catholic schoolgirls keep their uniform or only the ones who suspect they're heading for a career in the sex industry?
Took Lance to his game and they lost again – against a team they have handily beaten in the past. They've got into the habit of losing and can't break out; habits are like that.

Wednesday 10:
Another of our dwindling band of Canadian SVP's went today. I don't know what his crimes were but they must have been unforgivably wicked to have him go on a Wednesday morning.
Even this minor unpleasantness (for me anyhow) couldn't dampen my day. The gym now seems a beautiful place where happy people go to spend time with other blissfully happy people and do surprisingly suggestive things with sexy machines and on comfortable mats. That's how it seemed to me with Cassie as a companion -- but I could be wrong.
Other news today: Toronto residents are dumping garbage at City Hall to protest the municipal workers strike. Britain is to relax the laws against marijuana. American policemen beating a black teenager were caught on videotape, which has shocked no one except the media who were apparently unaware of such things. I now doubt they've ever had any reporters 'on the mean streets' as they claim -- whenever someone suggests the media aren't needed.
I understand Gwen drove herself to soccer practice after work but as no one videotaped the event I can't be sure anyone called Gwen actually exists – not in our house anyway.
Alys attended the parents' meeting for Lance's camp counsellors-in-training course, luckily Gwen wasn't around to cast aspersions on this. Lance remains unconvinced he would benefit from such training.

Thursday 11:
Transformation is back one week. 'We' are still not meeting 'our' dates.

It wasn't gym day so Cassie and I had to restrict our activities to reviewing her procedure at work and reviewing our gym-hardened bodies in the park.

Gwen and Lance's soccer teams had their photo night so I now have documentary proof a Gwen exists and possibly lives behind a door in our house.

Friday 12:
Work is still slow as everyone waits for 'transformation' day. Cassie and I got back together to review the changes I made to her procedure after our last word-for-word read through and then we retired to the gym. Cassie has heard from Lydia (isn't e-mail wonderful) that I also like all things Victorian, which isn't quite true. I only like the way they made everything sexually exciting, even table legs and women's ankles. We, on the other hand, have managed to do what Lenin said Communism would do, make having sex like drinking a glass of water (though since Walkerton that's become much more exciting now than it was in Lenin's time). Nevertheless, it has given Cassie and I a whole new range of things to talk about. Finding that Cassie and Lydia are corresponding about me, however, has made me suspicious. Does Cassie imagine she could end up, if you'll pardon the expression, in a rich man's bed by using me as a rung on the ladder to his bedroom window? A chilly doubt has crept into my mind, which makes me uneasy.

Macleans magazine has now taken to advertising aggressively on the radio, talking itself up as the source of Canadian truth and an alternative to the US media. We get Macleans too and I'm sad to say even if it is better than the American media, I don't find it entertaining reading. And to be honest, it could hardly be worse than US media because they all look like an American government propaganda unit while Hollywood simply makes 90-minute advertisements for the US arms industry. How could anything be worse?

Ontario news: the Government passed legislation ordering Toronto's workers back to work. The clean up has begun.

In world news, the man who taped US police beating someone they were arresting has been arrested, no doubt as a terrorist. Also in the

US, the National Debt Clock, which records the level of debt, was started up again yesterday. When the US government began running budget surpluses, it was switched off, now it's back on. Two British transsexuals have won their case at the European Court of Justice. They claim they are discriminated against because the British Government refuses to acknowledge their sex change. I'm with the government on this one. No matter how much surgery you have or how many pills you take, you're still the man or woman you were born as. Re-modelling your penis as a vagina, or vice versa doesn't give you ovaries or a prostate gland, or alter any of the hormonal or chromosomal differences. Despite what activists and quack surgeons will tell you, it isn't only plumbing that makes the man or woman.

Saturday 13:
Today, at the Extreme PC Warehouse, I ordered a 'student package' computer with Internet, CD, sound, DVD, and TV all rolled into one. "Saves space in their rooms," the salesman said. "So they have more room for books and things." I doubt that's a useful feature because most of today's students can't read. However, I'm pleased to relate that every one of the vital add-in components was 'Extreme' so I've finally joined the consumer mainstream.

Today was hot and dry, a pleasant change from sticky.

The Ontario Appeal Court ruled that the Federal law on marriages discriminates against gay people and says Ontario must register gay marriages. This is considered a great step forward in society, as I'm sure the first gay divorce will be.

Called dad. They've knocked down the gloomy, dirty, rundown, coal-burning power station in front of his house. I said great. He said, "Not really. Now I can see the cemetery that was on the other side!"

Sunday 14:
Went to a swimming pool store for a new cover and was amazed to find most of the pool products are 'Extreme' too. This is going too far. When the normal staples of life, like pool accessories and electronic components, are extreme, what hope is there for fripperies like fruit and vegetables? Also went strawberry picking and listened to the pickers complain, as they do every year, that the berries were small, had been too picked over, the day was too hot, etc. How come at our strawberry fields we never have elegant ladies in silky

summer dresses and sun hats who cycled there with a bottle of chilled white wine and a picnic in the hamper, like you see on TV?

Gwen went with her team to Minnesota to take part in the USA Cup tournament. We stayed behind and will keep informed by phone, Internet and e-mail.

Monday 15:
Involuntary separation packages were issued to management staff and shortly after the above announcement was made, Francine called and arranged for me to meet with Mr. Ogilvie 'last thing tomorrow'. As if the words weren't ominous enough, her voice took on a menacing tone as she said it. What will I tell Alys? I'm helpless, like a rabbit caught in the headlights of a car, unable to dodge. My breath comes in short gasps and my chest tightens. Am I the next heart attack victim?

I did try to work harder at the gym so I could get a Playboy spot when I'm fired but my discussions on Victoriana with Cassie kept getting in the way. Cassie has the same unhealthy interest in Victorian brothels as Lydia has, I'm happy to say -- but my doubts remain un-silenced.

I watched highlights of Gwen's first soccer game on the USA Cup's website with Alys, trying to find a way to warn her of the possible impending doom at work. No solution presented itself and she still doesn't know. I'm going to be like that manager in The Full Monty movie who pretended to go to work every morning to keep the bad news from his shrewish wife. If my efforts in the gym had paid off, I too could have become a stripper. As it is, I don't think I shall. Only in the movies could women like seeing plump middle-aged men taking their clothes off.

In world news, the king of Morocco has married a computer engineer and the editors of TV Guide have chosen the Jerry Springer Show as the worst TV show ever, which it could be but there's lots of competition for that title. Now I know why we have wars; it's to drive this kind of nonsense off the front page.

Tuesday 16:
My meeting with Mr. Ogilvie is postponed.
Cool morning but even hotter than usual afternoon -- 33 degrees C. Toronto's associate medical officer of health says today the heat alert of the past 5 days may be upgraded to a heat emergency.

Presumably, this will fast track you to a place at the doctors, at a time when one in five Ontarians say they have problems getting to see one. Spain and Morocco's armed forces are still facing each other down over some small uninhabited pieces of land Spain says belong to them and Morocco says they don't – and this while Spain is trying to recover Gibraltar from Britain. The hypocrisy of the average European State is mind-blowing. The British-born Islamic militant accused of killing Daniel Pearl, an American Journalist, was sentenced to death in Pakistan, while the American Taliban, John Walker Lindh, did some plea bargaining and got twenty years in jail in the US. It pays to choose where you're caught carefully.

Summer camps in Toronto began today as Toronto municipal workers go back to work. The Euro, after being way down on the dollar since shortly after it was introduced, has regained parity as the dollar slides. The Rolling Stones have arrived in Toronto to prepare for their North American tour. This is their third time of practising here before tours.

We reviewed Gwen's team's progress on the Internet, where the day's scores are posted on the tournament's website, so far so good for the girls. And on the web I got to see Gwen, something I could never do if she were at home.

Wednesday 17:
The postponement of my meeting with Mr. Ogilvie, which so terrified me a few days ago, has reduced its horror to ho-hum. It didn't impinge one iota on my happy hour in the gym with Cassie (though my gnawing suspicions do). The coffee shop wasn't crowded today (with so many managers gone, and the fear it has induced in our staff, most people are sitting at their desks pretending to work) but it didn't stop Cassie and me from sitting too close together. I'm now so used to her kissing me, I even kiss her back – sometimes I even get my retaliation in first.

When I got home, I went to the clinic for my six-month follow-up cholesterol blood test, results will be announced in one week. With luck, the stress hormones will have eaten the bad cholesterol and my doctor will stop grumbling about the one small deviation I have from the medical average. Doesn't the medical world understand about averages? Maybe modern doctors have all had a modern education and dropped math at Grade 2.

Gwen's team have progressed out of the 'round robin' stage and are into the quarterfinals. My workplace stress is now multiplied by my kids' sports stress.

Lance isn't thrilled with Camp Counselling and says so loudly. He also says, having learned to do this from Gwen, Nico and Alys were not at the training.

Thursday 18:
My meeting with Mr. Ogilvie is postponed.

Even if I'm going to be fired, this continual postponement of the meeting to announce it may mean I reach retirement before it happens.

Canadian news: Toronto has a Heat Emergency and four Emergency Cooling Centres have been set up around the city. Temperatures have hovered around the record mark for 4 days now. The Canadian Auto Workers union is to fight Ford's decision to close the Oakville truck plant, perhaps by working in it – or is that too much to hope for? A $6B class-action suit against Nortel, the fading telecoms giant, was started yesterday. The Complainants don't like Nortel's accounting practises.

Unlike past disasters, there's been no baby boom in New York in the wake of the WTC horror. Spain's soldiers have ousted the Moroccans from an island called Perejil, which Spain claims but which lies off the Moroccan coast. Maybe they could rename it Gibraltar and then everyone would be happy – except Morocco, of course.

Gwen's team are in the semi-finals of the USA Cup and my heart attack is imminent.

Alys is going out with 'the girls' tomorrow night and will stay overnight because there'll be lots of drinking involved. I was about to suggest I pick her up instead of the sleepover when my evil twin gave me a salutary smack. Maybe 'Cinderella Arthur' shall go to the ball as well.

Friday 19:
My meeting with my boss is now postponed until after my vacation so my prediction of reaching retirement before I'm sacked is looking good. This happy thought, when added to the pleasure Cassie demonstrated when I told her about my freedom for tonight, made the whole day sing.

Canadian news: The Pope's security people plan to be invisible when he visits Toronto; no doubt hiding out in Gwen's bedroom.

Canadian companies are rushing to help Cuba find gold lost in 'hundreds' of Spanish shipwrecks off their coast. It won't do the Cubans any good because gold never does anyone any good. The only way to become rich or even pleasantly prosperous is to work in a system that allows people to get rich, as the Chinese are proving with every day that passes since their leader wisely ditched Socialist economics.

Gwen's team won their semi-final and they are in the final tomorrow. It's lucky I spent so much time having the tension massaged from my limbs by Cassie at the gym today or I'd pass out from suspense.

Cassie's outfit for the Club was extremely appropriate for the summer weather we're having, or so I rationalised to myself as I helped her put it on. Why do they make the fastenings on women's clothes so fiddly? I was all fingers and thumbs and I'm sure it wasn't all due to lust. After that giggly time in my office, however, the evening though didn't go well. At first everything was as I remembered it with excited people greeting each other and playfully teasing; raising the temperature for everyone. Then a callow youth entered with a group of young girls around him. He was soon the center of attention and I was pleased when they all made their way to the farthest corner from Cassie and me, taking a large part of the female members with them. Cassie was incredulous when I asked who the youth was because apparently he's the hottest local singer around right now – he's a global star – and he's become a regular here recently. I couldn't help noticing her eyes strayed his way much too often and with a longing expression. My suspicions about her feelings toward me were allayed somewhat by her suggesting that, if we ran away together, we could play like this every day of our lives. In fact, I relaxed enough to go to the washroom sometime after this and when I returned Cassie was gone and a burly, leather-clad woman, some inches taller than me, occupied her barstool. She introduced herself as one of Cassie's friends and added Cassie had gone to the bathroom and asked her to keep our seats. This re-assured me at first but as time passed and Cassie stayed missing, her friend became friendlier and my nerves began twitching. It didn't help that almost everyone in the room was now fawning at the star's feet and Cassie's friend and I were practically alone. When she suggested retiring to her dungeon to play, I made my excuses and left but not before seeing a brief glimpse of Cassie through the press of bodies, literally grovelling at the youth's feet. The journey home on a midnight train filled with sad drunks removed any lingering romance in my heart, leaving me numb.

Saturday 20:
Fortunately, Gwen's team won the USA Cup!!! Without this to balance my misery, I might have succumbed to depression. It wasn't just the winning, the whole day kept us on edge, from the preview online to watching the score being updated online. The teams were tied when we went out for supper and Alys ran off halfway through the meal to see if there was a change. There was, Gwen's team won after overtime and a penalty shoot-out. We spent the rest of the evening at home wallowing in the web highlights.

Sunday 21:
Gwen arrived home late in the afternoon, after travelling all night and day, so happy and tired she spoke to us for over an hour.

Monday 22:
Now that Mr. Ogilvie doesn't want to see me anytime soon, it's a pleasure to go to work. No one wants anything from me, or from my department (except Cassie, who is still demanding her procedure be finished asap), my people are too busy socialising to grumble, senior management is shuttered in their bunker avoiding contact with the indigenous natives, and my time is my own. Consequently, after the gym, Cassie and I had a leisurely lunch in the sunshine where she apologized for abandoning me on Friday night and offered to make it up to me in a disturbingly satisfying way, which was followed by a swift jog to a nearby park with lots of privacy provided by leafy shrubs. The freedom that modern women have is incredible, for modern men; however, for me, the veil has slipped and I see only naked ambition behind.

Canadian news today: World Youth Day is underway and it may not cover its costs say the organisers, the Catholic Church. I suspect that's an opening shot in their request for money. The world's stock markets crumbled yesterday to levels not seen since the Nineties and the Rolling Stones crew chief died of a heart attack during the preparations for the upcoming tour.

Tuesday 23:
Canadian news: Stock markets and the Canadian dollar dived again. The Pope arrived today for WYD. Schools in Toronto are seeing reduced fighting and increased classroom civility since the mandatory suspensions of people who are verbally abusive. It proves the Arthur Lakelady law of manners, 'for every 1000 incidents of bad manners you get one murder'. Manners are what prevent violence. If Northern Irish Protestants or Southern American Whites, for example, had extended the same courtesy to ALL their fellow men and women, the world would have been a pleasanter place. And it's true everywhere around the world.

World news: An Israeli air strike has killed 11 people in Gaza. The Northern Irish are once again close to civil war as drive-by shootings follow riots. A massive snowstorm in South Africa has forced the government to declare parts of the country a disaster area. Spain and Morocco have returned the disputed islands to their prior demilitarized status. Normal loopy service has been resumed.

Normal service has also returned in the Lakelady house; Gwen was at work all day and soccer practice in the evening. I took Lance to his practice and wrote my diary. Lance's team has settled into a steady rhythm of wins and losses that will leave them close to, but not quite at, the top of their league so I'm leaving this subject for my diary and this year – unless something unusual happens to change that.

Wednesday 24:
Cassie and I missed out the gym today -- foreplay is no longer going to get in the way of real play. The afternoon was heaven, mainly because Cassie is trying hard to get back in my good books after her desertion. I think she feels my withdrawal. Even going later to the doctor to hear my cholesterol results wasn't a complete waste of time because I now have enough Viagra to get through this week and my upcoming vacation.

Here are the results of my cholesterol test: after 6 months of eating white meat, cholesterol-free margarine, watery milk, and all the rest of the doctor's good advice, my cholesterol is higher than when I started! Back to proper food and to hell with them. Even the doctor said, "Oh well, it isn't actually outside the range anyhow."

I'm sad my theory that my stress hormones would eat the cholesterol didn't hold up because that might have been my passport to untold riches; anything about health gets North Americans reaching for their purses.

Lance and Nico had a bust-up at the end of the Camp Counselling session and Alys took Nico's side – at first. When the argument grew more heated and more encompassing, she took Lance's side. They both came home vowing never to attend another session and Alys is going to complain to the Town Council about the 'people' who run the counselling course. I expect the Town's lawyers will recommend counselling for everyone. The best thing about it all is I think this should put an end to Gwen's suspicions.

Thursday 25:
In the news today: An asteroid is on a collision course with Earth. The last one let me down over the ACR process all those weeks ago but this one still may land before the Transformation kicks me out of the company. I'd like to go to heaven as an employed person. I don't know why it just seems important.

The Pope is in Canada and took a boat trip yesterday and WYD pilgrims are being urged to walk more rather than clog up the subways. The report into the US bombing of Canadian soldiers says the pilots were solely to blame. Britain is vowing to crack down on militants in Northern Ireland who threaten the 'peace process', ho hum.

Alys was surprisingly lovey-dovey in the morning and evening today; it was so similar to Cassie's recent behaviour I'm now beginning to think Gwen must have been right.

Friday 26:
During the day, I handed the department over to Mohammed. It's his turn for an opportunity to shine in front of my fellow managers. Unfortunately for him, there are absolutely no managerial events (aka meetings) happening right now. Once I was sure he had the reins, I went to lunch with Cassie and we only returned after everyone had gone home so I could help her dress for the Club tonight. Even that didn't entirely soften my hardened heart. Once doubt creeps in, lust and love seep out.

Later that evening, instead of the Club, I flew to visit Dad and the family in the UK. We go every two years and with every visit the UK is less like Britain and more like nowhere-land. The corrosive grip of Europe and US TV drips away the last remaining shreds of

British-ness like acid on flesh.

Saturday 27:
Life in the Fourth Reich.
Dad tells me that they've just released a local shopkeeper from prison for the crime of selling British vegetables to British people in Britain using British weights and measures. Only metric measures are allowed now and a fondness for your own ways is a criminal offence. Britons used to say they'd 'won the war but lost the peace'. That was before they joined the cosy Franco-German alliance, born in WW2 and forged anew when the self-proclaimed 'liberating powers' went home leaving this Unholy Roman Empire to gather back all its wartime puppets.

The truly sad part of all this is Europe has been here before. The EU was designed to stop a repeat of WW's 1 & 2 but it has returned Europe to the Middle Ages so Europe's grandchildren will have to fight and die to extricate themselves from this feudal fiefdom as their ancestors did throughout the 15-19th Centuries. It is my eternal shame I encouraged people to vote for this travesty. My excuse is I believed we were entering a Free Trade zone that would help us all get richer. First hand and bitter experience of the Biblical teaching; what profiteth a man that he gains the world but loses his soul?

Sunday 28:
Driving to the Norfolk Broads

Monday 29:
We go boating
Everywhere people are wearing England soccer shirts and the English flag, something I never saw as a child growing up, is flying from every other building. I wish it were a genuine outpouring of patriotic fervour and not just a hangover from the World Cup. Once the British people bestrode the Earth; they were pre-eminent in industry, commerce, finance, exploration, science, military prowess and, paradoxically, humanitarian ideals. Now they just wear the T-shirt. It's hard to believe a country that has shone so brightly for a thousand years can now be content aiming so low and being pleased when they only just achieve even the minuscule targets they've set.

The Lakelady family picked up their Broads cruiser today at the Golightly Family Boatyard and began 'messing about on the river'.

Our boat is called the Sinking Light II. After a nervous start, for everyone, particularly the instructor and other boaters, I finally drove away a boat as big as a bus down a series of streams known as the Norfolk Broads. No doubt to someone used to these waterways they look broad but to me, there never seemed to be room for me and all the other traffic. Now that we're safely moored near a pub, I can look back on our first day and laugh. I did laugh until Alys said, "Stop gibbering."

Tuesday 30:
There are some Golightly boats moored at the same pub. I'm not surprised. Compared to the bigger boat companies, the Golightly boats were an incredible bargain. I can't understand why they aren't better known or more popular. Today we saw Fading Light and Dying Light.

Wednesday 31:
On vacation so nothing happened -- Hallelujah
Today we saw Diminishing Light and Lowering Light moored (not parked, I'm learning the lingo) at the same dock we were.

August 2002:

Thursday 1:
I don't know if it's true of all British radio stations or only the Yoof-centric ones Gwen and Lance insist we listen to while driving in the car and boat, but Britain has really gone in for self-pity in a big way. It was always bad, now it's reached monstrous proportions. The reason Planet Earth has never been contacted by life in outer space is because a great column of whining shoots straight up into space from the UK and sweeps the galaxy every 24 hours, sending rational alien beings fleeing to the next closest galaxy for their interstellar trips. In Britain, radio competitions encourage people to call in and say how miserable their lives are so they can get free tickets to see groups called Bottomfeeder or Lagerpuke. The sicker and sadder you are in this masochistic culture, the more you're feted. Add to this the venomous jealousy of successful people by the media piranhas and it isn't any wonder talented Britons, like David Bowie, run for the door at the first opportunity.

Today we saw three more Golightly boats, Half-Light, Failing Light, and Waning Light, so maybe they are becoming more successful. Perhaps we've caught them early in their rise to dominance but it's strange we haven't yet seen Sinking Light I. I'm getting a 'sinking' feeling about it (sorry, couldn't resist).

Friday 2:
I've now been listening to today's music for over a week and it's really poor -- and I lived through the Jackson 5, Partridge Family, Monkees and Archies. The fact most modern music is a 're-mix' of all those old phoneys tells me all I need to know; by their heroes shall you know them. It's all pompous (yes, even at their age) self-important teenagers earnestly parroting things they've no experience of but they claim is a reality. Well, not in my neighbourhood it isn't.

Returned the boat to the boatyard and saw Low Light, Bad Light, Half-Light, and Stop Light. Still no Sinking Light I, so I asked the man who tied up the boat for us about our unseen sister ship and he said, "Don't ask." So I didn't.

Saturday 3:
After a long, painful drive north through holiday traffic, we went to the theatre with the tickets we bought over the Internet all those weeks ago, and we were very impressed. Mainly I was impressed that booking things over the Internet actually works!

Sunday 4:
North Americans like to boast everything is bigger in America, and they cite the giant redwood trees of the west coast as an example but it's a poor one. Trees in most of North America are skinny, stunted things, willows, larches, birches, or pines. They either get too much water or not enough, depending where they live. Trees in England tower over the countryside, overhanging roads and making natural tunnels of country lanes. It's the bit Gwen likes best about England. These days, it may be my favourite too.

Monday 5:
Britons love all things American. When English people put their England soccer shirts into the laundry, they put on something that says USA on it. And they eat and drink anything they think is American -- like Italian pizza, German hamburgers, French fries, and cola. In some ways, I wish the British would be more American. Why, for instance, don't they eat lots of salad and lightly cooked vegetables, attend church every Sunday, take an active part in local politics or volunteer for the PTA, Neighbourhood Watch, or Big Brothers and Sisters, as Americans do? All these things are worth emulating. Why do Britons only choose the greasy side?

Tuesday 6:
My gloom, still hanging on from home and work, is lightened by the weather. Every day the weather forecaster says 'Sunny periods WITH SHOWERS' and Dad hears showers. He looks anxiously out of the window and suggests we stay home and watch TV. Every day I say get in the car we're going out. And so far, apart from the day driving north, we haven't been rained on once. The British Met office is in league with the TV companies to keep people indoors and consuming advertisements.

Wednesday 7 to Friday 9:
Meeting more family and old friends and watched some pre-season professional soccer games.

Saturday 10:
All the British men in our combined Lakelady families are addicted to Psychoporn, an ugly lust for gratuitous violence devoid of life or humanity. I say this after a week of watching the films of Jean-Claude Van Damme, Arnold Schwarzenegger, and Sylvester Stallone. The fact these 'stars' are all Europeans who make their living in the US should be warning enough to rational Britons (if there are any left) of which way their future lies, and it shouldn't be toward either of these two ugly land masses.

Sunday 11 to Thursday 15:
More vacation stuff.
I miss Cassie and, with the too close proximity of the kids in vacation accommodation, Alys as well but on the whole, I'm enjoying the rest. Isn't that what vacations are for?

Friday 16:
Driving across the Pennines heading back to the airport was like a romantic's dream of England. The antique-gold setting sun burnished the hilltops and cast long shadows in the golden mist-filled vales, where sleepy sheep and cattle contentedly munched the rich grass. Everything lay still and quiet. It was as if 'Cider with Rosie' had left the mind's pages and entered the physical world. There's something magical about the light in Britain; it appears in every picture you see.

Saturday 17:
Back in Canada, unpacking and laundry, fixing the garden and sorting the mail.

Sunday 18:
Among the mail waiting for our return was Gwen's school leaving results and she can go to any of Canada's best universities. She has chosen to go to one on the East Coast, which is a couple of days of solid driving away. I expect we will see as much of her as we have this past year when she was living at home.

According to the Economist, also waiting for me when I got home, the German Chancellor looks like being the Euro's first victim. The 'one economic policy fits all' theory is keeping Germany depressed and he is losing ground in the forthcoming election. An old phrase, something about the 'biter bit', comes to mind.

Monday 19:

My return to work was the occasion for a stream of fellow-workers to wander through my office, each recounting in gory detail the recent firings of various middle managers or junior executives. It seems the cuckoo-managers were busy while I was away. Many of the fallen were colleagues from past departments or projects and my growing panic at this news was sent into outer space when Francine called to say Mr. Ogilvie would see me after lunch. At first, this relieved my fear. After all, the others had been marched out under Security escort with their belongings crushed incongruously in supermarket plastic bags, like the homeless people they were about to become. My relief lasted only minutes when I realised it might just be a trick to ensure I wasn't prepared for the Security guards when they arrived. By lunchtime, I was paralysed with fright and couldn't eat my sandwich (lean beef and lettuce to rid my waist of those frustratingly tenacious 2 inches).

Then the call came and I went, heavy of heart and leaden of foot, to hear my doom but after all my worry, it wasn't what I'd feared. Despite the premature rumours of my unlikely promotion or too likely demise, I was so happy with what transpired I almost cried. My past work in the documentation field has finally been appreciated. I've been 'hand-picked' for a place in the new organisation and I have to say it is perfect. It's very close to home, so no more commuter train, and I'm the only one there is in this role, so I'm indispensable. I am to become the corporate Governing Documents 'Conscience' (there isn't an official title as such) with an office in a small building the corporation has in the suburbs, along with my three staff.

I'm surprised to learn, from Mr. Ogilvie, that the corporation has 561 Governing Documents, 2348 Processes and 4873 Procedures, which makes my sections' efforts these past four years seem trivial by comparison. And, now the corporation is reorganised, they all need revising and maintaining. I'm the man to do it. Mr. Ogilvie says the office location was specifically chosen for my convenience so I wouldn't be disturbed while I work. People who needed to consult the documents can still get in touch, through the corporation's excellent e-mail and internal telephone system.

The Transformation team couldn't find a new manager for me to report to so it's still Mr. Oglivie. I don't mind, better the devil you know...

I went to the gym alone. It isn't the same without Cassie or Lydia. Cassie, you'll remember was 'safe' in her job but sadly her department and position were placed out in a western suburb of the city where none of them live. They moved while I was away. I called Cassie this morning to say goodbye (It's for the best really, things were never going to be the same between us) and learned her entire department is looking for new jobs or new houses.

I expected to weigh more after my three weeks eating stodgy British food and drinking British real ale but, to my delight, I'd lost a pound so I had salad and quiche for supper to build on this excellent result.

World news today: Canadian war veterans went to Dieppe on the anniversary of that ill-fated raid. Two British soldiers have been shot dead in Kabul but not, apparently, by the Taliban or Al Qaeda -- more friendly fire. Preparations are underway for the anniversary of Sept 11 and the NYSE will open late to allow traders to attend the ceremony.

Tuesday 20:
After the euphoria of yesterday, I'm sobering up. The downside of my new position is it is outside the Employees Association and hence no employment protection. It requires longer hours, no payment for overtime, a worse benefits package, and no pay increase. Also, I won't be downtown where the action, the restaurants, and the gym are. I learned all this from the letter I was given this morning outlining my new terms and conditions. Our company has changed a lot since I joined 15 years ago. I still have that first letter welcoming me to the company and hoping I will be very happy here, which I have been. This new letter has three paragraphs, two of which are veiled threats of dismissal.

A cool autumn-like morning, enough for mist in low-lying areas and prominent nipples on all the summery-dressed women walking to work. I'll miss the downtown women in their workday best clothes. I even miss Gerry, the morning walks from the station to work are quiet without him.

World news today: US Intelligence experts say Bin Laden is alive and planning to strike soon – they must also listen to the news but are obviously slow in mentally processing it. Chechen rebels claim to have shot down a Russian helicopter, killing the 80 soldiers on board. In Zimbabwe, white farmers who had refused to give up their land to Mugabe's men have been charged and imprisoned. Meanwhile, the population is starving because the farmers haven't been able to farm while this lunacy has gone on over the past year. We in the West are being asked to send food aid -- presumably, the Zimbabwe government doesn't mind white farmers producing their food over here. Two US soldiers were wounded in Afghanistan, this time actually by 'unfriendly' fire. In Nigeria, a young woman has lost her appeal against being stoned to death for having a baby out-of-wedlock – aren't foreign cultures wonderful. Four Canadian authors have made it onto this year's Booker prize list. Next year will be my turn I'm sure.

I had Caesar salad and grilled skinless chicken for supper to maintain the weigh loss momentum.

Wednesday 21:
The provincial auditor has criticised the Toronto public school board for its budget, which it overspent on trifling fripperies like operating 84 swimming pools, adult education centres, lunchroom supervisors in schools, and a student to computer ratio of 6:1 (the Auditor thinks 10:1 is the correct ratio, academically speaking). Living high off the hog this way will be the death of us all. Ontario's school system ranks only fourth best in Canada, says Parent magazine – I blame it on all those computers and swimming pools.

Went to the gym and weighed myself. Weight: plus 1lb. I blame that on salads. With stodgy filling food you don't eat much, with salad you eat and eat until you're as round as an iceberg lettuce.

Thursday 22:
The new location my group has moved to also houses the corporation's few remaining Quality Assurance people. They're very surly. I can understand it, however, because obviously their old boss wasn't as careful in finding them a spot as Mr. Ogilvie was for me. None of them live on this side of the city and, as they have to be out at our different facilities every day, they will never be able to be at

their desks anyhow so they could have stayed downtown or worked from home. They have 'nowhere to lay their heads' as one told me. I tried to advise him against using that phrase in case it is misconstrued but, as I said, they're very surly.

My office is nice enough; cosy would be the best description. It has a small window high up on the wall and, if I stand on tiptoes, I can see an abandoned lot, a seedy strip joint and bar, and a massage parlour. The office is a reasonable size, provided I don't get any visitors. My phone isn't connected yet and we aren't on a proper LAN, more of a desktop modem arrangement, but I've no doubt all that will be sorted out in time. The important thing is to get on with those governing documents because mayhem could break out at any time if the corporation's workers don't have the correct procedures.

We, my three remaining staff and I, began unpacking the documents from their crates. It almost looks like every copy of every document is in the mountain of 197 boxes they've sent. Perhaps the company is afraid that someone will use an out-dated procedure and have a terrible accident. I can't think what else would possess them to send actual documents. I'd rather expected electronic copies but, until the LAN is working, marking up paper copies is as good as anything. Unpacking is going to take a while.

Our Federal Prime Minister, Jean Chretien, says he'll retire in 18 months and he doesn't want to see any unseemly jockeying for power in the meantime. I agree. Arthur Lakelady will retire in 15 years so, please, no unseemly jockeying for my position either. I suspect Chretien means he'll begin his first final tour of duty then. Like The Who or Frank Sinatra, he'll keep retiring forever. In more relevant news, street workers (aka prostitutes and panhandlers) are suing the movie industry for loss of earnings. It seems they get pushed off their 'patches' when the film crews move in. The film people already do pay them for the inconvenience, just not enough.

I will soon be able to get Dad made into jewellery because a company says it can turn human remains into diamonds, only in Dad's case I fear the diamonds will constantly be developing flaws.

Friday 23:
Now that I've examined the new organisation charts and the old documents closely, I can see this documentation job is going to be tricky. We can't just strike out all the old department or job titles and replace them with new, or generic, ones because some of the titles

stay the same and some new departments have old titles but no longer do the work mentioned in the document and so on. We decide to unpack our own personal boxes instead. Getting the offices right will help us become more productive later when we get round to doing the manuals. In the meantime, I'll ask Mr. Ogilvie to prioritise them so we do the most important ones first.

The daily food bank's shelves are bare. Apparently we've all stopped contributing – I can't understand why. At least they will soon have a lot more new customers.

Our new premier, after his Auditor slammed the 'overspending school boards' has hinted more money may be made available. My prediction of an election is looking better each day.

The Saudis are denying they are pulling their money out of the US now that the US is turning against them. The US has started a new hunt for Al Qaeda in Afghanistan. They would be better off looking in Alabama.

World Youth Day security people didn't get paid and held a rally outside the security company's offices in Toronto.

Actor Liam Neeson, who played Michael Collins in the movie Big Fella, unveiled a statue to Collins in his hometown -- on the 80th anniversary of his assassination by his own side. Collins is a hero of the struggle for Irish independence and they still celebrate that. It will be another 100 years before an Irish historian writes a paper pointing out that the best thing that happened to the Irish (and those other Celts, the Scots and Welsh) was the union with England. If there had been no union, there would be approximately 8 million Scots and Irish Celts and 5 million Welsh Celts scratching a living on their barren rocks today as every one of the other tiny European peoples still do. The fact there are around a hundred million Celts in the world is because that union gave them access to England's colonies in North America, Australia, New Zealand and the rest, the only really successful colonies anywhere. We Lakelady's are Welsh but, despite spending two millennia down coal mines, we aren't totally blind.

Saturday 24:
Called dad. He's been resting this week after the exertions of the past three when he sat in our hire car and watched the countryside whiz by. Gawain also needed to rest so he took a week off work. The weather is terrible so they can't get out, Dad says, and they've been

forced to stay in and watch movies. There are days when I wonder how Britain managed to have an empire, considering the material Britannia had to work with. When I watch my British family, I understand the need for all that flogging and hanging. However, health-wise normal service has been resumed. Dad has a swollen gland in his throat and the doctor is booking him an appointment with a specialist.

Our pool was bright green when we got back from vacation and I started cleaning it up with Extreme Shock Pool Cleaner.

Sunday 25:
The pool is now cloudy and its chemistry is completely wrong. The Extreme Shock chemicals weren't quite the success I was expecting.

Monday 26:
Mr. Ogilvie says the processes and procedures are all equally important and we can start on anyone we like. He's right of course but it still seems odd that he can't provide better direction than that. Somebody must be screaming for the latest updated procedure, or perhaps it's too soon. The new organisation maybe hasn't had time to know what they are short of.

The news today: The Toronto school board still refuses to balance its budget. They want the Province to be the villains. Meanwhile, the Canadian right wing of Alliance and Conservative parties have, once again, failed to make a common front so we look set for years more Liberal governments at the Federal level.

Lance and I are definitely turning into Gawain and Dad. As Gwen says, I've got to stop it now, be firmer, stop taking life as it comes, and start shaping life to what I know to be right. When I say that out loud, I feel stronger and think it could be done. Perhaps Gwen takes after me?

Tuesday 27:
The Education Minister is urging employers to let their staff take time off to help their kids with the first day of school next week. This after 100 years of schoolchildren starting school! The Minister wants me to have time off to take Lance, to High School for his first day, where he'll be mercilessly bullied by everyone else's proto-thug and will in his turn bully other equally sensitive kids, but doesn't suggest I be given time off to take my daughter to University in

Nova Scotia, a 19-hour drive away.

Wednesday 28:
The province has taken control of the Toronto and Hamilton school boards because they wouldn't balance their budgets.

An Arab journalist with close ties to Islamic militants says Bin Laden is back in command of his guerrilla group after a long period of chaos following a US attack. A WTC survivor has been discovered alive and well and living in a New York health centre.

Thursday 29:
The US claimed the world was behind it on attacking Iraq, despite the whole world assuring the US they weren't. Meanwhile, in Afghanistan, they think Bin Laden is moving about on cloudy nights so as not to get caught -- the cheating rotter! Canada is to allow US troops into Canada in the event of a terrorist attack or natural disaster; Canadian politicians clearly don't watch TV or read the news because if they did they'd know allowing American forces into your country is a serious Health and Safety risk to your people.

A study in Massachusetts has found it only takes a few cigarettes a day for three weeks for girls to be addicted. Boys are so damn lazy they can take as long as 6 months to become addicted.

Friday 30:
I miss the train
That is, I miss getting on the train. I miss the civilised yet naked aggression to get 'your' seat and the offended glares when you don't and you sit in someone else's seat. I miss checking out the fellow sufferers to see who is missing and also listening to other people grumbling about their family life.

Immediately I got home from work, Gwen and I set off for Nova Scotia. We drove to Cornwall and stayed the night. Gwen slept most of the way; her farewell parties this week have tired her out.

Baseball players are threatening to go on strike again but the TV companies aren't rushing to stop them. Apparently, nowadays the advertising in baseball games doesn't cover the cost of purchasing the rights so TV companies will actually make money if there's a strike. To add insult to injury, the International Olympic Committee is considering removing baseball from the Olympic Games -- why was it ever in?

August 31, 2002:
The end.

It was a year ago, the company announced it would reorganise to be more efficient, reduce duplication, and focus accountabilities and now the process is complete. I really was the last to be placed. From past re-organisations, I know it will be another two years before people know what they're doing and have the working relationships in place to support them. By that time, our managers will have grabbed as much of the fuzzy pie as they can and will be duplicating the work of other sections when they don't get their way or can't work with the other managers. Important functions will be dropped, like small time bombs awaiting the right series of events to explode in our faces. As those explosions rock our small world, new or old processes will be grafted onto the slimmed-down organisation, thus closing the door after the horse has bolted. In three years time, management will start grumbling about how difficult everything is and, a year after that, they'll start campaigning for another re-organisation to make their meaningless lives interesting. We could solve the problems of executive tinkering by giving them real hands-on work to do – street sweeping, for example. All this ran through my mind while Gwen and I drove through Quebec and New Brunswick on a beautiful autumn weekend.

I'm glad my new office location hasn't got a gym nearby because it hasn't worked a millimetre off my waist never mind an inch. Perhaps for the next year, I'll try that neighbouring massage parlour but you will never know if it gives better results.

And why is that, I hear you ask? Simply that Gwen is at University, I'm safely in my new job at work, Lance is preparing for High School and Alys is content busily keeping us all on track. It has been an eventful and stressful year and now it's over I'm resolved never to keep a Diary again because somehow it makes things happen and I don't really care for that. I like my life uneventful.

September 2002:
Final Days and Final, Final Words

Sunday 1:
Arrive at University.

Gwen settled into her residence while I unloaded the car and fixed up her computer with its built-in TV, DVD, CD and burner. She stood in long lines to register while I paid her fees and attended a lecture on how a good parent behaves while your kid is spending your life savings and pension at University. There was a moment during the lecture when it looked like the parents may rebel. The Dean was explaining that despite the fact everyone in the room was paying the piper they were not going to be able to pick the tune. The University is obliged by law to deal only with the student. Parents can only get information from their children. This latest revelation of how the government has stolen our children, leaving us only the responsibility and costs of their upbringing, brought forth such a growl of discontent I thought it was the moment when the serfs storm the Bastille but it wasn't. The Dean followed with a joke and apathy was restored. Then the Frosh events began and I was dumped like an old, worn-out item of unfashionable clothing.

On TV, in the evening, I saw an advertisement for Pilates, which promise a sculpted torso in only a few weeks without any painful exercise. It's a thought.

Monday 2:
After a brief goodbye, ('must run Dad, there's a pancake breakfast in five minutes'), I made my way to the bus stop for the trip to Halifax Airport. The bus left half an hour late and arrived a quarter of an hour early based on the schedule they gave me – that's life outside the big city I guess. No matter, I waited patiently for my plane, dreaming of being a student again and staying in a co-ed residence. Gwen's residence looked like the Playboy mansion there were so many giggling girls with bulging bosoms, bare midriffs, and painted on pants. I flew home to Ontario to review my own torso.

Weight -- +3 lbs

Waist -- 36 ins., no change

BMI -- 28.5, up from 28 and well into the forbidden zone.

Abs -- no sign of any

Chest -- 42 ins., no change.

Folds of flab on stomach -- no change.

General 'blurring' around edges -- no change.

Conclusion -- something must be done.

On my way to work last Friday, I noticed an Extreme Pain Gym. Now that I won't be walking to work or spending so much time travelling I could get some serious training done, maybe an hour a day. I looked around the door. It was filled with muscular black men with loads of shiny jewellery and white men with shiny jewellery and tattoos (Do they make white tattoo ink for black people and, if not, why not?) It looked like people exercising in a gay bar. Many of the muscular black men seemed to be helping willowy blondes with their exercises. Could I get a job doing that? The willowy blondes were also tattooed and pierced (I suspect most were exotic dancers limbering up for the evening shift at that nearby strip joint).

Why, after my lack of success last time, would I return to this preposterous pursuit of bodily perfection? I'm glad you asked. The answer is because I did 'suffer' some improvement; by the end, I could run on the treadmill for 20 minutes rather than the walking and running as I did at the start. It still felt like death but there was progress; it just wasn't in anything I measured or wanted changed. Maybe, with another year or so, I'd get those other desirable improvements too. Who knows, maybe I could become a personal trainer, a Full Monty-style stripper or a co-ed residence student after all.

Epilogue:

December 2003:
Finally, finally finished and Another Important Life Lesson Learned

It's been over a year now since I laid down my pen but a part of the story suddenly sprang into life again and as it points to such an important life lesson, I feel you need to know. Lydia is divorcing Mr. S. and her lawyers are asking for a huge settlement, which she is going to use to raise Llamas on a ranch in the mountains. It seems she had one more achievement left in her and now it's happening. Plan A was the best one after all. I shall tell Gwen to make a plan for her future and stick with it no matter what contrary advice she gets from older, wiser heads. You only get one life and you may as well spend and use it as you wish, whatever well-meaning busybodies think of it.

And what of the future? 'Mystic Arthur' predicts that studious, hard-working Gwen will go on to become something worthy, admirable and unexciting, a doctor perhaps, while energetic, noisy Lance will find his role in something where those qualities shine, advertising or marketing maybe. As industries slip away to the East, I will be lucky to hang on at work for a normal retirement – but I still hope to anyway. 'Mystic Arthur' prefers to predict happy futures, despite the melancholic Celtic nature he was born with.

'Everyday Arthur', on the other hand, predicts I'll send this book to a publisher (one day), secure in the knowledge it will be lost in the mail, or fall off someone's desk, or get laughed into a recycling bin as pitiful and, consequently, Silky will not be catnapped, nor Lance abducted. Alys will be safe while shopping and Gwen will continue to be Gwen, only somewhere far away from home.

Author Bio:

Paul James grew tired of waiting for a literary agent or publisher to snap up his masterpiece so he began posting excerpts on social media and, when the reaction to those snippets was good, he published it himself (well, with a little help from his friends). He hopes you enjoy reading it as much as he enjoyed writing it.

Despite years of schooling and work in middle management, Paul can still see the funnier side of life. As well, living in central Canada with his wife and with the experience of raising two now grown-up and moved-out kids, he feels he can see both sides of any question – so much so that sometimes he can't tell one side from the other.

Paul feels he understands enough of the English-speaking world's concerns to comment on that in his writing because (1) he and his wife moved to Canada from Britain at a middling age and they still visit English family and friends frequently, (2) he has visited the USA a lot through vacations, his work and his children going to university there, and (3) through work and family visits, he has spent many months in Australia.

When Paul isn't writing, he can be found reading, traveling, or outdoors with a camera looking to capture amazing images of landscapes and wildlife.

Visit Paul's Facebook page here:
https://www.facebook.com/profile.php?id=1004838068

Visit Paul's Twitter here:
https://twitter.com/pauljames953

Paul's Amazon Author Page:
http://amazon.com/author/paulj953

And don't miss this other book of whimsical articles by Paul James and Lulu Publishing!

Random Musings

On Amazon:
https://www.amazon.ca/Random-Musings-Paul-James-ebook/dp/B0167ASO40/

On Lulu Publishing:
http://www.lulu.com/shop/paul-james/random-musings/ebook/product-22372492.html

On Barnes & Noble:
http://www.barnesandnoble.com/w/random-musings-paul-james/1122738585?ean=9781329543676

Made in the USA
Lexington, KY
25 March 2017